P9-AES-232

DATE DUE

DEMCO 38-296

Monkey King

Monkey King

PATRICIA CHAO

HarperCollins*Publishers*

HarperCollins books may be purchased for educational, business, or sales promotional use. For information please write: Special Markets Department, HarperCollins Publishers, Inc., 10 East 53rd Street, New York, NY 10022.

FIRST EDITION

Designed by C. Linda Dingler

Library of Congress Cataloging-in-Publication Data

Chao, Patricia, 1955–
     Monkey king : a novel / by Patricia Chao. — 1st ed.
         p.   cm.
     ISBN 0-06-018681-X
     1. Chinese American families—Fiction.   2. Chinese American women—Fiction.   3. Chinese Americans—Fiction.   I. Title.
     PS3553.H2765M66   1997
     813'.54—dc20   96-23703

97 98 99 00 01 ❖/RRD 10 9 8 7 6 5 4 3

For my mother and father

and for all my teachers

About my malady I can do nothing. I suffer a little just now—the thing is that after that long seclusion the days seem to me like weeks.

—VINCENT VAN GOGH, LETTER TO THEO

It is so difficult for me to be in this world.

—PHILIP GUSTON, NOTE TO HIS WIFE, MUSA

Acknowledgments

For making this book possible I am grateful to the Blue Mountain Center; The Millay Colony for the Arts; Virginia Center for the Creative Arts; my mother and father; my agent, Heather Schroder; E. L. Doctorow; Marty Lipp; Bill Mead; Miriam Beerman; Allan Hoffman; Ai jen Poo; Kera Bolonik; and everyone else who provided inspiration, suggestions, and encouragement.

For their faith and literary expertise I am especially indebted to Mona Simpson; my editor, Terry Karten; and my most constant readers—Karin Cook, Stephanie Grant, and the late Kenneth King.

Prologue

My father stands on a hill in a high wind, a strapped black bag at his feet. No, it's a dock, a stupendously busy dock, in the port of Shanghai, the most crowded city in the world. Anyone can see that he doesn't belong here, that he's a peasant from the outbacks of the north, from the style of his cheap blue serge suit, made by a local tailor, and his ill-fitting black shoes with their bulbous toes. Still, even among these city slickers he cuts a remarkably handsome figure. He is tall for a Chinese, nearly six feet, with the proportions of a tall person, lean-necked, arms and legs long for his torso. His full hair is slicked back in a side part, his eyes have the doey shape of a matinee idol's, with thick lashes. If you were to look into them you would see that he is terrified. This is the first time in his life he has seen a steamer. He has never ridden in a car, and the night express that took him from Wuhan to Shanghai is the only train he's ever been on. The shape of his lips is generously drawn, as if he were a sensual man, although he is not. He has the hands of an intellectual, pale-backed, narrow-palmed, with long, tapering fingers. His wrists are knobby, his Adam's apple unusually prominent, he is thin by any standards.

When the gangplank clangs down, my father hangs back from the crowd. Not out of politeness, or even tentativeness, but because he is sailing steerage and must wait for the first- and second-class passengers to board before him. He waits without aggression, the bag at his feet like a sleeping dog. He waits without heart.

The hill again. A cemetery by the sea. To the east the grass fades into cliffs and then there's the drop to the Pacific. After the funeral, my father was cremated and the ashes were flown to San Francisco, then transported down the coast to be buried. Behind my father sleeps his mother-in-law, my Nai-nai, buried in her best silk *chipao*—a violet one—and tiny black satin slippers.

The ghost's eyes are larger than the man's were in life. He has shed the blue serge suit jacket and now stands only in trousers and a loose white shirt. The black bag has decayed into shreds. His feet are bare. His hair is turning white.

White in China means death. Corpses are wrapped in white blankets, mourners wear white, white flowers are carried in funeral processions. White is bloodlessness, despair, the color of the sky on the March morning I tried to kill myself.

Part
One

1

Christ, it looks just like that prissy boarding school you went to. I could hear my sister's voice in my head as we started up the winding drive. A cluster of white Colonial houses, with several tasteful modern buildings thrown in. Near the gate to the left were half a dozen tennis courts and to our right was an amoeba-shaped lake surrounded by weeping willows. All the buildings were connected by neat flagstone paths. On one of these paths a group was walking with cheerful expressions, faces upturned to the weak sun. A teenage girl stopped, yawned, and slipped her sweatshirt over her head to tie it around her waist, casual, like any kid, anywhere, on an early spring day. It really could have passed for a campus, except for the wire fencing out front and the fact that it was much too quiet.

This was my second hospital in five days. The first was Yale New Haven, where I'd been admitted from the emergency room and they'd doped me up with something they usually use for psychotics. It made me not care so much when my shrink Valerie told me where I was going when I got out of there. She'd drive me up herself, she said.

I said, What if I don't want to go.

She shook her head. "I don't have a choice, sweetie. You broke our pact. You promised you'd let me know if things got this bad."

I didn't answer. Instead I said: "Maybe I should have stuck my head in the oven."

"If you'd done that you would have blown up every house on your entire block. This isn't England in the sixties. You're not Sylvia Plath."

The whole way up I'd been in a trance. We stopped at a Howard Johnson's for breakfast, but I didn't eat anything, just sipped black tea and chain-smoked until Valerie said, Come on, we're going to be late. The only thing I remember about the drive was watching the trees along the highway—maples with their massive trunks and dark snaky lower limbs, fatalistic lean oaks, spears of birches angling whitely and every which way against the lightening sky.

Admissions turned out to be in one of the Colonial houses. Again, the feeling was boarding school—the headmaster's study, where you reported to if you'd been caught drinking or with a boy in your room, or if they were going to tell you that someone in your family had died. Valerie and I sat in Queen Anne chairs upholstered in red velvet while a snotty-looking woman in half glasses took notes at a desk facing us. Her chair was a regular office swivel one, which she trundled ruthlessly over the faded pink and blue Oriental rug to retrieve forms from the file cabinet.

The information they wanted was simple enough:

Age: 27
Allergies: ragweed
History of psychiatric illness: none
Admission: voluntary
Status: suicide risk

Several official-looking documents, like leases, were handed to me on a clipboard. How civilized this was, nothing like I'd imagined. I signed, using the ballpoint attached on a string, not bothering to try to make out any of the small print. I can't tell you how my handwriting had deteriorated by then, I was lucky to be able to make any kind of mark at all. Valerie signed each form after me, her writing loopy and leaning, the kind my best friend, Fran, says indicates a generous nature.

"Okay, honey, I have to be getting back on the road now. I have a ten o'clock client." When she leaned to hug me, I felt the strength in her lean arms and shoulders. "They'll take good care of you here, Sally," she whispered. "And don't worry—remember, I'll be coming up to see you once a week."

When Valerie had left, Swivel Chair Lady peered over her half glasses, meeting my eyes directly for the first time. "Would you please hand me your suitcase?"

I thought: Customs, and heaved up the sagging bag that had surprised me with its weight, even empty. It was my father's; I'd found it on the floor of my mother's closet. While I was packing, Ma had come into my room. She sat down on the bed next to me looking plump and helpless in what my sister and I call her Chinese Communist outfit—navy turtleneck and matching elastic-waistband pants.

"That bag's falling apart, but I don't like throw away. Are you sure you want? I have better."

"No, this is fine."

In fact, it was appropriate, because I too was traveling to a strange land from which I might never return.

After a while Ma cleared her throat and said: "You don't worry about expenses. However long it takes, okay."

Her eyes were glassy. It made me uncomfortable and I looked away, pretending I hadn't seen.

The straps and buttons gave Swivel Chair Lady a little trouble but I didn't offer to help. She stuck her claw right in, rummaging, feeling everywhere—between my folded clothes, into all the corners, her nails scraping leather.

In Mandarin, my Uncle Richard once told me, there is a special category of nouns for long, skinny things like pencils, chopsticks, hair. All numbers modifying these nouns must end in zhi.

Swivel Chair Lady confiscated all my *zhi* objects: cigarettes, shoelaces, belts, hair elastics, the drawstring to my parka.

Also, contact lens solution, nail clippers, aspirin. She asked for the pearl studs in my ears and the gold watch Ma gave me when I got married. Then she picked up her telephone receiver and dialed four numbers. "The new admit is ready." She said to me: "An MH will escort you to the ward."

"MH?"

"Mental health worker. You are aware, aren't you"—she paused and gave me what I interpreted as a triumphant look—"that you're going to be watched twenty-four hours a day?"

The dayroom in Admissions resembled a primary school classroom, furnished in orange, yellow, and white plastic, with a linoleum floor and plaid curtains at the windows, which lined one wall. There were no bars, but the panes were reinforced with chicken wire and looked like the kind you couldn't open. At the far end of the room was a glassed-in booth, where a nurse in a pantsuit was sitting in a folding chair. Right outside the booth a man in a pale yellow button-down shirt was slumped in an orange chair, an ashtray smoking on the table beside him.

The MH, a woman about my age, led me over to one of the doorways opposite the bank of windows. Through the brown darkness, I could see that one of the beds was already occupied. Someone whose face was to the wall, long stringy hair—I couldn't tell what color—one hand dangling over the edge. The hand was so small and pale that it itself looked ill.

"Lillith," said the MH.

No answer.

"She just got in this morning too."

I set my bag down near the foot of the unoccupied bed, not knowing what to do next. I didn't feel like staying in this stuffy room with that creepy sleeper.

The MH was standing in the doorway, watching me. She

had a certain kind of Zen quality I've always admired, with her wire-framed glasses and bun and the Earth shoes that pulled down her heels as she walked, although on her the effect was oddly graceful.

I asked to use the bathroom. It turned out I couldn't even do that by myself—the MH posted herself right outside, the door slightly ajar. Sitting there, waiting, I looked around, wondering what possibly could be dangerous. It didn't occur to me that I could shatter the mirror glass, or even the frosted shower door, with my fist, and use the pieces to slash my wrists, or swallow them.

Christ, I was never going to be able to pee. I told myself this was just a job for her, she wasn't listening or anything. The disinfectant smell made me shiver, and I had to concentrate hard on the speckled white ceiling tiles until they blurred, before I could let go.

When I came out the MH said: "You're free to watch TV, you know. Or read, if you want."

Reading was another ability I'd lost—it was the reason I'd quit my job as an art director in New York City. I'd managed to hide it for a while, marking time at my drafting board, leafing through font books. The letters themselves still interested me, as abstract entities. I could still discuss what typeface would be appropriate for what kind of ad, and I could discern the shapes and textures of things, when a paragraph seemed too long or too dense, for instance, but if I read a sentence I couldn't remember a word of it ten seconds later. Then it got so I couldn't understand text at all unless I read it slowly out loud, and even that didn't always work. The letters started getting smaller and smaller, although the pica rule said otherwise.

A similar thing happened when I went back to Connecticut and tried to drive. I faked it for a while, but you can't fake a sense of timing. Ma put her foot down after the front fender of the Honda got swiped as I was trying to make a left-hand turn into oncoming traffic.

"I'm sorry," I said.

"Why are you sorry?" the MH asked.

"I'm sorry I can't carry on a conversation."

"This isn't a cocktail party. You don't have to be entertaining."

Where did you go to college? I wanted to ask her. Do you have a boyfriend? What makes *you* so normal?

The phone shrilled and the nurse poked her head out and announced there was another admit. I snuck a glance at the man in the yellow shirt. He hadn't said a word or even raised his head since we'd come in. While the MH was gone I picked up a *Ladies' Home Journal* from one of the tables and flipped through it aimlessly. I was dying for a cigarette but didn't have the nerve to ask. The man seemed like he maybe couldn't speak at all. I settled for secondhand smoke.

Since I'd been sick, a minute could feel as long as a day, or I'd blink my eyes and suddenly see that three hours had passed. The dayroom had one of those large school clocks where the seconds jerk along. It reminded me that my mother would be starting her own class at Yale about now, standing before the blackboard in her plaid skirt and white blouse. Ma had no compassion for the slow or the lazy or the simply unfocused. She could pick out those students in the back, the ones who hadn't done their homework, and she'd call on them. When my sister and I were small we'd do the dinner dishes while Ma corrected exams at the kitchen table. "This one gets a *C*!" she'd announce triumphantly. Or worse: "This one doesn't belong in my class, he's too stupid." She'd draw the *F* much bigger than any of the other grades.

My mother is nothing if not efficient. When she'd found me passed out on my bed and the mess on the floor beside it, she called 911 and then she called Valerie. I don't remember a thing about the ambulance ride, although they told me later the siren was screaming the whole way. In the emergency room they made me sit up in a chair and gave me this evil-looking black potion in a glass so I'd throw up again. It was Valerie who jerked me to my feet and hustled me down the pale green corridor to the bathroom, Valerie who knelt on the floor with me, grabbing back my hair and holding on to my nape with the other hand, as if she'd done it a thousand times before for other desperate women. It came up as easily as a trick, just colorless mucus by then, and I thought: It's all gone, I have failed. When I was done, she wet one of those coarse brown paper towels all public bathrooms have and pressed it against my forehead. We walked back that way to where Ma was sitting ready with a handful of Kleenex.

After her class was over, Ma would drive home for lunch, to the empty house. She'd change into her Communist China outfit and call Lally Escobar, who lived next door. Lally was a little older, divorced, with a son in Australia. *Come over for leftovers.*

"Bonnie, you're so lucky to have daughters!" Lally would tell my mother. "Sally is the willowy, sensitive one," she'd announce, even if one of us was in earshot, and then: "But of course that Marty is the beauty." We might have been species of iris in her garden.

By noon there were six new admits, including me and my roommate and the man in the yellow shirt. Lunch was brought in on trays. I asked one of the other patients if I could bum a cigarette. She looked surprised but shoved the pack across the table at me. It was a Lucky Strike and it made me dizzy, which I liked.

When my roommate finally staggered into the dayroom, she looked terrible, skinnier even than me, with hair that could have been dark blond if it weren't so filthy. Her eyes were a chilly washed-out blue—the kind Nai-nai used to call devil eyes. Laceless white sneakers sagged around skeletal ankles. She too had been deprived of *zhi* objects.

When we lined up for meds, I saw that her paper cup was

brimming with different colors. She swallowed the pills one at a time, moving the water cup to and from her lips in slow motion, as if sleepwalking. Once she gagged, but it didn't faze her, she just waited until she knew she was going to keep it down and then continued. A pro.

The brassy theme music of a soap opera blared out from the television set. I could hardly keep my eyes open—what had they given me?—and then I was dreaming that it was dark November and I was a child lying on my bed on Coram Drive, looking out at the dusk beyond the white-curtained windows. It was a dream I'd been having a lot lately.

The sound of clapping jolted me awake. We admits were ushered from the dayroom and down a corridor into a room with lime green wall-to-wall carpeting but no furniture, like a new house. This, we were told, was group therapy. The leader, a bearlike man in beard and ponytail, gestured to us that we should sit down on the floor in a circle.

"We'll start off by getting to know one another a little bit. Let's go around the room and hear why each of you are here."

Nobody was talking. Bear Man knew his stuff. One by one he got us to cough up our stories. He started by pointing at the woman who had given me the Lucky.

She was an alcoholic, she confessed. I envied her that simple label. She'd come home drunk one night, gone in to check on her three-month-old daughter, and accidentally set the crib on fire with her cigarette. Her husband had given her an ultimatum: rehab or divorce.

The next person, a young guy, was a sophomore at BU majoring in medieval history. He'd started having obsessive-compulsive thoughts about killing his girlfriend, who he was sure was cheating on him with the assistant coach of the soccer team.

A woman with short black hair and very red lipstick was a flight attendant who had been suspended from her job because she kept testing positive for uppers.

My roommate, sitting beside me, spoke in a stilted, breathy

voice, like a child reciting poetry: "My name is Lillith. I was living in a halfway house in Fairfield."

"What happened?"

"I had an episode." This close, I could see freckles. The skin under her eyes was fragile and purplish.

"Mmmhmm." The leader turned to me.

"My therapist thought I wasn't doing well enough on antidepressants."

A bear eyebrow was raised, hovering.

"And I tried to kill myself last week."

No one seemed impressed. Bear Man nodded and went on to the last person, the man in the yellow shirt.

His sleeves were now rolled halfway up his forearms, I guessed the overheated dayroom had finally gotten to him. In his late thirties, probably, with a black square haircut that made him look like Frankenstein. Propped up against the wall, a big muscular guy sagging like a sack of flour.

Bear Man saw right off that this one wasn't going to be easy and tried another tack. "What do you do for a living?"

Mumble.

"Where do you work?"

Mumble.

"What is your job?"

The man lifted his head, and his eyes were unfathomably dark. "Security guard," he exhaled, and then looked down again. That was all he said.

But now his badge of admittance to our group was plain to see—a deep purple vertical scar on the inside of each wrist.

My heart was filled with something like awe.

For dinner, they let us go out to the cafeteria. It was one of the modern buildings, an A-frame, all yellows and whites and chrome, appallingly bright and loud. Not a soul looked up as we entered. By the door was a tableful of teenagers, boys and girls, dressed in jeans and T-shirts, leaning over and shouting at one another. It wasn't clear who was in charge of them.

The menu, purple Magic Marker script on shiny cardboard with smiley faces drawn on the bottom, was incomprehensible to me. I fell behind in line and listened to other people rattling off what they wanted to the lady behind the counter: veal Parmesan, chicken pot pie, eggplant casserole, several different kinds of vegetables, a soup I didn't catch.

I slid my tray onto the chrome rack and said the first thing that came into my mind: "Eggplant casserole and rice, please."

"What? You'll have to speak up, honey."

I repeated it for her.

"No rice today. Listen, how about some linguine? With garlic and butter. You look like you could use some meat on those bones."

"Okay."

"Good girl," said a man's voice behind me.

I turned around. It was the evening shift MH, a man about my age, as handsome as a movie star, with longish dark hair.

Lillith, sitting across from me, didn't eat. She cut her veal up into splinters, which took a long time, since the knives, although metal, had no serrations, and then began methodically mashing the bits of meat along with the coagulating cheese into the linguine on her plate. It was hard not to watch her doing this. The man in the yellow shirt was sitting hunched over beside her, not eating either, his hands around a mug of coffee so that the scars were hidden. Every so often he swallowed, not the coffee, but his own spit. Bulging out of his white throat, his Adam's apple looked like a growth.

I took a cautious bite of my eggplant. It eased down and then settled gently into my stomach. The taste was odd, not wrong, but like it was coming from far away. I forced myself to keep eating.

*   *   *

After dinner when Lillith and I were lying on our beds, she surprised me by leaning over and asking casually: "Okay, so how'd ya do it?"

"Are you talking to me?"

Her eyes were hidden behind her veil of greasy hair, so I couldn't tell her expression. "Who else, Miss Priss?"

I turned a little so my back was to the door, pushed up the left sleeve of my sweater, and showed her my scars. Tiger stripes, I called them. Of course they were nothing compared to the man in the yellow shirt's.

I'd started in high school. Using the smallest blade of my Swiss Army knife to pick away at a spot until I couldn't stand it anymore. Only when I was alone. Didn't anyone recommend you seek counseling? Valerie had asked me, and I said, No, it was just something I did, a kind of tic. Certainly not as dramatic as bulimia, which one of my roommates was into. At least my habit was more discreet. I had it down to an art, savoring the very first sting of it, before my brain had time to distinguish pleasure from pain. Finally it would subside into something dull and predictable, a nasty little wound that I could have gotten by accident. Only a new cut would do the trick, give me that thrill again.

After I got married for some reason I just stopped, and I never even thought about it until those last few weeks at my job when I'd caught myself at it again. The delicate welling of blood, exactly one inch long—I had such a feel with my X-Acto knife I knew an inch without measuring.

Lillith propped her chin up with a fist to look. "Fuck," she said appreciatively. "But that's not the way you did it."

"No."

"I bet you took pills. You're the pill type."

"What about you?"

"Once I drank Lysol, but they pumped my stomach out. And I tried to hang myself. The only thing I haven't used is a gun."

"Too phallic, huh?" I asked.

It was supposed to be a joke but she didn't laugh, just rolled around so that her back was to me, signaling she didn't want to talk anymore. So I picked up that stupid *Ladies' Home Journal* and stared at it until bedtime meds were announced.

Lillith conked out right away. I lay there in the scratchy, overbleached sheets as the brown darkness filled up with her bitter breath. From beyond the wedge of light at the door came the sound of low conversation and occasional laughter. When I couldn't stand it anymore I got up and opened the door all the way.

"I have to use the bathroom."

The handsome MH turned from the doorway of the nurses' station where he'd been leaning and escorted me. When I came out he was standing with his arms folded over his chest, staring discreetly into space.

"I can't sleep."

I was afraid I was going to be scolded, the recalcitrant patient, but he simply gestured for me to sit down at a table. Then he sat too, as graceful as a cat. "What do you think the problem is?" A nighttime voice, soft, with subtle undertones.

"I never sleep well the first night in a strange bed."

"And why is that?" If the day MH's style had been supremely matter-of-fact, this one's was seductive.

"I don't know why. It's disorienting, I guess."

"Not used to a roommate?"

"I've been sharing rooms all my life."

"The dark, maybe?" He was treating me like a child.

"The dark is kind, why should I be afraid of it?"

"Ah." He smiled. "So what's on your mind then?"

"I miss my sister." I had no idea why I'd said that. I hadn't been thinking it at all.

"Where is she?"

"Usually she lives in New York City, but now she's out of

the country on business." That wasn't exactly true, but I didn't bother to correct myself.

"Aren't there phones where she is?"

I shrugged, something Valerie hated.

"Well, one thing's for certain. Someone's broken your heart."

"What makes you say that?"

"You've got an extraordinarily sad face. Like an ancient Kyoto beauty. Didn't anyone ever tell you?"

I shook my head. I wasn't up to flirting, if that's what he was doing.

"Look," he said, "I think you'd better try to get some rest now."

This time, maybe because I could feel the meds kicking in, I knew I was going to be able to sleep. It was a relief to crawl back between those stiff hospital sheets, back into that haze that had no part in time. I'd have given anything to be able to stay there forever, drifting, not dead, not alive.

In the dark I leaned down to the foot of the bed where I had placed my bag and groped around in the side compartment until I found what Swivel Chair Lady had missed, jammed down to where the seam was fraying. A slender cylinder wrapped in a scrap of velvet. It had the heft of an expensive fountain pen although it was slightly longer. It smelled of the bag, medicinal and musty. In the dark I fingered the folds of cloth aside, to feel the cool jade.

My Nai-nai's hairpin. Over a hundred years old, all the way from Shanghai, given to me for my ninth birthday. You would have thought the phoenix head would have been worn down by now, I'd handled it so much, but I could still trace the bulging eyes, the curve of the beak, as well as the wicked sharp point it slimmed into at the other end. My grandmother had once stabbed someone with it, one of her suitors who had gotten too frisky. I could picture his amazement as she jerked it out of her hair, which loosened in a gleaming, liquid black fall over her shoulders—for a split second he probably thought he'd gotten lucky—and then the mortal pain as she jabbed it in between his ribs.

I rerolled the pin in the velvet, wedged it back into its niche in the bag, and rebuttoned the compartment.

"Nai-nai," I whispered. "Keep me safe."

But even as I said it I knew: nothing in this world is safe.

2

Like most people I have many names. My father gave me "Delicate Virtue" in Chinese, but for the tough American world my parents decided that "Sarah Collisson Wang" had a ring to it. Herbert Collisson was the chairman of the Asian department at the Army Languages School in Monterey, where my parents were teaching then. But Sally is what I'm known as, Sally Wang-Acheson for the six years of my marriage, and since then I'm back to Sally Wang, those two flat *a*'s knocking against each other when Americans pronounce it, so graceless and so far off from what Daddy intended.

"What does it matter what Daddy intended?" I can hear my sister, Marty, saying. "He never gave a flying fuck about who we really were."

You should understand this: I am not the kind of person anyone ever expected to go crazy. That's more my sister's department. The only extreme thing I'd ever done in my life was to drop out of college to get married. I thought I'd never have to make a big decision again, except maybe whether or not to have children.

It's in my nature to hoard, and this turned out to be a godsend. My ex-husband, Carey, and I kept separate bank accounts, so when we got divorced the division of finances was simple. After I quit my job—telling my boss I wanted to freelance so I'd have more time to paint—I had enough savings to survive on for several months.

My new apartment in the East Village had a northeastern

exposure and no coverings on the windows, so that I could sit in the baby rocking chair nights with the lights off and stare straight uptown to the silver spire of the Chrysler Building. Carey had kept most of the furniture, since it was originally from his family. My clothes were hung on exposed racks like a department store and I slept on a mattress on the floor. I had one mug, one glass, one plate, one set of cutlery, a single pair of chopsticks. Spare, the way I like things.

I actually did try working at home for a while, but it was just as excruciating as the office. Mornings I'd switch on the TV and just lie there, not getting to my drafting board until early afternoon, sometimes not at all. They fascinated me, those talk-show guests, bad skin slicked over with pancake makeup, as they related their dramas in quavering tones. I'd have to remind myself they were getting paid to do this.

I decided that what I needed to do was make my life extremely simple. Every Friday afternoon I went grocery shopping, always with the same list: a whole chicken, brown rice, and frozen vegetables. I'd stew up the chicken and live on it for a week. That was an old Wang tradition—even my sister, who can't boil an egg, has been known to call my mother long-distance for the recipe. One day at D'Agostino's a stock guy came up to me. "Hey, lady, are you all right?" I guess I'd been loitering in an aisle or something. Looking into his face, I realized he thought there was something wrong with me, maybe that I was mentally retarded.

I was cracking up and I knew it and I couldn't stop it.

It got worse. I couldn't tell anyone what I was seeing then. For one thing, my father was everywhere, a shock of white hair in the periphery of my vision, and then I'd turn and it would be a stranger, even a woman, or worse, nothing at all. Footsteps up the stairs at night, although I lived on the top floor and there shouldn't have been any.

I took the bus to Chinatown and wandered around scrutinizing every single little old man on the stoops, hoping this would break the spell. They mostly spoke Cantonese. Daddy's language had been a pure, educated Mandarin. Walking those teeming sidewalks, I felt totally alien although the tourists thought I was part of the scenery. When they stopped me to ask directions and I told them I didn't know, they were always amazed and put off by the fact that I spoke perfect English.

I found the old *bao zi* shop where my parents would take Marty and me. Chinese McDonald's Ma called it. I sat on a cracked green stool at the Formica counter and ordered a pork—*cha shao*—with an orange soda, like I used to. But when the steamed bun came I couldn't eat it. I drank my soda from the can through a bendable straw and watched old peasant women come in and order dozens of buns stacked in boxes tied with string. The women scolded the bakery man if he didn't have exactly what they wanted. He just smiled and was cheerfully rude back to them.

Chinese man the best to marry, Ma would tell Marty and me. Like American, basically tenderhearted.

Except Daddy. I had killed him in my head long ago, long before he actually died. What he had done to me was horrific. Still, I'd recovered. I'd even gotten married. So what was the problem? Why was he plaguing me now?

USELESS GIRL. WALKING PIECE OF MEAT.

I crossed Canal and went into Pearl Paint. It was mobbed, as usual, with serious and not-so-serious artists. On the second floor I meandered into the mezzanine, where the priciest oils were. Without thinking I picked up a couple of tubes of Old Holland cobalt violet light and slipped them into the pocket of my parka. My heart began to thud so hard I was sure it showed, but as far as I could see no one looked at me twice. I just clomped down those rickety loft stairs and strolled out of the store with eighty bucks worth of paint in my coat. No electronic beeper, no security guard grabbing my elbow.

In a store window I happened to catch a glance of myself

and saw what a lowlife I looked, hair hanging down in a tangle. I hadn't even bothered to wash my face that morning. Amazing that I hadn't gotten stopped.

At a street vendor, I bought produce: pale chartreuse star fruit, persimmons, giant globes of winter melon. Then I went home and piled it all on a card table and tacked up a stretched canvas on my wall. Using a new palette, including the paint I'd stolen, I made several false starts. Nothing was happening—it was too static. I rearranged the fruit more gracefully, but this time it looked pockmarked and malevolent. I adjusted the light down and then the fruit looked dead again. *Nature morte.* Over the next couple of weeks I watched it all rot. It became a kind of pleasure to wake up and examine each new stage of decomposition. I almost couldn't bear to throw it out.

Fran suggested I try Chopin nocturnes. "Remember at school, when we'd get depressed? They always worked for you then." I dug out the tape and played it over and over, but the only thing it did was make me cry.

The bare night against the panes started to spook me. I unpacked one of my few boxes of marriage stuff, the steel blue Porthault sheets we'd never used, and stapled them up over the windows. The shroudlike heaviness of the drapery spilling down and pooling over the dusty floor was comforting. Now my apartment had two levels of brightness: dark or dim. I rarely turned on the lights.

I tried calling my sister. She was always out—at her job as a clown at the South Street Seaport, acting class, auditions, or the kinds of parties you read about in *New York* magazine. When I finally got hold of her she told me that her new boyfriend, a producer, had invited her to his villa in the south of France. The next thing I knew she was gone.

"Career connections," Ma explained to me from New Haven. By then I was hiding behind my machine, listening to the disembodied voices of the few friends who still called echoing in the empty apartment. My mother hates leaving messages and will just hang up and dial again, as if she could wear down the machine that way. She did this so many times in a row that one night I finally picked up, just so she would stop.

I told her I wasn't feeling well.

"New York City air," my mother diagnosed. "You come up to the country to rest. Stay as long as you want." Ma considers anything not Manhattan to be the country.

I decided it couldn't hurt. Although I had a set of perfectly good luggage Uncle Richard and Aunty Mabel had given me as a wedding present, I just threw some stuff into an old Macy's shopping bag. Maybe I wanted to make sure I wouldn't stay in New Haven long, which was a joke considering how soon after I arrived it became obvious that I would never leave.

Ma picked me up at the train station and then went back to Yale for a department meeting. We were in the middle of a January thaw, and I sat outside on the front steps and watched the snow melting off the eaves, plopping onto the gravel border. When you're clinically depressed something like drops falling can mesmerize you for hours. Then I wanted a cigarette and I'd forgotten to buy some before I left the city, so I went inside and up to my sister's room. Her desk was uncharacteristically bare, but in the top drawer I found used checkbooks, a letter from an old boyfriend ("My Winky" he called her), a ruffle-edged snapshot of the two of us on the swing set at our old house, and finally a pack of stale Larks.

The backyard was separated from the driveway by a concrete curb, beyond which the terrain sloped steeply into a flat meadow. I sat on the curb with my back to the house and lit up. Even in this season, through the acrid taste of old tobacco, I could smell the clean must of the evergreens. I felt a spark of hope. Perhaps after all it had been a good idea to come home. I could see myself leading a dull, comfortable life for a few weeks, doing errands for my mother until I got my brain back. I exhaled, watching the last of the smoke from my cigarette curl up in slow motion.

*   *   *

When I was still able to, I took the Honda over to our old
house on Coram Drive. In physical distance, it was nothing,
about five miles. When we lived there, the house, the last on a
dead end, had been painted forest green with black shutters. It
had changed hands a couple of times since my parents had
sold it, and now it was buttercup yellow, with a neat white
trim replacing the shutters. At some point the side porch had
been insulated to serve as another room, because I saw white
curtains at the windows. Thick ruffled curtains, not the delicate lace-trimmed ones my mother favors. The cozy effect was
completed by a calico cat sitting on the sill, something that
made me realize just how completely wiped out our presence
there was. We never had any pets. Daddy said that animals
belonged on farms, where they could pull their own weight
and weren't just another mouth to feed.

The bedroom Marty and I had shared had a closet with a
window. This had been my hiding place. From the window
you could see past the grass island with its hawthorn bush
and straight down the block to where the road made a sharp
bend, by Witch Dugan's. You could check out who was out
riding their bike, who was playing kickball, who was getting
yelled at by their mother on their front steps. I peered up at
the window but couldn't tell whether it was still being used as
a closet or whether they had decided to make it into another
tiny room.

It was too early in the season to tell if the daffodil bulbs my
mother had planted along the front walk had survived. The
hawthorn bush had been cut way back, almost to a stubble,
and I couldn't see any berries. I looped the car slowly around
the circle several times, wondering whether I should park in
front and knock. Someone who'd paint their house yellow and
owned a cat would certainly be friendly. Maybe they'd even
give me a tour. I hoped my circling wasn't conspicuous. People were always getting lost on Coram Drive, it was such an

odd little street, with its dramatic L-shaped bend and then suddenly the circle, which belonged to us, the neighborhood kids. We'd be out playing and have to scatter to the sidewalks or up onto the island when a stray car came by. "It's a dead end, stupid!" we'd hoot at the driver, who would either glare or look humiliated, depending on whether it was a man or a woman.

There were no kids out this time, not surprising on a bleak, tail-of-winter day. The Katzes' house next door had been knocked down a long time ago and someone had put up an ugly rawboned ranch that didn't go with the modest fake Colonials on the rest of the street. No doubt the goldfish pond out back had long since been filled in. I ended up not stopping at all but instead retraced my route out to Whitney Avenue, past St. Cecilia's and Lake Whitney and the wicked curve that was the last thing Darcy Katz saw in this life, and back home to the fancy house on the hill that contained only my mother, bent over the desk in Daddy's old study, paying bills. When she asked me where I'd been I told her out by the lake.

My lie gave me an idea. I needed to draw again. I couldn't read, and I couldn't paint, but there hadn't been a time in my life when I couldn't depend on that most elementary of connections between my eyes and the paper. I went up to the attic to look for the old box of drawing pencils and a half-filled sketch pad I knew were there from high school. The place was a mess: boxes brimming with schoolbooks, crates of Nai-nai's Limoges, which my mother thought was too good to use, packed in straw, ancient black fans with wicked-looking blades, bulging garment bags on hooks, moving cartons containing Daddy's old Chinese newspapers. Everything I touched brought up a puff of dust, making me sneeze.

And then I saw it, behind an old black trunk from China: the green plastic laundry basket filled with stuffed animals. They were battered almost beyond recognition, but I remembered them all: Buzzy the bear, Charlie the giraffe, Wilbur the donkey. I reached into the pile and pulled out the most raggedy one of all: Piggy. His fur, what was left of it, had been worn to a kind of sickly flesh color, the plastic snout with its two indentations still a garish orange. When his dark beady eyes caught the light from the overhead bulb, I felt a repulsion so great I almost dropped him.

In the next instant he looked benign, dirty and scarred, an old warrior.

I brushed him off and took him downstairs with me. For a while it would give me a jolt to see him sitting there on my pillow, plain and alone, but then I got used to it.

I had completely forgotten about my plan to go out by the reservoir and draw. By the time I remembered, it didn't seem worth it.

I began staying in bed all day. Every afternoon at one exactly Ma would come home from teaching, roaring up the driveway, clanging in the kitchen, and then rapping at my door. Without waiting for an answer, she'd push it open.

"You want cottage cheese? I make a nice salad, put fruit cocktail on it."

"No, Ma, I had something."

She knew I was lying and I knew she knew it, but we had to go through this ritual every day.

"Where all your grade school friends?" she asked me. "Maybe you call them, have party here."

"There's no one left," I said vaguely, and then I realized I had made it sound as if they were all dead.

I ventured out of my room only when I heard the door between the master bedroom and bathroom open as Ma went to bed and I could smell the soap from her bath in the hall.

Night was when I felt most comfortable. The house looked different then, the stark furnishings and Tudor arches friendlier in chiaroscuro. I wandered down to the kitchen and found food laid out on the counter: Chinese plum candies in blue and red wax papers, sesame crackers shaped like chickens, swollen-bellied pears in browns, greens, and yellows, tucked into the Rembrandt shadows of an earthenware bowl. Ma's own still life, to tempt me. The refrigerator was stocked with cottage cheese and plain yogurt, things that my mother herself never ate, but she must have remembered my vegetarian phase in boarding school. I sat down at the kitchen table and like an animal devoured what I had picked out, not knowing or remembering what I was cramming into my mouth, staring out at the black beyond the tiny window over the sink. Sometimes I'd take the food into the living room and consume it sitting on the floor with the TV on, sound off, even though I had no idea what was going on, watching simply in order to concentrate on something besides the static in my own head.

When even silent TV became unbearable, I went down into the basement and sat there in a dream until the sun came up.

My one-month visit had spilled into two. Ma made me an appointment with her doctor, who ordered a bunch of tests. The tests turned up nothing. I was underweight, but not seriously so. The doctor suggested that I see a psychotherapist.

My mother thought this was nonsense. "All you need is career. That takes your mind off personal problems. You seen my sewing scissors?"

"No," I said.

One afternoon Ma came to my room and announced that she had invited Lally Escobar to tea. "She especially wants to see you."

"I don't want to see her." I was lying in bed as usual, still in my pajamas.

"But she knows you're home. What am I suppose to say when she ask for you?"

"Tell her I'm asleep."

My mother said firmly, "You come down," and shut the door.

The only place I could think of to hide was the basement. I made it down to the first floor without Ma hearing. The teakettle began to whistle at the exact moment I opened the basement door and shut it behind me in a single motion. At the bottom of the stairs I held my breath. The kitchen floorboards creaked as my mother moved about above me. Then I heard the chimes of the doorbell and short quick creaks as she went to answer it.

I didn't dare turn on the light. When my eyes got used to the dark I edged my way deeper in through the maze of boxes and old furniture, the oil furnace growling in the middle, and finally reached the corner where I'd made a kind of nest for myself out of an old stadium blanket on top of several rolled-up rugs. I drew my bare feet up and tucked the bottom of the blanket around them.

Lally and my mother were talking. There was a package of Pepperidge Farm lemon nut cookies on the table between them. Because they were having Western tea, Ma was using her tulip tea set that had cups with handles. There was a bizarre rasping noise that I recognized as Lally's laugh. I pictured her in her gardening outfit—a pink-and-green-striped turtleneck and overalls—although she probably wouldn't be wearing that today.

I waited, growing colder. The dark pressed against my ears, so that I could hear my blood pounding. I covered the sides of my head and tried to slow down my breathing. The furnace rumbled. Lally wasn't laughing anymore. In fact, it was perfectly silent above. I imagined slowing down my breathing more, suppressing my heartbeat, like the yogis in India. Only I'd will it past suspended animation. I'd make myself die.

I reached down between the rolled-up rugs and felt for Ma's sewing shears. It wasn't the easiest thing to do in the dark, but I knew where there was virgin skin, up near the crook of my elbow. The feeling came, not as sharp as it would have been if it hadn't been so cold, and it didn't last nearly long enough.

There was one window high up in a corner that let in a bit of daylight, and I made myself concentrate on that. My cut began to throb. I pressed a corner of the blanket against it.

PIECE OF MEAT.

The window had gone completely dark by the time I finally decided it was safe. I unfolded myself from the rugs, stamped around a bit to get the circulation back in my legs, and then went up the basement stairs, slowly and deliberately this time. When I opened the door there was my mother sitting alone at the kitchen table, looking directly at me. The tea things had been cleared away, and the dishwasher was humming. I blinked hard, getting used to the light, and saw that my arm looked much worse than I'd imagined. I hadn't been so neat this time.

For a moment I thought she wasn't going to say anything at all. I turned to go on upstairs to my room.

"Lally gave me the name of someone. A woman doctor." I must have looked blank, for she added: "A doctor for your brain."

"A psychiatrist?"

"She has a medical degree from Yale. Good reputation."

So this was it. If my mother admitted it, I really was crazy.

I knew in my bones that no matter how brilliant this person was, she'd never be able to cure me.

3

We each got assigned to a unit. Lillith and I stayed together—
same unit, same treatment group. The alcoholic and the flight
attendant went to Rehab in its own separate building behind
the cafeteria, and the quiet guy who slashed his wrists ended
up being transferred to State. Lillith told me about State, how
the ratio of staff to patients was so bad they kept everyone
drugged up to the eyeballs. According to her, Willowridge was
a country club.

The point, it seemed, was to deinstitutionalize our surroundings so we could pretend we were normal citizens
instead of prisoners. The dayroom in our unit resembled an
upscale suburban living room, with its gold wall-to-wall carpeting, Ethan Allen furniture, and the baby grand Steinway
donated by a former patient. Where the dining room in a regular house would have been was the glassed-in nurses' station,
and across from it a kitchenette where people hung around
and drank coffee. But unlike in a regular house there was an
air of emergency, too many comings and goings, the phone in
the nurses' station constantly ringing.

I was on Status One, house arrest. Along with me was a
man who had to dress in pajamas because he was liable to
run away. "Elope," they called it. We got our meals on trays
and had single rooms on the first floor near the nurses' station, where the staff could keep an eye on us. Our day began
at 6 A.M. when we were woken up and taken for showers. In
my entire twenty-four hours, the shower door was the only

one I could shut behind me. I turned the water on full force and made it as hot as I could stand and then hotter, so that it steamed up the glass, obliterating the silhouette of the MH leaning up against the sink. We got exactly seven minutes in there—they actually set a kitchen timer. It was Lillith who explained to me the dangers of the bathroom. At State, she said, some guy had once managed to drown himself in the toilet.

In our first week at the unit, Lillith had advanced to Status Two and gotten her sharps back. She'd decided not to hold my unimpressive suicide attempt against me and became my buddy, bringing me honey packets from dinner, a necklace of tiny wooden spools she'd made in OT. It was Lillith I went to when I found I'd gotten my period. I'd lost track, I'd become so irregular, and during my shower I thought I had a stomach-ache and then looked down and saw it in the hollow of my thigh like a bloody oyster.

I found her in the dayroom and asked if she had a Tampax.

"Can't help you there," she said. "I had a hysterectomy." There was something about the way she said it that discouraged me from inquiring why.

I had to ask at the nurses' station. When I went back into the dayroom my treatment group was waiting there to go to breakfast. Lillith was reading a magazine. A couple of the younger guys, Douglas and Mel, were fooling around with a tennis ball, taking turns bouncing it off their heads.

When Douglas saw me he started chanting: "Wally Sang, Wally Sang, Wally Sang."

Douglas scared the shit out of me. Over six feet tall and built like a linebacker, he wore the same stained forest green polo shirt and crummy jeans day after day. He was in here because he had tried to murder his mother who was black and from Barbados. His father was white. Douglas would actually have been an attractive guy if it weren't for his personality. His thing was to hit on all the women—MHs, nurses, patients, even poor Rachel, who walked around with a teddy bear clutched to her bosom.

Lillith looked up from her magazine and patted the sofa next to her. "C'mere," she said. "I'll do your hair."

No one had done my hair for me since Ma at the breakfast table before school. She'd make my two long plaits with paintbrush ends, and bows to match what I was wearing. "Beauty routine," Daddy would mutter. My sister's face framed by its Dutch-boy cut rose smug across the table.

Lillith's touch as she combed was a lot gentler than my mother's. It made me feel dreamy and in danger at the same time.

"I think braids," she said. "I'm good at braids."

"Okay."

"How many?"

"Just one."

"Oh," she sighed, "I'd kill to have hair like yours." Douglas passed into our line of vision, making a pig face, lips bloomed up touching the tip of his nose.

Lillith ignored him. She said to me: "You know, you should talk more in group."

"I can't."

"Oh, come on. You're so smart, you can think of something." She herself had related harrowing tales of growing up in a mansion in Guilford with her pervert uncle and his string of boyfriends. Her stories were full of rubber gloves, hoses, and toilets. "When I get out I'm going to the beach every single day. Lie around and drink piña coladas and get a tan."

"Me too," I said.

"Seriously, if you want to get out you should talk. Why do you give a shit about what these people think? You're never going to see any of them again."

"That's true."

"Plus, you think they haven't heard it all before?"

"I guess."

"Okay, you're done," she said, snapping the elastic. I could see my reflection in the glass wall of the nurses' station. She'd been so neat it looked like I had short hair.

"Thanks."

"Tell me your opinion of this." She opened her copy of *Glamour* to a photograph of a do-it-yourself crocheted string bikini.

"Wowza," said Mel, looking over her shoulder. I liked Mel. At nineteen, he was the youngest in our group, transferred from Adolescents because he'd kept on getting into fights there. He wore macho clothes—frayed flannel shirts, work boots, a gold stud in one ear—but underneath I could see that there was something delicate, almost dandyish, about him.

Lillith said: "I'm going to send away for some shocking pink yarn." I looked at the browned, busty, gleaming model, and then I looked at Lillith, all frail bones with a caved-in chest and skin the color of skim milk.

"That would look great on you."

"You think?" When she smiled her teeth were stumpy, grayish at the roots. "Oops, gotta go," she said. The MH had just come in. Breakfast had already arrived in plastic wrap for Pajama Man and me.

"Have fun," I said.

I didn't really mind being stuck in the house while everyone else was out at meals or therapies. Pajama Man and I mostly watched stupid TV, and when I got sick of that I'd go curl up in my favorite spot, the bay window seat, where I could sit for hours, doing nothing. Staff didn't like that, they'd come over and try to get me to tell them my feelings.

I ate my breakfast at the window. The view was the flagstone path that led up to the front door, where another group was trooping back from breakfast. About fifty yards beyond shimmered the cold gray plane of the lake. On the near side were a couple of wrought-iron benches, where occasionally I saw someone huddled up, tossing bread to the ducks. On the far side stretched a line of weeping willows beginning to bud white. At least Willowridge really had willows. I imagined that if I could still paint I'd use a Chinese brush and ink—the kind you mix up in a stone—on the finest rice paper. Stark short strokes for the boughs, washed over with a broad sweep to indicate wind.

It was an audacious fantasy I was having, because I knew full well the absolute confidence it took to work in ink. You had to do it from your soul, and it had to be as natural as breathing.

Lillith's uncle sent her raspberry licorice strings. We all watched while she opened the package and made a disgusted sound. "He knows I hate this crap."

She put the tin on the sign-out desk in the foyer. After dinner Douglas took it into the dayroom and consumed every single piece while watching *Lifestyles of the Rich and Famous.* Then he went into the bathroom on the first floor and puked. Puking was a common occurrence at Willowridge. They'd note it down in the daybook: "Refused meds, reticent during group, vomiting 8 P.M."

On my way into the kitchen for a cup of tea I heard him retching and then the toilet flush.

The bathroom door opened and Douglas emerged, looking amazingly healthy.

"Hey, geisha girl," he said.

I pretended to be fascinated by a conversation in the nurses' station.

"You do have beautiful hair," he said. "Satin. Is it like that on the rest of you?" He came up slyly beside me and pressed his nose into the crown of my head. "Mmm. Smells good too."

"Get away from me."

"Don't be so skittish." He yanked at my braid and tears popped into my eyes. "Come on, I want to show you something." Still holding my hair, he dragged me along the hall a few feet into the recess where the phone was. We called it a booth, though it didn't have a door. He let go of my braid and turned me around so that I was facing him, and then he kissed me. I could feel the soft squishiness of his belly, surprisingly comforting, and also between his thighs where I was afraid to lean into. His lips were chapped. He twisted my head around to insert his tongue and despite his having been sick, his saliva was still as sweet as a child's from the candy, although I could taste the other too at the back of my throat.

He said into my ear: "I've always wondered about what they say about Oriental women. Is it true, Sally? Tell me, is it true? Are their cunts, you know, *slanted*?"

"Fuck you."

"Leave her alone."

It was Mel, coming down the back stairs.

"Ah, don't worry, she's not my type anyway. Too skinny." He released me.

Mel said: "Touch her again and I'll kill you."

"Christ, she let me do it."

I ducked into the bathroom without asking the MH on duty like I was supposed to. The faint stench of Douglas's half-digested dinner still clouded the air. I could report him, get him into a heap of trouble, but I knew I wasn't going to. I took a piece of toilet paper and scrubbed at the corners of my mouth, which were stained a carnival red from the licorice juice, like the little-girl lipsticks Aunty Mabel used to give Marty and me for Christmas.

In group Mel told us that when he was little his older cousins had locked him in the garage and pulled down his pants and tortured him by sticking pins into his buttocks. It was a kind of game, he said.

"How old were you?" the MH asked.

"I'd just learned to walk," Mel said tersely, not looking at anyone.

"Two?"

"Something like that."

"How often did this happen?"

"Every single Saturday."

"Did you tell your parents?"

What a stupid question, I thought.

"No," said Mel. "I couldn't talk very well."

"But they must have wondered about the scars."

Mel shook his head. "I don't remember."

"Hi, Ma. I got your messages."

"How are you? How is your health?"

"I'm okay. They're taking care of me."

"Enough to eat?"

"Yeah, there's plenty to eat. Ma, my group thinks it's better if you don't call me anymore."

"Ah? What's this? Who says this?"

"They think it's better if we have less contact."

"I don't understand this at all, Sal-lee. This is not clear thinking."

"Yeah, well, you can talk to them yourself if you want."

"I leave you alone the first two days, because Valerie says let her adjust."

"I know, Ma. Thank you."

"So what's this? They want to keep me away from my daughter?"

"They think it would be better if I didn't have any outside influences."

"Your mother is not outside. Next Tuesday I'm coming. They told me to come, for family night."

"Family therapy. That's right."

"You want me bring anything?"

"No, Ma, that's okay."

"How about clothes?"

"No, Ma, I'm fine, they have a laundry room here and everything."

"Valerie says there's tennis courts there too."

"Yes, Ma, but it's too cold to play tennis."

"Valerie says it's a very prestigious place." I wanted to laugh. Was Ma going to brag about me being in here? But then she continued: "You know your sister call me from south of France."

"Really?"

"She's having great time. She says maybe go to Africa on safari next. You sure you don't want me bring anything? Those plum candies you like so much?"

"Yes, Ma, I'm sure."

From my place on the window seat, I spotted Valerie right away, lanky in her big black coat, hair tied back in a fuchsia scarf, striding up the walk. There was a flurry in the nurses' station when she asked for me.

And then there she was, in the dayroom doorway, holding the battered brown briefcase full of legal pads she used to take notes. I was never so glad to see anyone in my life.

"Well," she said. "You look better. Your color has come back."

We had our session in my bedroom, she sitting in the visitor's chair while I lay on the bed. She leafed through the file folder that contained my chart. "I see you're still on suicide precautions."

"Yes."

"Is that necessary?"

"No."

"You don't have any more thoughts about killing yourself?"

"Not in the near future."

"Sally, this isn't a game."

"I'm not going to commit suicide."

"I see. So, what I understand, is that you're not contemplating suicide anymore, but you're not exactly jumping up and down at the prospect of living either."

"You got it." I couldn't figure how she'd done that, I'd thought I was fine, but now I couldn't look at her, I couldn't let her see that she'd made me cry.

"I'm going to have them ease up on the Stelazine. So you'll feel something, even if it is pain. Your appetite?"

"Okay."

She frowned, peering at something.

"It says here you've been having trouble sleeping. Nightmares?"

"I wake up a lot. But that's nothing new."

The unit was full of rustlings, and my bedroom door stayed ajar, so I heard all of it. The back and forth to the bathroom, the shivery emergency shrill of the phone in the nurses' station, staff pouring a cup of coffee or getting stuff out of the refrigerator in the kitchenette.

"Are you still seeing ghosts?"

I'd told Valerie about my father—what happened when I was eight, how I had learned to forget and not forget, how he'd started reappearing on the streets of Manhattan.

"He's not here," I told her.

"Have you talked about it in group?"

"Him. Not the ghost."

"I see," she said.

"When am I going to get out of here?" I asked.

"When I'm convinced you can act like a responsible human being."

I sighed. On the far wall I noticed faint tape marks where some other patient had once put up a poster. Was it possible that someone desperate enough to be on Status One would care that much about their surroundings?

*   *   *

After our session, I walked Valerie out to the foyer. In the mirror frame over the sign-out book was tucked a note telling Douglas to phone his mother.

"I'll see you next week, sweetie," Valerie said, laying her hand lightly on the side of my face. "Remember, we're cutting down on the meds. Let me know how it goes."

A little while later, when Pajama Man and I were eating our lunches, Douglas meandered into the dayroom, kicking at the door frame with his sneaker. "Sheeet," he muttered, and collapsed into one of the TV armchairs beside Pajama Man. *The Young and the Restless* was on. One of the older female characters had on a crescent-shaped gold necklace and matching earrings that I found gaudy but I knew Lillith would like.

"Don't forget to call your mother," I said to Douglas.

He turned around and gave me a level look. "You are such a fake, Sally Wang."

"Exactly what do you mean by that?"

He groaned and yawned, stretching his legs out in front of him. "I can see straight through that goody-goody act of yours. You pretend to be so fucking sweet, but actually you're wondering what the hell you're doing in here with all the loonies. You think you're so much better than the rest of us."

"I never said—"

"You don't have to *say*. It's in your expression."

"That's not fair."

"That's not fair," he mimicked me. "You know what you remind me of? One of those little dogs people have in their cars, the ones that bob their heads up and down. You're made of plaster. You're not real."

He reached over past Pajama Man and twisted the volume knob on the TV set until someone stuck their head out of nurses' station and told him to turn it down.

4

In the bedroom Marty and I shared on Coram Drive, the wallpaper was white apple blossoms on a blue background. I can feel the texture of the paper now—the flower petals were raised and striated. The blue was the oddest shade, not like sky, or anything in nature, but dull and dark, a Prussian blue.

I dream I'm back in that room and there's my mother sitting on the bed. She's a monster—her skin has become that wallpaper, completely covered with it, like leprosy. She has no features on her face, just indentations. It revolts me in a way I can't describe.

I want to kill her.

I wake up, but whether it's out of sleep or into another dream I'm not sure. Though the room is dark I can make out white lace curtains at the windows. Or are they ghosts? My heart is pounding my ribs apart, cold sweat runs down my sides. I'm lying on my stomach with every inch of my body pressed as close as possible to the sheet. Maybe if I lie very flat like this, staying still as if I were dead, I will be okay.

There is a beating in my head, behind my eyes, and I squeeze them shut, willing the sound to stop. If my blood is so loud, how will I be able to hear anything else? In the darkness I wait a long time, studying the shape in the next bed—a puddle of black hair, the body like a mummy. Is she asleep or dead? Is that the silhouette of a baby rocking chair, tipped or tipping, by the window?

Finally I dare to turn my head and look the other way, toward the door. There is a gold line at the bottom. I can hear people whispering. "There's an ugly one," someone says in a loud voice.

The door snicks open and my eyes close in the same instant. I turn away from the light as if in my sleep.

"She was awake, I heard her crying." I recognize the voice of one of the female MHs on the night shift. A male voice answers: "She just got off suicide watch."

After they leave I look over at the next bed and see that it's only my new roommate, Rachel.

14 March

Fran:

You can tell from this letterhead where I ended up. Thanks for listening to me all those times I called you in the middle of the night. You are a friend among friends to put up with me in this wretched state I'm in.

It's actually not so bad in here. The big news of the week is that I'm up to Status Two, which means I can smoke, wear contacts, and attend all the scintillating therapies they have here.

My concentration is still not up to writing long epistles. I hope first-year law is treating you well. Write if you have time.

Love,
Sally

17 March

Mar:

Happy St. Patrick's Day. I'm sending this to the address you gave me when you left New York, which I hope is still good.

Supposedly I'm here to rest but so far there hasn't been

too much of that what with all this therapy—art, music, occupational, dance (they play a tambourine and we do free-form movements to get in touch with our bodies), and something you would get a kick out of—psychodrama. One person casts the rest of the group as members of their family in order to reenact some kind of traumatic experience. So far I haven't gotten to direct but I've played a domineering mother, a bullying older brother, and an aunt dying of cancer.

Hope to see you soon.

Sa

20 March

Dear Aunty Mabel and Uncle Richard:

Thank you for the get-well card. I'm sorry that Niu-niu can't climb up the trellis anymore. You could just set her in the kitchen next to the picture window to watch the starlings from there.

Yes, I'd love to come visit you this spring, if I ever get out of here.

Love,
Sally

What I remembered about Florida: the flat clarity of light over white sand as I walked barefoot, edging my toe into the mild surf of the Gulf. A fragrant wind. The sun on my back.

The sun.

My stomach contracted with desire.

It was just over a week until Easter Sunday.

The art therapist told us to make a self-portrait.

I couldn't do it. Every terror of the blank canvas I'd ever felt was multiplied a million times as I sat there at the big table with a sheet of newsprint in front of me. For everyone else it was a cinch, just another therapy. They were all working busily, Lillith with her arm coiled to hide what she was doing, Douglas chunking down like he was making polka dots, Mel leaning back with a cigarette in his mouth, and even Rachel— I could see from across the table that she was sketching an enormous face, in choppy lines.

It didn't do any good to remember the first drawing class I took in college, with life poses for one minute each, where you wouldn't even look down at the paper as you drew, fast, without corrections, following the curve of a spine by feel. No time to think, before the instructor's "Next!" and the model would switch poses. Letting the sketches fall to the floor until by the end of the class you had dozens which you could look over later and say to yourself—"Yes, I caught the arc of that muscle" or "The proportions are wrong here, but the feeling of weight is good."

I picked up my charcoal.

I was stupid now, and couldn't see, but there had once been a time when I'd had the divine fire.

Senior year at boarding school, after the standard program of charcoal, pastel, and watercolor, we graduated to oils. It was a completely new language, the box of miniature paint tubes marked with colors I'd never heard of—burnt sienna, titanium white, cadmium red, Indian yellow—the fat stiff-bristled brushes that felt clunky in my hands after the slender supple-tipped watercolor ones.

For the first time, it didn't come easy.

My problem was with the paints themselves, lying like gobs of frosting on the wooden palette. Our teacher ran us through some basic color theory before letting us mix. On the palette my colors looked okay, but transferred to canvas the effect was mud on a dark day. An unforgiving medium on an unforgiving surface. I didn't understand impasto yet, and any slip in judgment meant I had to scrub with a turpentine rag.

I spent a lot of time torturing myself by leaning over other people's shoulders and watching them work. In content, they didn't seem any more inspired than me, but their paintings had already begun to show texture and control. One day I walked into the studio and found an old still life someone had set up, a misshapen brown pot, probably a reject from the ceramics studio across the hall. It was crammed with daisies picked from the senior garden, already dying.

To hell with it, I only knew how to do what I could do. I put away the large landscape canvas I'd been working on and picked up a small new one. With my finest brush I began to work from the outside in, sketching the edges of the spiky petals protruding from the clump, using the white of the canvas as if I were working in watercolor. It looked too spare, so I mixed up some turpentine washes, blue and gray and brown, the tints of decay. The teacher had come in, and he strolled by a few times, looked, and moved on. I don't know how long I played around the periphery, concentrating only on the flowers that interested me, but eventually my old impatience took over.

I laid out a new palette of the most improbable colors I could find: magenta, emerald green, electric blue, cobalt violet. With a fatter brush I blocked in the squat shape of the vase as it listed to the left, almost off the painting, and then the interior of the bouquet, where the petals were mashed, their yellow hearts rotting. I mixed the paints on the canvas itself, tossing down my brush when it got too grimy and picking up a new one. I worked fast, without care, approximating. In five minutes I was finished.

The teacher had been standing behind me watching for I don't know how long.

"You caught it" was all he said.

Of course, as I learned later, that's what Van Gogh did, slather on the raw colors and work them into each other on the canvas, only he used a palette knife instead of a brush. He

couldn't bear the distance between the medium and the subject, the medium and himself, the subject and himself.

The art therapist tacked our drawings up on the bulletin
board, with mine in the middle.

"What do we think about these shapes that Sally has created?"

"Trees," said Rachel. In January her boyfriend had been
thrown from a motorcycle and killed as she stood waiting for
him on the porch of her parents' house half a block away.
When she first got here pieces of the accident were still in her
mind, but now she just looked blank when people talked
about it.

"What else do we see in Sally's drawing?"

"Blood vessels." Lillith, of course.

I myself was surprised at how thick and violent the lines
came out, because I'd started each time with great delicacy,
tracing a faint curve and then working it gently into the paper
with my fingers.

"Does anyone notice a *human shape* about this?"

A couple of stools scraped.

"Douglas?"

"I definitely see a tit."

"Excellent! There's a head, and a torso—see? And here as
you said the curve of a breast, but it's hazy, like it's just beginning to emerge." The art therapist folded her hands in front of
her stomach and beamed at me—her newest discovery. "Okay,
honey, this is what I want you to do. I want you to study yourself in a full-length mirror. And the next time we meet, draw
exactly what you see there, draw from memory." I could hear
Douglas snickering.

As we were leaving, Rachel went up and studied my drawing.
"Sally. If this is the face, here, you forgot to put in a mouth."

One of the upstairs bathrooms had a full-length mirror on the
back of the door. I closed the door behind me—I could do this

now—and dragged a footstool against it. The only locks in the unit were on the outside doors.

I am tall, even for an American woman, though not as tall as my father. My hair has a reddish undertone, not the pitch black people expect of Asians. I have a big oval face and a square chin—an overdeveloped jawbone, my dentist used to call it. My eyes are long and narrow, with no lashes to speak of, and I have the kind of lips women's magazines say you should wear very pale colors on, to de-emphasize. The only truly beautiful feature in my face is my nose, which is small and straight, and has more of a bridge than Marty's—she's always complaining about her sunglasses slipping.

As for body, I'm big-boned and long-waisted. Hips and thighs, but no chest to speak of, unlike Marty and my mother, who are buxom. My hands are freakishly large—long palms and fingers—bigger than most men's.

I was not meant to be looked at; I was meant to be one who looks.

Thank God I could still draw.

It was family therapy night. By six-thirty, when we got back from dinner, the dayroom had already begun to fill up. Lillith pointed out a well-dressed couple—Rachel's parents. Mel, who was from a large Italian family, had a retinue: mother, father, siblings, an aunt or two, even a grandmother. I noticed a man who looked like a haggard Jack Lemmon moving uncertainly around the edges of the crowd. His deep-set eyes, darkly shadowed, were just like his son's. Douglas. The two of them huddled in the corner, as thick as thieves, the son dwarfing the father.

There was my mother, stopped in the doorway, peering around, sure she was in the wrong place. She was still in her teaching clothes, carrying two Lord & Taylor bags, and she was alone. What did I expect, my sister wasn't the type to cut a vacation short to go see someone in a loony bin.

When Ma saw me her mouth turned into a line.

"Sal-lee." Without inflection, as if I were a student she were calling on in class.

Still, she was worried. I could see that.

"Hi, Ma. Come in and sit down."

As she lowered herself into one of the TV armchairs, my mother inhaled deeply and pulled the hem of her skirt over her knees.

"You gain weight." I was conscious of her accent, as I always am when I haven't seen her for a while.

"Maybe next time you could bring some of my fat clothes."

She snorted, looking more comfortable. "You're not *fat*." She held out a shopping bag. "Some jeans you left, a sweat-shirt I found you used to wear at boarding school. Also grape-fruit. Your Aunty Mabel sends a whole crate, I don't think I can finish it all. And look." From the other bag she plucked an old silk dress I'd bought to wear on my honeymoon, that I had forgotten I owned, even. It was a black-and-pink flower print, wrap waist, with puffy sleeves. I didn't have the heart to tell her I wouldn't be caught dead in it.

"Thanks, Ma."

She leaned back a little in her chair, appraising the furnish-ings. "Not so bad, huh? Doesn't look like hospital. But darker carpet would show dirt less."

The MH who was going to lead our session came over to introduce himself. To him Ma probably looked like a harmless little old Oriental lady in her pixie hairdo and schoolmarm out-fit. I'd heard that her students routinely made the same mis-take at their first class—grossly underestimating her.

"I hope Sally is doing all right," she said to the MH as if this were a PTA meeting and he was my teacher.

"Oh, we think she's making great progress," the MH told her, and smiled at me.

Ma leaned toward him confidingly. "How much longer she has to be in here?"

"It depends on Sally, of course. But I think she still has a lot of work ahead of her."

My mother looked disappointed. It was the same expression she'd worn when she told her friends I hadn't gotten into Yale.

"I have theory about why Sally gets sick," Ma said.

"And what is that, Mrs. Wang?"

"She's the type who needs a husband. It's so traumatic for her, to divorce."

"Why do you think she is the type who needs a husband?"

"She's an American girl but she has old-fashioned Chinese mentality."

"And what exactly is that mentality, Mrs. Wang?"

"Oh, you know, be a good daughter, be a good wife. Obedience. Confucian law. This is what her father teaches her."

I looked down at my hands and saw a bit of charcoal under one thumbnail. Surreptitiously, I began to scrape it out.

"I notice this especially when her father died," Ma went on.

"Excuse me, Mrs. Wang, but why do you always refer to your husband as 'Sally's father'?"

My mother looked surprised. "We're talking about Sally, right?"

"We're talking about you too."

"Okay." I could tell Ma thought the MH was stupid.

"Let's talk about exactly what happened when your husband died. How did you feel, Mrs. Wang?"

"Of course I grieve, he was my husband. And my younger daughter, she cried for days. But it's Sally who has really hard time. No crying, no speaking."

"Is that true, Sally?" the MH asked.

My father had his first stroke near the end of my senior year at boarding school. It was right after I got rejected from Yale, and although no one ever pointed this out to me, they didn't have to.

At my graduation, Marty showed up as the lone family representative, boyfriend in tow. She was wearing a very tight sheath splashed with purple cabbage roses and lipstick to match. "Egad," she said, looking around the lawn, which was strewn with girls in airy white dresses. "You went to school in this place? What did they feed you—strawberries and cream?" She waved the old Instamatic at me. "Honey, they made me bring this, but you don't really want a bunch of pictures of you and your virginal friends standing around looking goofy, do you?"

I told her I didn't care.

"Let's go find the champagne," my sister said. She winked at the boyfriend. It was still Schuyler then, a hulking blond who maybe said five words the whole time he was there.

I never went home that summer but took the train straight into Boston, where I had a job at the chocolate chip cookie booth at Quincy Market. Ma called every couple of days to keep me posted. Daddy was home, Daddy was sitting up in the living room reading newspapers, Daddy had taken a walk around the block after breakfast, the doctor said that Daddy was well enough to teach the last session of summer school. When I got Marty on the phone she said that you couldn't tell anything had happened to him at all, except that it took him a beat longer to answer when spoken to.

"Just as well," I said.

Fran had invited me to her cousins' house in Wellfleet for the last couple weeks in August, and I went to Providence from the Cape, taking the bus with my two suitcases, one filled with clothes, the other with art supplies. All the other kids had parents with station wagons or U-Hauls. I settled into my first semester at the Rhode Island School of Design, taking it seriously.

I hadn't seen my father in over a year when, the Saturday before Thanksgiving, I got a message to call home.

At breakfast that morning, Ma had looked out the kitchen

window and seen that the last rain had stripped the oaks in the front yard. "We have to get the boy to rake," she said to my father. When he didn't answer she turned to look at him. His jaw was slack, as if he were amazed at what she had said, but his eyes were pinched, focused on something behind her, beyond the window. He was dead by the time the ambulance pulled up in front of the emergency room entrance.

This is the official story, the one Ma told driving me home from the train station. I remember that she was wearing a rust-colored turtleneck sweater, a Christmas present from me, and a tweed skirt, lipstick on perfectly. She drove as smoothly as always, signaling in plenty of time before all her turns— thwack! and the clicking—and this somehow seemed to me the most astonishing thing of all.

But I shouldn't have been so surprised. Ma was always businesslike about death. I'd come home for summer vacation my junior year of boarding school and Marty told me she'd flown to San Diego the day before to bury my grandmother. That was how I'd learned of Nai-nai's death. I called California and begged Ma to let me come. "Not for kids," Ma said. "You remember your Nai-nai like last time you saw her."

The day after my father died, Marty was at the front door of our Woodside Avenue house, leaning up to hook her arm around my neck. It was the most affection she had shown me since we were kids. "Honey, I'm glad you're here," she whispered, and when we pulled apart I saw that she was holding a dustpan and brush. "I'm cleaning," she said. "I guess that's our job, you and me."

That night Aunty Mabel and Uncle Richard came over from the Holiday Inn with Chinese takeout. Marty and I spooned food into serving platters and the rice into bowls, while Ma sat at the head of the dining room table and spoke in exhausted tones to her sister and brother-in-law.

"This is time when it's good to have daughters," she said.

The morning of the funeral, as I was getting dressed, I

looked out my bedroom window and saw Marty standing in the driveway, one foot up on the stone curb. At first I thought she was smoking a cigarette and then I realized that it was a joint. She lifted her chin steady after each toke, to hold the smoke in. For the first time since I'd heard Daddy was dead, I wanted to cry.

The service was held in the old Congregational church with its long light windows and plain furnishings that Marty and I had attended as kids. We went with Ma except at Christmas, when she'd drag Daddy along and he'd shift embarrassingly in the pew, not knowing when he was supposed to stand up or pray or open the hymnal, much less the words to any of the hymns. Daddy's old friend Mr. Lin gave the eulogy in Chinese. Even though I couldn't speak the language, I could tell that his accent was the same as my father's. It was odd to hear the separate precise syllables of Mandarin in this stark white Christian chapel. Mr. Lin ended the speech in English: "Such a brilliant man, could have gone on to distinguished career in physics, he sacrifice to make good life in the United States for his daughters. We all miss him, eh?"

Sacrifice, I thought. Who exactly had sacrificed? Or been sacrificed?

Ma's face was pale and perfectly composed over the white collar of her navy silk shirtdress. In the middle of the eulogy I happened to look over and saw a small glistening tear collect at the inside corner of one eye and begin to slide, oil-like down her cheek. She reached into her handbag and stopped it cold with a folded Kleenex. I don't remember much else— mostly I was concentrating on not looking at the casket, because I thought I would throw up if I did.

At the house we served small glasses of sherry and fried sugared walnuts and hundred-year-old duck eggs that Aunty Mabel had sliced into quarters. "Everything from Sung Trading Company," she whispered to me. "Remember to thank Aunty Lilah."

All my parents' friends were Aunty and Uncle, though Aunty

Mabel and Uncle Richard were the only blood. Ma stood resolutely straight as the guests came to pay their respects, leaning to kiss her and then me and Marty. My sister's face looked ravaged, from grief or being stoned, I couldn't tell which. Rosy-cheeked Mimi Sung was being helpful as usual, passing dishes and showing people where the bathrooms were. She had gotten quite busty, I noticed. And there was our old enemy Xiao Lu, in line with his mother and father. At nineteen, he towered over everyone else in the room. "Sorry" was all he said to us. His tone sounded preppy. Marty turned to roll her eyes at me. "What the fuck is he doing here?"

Toward the end Ma's calm broke. She nudged my shoulder and said in an odd rushed way: "You're in charge, you take care of everything," and then she disappeared upstairs. Fortunately, people took this as a cue to leave, and finally Marty and I were alone in the kitchen loading the dishwasher.

"God, I'm glad that's over," I said.

My sister drew a deep breath. "Sa, listen, I have something to tell you."

"What?"

"It didn't happen the way Ma says."

"What do you mean?"

My sister turned her swollen eyes toward me to make sure I understood the importance of what she was about to say. "They were having a fight."

"What were they fighting about?"

"Me."

I slammed the dishwasher door shut and pushed the buttons. The hum and gush filled the house and then settled into a steady rushing.

"It doesn't matter, Mar. You didn't kill him. You know how he was. He would have gotten overexcited somehow, over something, eventually." But what I was thinking was: I gave him his first stroke, you gave him his last.

My sister nodded, slowly, and arranged herself on a stool

by the stove, watching me wipe off the counters and kitchen table. Her eyes were half-closed, as if she were in a trance. Upstairs we heard the toilet flush. "Do you think we should check on her?"

"No. I think she's all right."

I went into the dining room to pour myself a glass of sherry. Back at the kitchen table, I said, "I thought Roger was sweet." Roger was Schuyler's replacement, a Yale rugby player, who had shown up for the reception. I could tell he saw my sister as some delicate Asian flower. On my way upstairs to get more hand towels for the downstairs bathroom, I'd brushed past the two of them sitting on the landing. He was kissing the top of her hair and murmuring, "Baby, baby." In my entire life no one had ever called me baby.

"Yeah, he is sweet," Marty agreed absently, her voice trailing off and getting lost in the racket of the dishwasher.

The Formica of the table was a tan and cream design that resembled birch bark. Rubbed into the pattern I saw a faint soy sauce stain I had missed.

"To die in your own kitchen," I said.

"He died in the *ambulance*."

"But he was probably completely out of it by then."

Marty stuck her hand out and I passed her the glass. She took a swallow and then said in a muffled voice, "This is what people drink at funerals, this wussy stuff. No, I saw him, there, before they carried him out." She pointed to the floor below the kitchen table, across from where I was sitting, where Daddy always sat. "His face was a mess, he was drooling and everything. But he was looking at me. He knew what was happening all right. Ma was the one who called 911. She woke me up and said: 'Come down and stay with your father.'"

My sister looked up and repeated: "'Stay with your father.'" Her mouth twitched and I thought she was going to cry.

I pictured the chair with its back to the floor and then, like an echo, my father lying beside it, half under the table. His long body fallen like a crooked tree. I could imagine his upturned face as my sister described it, all pulled down on one side, far worse than the first stroke, the gray skin quivering where it had been stretched. One eye staring straight up, embedded in a nest of wrinkles, and black with terror.

After a moment, Marty said dreamily, "Sa, do you think you'll ever get married?"

"Maybe," I said.

My sister tipped her head back so that I could see the clean line of her jaw and her throat convulsing as she swallowed the last of the sherry. She set the glass down on the stove with a little click. "Well, I'm *never*. I don't see why I can't just live with people."

"Ma would love that."

"Ma doesn't care as much as you think."

The dishwasher hiccuped and eased into the dry cycle. Now we could hear a car climbing the hill outside before making the turn down our long street, and then upstairs a slow, sighing creak as our mother turned over in her bed, alone. I was exhausted, but at the same time ready to stay up all night with my sister. I thought that if we sat there long enough, Daddy would be completely erased from the room.

Ma was ominously quiet as we walked side by side down the hallway to the foyer. Out of the corner of my eye I caught a glimpse of Lillith and her uncle. He was much younger than I'd expected—thin fair hair slicked back from a high forehead not unlike Lillith's, wearing a white-and-purple-striped shirt and a green Hermès tie. Fastidious. Certainly not someone you'd think would stick tubes up someone's anus or play with their shit. Lillith had her hands pressed to either side of her face and was mouthing something up at him.

My mother opened her purse and took out her car keys. "I forgot to tell you. Carey called."

"Did you tell him where I was?"

"What do you want, everyone to know you're in a place like this?"

"He was my husband, Ma. He can know." When she didn't answer I said, "Come on. Aren't there psychiatric hospitals in China?"

She muttered something I didn't catch.

"What?"

"I don't like these rules. Why can't I call my own daughter?"

"Next time, Ma. I'll see you next time, at family therapy."

"Your sister is coming home."

"When?"

"I tell her soon. It's too hard for old lady all alone."

"Oh, come on, Ma. You're not old." But as I said it I saw her paleness, paler than the powder that covered it. When had she started wearing powder?

An MH was standing in the foyer, seeing the families out. She smiled at my mother. "Hello, Mrs. Wang. I'm glad to see you made it tonight."

"That girl has good skin without foundation," Ma said to me.

The front of our unit had a sliding glass door that was controlled electronically from the nurses' station. As it whooshed open for my mother the smell of wet earth and trees came gusting in, and for the first time in months I remembered what it felt like to be well.

5

Remembering.

That was how they judged you in the loony bin, by how much you remembered and how well you related it. My group was getting frustrated. You would have thought I was betraying them in some way. I'd given them every single detail and they wanted more.

"Sally, you're not a reporter. This is your life."

"You can tell us. You may fall apart, but you won't die."

I knew what they were after: rage.

They pointed to my tiger stripes: this is what happens if you don't scream, beat on a pillow.

"When are you going to confront your mother?"

"When are you going to confront your sister?"

Valerie was more patient than my group, taking down all the pieces I could conjure up without immediately wanting to fit them together. Her scribbling was especially prolific, I'd noticed, when it came to my dreams. But what, exactly, was the point? What was the use of calling up the past when you were drowning, how was it going to save you? Take Rachel—she was better off than any of us, because she'd figured out the time when her life was perfect and moved back there. Why should she have had to hold something in her mind like her boyfriend's brains splashing all over a tree trunk if she couldn't bear it?

And Lillith. She'd developed her memory into an art. How many times had she told the story of her uncle, with how many variations? She took out all this drama and wore it like a shawl, flinging it about her for everyone to gasp about. She never failed to weep at certain points in the telling, as if she were reading the sad part of a book over and over. But I couldn't see that her remembering had helped her any. She was either crazy and unreachable or obsessed with the past. Either way she was trapped.

Valerie said you remember in order to understand. I wished it were that easy. I wished I could step back from my life, as if it were a painting in progress, study it from different angles, in different lights, so I could figure out where to put the next brush stroke.

In OT I tried my hand at the potter's wheel, making bowls, which I flattened down afterward. I loved the feeling of the cold slippery mass disintegrating beneath the pressure of my palms.

"Masochist," said Mel. He was sitting at a table behind me rubbing a copper sheet over a mold.

"Destruction is the flip side of creation."

"Right," he said, smirking.

On Easter Sunday he'd introduced us to his ex-girlfriend Bethie, a slight blonde in a ratty rabbit coat who couldn't take her eyes off him. She was partly responsible for his being in here. They'd been arguing in the car when a cop pulled them over. In a classic case of displaced anger Mel had punched the policeman in the jaw.

Lillith came by carrying a tray of sculptures for the kiln. They were miniatures of food: a plate of spaghetti and meatballs, a hot dog in a bun, an ice cream sundae with an outsized maraschino cherry tilting off the top.

"Want a bite?" she asked us.

"I'll wait till they're baked," I said.

"Dibs on the sundae." Mel reached over and poked the cherry, making a dent.

"STOP IT." Lillith snatched the tray away. She was acting anorexic, making food instead of eating it. As she marched toward the kiln, it struck me that she had the bearing of a mad queen, all bones and misplaced energy. Her hair, which she was wearing in twin skinny braids plastered around her head, even sort of looked like a crown. Although it wasn't a particularly cold day she was covered in layers—two turtlenecks, a button-down shirt, and a sweatshirt—at least that's what I could see—which somehow managed to accentuate, rather than hide, her skeletal form.

The next thing I made on the wheel I kind of liked, and it was getting close to the end of the hour anyway, so I put it aside to be fired, then washed up. I meandered over to where Lillith was standing by some wooden racks displaying the work of other patients. She wasn't looking at them though. She seemed concerned with something on the knee of her jeans, rubbing at it furiously.

"What's the matter, do you have a stain?"

"Got to put it out."

"Put what out?"

"I'm on fire," she said.

At breakfast the MH, a new one, asked where Douglas was.

No one knew. It wasn't unusual for one of us to be missing mornings: bad nights were common, and there were always shrink appointments. Still, they kept pretty close tabs on us. He must have planned it down to the last gesture and worked without pause.

By eight-thirty it had already hit seventy, one of those freakish March days where at school you'd see people in tank tops and cutoffs lounging on the grass. Forcing spring. We were all in good spirits. On the way back from breakfast Lillith and Rachel linked arms and did the "We're off to see the wizard" gallop down the flagstone path toward the house. I was lagging behind, watching the ducks on the lake. Even when I saw the ambulance it didn't occur to me that anything was wrong. We were used to them at all times of the day gliding up the snaky drive to the admitting ward. Two men in light green uniforms emerged from the front door of our unit carrying the stretcher. They went by so fast all I got was a glimpse of the enormous wrapped body and blue eyelids. I thought the person must be dead until I saw that he was hooked up to an I.V. bag.

Later they figured out he had gotten the razor blades from his father on family therapy night. Usually blades were doled out one by one, and you had to turn them into the nurses' station when you were through. A casual request: "Dad, the blades they have here really suck, could you bring me some Wilkinson's?"

In the downstairs bathroom where he'd puked up raspberry licorice, not ten yards from the nurses' station, Douglas had shaved his head completely bald. Then with a new blade he'd sliced open his carotid artery.

"Right here," explained Lillith, sliding the side of her index finger diagonally down the front of her own skinny neck.

Douglas made the kind of mess you didn't want to hear about. Five more minutes, they said, and we would have lost him. Five more minutes, and there would have been more of him outside his skin than in. They blocked the end of the downstairs hallway to clean up with mops and buckets, and a section of carpeting had to be cut away.

Compared to Douglas I was an amateur.

We had an emergency group meeting and then we went to dance therapy where we lay on our mats and listened to spacey music. Mel didn't participate. He stood in the doorway and chain-smoked. His face had a closed-in look, which I took to be a bad sign.

Sure enough, that night after dinner he and Pajama Man got into a fight. What I saw was Mel twisting the guy's arm around his back and pounding his forehead into the carpet. The door to the nurses' station opened and two male MHs emerged, taking such big strides they looked like they were moving in slow motion. One of them pinned Mel to the floor by sitting on his back, the other got him into the straitjacket. I'd never seen one before. It was strangely innocuous, pure white with laces, like a corset. Mel looked like he was hugging himself.

The nurse brought out the syringe. I knew I shouldn't watch but I couldn't help it. They pulled down the back of his jeans, and as the needle slipped in, he threw back his head and howled. It was the most primal sound I'd ever heard a human being make, raising the hairs on the back of my neck.

For the first time I could truly believe I was in a loony bin.

Mel was knocked down to Status One, standard procedure for such a major acting-out. Before lunch Lillith and I went into the dayroom to see how he was doing. He was out of the straitjacket, looking normal, his tray already set up on the coffee table, as far away as possible from the TV, which was Pajama Man's territory.

"How're you feeling?" Lillith asked.

"Nothing like a Thorazine hangover," he said breezily. But the only clue to what had happened the night before was a slight darkness under his eyes. He was nineteen, after all. We watched as he unfurled the paper napkin as appreciatively as if it had been made of the finest linen, spreading it out on his lap with a flourish. He ate European style, cutting the food into tiny bites before popping them into his mouth like kisses. It was grilled chicken, garnished with sprigs of rosemary.

"That's what I'm having," I said.

"I'm afraid it's not on the menu."

"What do you mean?"

Mel wiped his mouth with his napkin, looking a little embarrassed. "My dad sent it over. He owns a restaurant. Here—" He speared a morsel of chicken on his fork and held it out to me.

"No thanks."

"You sure? It's awfully good."

I saw that his eyes were not green, as I'd first thought, but a clear hazel with a dark gray rim around the pupil.

A badly photographed postcard of a town square with cobblestoned streets and window boxes full of garish red flowers. It could have been anywhere in Europe. But the handwriting was just as I remembered it—small and careless, with uncrossed *t*'s and dots from the *i*'s flying all over the place.

> Sa—I wanted to send you Monet's poppies but it's not the season. Denny is spoiling me to death with home cooking and an extremely well-stocked wine cellar. I'm in charge of the daily marketing and my French is becoming *extraordinaire*. Tomorrow we're getting up at dawn to see the lavender harvest. Hope you're better and happy. *Mille baisers*, Mar.

On Saturday night I attended a dance. Mixers, they called them. The only thing I could think of were boarding school mixers, where you wrote down your height on a list and were then bused to a boys' school and matched up with someone who tried to ditch you right after dinner. I put on an old cardigan of Nai-nai's, smoke blue with pearl buttons, to wear with my regular jeans and sneakers. Some people in our unit got really decked out—walking through the foyer I got a strong whiff of mingled cologne and aftershave.

The gym where we had rec therapy was darkened and blasting with old disco from a sound system set up near the bleachers. The adolescent girls leaned up against the walls behind the basketball hoops, smoking and talking mostly to each other. They seemed one of two types: big-boned and mannish, or anorexic, with jutting wrist bones and long wispy hair. Hard cases, a lot of them had been kicked out of juvenile homes. One separated herself from the pack and sauntered over to the bleachers, where Lillith and I were sitting.

"Any news about Id Squid?"

"Who?" I asked.

"Duggle-*ass*."

I told her what we'd been told that morning—he'd been upgraded from critical to serious.

"Gruesome what he did, huh?" The girl shook her head, hair flying—she was one of the wispy ones—and gave a few hard chomps to her gum. The heels of her cowboy boots scraped the freshly waxed floor as she turned to stroll back to her friends.

Lillith got up and started dancing all by herself, on the edge of the floor. She shut her eyes and whirled with her arms outstretched, at the same sultry tempo no matter what was playing. Every so often she'd stop and scratch herself—her nose, under the arms, behind the knees. She was wearing layers again, and her hair was still up in braids—it didn't look like she'd washed it for the entire week she'd worn it like that. Watching her, it hit me again how scarily thin she was, in a different way from the adolescent anorexics. They were taut with the control needed to warp their bodies into art. Lillith seemed at the mercy of something bigger than herself, becoming more and more brittle under its centrifugal force.

There was a guy there who might have been about fifty, all dressed up in a herringbone jacket and tie, wire-framed glasses. He looked like a dork doing the twist—his face got so red I was scared he was going to have a heart attack. But when they started playing Glenn Miller he got out there with this woman in our unit and all of a sudden they were gliding and dipping like something out of a 1940s movie. Then he asked someone else—just another woman out of the crowd— and I couldn't stop watching, it was so beautiful. When the next song started he was in front of me, holding out his hand and bowing.

Dancing with him was like riding in a car, it was so smooth, the steering mechanism in the small of my back, where his palm was pressed. He hummed along in a pleasant, absent-minded way, and I thought, This is what it's like for other girls to dance with their fathers.

Afterward I went over to the refreshments table, where I ran into the alcoholic we'd been with in Admissions. She was all the way up to Status Four, weekend passes and everything. "They're going to spring me soon," she said.

"You going back home?"

"My husband and I have some friends in Albuquerque. We're going to leave the baby with my mother and spend some time there, try to figure out if we want to stay married. What about you?"

"I thought maybe I'd go down to St. Pete."

She wrinkled her nose and exhaled a stream of smoke. "Old people and no surf."

"My aunt and uncle have a house down there."

"At least it's not New York City. Jeez, what a snake pit."

In front of us a slender man with long dark hair was dancing with a wispy adolescent. The alcoholic said, "Remember him? Can't keep his hands off the girls. Rumor's he's on probation." I looked closer and recognized the catlike confidence: it was the MH from Admissions, the one who looked like the romantic lead in a movie.

After the dance was over he leaned down and said something to his partner, who pouted but went back to the group behind the basketball hoop. Then he was striding in our direction. The song coming on was "Boogie Woogie Bugle Boy." He extended his hand and I thought about refusing, but it seemed easier just to go along. We stood there for a moment feeling for the beat. "You're thinking too much," he said to me. "Just follow." Before I knew what was happening he'd rolled me out into a spin and then back in again against his chest. It was so fast and easy, I felt like one of those paper-tongue party favors. "Okay?" he said into my ear.

I decided to take his advice and let him lead. As the song progressed we did other, complicated things I'd seen people do, and I saw that he, like the Glenn Miller guy, knew where a woman's center of gravity was. The difference was that the MH would use this knowledge for his own nefarious purposes.

Nothing, he's nothing, I told myself. Can't hurt you.

"I bet you don't even remember who I am," I said, when we were dancing close.

He spun me so that my back was against his chest and said: "Ms. Broken Heart. The one with the sister."

"That's right."

"And I know you're an artist."

I spotted Lillith sitting alone on the bleachers. She was watching us.

A few minutes later the MH said: "I saw that drawing of yours they put up in the cafeteria."

"My abstract period."

"No kidding, you're very good."

"Mmmhmm."

"Professional?"

"I was in school, but I dropped out."

"You should go back," he said.

Who are you to give me advice, I thought.

When the dance was over I thanked the MH and then I climbed up the bleachers and sat down next to Lillith. She looked exhausted and a little crabby.

"You're the fucking belle of the ball," she said.

"Right."

Then she leaned up against me so that I could smell the rankness of her unwashed hair and whispered, "You ever do it with a girl?"

"What did you say?"

"You heard." I was staring straight ahead, but I could feel her fingertips slide between the buttons of my cardigan. They were so cold I had to suppress a shiver. "You and your sister never . . . ?"

I looked down. Her crossed feet in dirty white ballet slippers were so tiny I knew I could crush one with my hand. "No."

"But you have the look."

"What look is that?"

"Hungry. Like you'd do it with anyone."

"It's exactly the opposite. I never do it at all."

"It's not so bad, you know. It's actually pretty nice. More *subtle* than with a boy, if you know what I mean."

I wanted her to continue and I didn't.

"Quit it."

Slowly, her fingers withdrew. When I looked at her again she was back behind her own eyes, unreadable. As I watched she began to scratch herself viciously again, this time on the palm.

Back at the unit, I went straight upstairs to get ready for bed. I was on the way to the bathroom to brush my teeth when someone called up the stairs that there was a phone call for me.

I couldn't imagine who it would be. I went down in my bathrobe.

"Hello?"

"Oh God, it is you."

"Carey."

"I kept getting switched. There's another Wang in that hospital."

I knew who it was—a seedy adolescent who gave me the eye in the cafeteria. Thank God he hadn't been at the dance tonight.

"Ma told me you'd called."

"Yeah, well, you know she's not a very good liar. I got hold of Fran and she told me where you were." A pause. "So. I guess you went off the deep end."

I pictured my lanky ex-husband sitting at his desk, pushing his glasses up and rubbing the bridge of his nose, something he did when he was nervous.

"I guess I did."

"So what happened? You could have called me, you know."

"I know."

"Are you okay now?"

"I'm better."

"Sally . . . listen, I hope it wasn't because of what happened with us. The divorce, I mean."

"So that's the reason you called? Because you feel guilty?"

"I called because I care about you, Sally."

"Right."

"Look, do you want a visitor?"

"No," I said. "I don't think I do."

"Well, you can call me anytime you want. For anything, to talk, whatever. I have a new number. That's why I was trying to reach you in the first place."

"You moved?"

"Yeah. You have something to write with?"

I exhaled. "No. Wait a sec."

The door to the nurses' station was closed for the shift-change meeting. I peeked into the dayroom and Mel was sitting placidly in an armchair reading a paperback. I wondered if they were still giving him Thorazine.

"Do you have a pen?"

"Here." He handed me a pencil stub and tore out a leaf from his book. I was surprised to see that it was the title page of a poetry anthology.

Carey gave me the number and said: "During the day is the best time to reach me."

"So you're living with someone." I felt very calm and very cold, like I did sometimes when I was painting well.

"Um. Well. Yes."

"I'm happy for you."

"Listen, when you get out of there, we should have dinner."

"All right," I said. "Thanks for calling."

"Sally, I still love you."

"Good-bye, Carey."

I went back to the dayroom. "Thanks," I said to Mel, returning the pencil.

"Anytime. Hey, are you all right? You don't look so good."

"Ex-husband."

"Rough." He picked up a pack of Marlboros and offered me one. I shook my head and watched him light it, and then the way he smoked, snatching the cigarette away from his lips after each drag. I had never noticed before how sexy it was.

"What're you reading?" I asked.

He picked up the book. "Yeats. Listen to this:

There is a queen in China, or maybe it's in Spain,
And birthdays and holidays such praises can be heard
Of her unblemished lineaments, a whiteness with no stain,
That she might be that sprightly girl trodden by a bird;
And there's a score of duchesses, surpassing womankind,
Or who have found a painter to make them so for pay
And smooth out stain and blemish with the elegance of his
*   mind:*
I knew a phoenix in my youth, so let them have their day.

"It kind of reminds me of you," he said.

I felt my face get hot. Not because of the poem but because of the way he was looking at me. It reminded me of someone—not Carey, or the movie-star MH, or Lillith, but someone from much longer ago, at that moment I couldn't remember who.

6

Dream: I am in a rowboat on a river. I row under a bridge into a very dark glassy lake. Black water. In my hands I have a book, but the print on its pages is indecipherable. I get the idea it's mirror writing, and hold the open book over the water, looking down to read.

What I see is too dreadful to take in.

I hadn't seen my mother in three weeks. She refused to come to family therapy. "Too busy" was her excuse. Staff was working on her.

"Your mother loves you," one of the MHs told me. "She'll come when she realizes how important it is to your recovery."

As a reward for talking in group, I was moved up to Status Three, which meant I could go anywhere on the grounds with staff or a Status Four person. Mel was taken off house arrest. The only one who got worse was Lillith.

It turned out she thought she was Joan of Arc. The scratching had become constant: palms, elbows, and finally the underside of her chin, leaving garish pink welts. I asked her if she had a rash, and she turned to me with a cynical expression.

"Can't you see. Burned at the stake."

"Who?"

"Who did it? Grindel Grundelwald. The dragon."

"Dragon?"

Exasperated sigh. "Look, I'm going to take up arms. Despite

what that fat-assed genitalic general says. And I don't speak French! I'm not French, that was all a big lie!"

In group she stretched her stick arms out in front of her and pronounced: "The molecules are singing."

"That's not real," the MH admonished.

"What are the molecules singing?" I asked. The MH gave me a warning look.

Lillith looked around gleefully. "Liar, liar, liar."

They'd started her on a different drug, but it didn't work. There was no choice but Status One and suicide watch. She sat kneeling on the carpet in her yellow flannel nightgown, so pale that every single amber freckle stood out in relief. The MH bent to look her in the face. "Do you understand why we're doing this, Lillith? Do you see that this is not a punishment?"

Her eyes were as blank as marble.

"Lil, you're going to be all right," said Mel. At that her head snapped back, and I was afraid she was going to explode, but she didn't.

At times she was still normal: admiring Jane Pauley's outfit, or we'd split a giant chocolate chip cookie I brought back from dinner. But I was afraid to look her in the eye. I understood that no matter how alone I had ever felt in my life, it would have been nothing compared to the isolation I would have seen there.

I knew so little about psychosis. I'd thought lunatics had fits, or outbursts, like Mel, and were confined to padded rooms until their minds wore themselves out. In the hospital I began to see that it wasn't so simple. The brain could fasten itself on a character from history, some kind of metaphor for the soul's illness. Jesus, who dies for everyone's sins; Galileo, who wants to see heaven. Why had Lillith chosen Joan of Arc? If I'd been her I would have picked my own namesake, Lillith, the real first woman, pre-Eve. The one who was fashioned out of a lump of clay, like Adam, and thus Adam's equal. Who escaped Paradise and had lots of interesting demon lovers.

Lillith's uncle came and went one afternoon while we were at rec therapy. The word was that he was giving her one more week. One more week, and if she didn't snap out of it, he was putting her into State.

I came back to the room just before lights out and Rachel was lying on her bed sobbing her head off.

"What's the matter?"

"I can't find my teddy bear. Someone took him."

"Who would have taken him? Come on, I'll help you look."

Together we combed the room. I opened the closets and looked first in hers, then in mine. Nothing. At the back of the shelf in her closet there was a stuffed Peter Rabbit, complete with jacket and trousers, that her parents had given her for Easter. I took it out and handed it to her. She slammed it back at me as if it were a hot potato.

"What are you two doing?" It was the MH, coming around for bed checks.

"Rachel can't find her bear."

The MH put her arm around Rachel and said, "Honey, we'll search for it in the morning, okay?"

"Someone stole him."

"No one stole him. If we can't find it, you can ask your parents to get you another, okay?"

When the MH left, I picked the rabbit up from the floor and took its clothes off, remembering that the teddy bear had been nude. I set the stuffed animal on the foot of Rachel's bed and she ignored it, but at least she didn't throw it back on the floor. In the night when she reached out at least she would find something to hold, something soft and familiar, that could soak up tears.

It had been two weeks since Douglas had tried to do away with himself in that spectacularly horrible way, and I still couldn't bring myself to use the downstairs bathroom. People were leaving our group, new patients were coming in, people who had never met Douglas.

In dance therapy we did backbends. Mel and I were partners, spotting each other. He was much better than me. I watched him go over easy, with a slow twist of torso, his faded black T-shirt slipping to show faint ribs. His hair hung down over the gym mat like a drowned person's and his face filled with blood—I could see it in the wall of mirrors behind us.

The therapist applauded. "It's unusual for a man to be so limber."

I did mine the sissy way, starting from a lying-down position.

"Good," the therapist said. She went over to the other side of the room to help some older woman who was griping about her arthritis.

"Come on," Mel said to me. "Stand up."

He cupped his hand at the small of my back, as if we were going to dance. "Okay, fall."

"I can't."

"Just trust me."

"Why should I?" I said, but I closed my eyes and as slowly as possible let myself arch back over the still point that was Mel's tensed palm. I could see the blood behind my shut eyelids as it reversed its flow. Crimson, violet, and finally chartreuse. My head was a boulder, my spine ready to snap. A million miles away, I felt my fingertips touch the cool dank plastic of the mat.

"See? You can do it."

His blue-jeaned crotch rose above me. I closed my eyes. "Not by myself."

"Stop putting yourself down, Sally," he said, and his voice was sharp. I opened my eyes and there was that look again, that I couldn't place.

"I'm dizzy," I said truthfully.

"Now straighten up."

I straightened up, which was a lot harder, and even when I was standing it took several minutes for the light-headedness to disperse.

I was sitting in the alcove next to the kitchen before breakfast sketching the profile of an MH through the glass window of the nurses' station. Lillith came trailing down the hall, fresh from her six A.M. shower. At least now they'd make sure she took a shower every day. The twin wet hanks of hair stained the shoulders of her blouse, which was about four sizes too large for her. For the first time in days her eyes looked almost lucid.

"Can I talk to you?"

"Sure."

She lowered herself down beside me on the love seat, so light I could barely feel the springs give, and pulled her legs up so that they were in the same position as mine, tucked under. Instead of talking she just watched me. I could feel her breath fluttering the edges of my hair.

"It's hard to concentrate with someone staring at you like that."

"Sorry."

"That's all right."

"It's just that you look so normal. You even looked normal in Admissions. You're the most normal person here, you know. I want it to osmose to me."

That was the kind of talk we weren't supposed to encourage. But I knew what she meant. Also, that it worked sometimes. Moral strength, lightheartedness, ease with your body—all these things were contagious.

"You really ought to eat," I said.

She gave me a sharp look. "What do you care? You're going to Florida to visit your relatives. I'm going to hell."

"That's a stupid way to think."

"At least I call a spade a spade. I don't cover things up."

She was right, Douglas was right, my sister was right. I was a fake. I did things from my head, not from my heart. For all my sincerity I was the least honest person I knew.

On the way to breakfast I walked by myself, noticing that beyond the lake the willow strands hung light green and delicate shivering with wind. Mel came up beside me and linked his arm through mine. We continued on, not speaking, not missing a beat, and I noticed, among other things, that he was exactly my height.

That week Valerie wanted to talk about sex.

"Sally, what's your experience when you make love with a man? What do you feel?"

Incest survivors will tell you they focus on something outside themselves during sex in order to escape. In my case, it was ceilings. At college, Carey's off-campus apartment had a yellow ceiling with tiny bumps like chicken skin. There was a hairline fault running down one edge, which sometimes would seem to have gotten wider, although in reality I'm sure it stayed the same. The window shades in his bedroom were translucent, and at night the watery red reflections of taillights would glide above us like the planaria I'd watched slipping to the edge of a microscope slide in high school biology.

Once, I can't remember why now, we spent a night in a fancy hotel in Boston. The ceiling gleamed metallic, matching the rest of the room, which was high-tech and spacious, with a thrilling view of the Charles River. The lights from the outside were reflected in the ceiling in a muddled way, like movies at camp.

On our honeymoon in Japan, the inn ceiling was low, ominously so, a pale Zen green. I had the feeling as we lay there innocently in our sleeping rolls that it might slowly lower until we were crushed to death, like the room in the Edgar Allan Poe story.

The ceiling of our first apartment in New York was made up of little decorated squares—tin painted over white. Carey liked the light on while we made love, and I could sometimes see the tips of our shadows slipping up along the molding where the ceiling and wall met. This would make me so uneasy I would have to close my eyes.

"What about his body? Could you feel him? His penis?"

I shook my head.

"Sally, concentrate. Could you feel Carey?"

Mel leaning over me in rec therapy. His breath so sweet it was almost narcotic.

"Sally. Could you feel him?"

My sister in the room on Coram Drive. Her face in the morning, eyes wide open, hair flying up with static over the collar of her nightgown, coming over to my bed to wake me up, although I'm already awake.

Sa-sa. Sa-sa.

Another ceiling. Moonlight defining twin parallelograms. It is Indian summer, the windows are open, and the white lace curtains have been drawn back, out of the way, to let all of any breeze into the room. There is the noise of the shades flapping up, making the pattern on the ceiling shift in an unpredictable way, with no rhythm.

I am no longer on the bed. I have shrunk to the size of a mosquito and float up to the ceiling, where the life-preserver shape of a shade pull dangles. I grab on to the O of it and swing, as if it were the tire in the school playground. Hold my breath. The play of light inside my closed eyes is dazzling.

My wrists pinned to the sheet. Carey lets go, his chest collapsing on mine.

"Sal."

"What?"

"You still don't like it, do you?"

"Of course I do. I told you I did."

"You don't stay with me. At first I can feel you, you know, that you're getting hot, and then you kind of disappear."

"It's getting better, Care, I swear."

"If we got married, would you feel more comfortable? Is that it?"

I think of my sister, fucking man after man.

For pleasure.

Tou-fa, tou-fa, tou-fa.

Over and over again, in a whisper, like a spell.

I know this means hair. But we didn't learn it in Chinese school.

"Sally, you have a visitor."

Since I'd been at Willowridge I hadn't had any visitors at all except for my mother that one time for family therapy. I dragged myself up from the bed and glanced in the bureau mirror. "In the dayroom," the MH said as I followed her downstairs.

But she wasn't. She was standing in the foyer, head down, reading the sign-out book, maybe looking for my name. Her hair had been cut very short, like a boy's, and I could see the shape of her shoulder blades through the suede jacket, which was the color of butterscotch, one I had never seen before. At the sound of our steps, she turned and looked up.

"Sa." She was wearing lipstick—in her tanned face her mouth looked like a little flame.

I couldn't say a word, there was so much heart inside me. I tried very hard simply to continue breathing while I walked the last several steps that would bring me to my sister.

7

"You look better than I thought you would," she said. We were sitting on the window seat in the dayroom.

"You cut your hair," I said. She took my breath away, I couldn't stop staring. I'd forgotten how small she was.

"Yeah, my agent's going to kill me." She pulled out a pack of Gauloises from her purse and shook two out. The backs of her hands were as tanned as her face, and she was wearing a pink cameo ring that looked vaguely familiar. There was a faint, tangy aroma about her. I couldn't remember the last time I'd worn perfume.

She lit our cigarettes and took a deep drag. I coughed on mine.

"Camel shit, honey, but it does the trick."

"When did you get back?"

"Last Thursday." She'd been back for an entire week and hadn't bothered to get in touch. "So when are they cutting you loose from here?"

"My shrink says soon. A couple of weeks at the most."

"You coming home?"

"No," I said. "I'm going down to visit Aunty Mabel and Uncle Richard." I had already called a travel agency asking them to find me the cheapest ticket to St. Pete.

My sister teased a bare brown foot out of its shoe and frowned at her fuchsia toenails. "How come they won't let you talk to Ma?"

"It's only temporary."

"It seems weird to me. Ma is very, very upset, you know."

"You mean because she can't call me?"

"Well, that, and because she thinks it's her fault that you're in here."

Before I could respond to this Mel came into the dayroom. He was clowning around, dribbling an imaginary basketball. When he saw Marty he stopped cold and straightened up.

"Howdy," he said, too casual. I knew what he was thinking. It was what everyone thought when they first met Marty. *That's* Sally's sister?

Marty barely gave him an appraisal. For the first time I realized how Mel would seem to my friends—there was no getting around his clipped, small-town accent, his slicked-back hair, the fact that he wore his jeans too tight. To give Mel credit, he summed up the situation right away.

"Later," he said, and went over to the TV armchairs, where Lillith was swathed in blankets. What I didn't understand was, why was she always so cold if she thought she was on fire?

"What's wrong with that one?" Marty whispered to me. I knew she meant Lillith. I thought it was lucky that Pajama Man had been discharged.

"She thinks she's about to be burned at the stake."

"Christ. Isn't there anywhere else we can talk?"

I took her up to my bedroom. My sister plunked herself down on Rachel's bed, kicking off her flats and taking the pillow out to settle it behind her head. "Sorry I didn't bring you anything," she said. "I thought about it. I thought you might need a joint, or a drink, or something."

"There're enough drugs in here."

"Anything good?"

"Nothing that I'm getting."

"I always thought Thorazine might be kind of cool."

"Well, it's not."

"You know we're coming tomorrow night and everything. Me and Ma, I mean."

"For family therapy? No, they didn't tell me. Well, that's good, I guess."

"So what *is* this thing, anyway?"

"Really, it's no big deal, just talking. We all sit around in a little room and a mental health worker leads the discussion."

"What are we going to talk about?"

"You know, stuff that happened when we were kids."

"Oh." My sister closed her eyes.

"Remember Monkey King?"

My sister didn't move a muscle. Her eyes were still shut.

"Mar, did you hear what I said?"

"Yes." She sounded irritated. "Why do you have to bring that up again? He's dead, for Chrissake. And you know it's going to upset Ma."

"I think we should talk about it. Exactly what happened. How he used to come into our room at night. Don't you remember?"

"We had separate rooms, honey."

"You're not paying attention. It was on Coram Drive. Don't you remember? He'd come in and sit on my bed and we'd both wake up and he'd tell us not to make any noise."

My sister opened her eyes. "I don't want to talk about it. It's over and done with."

"I bet you don't even remember," I said, to goad her. "You were only seven. You were just a baby."

"Of course I remember. Monkey King. Monkey King. Monkey King." The way she said it made a thrill start at the base of my spine. "It's no big deal, Sa. It doesn't matter anymore. I've gone on with my life, you should go on with yours."

"We should have told Ma. Back when it happened, I mean."

"But we didn't. So why bring it up now? I think she's going bonkers, Sa, I swear, she's the one who should be in here, not you."

"She knows anyway."

"No way."

"Remember when she took me to that faith healer in China-town? Remember, you were so jealous, when you found out about it you wanted to go too. She knew then. I think she and the faith healer even talked about it, only I'm sure they didn't actually say the word 'incest.'" I was talking too much, too fast.

Marty was quiet for a moment. Then she said: "You just had dyslexia in school, or something."

"Jesus Christ, Mar, you have to help me out."

"I never understood why Daddy had a thing about you any-way." Her voice was accusing. "You're not even that pretty."

"You're so fucked up," I said. "Pretending it never hap-pened."

"I'm fucked up? Who's the one in the mental hospital?" Marty got up off the bed, shrugging back into that fancy suede jacket I was sure she hadn't paid for, it was either shoplifted or a gift from some boyfriend. "I'm sorry I came back," she said. "I was having a great time in France."

"I never asked you to come."

"I only came for Ma's sake."

"So go back."

My sister dug around in her purse and pulled out her sun-glasses. But before she put them on I saw how our conversa-tion had changed her face.

For the first time I saw our father in her.

Mel and I stood by the window in the dayroom watching as the ambulance pulled up and the attendants jumped out and went to open the back doors. Lillith was at individual therapy, probably a good thing. She didn't need this kind of shock. There was no stretcher this time. They whisked him into the building and then the fuss started in the foyer. "You're a sight for sore eyes!" I heard the day nurse say.

It took him a few minutes to get through the crowd. It was

funny, but all the patients there were popular. Everyone had had a bizarre enough life to be a star—we who were shunned in the outside world for being peculiar.

Finally Douglas walked through the doorway, the early afternoon light hitting him full on. He had put on even more weight, his bulk emphasized by the fact that his head looked smaller because he had no hair, just a kind of stubble. He was wearing a polo shirt—purple instead of the old green one, which probably had gotten ruined—and it was open at the neck, fully exposing the main scar. Since I'd been at Willowridge I'd seen a number of razor cuts, but none this fresh. It was puffy and violet colored, traveling in a curve under his chin like a nightcrawler.

And there were other scars, too, that they hadn't told us about. One on each temple, slightly less garish, shaped like parentheses. The skin on the rest of his face and the scalp showing through was a sickly grayish brown color.

"Hey, buddy," said Mel, too casually I thought. "Those are some tattoos."

"Welcome back," I said.

Douglas ignored us both. He went over to the TV, turned it on, and then sat down, calf crossed over the opposite knee. His trouser leg was pulled up to expose a bare, raw-looking ankle. Then he burped. Long and juicy. In character, for sure. But there was a difference from the way he'd been before. He didn't check to see anyone's reaction. He was beyond arrogance, I saw.

He was utterly bored.

That night it finally came down: Lillith was going to be transferred to State.

I skipped breakfast to hang around and say good-bye. She had my old Status One room, the single next to the nurses' station.

"It's too bad your uncle couldn't give you one more chance."

Cross-legged on her bed, she seemed not to have heard. Her hair was down, uncombed, as it had been when we'd first met. She stared straight ahead, her jaw working subtly.

"Is she going to throw up?" I asked the MH who was helping her pack. More like packing for her, since Lillith herself showed no interest in the process.

"Drug tremor," the MH told me. She set Lillith's black-and-white-tweed suitcase on the bed and unzipped it. "Sally, would you take out the things hanging in the closet while I check through these drawers."

Feeling like I was invading Lillith's privacy, I slid back the closet door. There wasn't much in there—sneakers, a smocked corduroy dress that would have been more appropriate for a twelve-year-old, several pairs of jeans. Also a stack of *Glamour*s. I wondered where the string bikini she'd been working on was and then remembered that of course it would have been confiscated because yarn was *zhi* and the crochet needle was a sharp.

As we filled the suitcase I asked the MH: "Is there a patient phone at State? Can I get in touch with her?"

"Of course you can."

"She's going to die, isn't she," I said. My voice was matter-of-fact.

"We're all going to die, Sally. We've talked to the nursing team there. She'll be in medical first, until she gains some weight. The first thing they're going to do is put her on a glucose I.V."

Someone shouted from the nurses' station that the MH had a phone call. "Keep an eye on her," the MH said to me. "And keep packing. Her uncle's going to be here in ten minutes."

"Look," I said to Lillith. She didn't move. I picked up the clay food sculptures from the top of her bureau, the hot dog and the ice cream sundae. "I'm packing these for you, okay? In case you decide to start eating again." I tucked the sculptures into corners of the suitcase, cushioning them with balled-up socks.

There was something under the bed, some dark baby-size shape. I reached down, slowly, so as not to alarm her, and carefully extracted it.

Rachel's teddy bear.

Although she'd grown attached to her rabbit, Rachel still mourned for the bear now and then. The poor thing looked even more chewed up than I remembered, perhaps she wouldn't even want it anymore. But really, it was hers.

Lillith was still sitting bolt upright, as if she were meditating. God knows what was going on behind those eyes. Was she still Saint Joan, tied to the stake? She turned her skull head, ever so slightly, caught sight of the stuffed animal in my arms. And did nothing. Just waited, to see what I would do.

I blew some of the dust off, ruffled up the honey-colored fur, which smelled slightly moldy, and then leaned to tuck the bear inside the suitcase. It just about fit.

When I looked back at Lillith her eyes were closed.

Before family therapy, when people had just begun to gather in the dayroom, I went into the kitchenette and made myself a cup of chamomile tea. I looked up and saw Mel lounging in the doorway, watching me. There was a hair sticking up at the back of his head like an exclamation point. I wanted to smooth it down but didn't quite dare.

"Want some?"

He leaned over my arm to sniff the mug. "What the hell is it?"

"It's supposed to calm you down."

"Maybe I could have a sip."

I tore open a packet of honey and watched the gold strands swirl like clouds through the lighter gold of the tea. "Did you know that *mel* means honey in Greek?" I didn't know if this were true or not, but it sounded right.

"You know Greek?"

"Not really. So what did you think of my sister?"

"Cute," he said in an offhand way.

"Not beautiful?"

Mel shrugged his shoulders, a connoisseur. "You built her up so much in group I expected this bombshell. Truth is, she can't hold a candle to you." He reached around me and picked up the mug, which he balanced on my shoulder.

"Ouch, that's *hot*," I said.

"Sorry," he said, lifting it off. Sipping, he said, "Tastes like dandelions. She's not as pretty as she thinks she is. You, on the other hand, don't give yourself enough credit. Still nervous?"

"A little."

"Go get 'em, Tiger." He gave me a rakish smile, the one I'd seen him use on his rabbit-coated girlfriend. "So, we gonna see each other on the outside?"

"You mean, like regular friends?"

"I'm asking you if you want to see me on the outside."

"I guess so," I said.

"Pul-*leeze*, Miss Wang," he said. "Don't do me any favors."

"I mean, yes, of course."

"You dummy. Don't you know how much I'm going to miss you?" His face was so close to mine I thought he was going to kiss me, but then he just handed back the mug and turned and walked out of the kitchenette. For the first time I noticed that his calves were slightly bowed, like a cowboy's.

This was it, the moment I'd been dreading.

"Sally has something in particular she'd like to share." The MH was smooth, using a casual tone so as not to alarm anyone. Not that this place didn't give Ma the creeps anyway. Like last time, she was wearing her school clothes—a blue cotton blouse and brown linen skirt with a kick pleat in the front. I watched her smooth a tiny crease over her belly. Her hands were so like Marty's, only paler and plumper.

My sister was wearing wide white pants, like a sailor's, and a red-and-white-striped T-shirt. I could see her looking around furtively for an ashtray. When she didn't find one, she looked peevish and began swinging one leg over the other. She twisted the cameo ring on her right hand.

"Go ahead," the MH commanded me.

I did. I think I used the word *molest*.

"Do we all understand what Sally means?" the MH asked. "Mrs. Wang?"

My mother had no expression on her face. It was as if I'd said nothing at all. I noticed that the roots of her hair, which she dyed, were a copper color, instead of the white you would have expected.

The MH leaned forward in his chair. "We're talking, of course, about sexual molestation. We need you to help fill in the picture."

Ma finally spoke up. "There is no such thing in our family."

"Are you sure, Mrs. Wang?"

"I don't know where she got the idea. Maybe from all the books she reads."

It was strange, but all I felt was relief.

"Yes, she makes this up, she has a big imagination. Both my daughters have big imaginations." My mother's face remained perfectly bland, as if she were giving out a recipe.

"All right," the MH said. "And what about you, Marty? What do you think?"

"She is an actress." My mother was smiling. "She doesn't know."

It struck me that Marty was right, Ma had gone insane.

My sister said: "Well, he did hit us, I'm sure Sally's told you about that. Actually, me more than her. I talked back a lot."

"And?" the MH asked, encouraging.

Marty leaned back in the molded plastic hospital chair, arms crossed over her chest, and shook her head. I wished for once I could see into her brain, past the smooth brown diamond face, the almond eyes that had grown double lids, to my mother's delight. She wouldn't look at me. "He gave me a black eye once. The first time he caught me shoplifting." I hadn't remembered about the black eye, but of course it was true. We told everyone she'd fallen off the swings.

"It seems we have a difference in perspective here," the MH said.

I was watching my mother. She was fidgeting quite a bit, with her skirt, the flap on her purse. At one point she took out a wad of Kleenex and blew her nose.

"Monkey King." My sister was sitting too far away to kick, so I glared at her as I said it.

"What's Monkey King?" the MH wanted to know.

"Just a story," Marty told him. "A Chinese folk tale." I noticed with interest that she was digging the nails of one hand into the palm of the other.

"My husband was a good father," Ma said. "Sal-lee was his favorite. He never hurt her."

"Why won't you talk to me?" I asked Ma. "Why are you still protecting him?"

"He was a good father," she repeated. "Look what he sacrificed for you."

That word again. "What? What did he sacrifice?"

"Work so hard to pay for your education. Then what happens. No-good daughter. You disappoint him so much, he can't say."

"I think 'no-good' is a loaded word, perhaps we could—"

Ma went on as if the MH hadn't spoken. "Children supposed to give you peace in old age. Your daddy was never peaceful. He talked this all the time, maybe he's better off back in China, shouldn't have come to the United States at all. Never have children."

"Why do you hate me so much?"

"Love, hate, this is so American. You say I love you, what does this mean? Action is important, not words."

"Listen, we're getting off the topic," the MH said. He was practically shouting. "Obviously there's a lot to be worked out here. Let's go back to Sally's original statement about her abuse memories."

"She knew about it." I pointed at Marty. "Your precious Mau-mau was in the same room and never said a word."

My mother clammed up, making her mouth into a line. I knew, if the MH didn't, that this was absolute. I'd seen her do it too many times in childhood. It scared me worse than anything, than her yelling, than Daddy yelling, even.

"I don't think incest is the point," my sister said. "We're never going to agree on it, so why bother talking about it?"

I wondered if she and my mother had discussed strategy. It seemed possible.

Afterward I walked them to the front door. As soon as the MH was out of earshot, Ma gripped my upper arm so hard I almost screamed. "Your father is dead," she hissed. "He is an ancestor. You must have respect for your ancestors."

"She's been in this place for too long," Marty said. "I told you, Ma, it's all these crazy people, they're a bad influence." She turned to me making big eyes and I felt like saying, I'm not one of your gullible white boyfriends, this act doesn't work on me. "Honey, there's no use brooding about the past. You just have to pick up and go on. Lots of people have breakdowns. It makes them stronger. Like a bone that's been healed."

"Your sister's right." Ma let go of me and smoothed her hair back with one hand. "And now the insurance is running out. You think about that, Sally. You discuss that with your smart psychiatrist."

"You know I'm not staying in here," I said. "You know I'm going to St. Pete."

"I could call and tell them not let you come," Ma said.

From the front door I watched the two of them proceed down the flagstones. I could tell they were arguing about where they had parked the car.

*   *   *

I'd just been moved up to Status Four, which meant I could go anywhere on the grounds by myself. It was only eight-thirty, plenty of time for a walk before lights out. I went upstairs to my room and grabbed a jacket. On the way out the door I remembered Nai-nai's hairpin. I found it in my bag and slipped it into my inside pocket.

The lake was absolutely still. It was a mild, clear night. I lay down on one of the benches and looked across the water to where the willows poured down in Gothic arches. They were white, ghostly, in the light from the parking lot. Around me the shapes of the buildings lay cozy and familiar: the A-frame dining room that had so disoriented me the first night, the gym, the barrackslike adolescent unit, all those Colonial houses, including the admitting ward.

I took the hairpin out and laid it against my cheek. It was much colder than the air, colder than anything alive.

I was ready to leave.

In eighth grade, I had finally announced to my mother that I didn't want to take piano lessons anymore.

She gave me a lecture on how important it was to have a music background. "You don't have one," I said. "Nai-nai didn't make you sing."

Ma told me I was selfish.

"You never get a husband, Sally. You don't know how to give in. You don't know how to love like a wife has to love."

I guess she'd know.

There were so many tragedies. At Willowridge, after a while you got numb. The amazing thing was that anyone survived at all.

The parking lot lights went off.

The dark is kind; why should I be afraid of it? I made out the Big Dipper, easy, over the trees, and then the North Star. Part of Orion stuck up over the horizon—he was a winter constellation, and on his way out. My favorite star was the cold blue brilliant light of Vega, but I couldn't find her, it probably wasn't the right season. And then I saw, upside-down from how I usually did, that bold glittering *W*, an *M* now, smack in the middle of the Milky Way. Queen Cassiopeia, brighter than anyone else, and the most abstract.

I got down off the bench and lay on my back on the wet grass and wept.

Part
Two

8

My mother grew up the youngest of five daughters in a wealthy Shanghai family. My grandfather was a scholar who had studied in Paris, and by the time my mother was twelve she could speak English and French as well as Mandarin, and of course the soft, slithery local dialect. Shanghainese is elegant and musical, a feminine tongue—it is to Mandarin as Portuguese is to Spanish.

Before Communism, my mother watched her three oldest sisters get married off one by one to boys of good birth, carefully chosen by my grandparents. The year my mother turned fifteen the revolution began, and like so many of the aristocracy, the family packed up and went abroad. The Mas moved to San Diego to live with my grandmother's cousin Su-yi. My grandfather had died in a tuberculosis epidemic, so it was only my grandmother and her two youngest daughters, Ming-yu and Bau-yu—Clear Jade and Precious Jade. They were forced to leave most of the household goods in storage. I think Nai-nai must have known that she would never see them again, for she brought all her favorite mementos with her. "So much junk," my mother would say, rolling her eyes, when she told the story to Marty and me.

I can picture Nai-nai, tiny even in high heels and the 1940s-style navy cinched-waist suit her Shanghai tailor had copied from French *Vogue*, hair swept into a bun with ivory pins making an X at her nape, gold hoops in her ears. In her youth, she'd been a well-known lieder singer, traveling to Paris and

Vienna on tour, so this new port didn't faze her. I can see her standing on the dock in San Francisco watching anxiously as they unloaded the luggage—heavy brown trunks with the family character, *Ma*, painted in white. Although my grandmother's English was heavily accented, she was a mezzo-soprano after all, and she shrieked at the men as they trundled the trunks down the gangplank. "Attention! You pay attention!" The Chinese Princess, the crew had dubbed her, which mortified my mother. She and her sister stood huddled together, arms linked, as the dockworkers stared at them and joked, using words my mother didn't recognize but knew were dirty.

Their first year in America, Ming-yu, my Aunty Mabel, was sent east to college. My mother had to adjust to American high school by herself. Her spoken English was not up to her reading ability, and since spoken Chinese has no genders, *she*, *he*, and *it* were interchangeable to her. One day, from a stall in the girls' bathroom, she heard a classmate mocking: "Mis-tah Bee-vah, she def-in-i-lih my fa-vor-ih tea-cha."

"They are stupid," she raged to Nai-nai. "I read *Pride and Prejudice* when I was thirteen, and they cannot spell."

My grandmother frowned at her youngest daughter. "Eh, Bau-yu, you may be intelligent, but you don't comb your hair properly. It's no wonder you don't make friends."

Nai-nai stayed in the guest bedroom, but my mother had to share a room with the cousin's daughter, who was attending secretarial school and silly beyond belief. The daughter had dropped her Chinese name for an American one—Grace—and her Shanghainese was so bad that my mother was forced to converse with her in English. "She has twenty kinds of nail polish on the dresser," my mother wrote, half in scorn, half in envy, to Aunty Mabel. As ridiculous as Grace was, however, it was she who thought to take my mother shopping for plaid dirndls and shirts with Peter Pan collars so that she could blend in better.

Su-yi, my grandmother's cousin, was from a different branch

of the Shanghai family, one that was not as illustrious as Nai-nai's. She was nervous having her overseas relatives staying and was always cooking, creating feasts of eight courses or more for weekday dinners. She always took care to include at least two seafood dishes, my grandmother's favorite.

"You don't have to go to all this fuss," Nai-nai would say every night when they sat down to eat.

"No trouble, no trouble. You're used to much better in Shanghai, I'm sure."

Su-yi's husband was as quiet as a tomb. In China he had been a pediatrician. He worked very long hours at his American job, which was managing an Italian bakery, and when he was home he'd park himself in the La-Z-Boy and read Chinese magazines. When TV came the husband would watch whatever was on until he fell asleep in the recliner. After dinner my mother and Grace would sit together on the sofa behind him while Nai-nai and Su-yi argued in the kitchen about who would do the dishes.

"You girls finish homework?" the husband would ask, without turning around.

"Yes, Ba-ba," Grace would answer, for both of them.

My mother's favorite was Jack Benny. The glasses and laconic delivery gave him the demeanor of a Chinese scholar, like her father. Jack Benny made her laugh, even when she didn't get the jokes.

By the time my mother joined her sister at Smith, she too had an American name—Bonnie. In her high school graduation photo Ma is wearing a blue-collared sailor's dress and she brandishes her diploma, all her teeth showing in a broad American grin, hair ribbons flapping behind her. She'd worn a cap and gown like everyone else in her class, but Nai-nai thought they were ugly and made her take them off for the camera.

Meanwhile, my Aunty Mabel had met a nice Chinese man. He'd been impossible not to notice, since he was the only other Asian in town besides old Mr. Lee, who ran the Chinese laundry. Pau-yu Wang was teaching introductory Chinese to rich white girls who still had missionary fantasies, despite the fact that China was now Communist. Being a well-brought-up Shanghai girl, my aunt hadn't dared speak to Professor Wang her entire freshman year, and he had shown no signs of wanting to make her acquaintance. She found him uncommonly handsome—many of his students had crushes on him— although his height was disconcerting to her. The two were officially introduced at a party for foreign students, and by the time my aunt was a junior, they had progressed to meeting for tea now and then. But once my mother swept into the campus coffee shop in her powder blue cashmere sweater set, newly permed curls bouncing off her shoulders, my Aunty Mabel didn't stand a chance.

In China my parents would have been considered no match at all. Daddy was from the north, a poor farming village in Shandong province, and because he had no relatives in the States, my grandmother couldn't check up on him. My mother teased my father about his nasal Beijing accent, and he, the intellectual, would merely smile. "Although your mother never admit," Nai-nai told me once, "Beijing Mandarin is most exclusive, like Parisian French."

Nai-nai approved of my father, despite his dearth of credentials. Perhaps she was impressed by his refined air, unusual in a man of his background. Or perhaps, after marrying off three daughters, she had relaxed her standards and decided it was all right for my mother to be adventurous—they were in a new country after all.

My parents were married in San Diego, a week after my mother's college graduation. In the official wedding portrait, my father is standing, his boxy dark jacket a little too loose, hair slicked off his brow in a side part, not smiling exactly, but his eyes are shiny with excitement. My mother is seated in front of him. She is wonderfully pale—rice powder, Nai-nai told Marty and me—dressed in a white tailored suit to which is pinned a corsage of tiny light flowers. Her expression is haughty, even severe, gloved hands folded in her lap, white pumps pressed together. She looks decades older than the girl in the high school photograph.

My parents got jobs teaching at the Army Languages School in Monterey, where they rented a bungalow half a mile from the Pacific Ocean. One day, smack in the middle of her morning class, while she was standing at the blackboard writing the characters for sun and moon, my mother felt deathly ill. Somehow she made it to the bell and hurried to the ladies' room, where she was crouched over the toilet for an hour. "Every day like that for six months," she told me. "I think I rather die than be pregnant."

My father was certain that their first child would be a son. It was 1958, the year of the dog, which means strong and reliable. He was so sure that when my mother went into labor he dropped her off at the hospital and then went out to buy four dozen eggs to hard-boil and dye red, as is the Chinese custom for a new baby boy. When they told him it was a girl he walked out of the hospital and got into the sky blue Pontiac my parents had just bought and made the rounds to distribute the eggs anyway. "Maybe next time," their friends consoled him. Because my parents had not been prepared for a girl, I had no name for the first two months of my life.

Ma is an inconsistent storyteller. Once she claimed that she and my father first set eyes on each other in San Diego, while she was still in high school, sweet sixteen, never-been-kissed. He was there for a conference and had stopped by the house to visit Aunty Mabel. When I challenged her later, she replied: "You dream this, Sally. Of course I meet your Daddy at Smith. Ask your Nai-nai."

But my grandmother claimed she couldn't remember. Nai-nai wasn't the type to sit down and relate tales, although now and then she would toss out a gem for Marty and me to ponder: "Did you know your mother buy her wedding outfit off the rack?"

In contrast, my father's frequent stories of childhood were ruthlessly unvarying. Each one was designed as a lesson to Marty and me—study hard, respect your elders, clean your rice bowl.

The house where Daddy was born had dirt floors and the family drank hot water because they couldn't afford tea leaves. My father was the middle child, sandwiched between two sisters. His parents both died shortly after their third child was born and the orphans were shuffled from relative to relative, a miserable existence. Especially for my father, who was always ailing; there wasn't a disease you could name that he hadn't suffered: malaria, tuberculosis, pneumonia, rheumatic fever.

In all those strange poor beds he read voraciously, everything from the classics teachers would lend him to the big-city newspapers visitors would bring to the village. And Western science textbooks so beat-up their covers were gone. At sixteen, in the hospital recovering from influenza, he composed a five-page essay on the new role of technology in China. It won him first prize in a provincewide contest and brought him to the attention of an American missionary couple stationed in Beijing. They arranged for him to study in the United States after he had gotten his undergraduate degree.

What seduced my father above all else was the elegant metaphor of physics, which had a language of its own so that no matter where in the world he went he'd find someone else who could speak it. He'd be respected, even if his English wasn't perfect. So there he was at Berkeley, fresh off the boat, knowing no one, with only a single change of clothing and ten dollars spending money a week. For the first time in his life Daddy felt at home, not in the shabby off-campus apartment he shared with two other male grad students, a Czech and a Russian, but in the chalk- and dust-smelling physics lab, surrounded by giant blackboards dancing with equations he could not only understand but elaborate on. Out of the lab, his life felt more precarious than ever, but if it were possible for my father to be happy, he was happy then.

Happiness precedes loss. This is the main lesson I have learned from my father. When the telegram arrived, Daddy knew at once that it meant the end of his dream. His sponsors had been killed in a car accident. Good-hearted as they were, they'd never changed their will and everything went to a son who lived in Minneapolis. The son did not return my father's phone calls or letters. As a stranded student my father could stay in America, but he had to support himself. The lawyer who was handling his sponsors' estate wangled an interview for a teaching post, beginning Chinese, no experience needed, at a prestigious women's college on the East Coast. My father accepted the job as soon as it was offered. He had nowhere else to go.

If the sponsors hadn't died. If my father had been more enterprising and hunted around for new benefactors instead of accepting a second-rate fate. Why did he give up? Daddy gave no clues, he never talked about his early life in America. I suspect that it was humiliating in a way that my mother, who was thirteen years younger with her family to shield her, had never experienced. Daddy's skin stayed as white as if he were still starving, unlike my mother, whose pallor was milk with a tinge of cream, the complexion of a Chinese beauty.

But my father, even in his ghostliness, still turned the heads of women on the street. Had he been bolder he could have courted one of his students, the ones who sat in the front row mesmerized by his full mouth as he formed each precise syllable. But I know my father did not find those girls beautiful. Too big and eager and uncontained, with their heavy breasts and muscled calves and light frivolous hair. The two Ma sisters with their aristocratic looks must have felt like a dream to him. Especially my mother, whose formidable will was hidden by a kind of vivacious delicacy.

It is true that I resemble my father, especially as I get older, except for my eyes, which Nai-nai said were my maternal grandfather's. But what was striking in Daddy feels cumbersome in me: my height, my long solemn face and full mouth, my large hands and feet. The shoe salesman would ask my size and Ma would put in: "You can see, she has enormous ones." She once told me there might be some Manchurian or even Hakka on my father's side. Hakkas were misfits who had no home province, big-footed because they were nomads and did so much walking.

If I am my father's child, then my sister is my mother's. Born barely twelve months after me, she was named after Martha Washington, my mother's favorite character from American history, which my parents were studying at the time to obtain their citizenship. Even as a girl my sister had an arresting face: diamond shaped, almond eyes set wide apart, a thin-lipped, stubborn mouth, Ma's kitten chin. Typical Shanghai, my mother pointed out. Her nickname for my sister was "Mau-mau," which means "little cat." Marty's official Chinese name is "Joyous Virtue" and indeed she was a sunny child, when she wasn't having tantrums.

"But you, you have your father's blood," Ma told me. "So pessimistic, those peasants."

And so I'd picture that melancholy running in our veins, like some rare blood disease.

When I was four and my sister three, Ma, who had been staying home with us, went back to teach summer school and Nai-nai moved in. It was my father who decreed that we should call my grandmother "Nai-nai," which is the word for a father's mother, instead of "Ha-bu," which means mother's mother. That way, Daddy said, she could stand for both grandmothers.

Nai-nai in no way resembled the plump bespectacled grandmothers in our fairy-tale books. I remember exactly how she looked the first time we met—the cream-colored kid gloves, ivory hairpins, miniature feet in black embroidered slippers dangling daintily over the edge of the sofa. "Not bound," she said when she caught me staring, "but still very nice."

I used to imagine that in China, beauty did not have a sexual connotation. If a woman was beautiful, she was beautiful like a flower or a good horse. A man wanted to write poetry about her, not to have her. My grandmother was beautiful in that way, with her pristine clothes, her long hair wound into its pincushion bun every waking hour, not a strand out of place. Her face was a perfect oval, like a cameo, her pursed lips dark red, and she had a mole on her neck that embarrassed her, to the point where she usually wore high-collared blouses. When I was older, I'd watch her hobble down the sidewalk and wonder how such a delicately made woman had survived the birth of five children.

My grandmother liked to take walks. After lunch it was our habit to meander down to the rocky beach to feed the gulls or explore the woods across the street or my favorite: stroll two blocks over to the primary school Marty and I were still too young to attend. It was deserted for the summer and my grandmother would lift me and my sister up in turn so that we could peer through the windows. The bulletin boards and countertops were bare, the chairs upturned on top of the tables. "Next year," Nai-nai promised me. The school was surrounded by pines, which threw cool shadows, and the ground below us was cushioned with fallen needles. My grandmother was wrong. By September we'd be in Connecticut and Nai-nai and the school in the pine grove would seem a thousand years away.

I remember all the days of that last summer in California as being sunny, every room in the bungalow filled with golden light, so that during nap time, even with the shades down, I could never sleep. I'd lie there making up plays with my stuffed animals while my sister snored her purring snore in the next bed.

I understand now that, like my father at Berkeley, I was happy.

9

Memory begins with an image.

I see my sister sitting on the front steps of our house on Woodside Avenue, waiting for her boyfriend Schuyler. She has on an old navy sweatshirt and a short denim skirt, one thigh—so slender I could die of jealousy—crossed over the other. A loafer dangles off her big toe, and her eyes are narrowed in that way that means she can barely contain her impatience. Her hair is parted on the side, the sweep of it following the sweep of her cheek.

She is thirteen, and just beginning to realize her power.

I'd left home by then.

Boarding school is my way out. By seventh grade, pamphlets have begun to arrive. Daddy has his heart set on Farmington, where Jackie Onassis went, but I fall in love with the quaint little school by the Sudbury River in Massachusetts. The day we visit, the autumn foliage is at full pitch and the shouts of girls on the hockey field float in through the open windows. We tour the fancy new performing arts center with its bubble dome, the white clapboard chapel that once was the centerpiece of a Vermont town (it was shipped down piece by piece and rebuilt by students), the dining hall with its French windows and pepper mills on each table. But what steals my heart is the art studio, with the skylight and balcony where you can go out and sketch on sunny days.

"That's where I'm going," I announce on the car ride back. In the rearview mirror I see my large face foreshortened with my hair whipping about in the draft from the open window.

"Get in first," Daddy says.

"I'll get in." It's the first time in my life I've ever been so sure of anything.

Before I know it, it's August, the month before I leave, but no one is paying attention to me because they're excited about the new house we just bought. It's on Woodside Avenue, a much fancier neighborhood than Coram Drive, closer to Yale. The down payment came from the sale of some land that my parents bought in Monterey and kept all these years. Some big developers want to build a spa there. The move will take place in September, while I'm away.

There are open boxes all over the place and Ma's frantically going through her lists. Marty has to remind her we need school clothes. Saturday afternoon we're off to the mall in our gold Ford Fairlane, my sister in the front seat next to Ma, her bare forearm lying along the open window. I listen to them arguing about the radio.

"No wah-wah-wah music," Ma says.

"It's good stuff," my sister snaps. Overnight she's become sophisticated, spouting off the names of foreign sports cars and haute couture designers. She goes to the kinds of parties to which I'm not invited. One time she's dropped off after midnight, drunk, and I have to sneak her into the bathroom to wash the puke out of her hair. She keeps giggling and I tell her to shut up, she'll wake Ma and Daddy. "Oh, Sally, you're so boring," she hisses at me in a stage whisper. "Fucking afraid of your own shadow."

Marty wins the music fight, and "Sugar Magnolia" floats back to me in snatches. "Isn't this pretty?" she asks.

"No meaning," says Ma.

She makes us start at Alexander's. Marty groans. "There's

not a single item of clothing in here I'd be caught dead in," she pronounces. "Not even a sock." She looks at me for support.

"Not even underwear," I say.

"Stop it," my mother says sharply. "Sally, I'm surprised at you."

We spin circular racks of skirts and sweaters that are all heavy on burgundy, navy, and forest green, like the banners of Ivy League schools. My mother automatically picks out the same things for Marty and me to try on, as if we were twins. She holds up two kilts in our respective sizes, both in the same burgundy and blue tartan.

Marty barely gives them a glance. "Geeky, Ma." My mother hands me the one in my size and I take it because it seems like something a boarding-school girl would wear.

After Alexander's Marty wants to go to Casual Corner. A rock station blasts away in the background and the saleswomen stand around like poles, gossiping and jingling their silver bangles. My sister heads straight for the angora sweaters, and my mother, after a considering glance around, starts poking through a rack marked SALE. I pick out the first thing that catches my eye—overall shorts—but when I try them on Ma says: "They don't bring out your best features." She means they make my legs look fat. Marty ends up with a couple of tight sweaters and a miniskirt. Ma puts her foot down about a gold chiffon scarf. "Looks cheap." Like the other stuff doesn't.

When we get home Daddy is in the living room reading. My sister crackles her shopping bags at him. "Look what we got."

Our father doesn't look up. "You spend too much money."

I don't say anything. Daddy and I never talk unless it's absolutely necessary and then only with my mother around.

The phone rings. It's for Marty, it's always for Marty.

"Hello?" she answers in that breathless voice she saves for boys, then she pulls the phone into the hall closet and closes the door as far as she can.

I go upstairs to try on my new clothes. I draw the blinds—David Katz probably isn't home on a Saturday afternoon but you never know—and put on the kilt and the cream blouse with mother-of-pearl buttons I got to match it. The mirror over our dresser is so short I can only see down to the tops of my thighs, but I think it looks okay. I crack open the door to the hall and it seems like everyone's still downstairs. It's safe to go to my parents' room to use the full-length mirror on their closet door.

Standing there, I fold up the kilt hem to see how I would look in a miniskirt and decide that Ma is right, I don't have the figure for short. My hips have swollen so fast I can barely fit into my skirts from last year, but I'm still so flat I don't need a bra, unlike my sister, who's almost up to B already, even got her period before me. I unbutton the blouse halfway and scrutinize myself. Even when I press my breasts together I have nothing that can possibly be construed as cleavage.

I don't hear the door open. I don't know anyone is there until I hear his sound, a kind of gasped grunt. His face is in the mirror behind me, eyebrows drawn down into a V, mouth slack. The expression is disgust.

I pull the blouse shut and whip past my father, down the hall, back to my own room and into the closet where I sit hunched on the floor, hands crossed over my chest, willing my heart to stop pounding. Out the window I notice the Cuddy twins, Michael and Shauna, wheeling around the dead-end circle on their battered tricycles. They look ridiculous.

I hate my body. It's too big, it was always too big. I want to be small like my mother and sister. At boarding school they won't care that I'm built like a boy except for my fat hips and thighs. I'll be an artist. How I look won't matter. One more month. One more month and I'll be out of here forever.

From downstairs I can hear my sister shrieking with laughter.

*   *   *

The week before I leave I decide to cut my hair. Darcy Katz does it for me in her pink room in front of the vanity mirror. "You sure?" she keeps asking over and over again until I want to scream. She cuts it in degrees, in case I change my mind, first to the middle of my back, and then, when I insist, all the way up to the nape. I wrap the snakelike hanks in tissue paper and hide them in the bottom drawer of my dresser.

At boarding school I make the best friend of my life: red-headed Frances Fischel, whose parents are divorced. Her father lives in the Virgin Islands with his new, much younger wife while her nutty mother languishes in a barn of an apartment on the Upper East Side of Manhattan. Fran always has a supply of the best hash money can buy, thanks to the generous guilt allowance she gets from her father. After night study hall, the two of us go down by the river to get high sitting on the cold rocks among the willows. A few yellow house lights glimmer remotely across the water from us. When the hash is laced with acid the lights break free like fireflies, streaming up into the violet sky. The first time this happens it freaks me out, but then I get used to it, even try to draw it from memory.

The two of us develop elaborate philosophies. I'm going to be a painter and she's going to be a poet. We make a pact to wear only silver jewelry for the rest of our lives. Silver represents dedication to art, while gold stands for worldly things.

The first time I go home is for Thanksgiving vacation. It feels like a dream. For one thing, we've moved from Coram Drive to the rambling Tudor house on the hill. On the way home from the train station Ma tells me: "So much trouble to move! You should be here to help. But now everything's fine, we're all settled in. Your daddy's study is so beautiful, with wood panel."

But when we pull up he's not in his study, but down in our

new living room, ensconced in his old oxblood chair with his Chinese newspapers.

"Hi," I say.

He mutters something about my hair, which has grown out ragged to my chin.

I go upstairs and open the first bedroom door I come to, which turns out to be my sister's. She's lying on her bed talking on her new Princess phone. "Hey!" she says, annoyed.

"Sorry." I close the door.

Later, when she comes into my room, she pulls a face. "You have zits."

"So."

"You shouldn't eat chocolate. I bet you stuff your face at that school."

"Up yours," I say, an expression I picked up from Fran. It surprises Marty.

"Uh-huh. Well, you missed all the excitement. The move and everything. I got the best room."

"Like I care."

She smiles at me secretively and leaves.

My first night home, Ma makes my favorite dinner: spaghetti and lima beans. We've just started to eat when Daddy begins talking. Not to me exactly. It's more like a quiz. Nothing's changed.

"How you doing in your subjects at school?"

"Fine."

"You get all As this semester?"

"We haven't gotten our report cards yet."

"How about tests? You get As on your tests?"

"Yes," I lie.

Marty has picked up her plate and is leaning across to shovel her lima beans into mine, as she has done since we were children. I let her because even though she's acting like a jerk, she's still my sister.

"Mar-tee isn't doing so well," Daddy announces.

"Daddy," Ma says.

"I think she wants to be a dropout. I think she doesn't care about getting into a good school like her *jie-jie*."

"I don't want to go to *boarding school*. I want to stay at home."

"Stay at home and fool around."

My sister lets out a sigh that flutters her bangs.

There's a silence, and then my mother says brightly: "Marty has star part in the Christmas pageant."

"I'm the Virgin Mary." My sister's smile is ironic.

"I won a prize," I say casually.

"Oh, what?" Ma asks.

"It was for a pastel drawing. They chose from the whole freshman class. They're going to put it in the spring art show."

Daddy clears his throat. "Yale only takes the best grade point average."

Ma nods. "When I was young, you know what I wanted to be? A neurologist. I wanted to learn all about the brain and nervous system and perform surgery."

My sister and I exchange glances. This is news to us.

"You could become academic, do research," Daddy suggests to me.

"I don't like math."

"Who's talking about math? This is science."

I don't want to be you, I think. Never. I hate you. My father is sucking up his spaghetti like Chinese noodles. I think how ashamed I would be if Fran, if anyone I knew at boarding school, could see him.

"You keep on," Ma tells me. "Be determined. Not lazy, like you did with piano lessons. You don't understand, you try again."

Daddy points his finger. "That Xiao Lu, he's entering the Westinghouse competition. You know every year who wins?" No one answers. "Chinese," my father says triumphantly. All our lives we've been hearing about Xiao Lu. I wonder who his parents hold up to him as an example.

I ask my mother if Nai-nai is coming for Thanksgiving.

"No," Ma answers. "Her hip is bothering her. Your Nai-nai doesn't like turkey anyway. That Su-yi will cook a big fish."

Our own Thanksgiving dinner is fancier than usual. Ma actually buys fresh cranberries and simmers them with orange peel and honey. I have two helpings of everything, including the pumpkin pie home-baked by our new neighbor, Lally Escobar. Marty's acting friendlier now. After dinner we put on our down jackets and mittens and go for a walk up to East Rock, where she tells me about her new boyfriend. His name is Schuyler, he attends the private day school in town, he's fifteen and has his learner's permit. The cigarettes we're smoking were stolen from his older brother. "Dad can't stand him," Marty says. She takes a long drag and stares out into the dusk and then she says: "We're doing it."

To tell the truth I'm shocked. Drugs is one thing but sex is something else. Who would want to? We're sitting out of the wind, on a gigantic flat rock that's famous in the area as a glacial formation. I wrap my arms around myself, squashing the down until I hear it sigh. "What's it like?" I ask, trying to keep my voice normal.

"Mmmmhmmm," she says. Schuyler's parents are always away on cruises and safaris and he and his brother are left the run of the house, ostensibly under the care of the maid. Marty tells me about the parents' bedroom, the sheets with the giant chrysanthemums on them, how they always put on the Rolling Stones.

"Do you like it?" I ask.

"It's okay," she says, so offhand that I want to belt her. She's perched on the edge of the rock, her blue-jeaned legs—grown long for her height—dangling over. The hood of her parka is thrown back and in the fading light her lashes cast half-moon shadows against her cheek as she contemplates the smoke from her cigarette. I picture her lying back naked on a giant four-poster bed, entwined with some silent clumsy boy.

It makes me so upset that I have to look away.

"I'm the only Oriental at school," I tell her. "Except this girl, Jane Chu, who's from New York Chinatown. She was born here but she talks with an accent."

"Kind of like Mimi." Mimi is our age, the youngest daughter of the family who owns the Sung Trading Company downtown.

"You could go away to school too, Mar. It's a lot of fun." It's almost dark now, but I can feel her watching me.

"No, I'm okay here. Besides, Ma wants me to stick around. Not that she says anything, but I can tell." Marty crunches her cigarette out and with a practiced motion flicks it over the barbed wire into Lake Whitney.

"How about him?"

"Oh, he's nothing. He just yells a lot. He can't do anything. I don't give a fuck about him." She turns directly to face me. "He's an old man now, can't you see? He can't hurt us anymore."

Since we were kids we've never talked about Monkey King, my sister and I, and even now I'm not sure that she remembers exactly what happened. I'm not sure what she's telling me. I look away from her again, because if I don't, I know I'm going to throw up my Thanksgiving dinner.

During Christmas vacation Marty makes herself scarce. Schuyler has turned sixteen and gotten his license. I meet him a couple of times—he's blond and beefy and taciturn, the prototype of all my sister's subsequent boyfriends. I notice once that my sister is wearing the gold scarf Ma refused to buy for her. Sometimes when she comes in late I hear Daddy yelling. "You are useless! Useless girl!" His voice grates, getting more and more high-pitched until I want to scream. Somehow, my sister manages to ignore him.

One evening Ma knocks on my door and says she needs help deciding what to wear to the faculty Christmas party. I lie on my stomach on her bed as she stands in front of her closet flipping through hangers. "You think I should wear dress or pants?"

"Pants. It's chicer." I'm flattered that she wants my opinion.

She pulls out a pair of black trousers, and after some consideration, a cherry-colored tunic, and puts them on while I watch from the bed. She catches my eye in the dresser mirror.

"You know, Sal-lee, you could be nicer to your daddy."

"How am I not nice to him?"

"You disappoint him. He try to be kind."

"He's always been crabby, Ma. It's not my fault."

Ma twists to examine her backside in the mirror. "Your father is not a cheerful man," she admits.

"Maybe he should help around the house once in a while instead of just sitting there reading his newspapers."

"I know Marty and Daddy don't get along, but you were always his favorite. Don't you remember?"

"No." Ma's up to her tricks again, trying to pretend that everything's hunky-dory.

"When you were born, he did everything. Change your diaper, give you bath. Even make your baby formula."

"I don't remember."

"It's true. You know Chinese don't talk about love, but there's nothing like a Chinese father. In Monterey every Sunday he take you to the beach to watch the seals. You really don't remember? Sealy. Your nickname is Sealy."

"So what."

Ma fiddles with a jet necklace lying on the bureau. "Most children love their mother more, but not you. You wait all afternoon until he comes home and then you bring him his tea in the living room, ask him how his school went." She picks up the necklace, loops it in double strands around her neck, and turns around. "What do you think?"

"Looks good," I say.

"And these earrings to go with? Or should I wear the black pearl ones from Nai-nai?"

"No, stay with the jet."

"Ma, are you ready?" It's my father calling from the bottom of the stairs. "Just a minute," Ma calls back, annoyed.

The house itself seems to breathe a sigh of relief when they are finally gone. I put on an old nightshirt that belonged to Fran's grandfather—white flannel with very pale blue stripes. She gave it to me when I admired it. I feel that it's armor, that it will protect me somehow. I take out my pastels and a sketch pad and set up my easel by the window, planning to draw a view of our new yard, with its dramatic trees that I can't yet name, but soon it's too dark to see. I turn out the lights and light a candle and with a broken-off piece of indigo begin to sketch in the shapes of my room: the bed, the baby rocking chair, the row of miniature Peking opera masks, the quivering giant shadow of the carved wooden horse on my bureau. I'm still at work when my parents come home.

Two weeks later, when I show it to my art teacher, he says: "You have made the object into a subject. And the mood! Such foreboding."

"Thank you," I say, thinking, I can do this. At least I can do this.

After that the vacations start to blend together in my memory. On the way home from the train station, I think it's spring break my sophomore year, Ma tells me two things. First, the accident. Since moving from Coram Drive we've completely lost touch with the Katzes. Dusk on a rainy night, the blind curve around Lake Whitney where Ma herself once scraped a fender trying to avoid a crossing turtle. The boyfriend was driving. He lived two days, but Darcy was killed instantly.

I keep trying to picture Darcy with a boy, and failing.

"Did you go to the funeral?"

"No. But I send flowers. White carnations."

"Ma! That's like a wedding."

"You know white is mourning color in China. And besides, it reminds me of Darcy." Ma is silent for a minute and then she says: "I'm worried about your sister. You know we send her to the best private school in New Haven." Marty has finally conceded to this, because it's where Schuyler goes.

Into my brain jump possibilities: flunking out, drugs, pregnant.

"She got arrested," Ma says. "At Macy's, with her friends. She was shoplifting."

I think of another time she got caught shoplifting, with me. I say: "That's not so bad."

"Not so bad? I had to go down and pick her up. So shameful! She and those girls, all their parents so rich, can buy anything they want."

"What did she take?"

"Some kind of jumper, not even nice-looking. She tried to wear it under her clothes."

"Did they press charges?"

"Not this time. I think she won't do it again."

"What did Daddy say?"

Ma presses her lips together. "Of course he's very upset. But she doesn't listen to him. Maybe you talk to her."

When I go up to her room, Marty is sprawled out on her blue-and-white-checked comforter, leafing through *Vogue*.

"That's sad about Darcy, isn't it?" I sit down next to her, noticing she has on way too much eye makeup.

"The guy was shitfaced." She yawns and turns over onto her back, stretching like a cat. "Christ, am I hung over."

"You knew him?"

"Not personally. He was a townie."

"You're a townie."

"Fuck you."

"Ma told me about your crime," I say.

"It was stupid."

"Why'd you do it?"

"For Christ's sake, Sa. I've already had all the lectures."

"Ma thinks you're sorry."

She laughs, flipping her hair out of her eyes.

I'm losing patience. "Are you going to keep on acting this way?"

"What way?"

"Like a self-centered bitch."

"Oh God, I don't believe you. Who's the one going to the fancy-schmancy boarding school?" She sits up. "You know, I read your journal last summer. I know all about your jaunts by the river, how you get your liquor and your pot."

"What?"

"You know what Ma and Daddy would do if I told them?"

"I can't believe you read my journal."

"I can't tell you how sick I am of hearing how perfect you are."

"At least I don't UPSET them."

"Because you're a hypocrite."

"You could have gone away."

"And leave Ma? No way."

"Ma can take care of herself."

"How do you know? You're not around." Marty flops back onto a mound of pillows, her arms folded behind her head. "But you know what? I wouldn't be you for all the money in the world. You're so goddamn passive. You can't stand up for yourself. You have no personality."

I lean over and punch her, hard, in the soft part of her biceps. She's caught off guard and tries to hit me back, but misses and goes toppling off the bed. The way she falls is overdramatic, just a little too graceful.

"Get out of my room," she growls, facedown on the rag rug. I can't tell whether she's crying or not.

"No one's making you stay in this dump."

"GET OUT OF MY ROOM." She jumps up and then her hands are in front of my face and I feel the biting pain of her fingernails in the flesh of my neck. I reach and slap her fingers away, slap until my own hand bones sting. I'm still bigger, after all. She lunges forward and with all her weight shoves me toward the door. "GET OUT."

"You're such a baby," I shout back. "Just wait until you're out in the real world without Ma to protect you. You'll be a big failure."

She slams the door in my face.

I begin spending more and more of my breaks with Fran at her mother's apartment in New York City. During the day we go shopping or to museums and at night we get stoned and send out for Chinese food and watch old movies on TV. Sometimes we go out with the boys Fran grew up with, who like her are smart-alecky and good-looking. The two of us dress up in our best thrift-shop outfits—Fran in a lime miniskirt and an orange chiffon blouse, me in a pink strapless gown threaded with silver beads. I have to stuff the top with Kleenex to make it stay up. Fran scrutinizes the effect. "You have a beautiful neck," she says, "but maybe next time you should wear evening gloves." She never directly refers to the scars on my arms.

My boy is always excruciatingly polite. Fran says not to worry, these guys aren't sophisticated enough to handle someone as exotic as me. What reassures me most is that she doesn't seem to take them very seriously herself. Once a couple of them come to visit us at school and we go skinny-dipping in the river. Fran's pale round breasts, illuminated by the moonlight, fascinate all of us. "You're thinner than you look," my boy remarks to me, and I know it's not a compliment.

Summers, when I have to go back to Woodside Avenue, I hide out in my bedroom, avoiding my parents as much as possible. I do volunteer things: arts-and-crafts counselor at a day camp, teaching life skills at a shelter workshop for the mentally handicapped. Maybe my sister is right, I'm a complete wimp, and helping people worse off makes me feel better. Weekends when the weather is good I'm out in the back yard drawing or painting. It's the one thing I do that takes me away from this world. I buy a field guide to learn the trees: silver maple, sugar maple, pin oak, blue spruce, and my favorite, the two black walnuts that form a kind of gateway to Ma's garden. A matched pair, the tree man says to Daddy, the wood worth twenty thousand dollars at least. One summer one of the trees is struck by lightning and has to be carted off in huge splinters, worthless. I notice Daddy doesn't brag about the one that is left, as he had with the pair. It seems that symmetry is terribly important to most people.

Marty has a string of summer jobs—the longest as hostess at a fancy steakhouse downtown, but she quits after a fight with the owner. "He wanted me to be goddamn Suzie Wong," she says.

"Useless, both of you," Daddy says at the dinner table. "Walking pieces of meat." He points out that the younger sister of one of his summer school students is a page in the U.S. Senate. Not to mention Xiao Lu, who is going to physics camp in the Adirondacks.

I have trouble sleeping, those summer nights at home. I read till I'm too restless to lie in bed anymore and then I go out to the backyard and smoke, and sometimes I even dream about this boy or that. It's not sex I'm thinking about. I want them to want me. That would be enough.

Back at boarding school I keep working on my portfolio, and on April 15, senior year, I get in line for the dorm phone to tell my parents I didn't get into Yale. Ma is the one who answers.

"That's a shame," she says. "I don't know what you're going to do now."

"Half our class applied, you know, and they took only seven people."

"Your father will be very disappointed."

"I'm going to the Rhode Island School of Design, Ma. It's a very good art school. Maybe the best in the country. They gave me a scholarship and everything."

"I just talk to Xiao Lu's mother. He got into Harvard and M.I.T."

For graduation I give Fran a hammered silver bangle and she gives me a pair of silver earrings shaped like teardrops.

10

Some memory you keep underneath, so you can get on with your life.

It doesn't work. What happens is that you end up moving from dream to dream.

But you, you have your father's blood.

He walks away into the night, his white shirt a flag. As in life, his shoulders are bowed and he travels hunched forward, not looking back.

I want to call out to him but realize that I don't know his language.

It's my ninth birthday. Ma doesn't get a cake or presents because we're busy getting ready to go to visit our Nai-nai in San Diego. That is, Marty and I are going while Ma and Daddy spend the summer in Taiwan, where my father has a teaching job. "We celebrate when we come back," my mother promises me. In the front of the tunnel to the plane she hands us over to the stewardess, who wears white gloves like Minnie Mouse. Marty cries but I don't. Daddy stands behind Ma, mixed in with the crowd. We don't say anything to him and he says nothing to us. When he raises his hand to wave good-bye I look away, and that's the last I see of him.

During the flight the stewardess keeps coming over with *Jack and Jill* magazine, coloring books, magnetic tic-tac-toe. Not that we need distractions; we sit quietly, buckling our seat belts when the sign says to. Most of the way I read *Eight Cousins*, feeling my sister's hot skull pressed against my shoulder as she sleeps.

My Nai-nai is so glad to see us, she has tears in her eyes. "*Ni kan!*" she says to her cousin Su-yi, who has come to the airport too because our grandmother doesn't drive. Nai-nai used to live with Su-yi, but now she has a separate house on the same street. Su-yi has a dough face and smokes cigarettes. Her hair is curly and black—dyed, I can tell.

Ma has warned us: "Nai-nai old lady, don't tire her out." But my grandmother is inexhaustible. Mornings, when she comes to wake us, she's already dressed, hair up, face powdered, lipstick on. The first night when she tucks us in Marty asks, "When do you go to bed?" and Nai-nai answers: "Very, very late. Old lady doesn't need much sleep."

Over my grandmother's shoulder I am watching the curtains, patterned with cobalt and fuchsia primroses, dancing over the open window. I have brought Piggy, although I am way too old. Marty left her Raggedy Ann on her pillow at home. Nai-nai doesn't make fun of me. "Poor old man," she says, when she notices Piggy's tattered chest. She looks in her drawers and finds a baby T-shirt I can dress him in.

Every morning the three of us go marketing, Nai-nai handing Marty or me the netting bag when it begins to fill up. We walk the ten blocks to the supermarket, where Nai-nai leans over the mountain of oranges to haggle with the produce man, who is fat and wears a white apron. Her voice is so loud that the other customers stare. "In China, I have maid to do this," she explains as we leave the store, Marty stomping hard on the rubber mat to make sure the electric door opens.

At the fish store I drag my sister over to watch the lobsters bumbling over each other in their tank. Although I would never admit it, it makes me a little sick to see my grandmother glaring into the eye of each fish as if it were a lifelong enemy and then pointing—"This one, and this"—and the fish lady slaps each carcass onto the sheet of butcher wrap she has laid across the scales. At home Nai-nai chops the heads off and puts them in a pot to make stew. "Good food for old lady," she says, and that's her lunch, while Marty and I get the bodies, steamed in a brown sauce so sweet that, when Nai-nai isn't looking, we stick our faces into our bowls to lick up the last drops.

Our grandmother has lots of opinions.

"Sal-lee going to be tall. Tall girl not so beautiful, but stands out." She looks me up and down. "You press your clothes, you're fine."

To Marty: "You like your mother. Sloppy."

"WHAT?" Nai-nai is the only one who can make my sister squirm.

"Mar-tee, you walk like water buffalo."

"Crabby old lady," my sister mutters under her breath.

"You don't talk back to elders," Nai-nai says serenely. "Now please wash rice for lunch."

I ask my grandmother about Chinese ghosts.

"Two kinds," she tells me. "Men ghosts and women ghosts."

"Which are worse?" We are in the kitchen making *jiao zi*, pork dumplings. Marty and I call them boiled ears, but we can eat two dozen apiece, dunked in a sauce of soy and vinegar, in one sitting. Nai-nai examines each one I make, frowns at some, smiles at others. Not in a million years could I pleat them shut as quick as she does—pinch, pinch, pinch—without even looking.

"Men ghosts are very strong. Make a lot of noise, like child. Women ghosts charming and often beautiful. Some say women ghosts worse."

When I first get to California I sometimes bolt awake in the middle of the night. I pad down the hallway to my grandmother's room and slip through the door, which is always ajar. "*Ai-yah*, awake again!" Nai-nai whispers, lifting the covers so that I can climb in.

"I heard a scary noise."

"Nothing, nothing, just the wind, so many big bush around this house."

"It didn't sound like wind."

"So what if ghost? They're dead, you're alive. They can't hurt you. You should feel sorry for them. They're like your sister, tease because they're jealous."

But it's not ghosts I'm afraid of. I can't tell her, but it helps to lie there in the sweet musty-smelling bed, listening to my grandmother breathe. She's the same height as me but sharpboned. Tough. I imagine being old like her, so that nothing can hurt me.

The kids on our street are easygoing, unlike those in Connecticut. No jumping out of the hedges and making Chinese eyes or yelling, We beat you Japs in World War II. There is even a family on the block with an American father and a Japanese mother. Their two daughters are teenagers, beautiful, longlegged, with red-brown hair parted down the middle. They always call out to us: "Hey, you two!" About Marty they say: "Isn't she precious?" After dinner we lurk on Nai-nai's front porch to watch their dates come pick them up. The boys are indistinguishable from each other, with booming American voices and faded polo shirts to match their faded blond hair.

We play softball and kickball. One girl takes me into her house and lets me borrow from her Nancy Drew collection, which is the largest I've ever seen. Sometimes we go to the beach, along with a lot of other kids in bathing suits, crowded into the back of a station wagon that smells of hot rubber and coconut suntan lotion. When we get there the mother sets up the umbrella and lays down the beach towels and says, "Shoo!" and we all run screaming like crazy people to the ocean, waving our arms. It is the most beautiful ocean I have ever seen, with all different kinds of blue in it, rolling like fluted glass toward us.

I tell the other kids about the Gulf of Mexico, where Aunty Mabel and Uncle Richard live. There were things waiting there in that warm flat water, crabs who'd clamp your toes no matter how carefully you stepped. Then I tell them about the beach in Monterey, where I was born, with all the wildflowers in the spring, and of course the seals. I say that when we went swimming they'd slide off their rocks to join us. Actually we never went swimming in Monterey—the water was much too cold.

Marty and I get very tan, and Nai-nai scolds us. "You become like peasants. Why don't you stay under umbrella?"

But she softens when she sees how hungry we are after our days at the beach, how we wolf everything down, no matter how strange. When we first got here we were picky, polite. Nai-nai corrected the way Marty held her chopsticks and made her cry. Our grandmother serves the meal in courses, unlike Ma, who sets everything down on the table at once.

Now we compromise. Marty is allowed to use a fork, and Nai-nai sometimes gives in to our pleas at the grocery store. "Hawaiian Punch? You sure you want red drink?" One night she even makes hamburgers, following the recipe from *Joy of Cooking*, although we forget to get buns so we have to have them on toast.

On the first rainy day, Nai-nai climbs the stepladder and takes out boxes from the top shelf of her bedroom closet. They are filled with presents from her admirers, back in her youth when she was a lieder singer. She kept everything: dried sprays of orchids, brittle and black-edged; a collection of music boxes from Switzerland; perfume, never opened, the bottoms of the crystal flasks coated brown. I imagine the perfume to be like orange juice concentrate: if you added water it would be as good as fresh.

Nai-nai lets us try on the silk shawls embroidered with dragons, phoenixes, and butterflies. "You girls so big," she mourns, measuring with her hands the breadth of my shoulders as I stand before the dresser mirror. "Your mother big too." Even Marty can't fit her feet into the black satin slippers, so tiny they're almost round, stacked neatly in a bottom drawer. My grandmother keeps her jewelry tucked into the toes of the slippers. Mostly earrings, heavy gems in elaborate gold and silver settings, although I've never seen her wear anything but plain gold hoops.

She shows us photographs of our parents' wedding. "Handsome couple," she says. My mother doesn't look too different, except for more makeup and wavy hair, but my father is unrecognizable. The man in the picture has dark, thick hair and a smooth confident face, as if nothing bad had ever happened to him.

At the wedding my grandmother is wearing a tight highnecked silk gown from her singing days, a gardenia pinned at the breast. "Why didn't you have an orchid?" I ask and she shakes her head. "Some flowers for youth only," she says.

From the glass-fronted bookcase in the dining room Nai-nai takes out an old book called A Dream of Red Mansions. We can't read it, it's in Chinese, but my grandmother shows us the color plates beneath their crumbling tissue. Princes and princesses wear elaborate headdresses like little Christmas trees, and flowing robes of turquoise and crimson sweep over their feet so that it looks as if they are floating from courtyard to courtyard.

Marty points out that the princesses have their hair loose.

"They're royalty," Nai-nai explains. "They have servants to comb."

My hair is as long as the princesses' but I am not allowed to wear it loose except at night. Nai-nai washes it for me in the kitchen sink. "I'm not going to hurt you," she says the first time because I'm shivering so much. I force myself to stand very still, although I get a crick in my neck and the water from the spray nozzle tickles. "In China, now, it's not the style for girls have long hair like this," my grandmother tells me. "Everyone the same, short, like your sister."

Once, after my hair has dried enough to brush out, Nai-nai puts it up into a bun like hers. I watch her in the dresser mirror, trying to memorize the motions, but my grandmother is too fast. When she's done she gives me the hand mirror so that I can examine the back of my head. I see that she has anchored the bun with a single pale green hairpin, like an arrow through a valentine.

"It's jade," my grandmother says, patting my shoulder. "You keep."

People ask about Connecticut: how's school there, do you like your teachers, who are your friends, and I lie, like I did about the seals in Monterey. I tell them I skipped two grades. I tell them there's a girl in my class who got pregnant and kicked out of school. If my sister happens to overhear she just looks at me with a frown.

I feel like I've been here forever in my grandmother's house, among these wide streets, with flowers crawling over the weather-beaten picket fences that separate the yards, the salt smell in the air, especially strong in the mornings when we go grocery shopping. It's Marty who counts off the days on the opera lady calendar hanging on the refrigerator in Nai-nai's kitchen, who starts saving shells in a plastic bread bag to take back to Connecticut. "Don't you remember when David Katz fell off his bike and broke his arm?" she prods me. "Or when Mrs. Augustine gave me detention?"

"No," I say.

The Nancy Drew girl and I start a magazine about our street—she does the writing and I draw the illustrations out on the picnic table in Nai-nai's backyard. "So talented," my grandmother says. We show it to the two teenage girls, who say, "Fantabulous" and giggle at the picture I've drawn of them, in miniskirts and gold chain belts. My sister scowls and bounces the kickball so hard against the foundation of Nai-nai's house that it leaves a black scar.

I draw other things too that I don't show anyone, not even Marty. If they were to find them and ask, I would tell them that this is Monkey King, this is his tail, this is the stake through his heart and the blood pouring out. But no one finds them. I do my drawings secretly, in the morning before Nai-nai comes in and my sister is still asleep, and afterward I rip them up into tiny pieces and flush them down the toilet.

The Monkey King is crafty, my mother said. Because he is a god, he knows everything, but he never tells it unless he has to.

Almost every day, postcards arrive: a Chinese cabbage made of jade sitting on an ivory stand in a glass case, a stone lioness with curly hair and a cub under one paw, red and black buildings with winglike roofs stacked on top of one another. On the back are messages from our mother in her angular printing: "Today we go to museum" or "Last night we have dinner with my cousins, there were nine courses and cherry soup for dessert."

"Relatives," Nai-nai sighs. "So many Chinese relatives."

Late one evening the phone rings and in the kitchen I can hear Nai-nai speaking loudly in Shanghainese, her telephone voice. She shouts for us to come. "Your ma-ma and ba-ba, hurry, hurry."

It's the next morning there, Ma tells me. Her voice sounds so close by, I suspect a trick, until my mother says it is 105 degrees outside and they have to sleep underneath mosquito netting. Then I can imagine so much blistering sun, a humid hotel room with a fan on the ceiling, the pedicabs Nai-nai has described clattering by the window.

Marty gets on and tells about the beach, about the school of dead flounder we found washed up the last time we went. She talks fast, kicking the rungs of the chair, biting her knuckles the way she does when she's excited.

She hands the phone back to me.

"Hello, Sally, it's your daddy."

"Hi, Daddy." My voice sounds creaky. I try to swallow, and I can't.

"You reading a lot of books?"

"Yes," I say. I don't tell him it's mostly Nancy Drew.

"When we get back, you tell me about them, all right?"

"Okay."

My mother again. "Sally, remember you're the elder. Be sure you help your Nai-nai. I count on you."

"Okay, Ma."

Our grandmother makes us sit in the living room after dinner instead of going out to play. I look at *National Geographic*, but even leopards can't hold my interest. I imagine announcing to my parents: "I'm not going back. I'm going to stay here with Nai-nai. I can go to school in San Diego."

The doorbell rings and there is Ma in a pastel-striped dress, pale, but not so pale as Nai-nai. Her hair is longer and straighter than I remember.

My sister is tearing over for a hug.

"You girls good? You're not too much of a bother to your Nai-nai?"

"Say hello to your ma-ma," Nai-nai whispers to me. I can't move, although I feel my eyes filling with baby tears. I watch my sister, who is now pulling at my mother's skirt and clamoring, "What did you bring back for us?" Now here is Daddy in his summer clothes—white short-sleeved shirt, khaki trousers— ducking his head in the doorway of the tiny house. It feels like when I had pneumonia: opening my eyes midmorning and the room was much too bright.

I can't look at him. But he is not paying attention to me. "Not good manners," he scolds Marty, who has climbed on top of an ottoman and is pulling up the leg of her shorts to show Ma a scab.

My mother makes a big fuss over Nai-nai, making her sit

down, bringing her a new cup of tea, although the one she has is still hot. Our grandmother gets her present first, a small package all wrapped up in white tissue paper. It contains what looks like several enormous pieces of gingerroot.

"Life-giving force," Daddy says grandly.

Nai-nai nods in a dignified way.

"You make tea with this, you feel strong," my mother explains to us.

My sister and I each receive a fine gold chain with a pendant made of a stone covered in gold filigree to resemble an animal: Marty's is an amber butterfly, mine a jade turtle. In addition, Marty is given a long slender box with Chinese characters on it which turns out to contain a wooden flute. She immediately starts puffing, but only a tortured rasp emerges. Ma demonstrates how to hold it, spreading my sister's small fingers over the holes, showing her how to make her lips into a kiss and direct a tight stream of air across the mouthpiece. She still can't get the hang of it.

The flute should have gone to me. I know I could play it.

My other present is a carved wooden horse just about the size of my hand, dark and smooth and long-legged with bulging eyes and bared teeth. Holding it up to the light, I see how the artist has let the grain of the wood suggest the curved muscles of the horse's shoulders and flanks.

"Your daddy pick this out," my mother says. "Extra special, for your birthday."

"Antique," my father adds, the first word he's spoken directly to me.

I don't dare look up, even though what I want to do is give it back, tell them that I hate it. But that would make me seem spoiled, and Nai-nai is sitting across the room beaming.

I don't thank Daddy though. And in the commotion of Marty trying to learn to play the flute, no one seems to notice.

Later, in bed, when everyone else is asleep, after I have tucked Piggy in beside me, I reach under my pillow and take out the hairpin Nai-nai gave me. Even as a child, I know it's a much finer jade than my turtle. The weight of it sits cold in the palm of my hand, and lying there in the dark, I think that it's as cold as the ocean in Monterey where I swam with the seals. I can see their gray-blue bodies gleaming in the water above, through the fractured sunlight on the waves. Once in a while they brush up against me, sleek dark flesh, a caress as gentle and unthinking as a breath. I am not afraid. Under here, I can hold my breath forever, and the cold does not bother me.

11

It's fall. I've just started third grade. After school it's still light enough to play outside until dinner. When Daddy asks us if we've done our homework we lie and say we don't have any yet.

There's always someone to play with. Coram Drive is in a Catholic parish, St. Cecilia's, and almost every house on the block has children. The Cuddys, two houses down from us, already have five, one right after the other, and their mother is always pregnant. In the summer the older ones sleep on the screened porch. All the names on the mailboxes are Irish and Italian till you get to the dead end, and there are the Wangs and the Katzes. Mr. Katz owns a bakery in Cheshire, a couple of towns over, and every dawn we hear his truck chugging out of the driveway. My father says that Jews are almost as smart as Chinese.

The Katz kids are our best friends in the neighborhood, although for a while my parents wouldn't let us play with them because of what happened last year.

David Katz is two years older than me, the bully of the block. He's big for his age, chunky, walks with a swagger. One Fourth of July he blew off the tip of his thumb with an M-80 and had to be rushed to the emergency room in his father's truck. The thumb grew back like a golf club, which just made him scarier, and the way he wears his hair, in a marine-style crewcut, doesn't help. My mother is the only parent on Coram Drive who is not afraid of him.

"David, how you ever going to find a wife, you have such bad manners? I know you have a heart of gold, but nobody else knows. Have another plum candy, it's good for blood circulating."

"Yes, Mrs. Wang," David mumbles to my mother. I think in a weird way he likes her.

Darcy Katz is my age, lank-haired and freckled and as skinny as a rail. She does everything Marty and I tell her to, including peeing into a hole we dig under the swing set in our backyard. But no matter what she does, the skirts of her smocked flowered dresses stay perfect starched bells over her knobby knees. Although Darcy and I are in the same grade, I am in the A class and she is in C. Despite what my father says, Darcy is not very smart. She likes me because I draw pictures for her—horses, kittens, pretty white-girl faces with long lashes and pouty lips—and doesn't even mind when I make a caricature of her father with a big white chef's hat on. She has a giggle that starts shyly and then turns into an uncontrollable stream, like her peeing.

Our backyard has the swings, but the Katzes have a stagnant little pond that Darcy claims holds goldfish, although we've never seen any. Sometimes when the four of us are hanging out back there, the bad boys come up to the wire fence that separates the Katzes' yard from the back lots, where they live. They holler at us, make machine-gun noises.

David screams: "Your mother eats shit!"

What I'm thinking is that it's no sweat to be Jewish. Although they attend Hebrew school, unable to wheedle their parents out of it like Marty and I did with Chinese school, David and Darcy with their fair skin and freckles blend in with the other kids. Plus their parents speak perfect English.

We climb over the fence and swipe things from the bad boys' backyards: a garden hose, crabapples, a new baseball glove left lying in the grass. Once we fill an old rice sack with rocks and throw them against someone's double basement doors until a window flies open.

The bad boys get back at us by ripping a hole in the Katzes' fence and pouring detergent into the goldfish pond. They run through our backyard, deliberately trampling the violet bed and Ma's tomato plants. Daddy leans out the back door screeching: "I call your parents! I know who you are!"

"You old chink!" they yell, and run away, laughing their heads off. They know he's chicken, that he'll never carry out his threat.

On the refrigerator my father tapes up a page from a magazine that shows a sad-looking black boy leaning up against a brick wall. Underneath it says: "He hasn't got a Chinaman's chance."

Daddy tells Marty and me: "That's what Americans think of us. "

"We're American," I say.

"You are American citizen. In your heart you are a Chinese."

I'm not listening. I've learned not to listen to my father. What I secretly know is that I am the most American kid I have ever met. In second grade when Mrs. Augustine has the whole class write down the Pledge of Allegiance from memory I'm the only one who gets every word correct. I pretend I am Natalie Wood in *West Side Story*. She is really American, my mother says, only playing the part of a foreigner.

But this doesn't solve the problem of eyes. The bad boys, sometimes kids we don't know at school, jump out at us, pulling the corners of their own eyes back toward their temples. "Ching chong Chinaman."

Everyone loves Chinese hair. Mrs. Augustine tells my mother that she looks out over the second grade and sees the sun shining off my sister's pixie. "Just like an angel, that one."

Eyes are a different story. Of course the best type to have are round and as large as possible. Even Ma thinks so. By her bed she keeps stacks of Chinese magazines with movie stars, and they all have great big almond eyes, outlined in black, with fluttery lashes. Some Chinese people, like our Nai-nai, have naturally Western-looking eyes, with double eyelids, but most have a single lid, which makes the eye look flat and slanty. Daddy has a single lid, though his eyes are big. Even Ma, who was a beauty in Shanghai, has single lids. She tells us that in Japan they have an operation where they take skin off your thigh to give you double eyelids.

"You have single," she announces to me. Marty she studies with more attention. "Too early to tell," she concludes. "You could be double when you grow up."

Ma cuts our eyelashes to make them grow fuller. The stubble hurts every time we blink, and Marty gets an infection. Finally the school nurse writes a note to our mother telling her that it's dangerous, so she stops.

"Foolish," Daddy says to Ma. "Why you want them to look cheap?" He points at me. "She has natural beauty, like all unmarried Chinese girl."

The way he says it makes me feel ugly.

At breakfast when Ma makes my braids she complains about the knots. "What's the matter with you, Sal-lee? Such a big mess! You look at that Darcy, always so neat."

I don't say anything.

Daddy is reading a newspaper, an American one, the *New Haven Register.*

"You don't eat," Ma says to me. Usually it's my sister who's the finicky one; I have a big appetite, a Chinese appetite.

When we come home from school Ma is out in the backyard raking. "Help your mother," Daddy says, so my sister and I change into our play clothes and go join her. The metal prongs of the rake scrape the grass, turning up curled bewildered worms. My sister says they make her want to throw up.

By the stone fireplace we make two huge mounds of leaves: spiky brittle brown oak, red maple with delicate points, yellow almond-shaped dogwood. I'm almost sorry we have to burn them. Our mother feeds armfuls to the fire while my sister and I watch.

Ma goes in to start dinner. It's almost dusk, and Marty and I light the ends of twigs and twirl them to make orange figure eights. My sister's hair flies up behind the collar of her gold corduroy jacket as she screams: "Look at mine, look at mine!" Waving our sticks, we jump onto the picnic table bench and then onto the table itself, leaping down so it gives us shocks in our ankles, then hurtle over the springy grass to the swing set. It's then that I spot it, the biggest worm I've ever seen, curled up under one of the swings. I stoop down and nudge it onto my twig with my finger. It doesn't really want to move, but I angle the stick to force it.

"What's that?" Marty demands, nosy as usual.

I hold up the stick and my sister shrieks and takes off, streaking along the fence that separates the Katzes' backyard from ours. I chase her, twig held up like the Statue of Liberty's torch. "Baby! Baby! It's just a worm!" She's close enough so I can hear her panting, or sobbing, I can't tell which.

"Get that away from me!"

On the patch of ground that is our vegetable garden in the summer, my sister trips on a weed and falls sprawling. I pretend not to see and keep running, past her, back toward the piles of leaves. By the dying fire, I see that the worm is gone, and I toss the twig away. I fling myself onto one of the piles spread-eagled and lie there, breathing hard, inhaling the sweet dusky smell.

Across the yard, I can hear Marty wailing, and then the back door slams.

"Sally, what happen?"

Instead of answering my mother, I turn over onto my stomach and bury my face in the leaves. They are cold and itchy.

"Sally, STAND UP. It's dirty there. Answer me. Did you push your sister?"

I have no words for her. I wait, counting One Mississippi Two Mississippi, until suddenly my head is jerked backward as my mother pulls me up by the braids. "You're acting *crazy*," she hisses.

Sitting up, I watch her march across the yard to where Marty is. My sister is crying even louder than before. Ma stoops over her, asking questions. Then she picks my sister up, grabbing her under the arms and hoisting her over her shoulder like she does a bag of rice. "Sally, open the back door!"

I can't move. Somehow my mother manages to get the door open herself.

I lie back into my leaf bed. The sky is now almost completely black, but the tops of the trees are blacker, like fingers reaching up. Although the fire is so low I can no longer see it, I can still smell the smoke. It feels peaceful to lie here like this. It feels safe. There are things going on in the house: Ma's loud voice, Daddy grumbling from his chair in the living room, my sister whining. They have nothing to do with me. I feel sleepy.

I hear the roar of the bakery truck pulling into the driveway next door, into the garage, the truck door slam. Mr. Katz is home from work. "Oh, look at the Wangs' yard, so nice and neat," I hear Mrs. Katz say as she opens the back door for her husband. Neither of them see me in the pile of leaves.

I think of different animals I can be: a chipmunk, a squirrel, even a bear.

But all I feel like is myself, a big fat human being.

In our house the kitchen light goes on. Ma's face is at the window, peering out. Then it disappears. The back door opens. I wait, listening to the padding footsteps across the swept grass.

"I think your sister has sprained ankle," she says. "I called Dr. Di Leo and he's coming over."

Nothing about it being my fault, although I can't imagine Marty not telling on me.

"Sally, get up. Come in and eat your supper."

I sit up and rub at my face, which is wet. My mother doesn't seem to notice. She simply stands and waits for me to get to my feet and follow her back to the house.

My sister is careless, a tomboy, her bed has lumps after she makes it. I always take care to smooth mine out, tugging the corners so that the white chenille spread lies perfectly flat, the fringe hanging down evenly all around. My mother doesn't notice. In fact, although Saturday is the day for changing the sheets, sometimes when I come back from school I see that she has changed my bed on a weekday. I know because Piggy is sitting smack in the middle of my pillow like a throne. I like to leave him lying down with his head propped up.

After school I lie on my perfect bed and listen to David and Darcy calling from outside: "Oh, Sal-lee! Oh, Mar-tee!" I heard Mrs. Katz say I must be going through growing pains, that is why I am always so tired.

My sister pushes open the door. Her ankle is completely healed now, although sometimes she stands on one foot, like a stork, to remind me. "You want to play kickball?"

"No."

"David said you could be first up."

"I don't want to play."

"What's the matter with you?"

"I don't feel well."

I look past her to the baby rocking chairs, to the window framed by curtains just a shade whiter than our bedspreads. The curtain borders are edged with the same lace as Raggedy Ann's apron.

"You are *bor-ing*," Marty says to me, and slams the door on her way out. I hear that irregular clomp that means she is taking the stairs two, sometimes three at a time.

*   *   *

Mrs. Lister, my third grade teacher, writes my mother a note:

> Although Sarah has always been a reserved child, for the past month or so she has been unusually withdrawn, and I'm a little concerned. When I called on her today, she put her head down on the desk and refused to answer. When I asked her if there was anything wrong at home, she said no. I suggest you make an appointment with your family doctor.

The doctor says that I am healthy as a horse. I sit outside in the waiting room, while he talks to Ma, wishing I really had a disease. I just know she's going to say something about waste, wasted money. But when the door to the office opens her face is normal.

"Come on, Sally. We go home now."

I know for sure she's not mad when we get to the car, because she lets me sit up in front with her. When we're out on Whitney Avenue she begins to hum to herself—some old Chinese tune. In church Marty and I used to be embarrassed because she sang way louder than anyone else, with shakes in her voice. Then one day at coffee hour the organist came up and asked whether she wanted to join the choir. "Your mother has perfect pitch," he told Marty and me. She didn't join, but I noticed she sang more in the kitchen. Hymns, old-time songs like "Someone's Rocking My Dreamboat."

"You know what this is, Sally?" she asks me now.

"No," I say, although it sounds familiar. Sad, like all Chinese songs.

"It's a folk melody called the flower drum. They made it up in China a long time ago. The empress decided that she wanted all the flowers in the summer garden to bloom, even though it was winter. So she called out all the musicians and told them to play play play until the flowers come out."

"So what happened?"

"It worked. In the middle of winter, the peonies and jasmine and plum blossom, they all burst into bloom. Your Nai-nai used to sing this to me when I was a little girl."

We are going past Lake Whitney now, a couple of blocks before we make the turn onto Coram Drive. It's winter, like in Ma's story, but everything is flat gray or white—the lake water, the lone seagull huddled on the wire fencing. The gull makes me think of the ocean.

"I wish we could visit Nai-nai," I say.

"Sealy," my mother says. That was my nickname, from a long time ago, when Daddy still liked me. "You know what I think? I think we need a treat." Instead of making the turn onto our street, we keep going straight and then turn right and head all the way up to Ridge Road.

"Where are we going?" I ask, but my mother just smiles.

It turns out to be Knudsen's Dairy, where we go in the summer, on Sundays, when Daddy is in a good mood. Next to the ice cream shop is a giant milking barn, and our family usually sits on the terrace where we can watch the cows being led up the ramp. Once Mr. Knudsen, bald and pink-faced like Mr. Clean, gave us a tour of the barn. It smelled awful, like throw-up. Today Ma and I sit inside at one of the sticky yellow tables.

"You used to have so many friends," she says, poking at the bulb of orange sherbet in its metal flower. She always gets a different flavor, though it has to be sherbet. Sometimes I think my parents like Knudsen's more than Marty and I do. I have a double scoop of chocolate almond fudge on a sugar cone.

I eat and say nothing. Ma reaches over and flips one of my braids over my shoulder so I won't get ice cream on it.

"Remember, you always play with Darcy?"

"Darcy's boring."

"How about school? Don't you have friends at school?"

"Some."

"Why don't you bring them home?"

"I don't feel like it."

"Next Saturday I take you to see Mei Shie."

"Who?"

"Mei Shie is special lady, can help you."

"A doctor?"

"Better than a doctor. She lives in Chinatown. We go there, just you and me. No Daddy or Marty. You can wear your play clothes."

We take the train in and then a taxi. The place where Mei Shie lives is over a noodle shop. The downstairs foyer has pale green walls like the nurse's room at school and the floor is dirty white tiles. As we climb the stairs skeleton cats brush against our legs.

My Nai-nai is the only other old person I know, and the woman who opens the door doesn't look anything like her, although she has a bun and wears the same shoes, shuffly black slippers. Big red spots bloom on her cheeks. She puts her sagging face right down in front of mine and says something in Chinese that I recognize to mean "Come in, come in," although her voice is loud and crabby.

The main room of the apartment is full of low, black carved furniture, and over at one end there is a beaded curtain, like they have at the Sung Trading Company. It's dim, there don't seem to be any windows, the only light comes from small pink glass flower lamps along one wall. The smell in the air is sweet and rotten. Ma and I sit down on a scratchy black couch and wait for the lady to bring us Chinese tea in tall glasses that have plastic webbing around the bottoms. Ma picks up her glass and takes a sip. It always embarrasses me, the way my parents slurp when they drink tea, but then the lady does the same, making an even louder noise.

Ma and the lady are talking in Chinese, and I hear my mother tell her my Chinese name.

"Ah," the lady says, making a clicking sound with her teeth. She leans over to peer at me, and now I can see the wrinkles on her cheeks like spiderwebs beneath the makeup. Then she reaches across the coffee table and puts both her thumbs hard right on my eyelids and stretches them up. It feels like getting sand in my eyes at the beach. Finally she lets go and says something to my mother. Then she scuffles into the other room, through the clicking curtain.

"Mei Shie says your energy is too yin," Ma tells me. She lowers her voice and adds: "Mei Shie not completely Chinese, you know. Her mother is Greek."

The lady comes tottering back, carrying something carefully in both hands. When she gets close I see that it's a tall glass jar with a screw-on lid, filled with some kind of murky liquid. My mother tries to help her with it, but Mei Shie nudges her away. She sets the jar down on the table in front of me and says something to my mother.

Ma translates: "Sally, you put your hands on the lid."

I do as she says, and it's just an ordinary lid, like on a peanut butter jar, only bigger.

"Close your eyes," Ma whispers.

With my eyes shut, the smell in the room is worse, and my throat swells so I think I might choke. The metal of the jar lid is cool beneath my palms.

It's the smell. I open my eyes to dark and there's a change in the air, a new body in the room. The bed sagging gently as someone sits down.

In the faint light from the window I can see his outline: the long curving torso, the bulbous head set onto a thin neck, just like pictures in the book. There's no tail, but I imagine it curled underneath like a worm.

"Be quiet," says Monkey King.

Look, Marty, I want to say, but of course Monkey King is right, I am not allowed to talk. It would break the spell.

So I lie still, as still as if I were dead. The hand, pushing up my nightgown. I can feel the ridges on his fingertips against my skin. Then my underpants are dragged down to my ankles, a flood of cold, and I think I might wet myself, but I don't.

Nails as rough as crab claws between my thighs. That stick he has, that he can make bigger or smaller when he feels like it. Or is it his tail? I can't tell. Ma said it hurt like this when I was born. Like she wanted to die. Like it would never stop. It cracks my bones apart. The curtains are flapping. Go to the ceiling. But sometimes I don't fly up there fast enough, or else drop down too soon.

With one hand he holds my wrists together over my head, with the other he covers my mouth. He is the Monkey King, he is immortal, he cannot be stopped. Tears wet my hair, but I do not make a sound. He doesn't need to cover my mouth, he doesn't need to whisper that he will kill me if I say anything to Ma. He lets go of my wrists and I feel his fingers in the hair at the back of my neck. This is the sign that it is ending. The first time I thought he was throwing up, but nothing came out. When he is quiet I let my eyes fall closed.

Now the smell is like the Katzes' goldfish pond in the summer. I am being put back together, my underpants pulled up with the elastic making a little smack against my stomach, the skirt of the nightgown arranged over my legs again carefully, in a way I would never do myself. Like Darcy dressing her dolls.

I hate dolls, I never owned one my entire life.

Piggy is back in my arms.

I open my eyes to dark.

He is gone. I can see the fuzzy gray lump in the next bed. I can hear the staccato puffs of her breathing.

"Mar?"

She doesn't answer, although I know she's not asleep.

*   *   *

"Aiih!" The lady's voice is right in my ear and I want to wince away but I can't, I'm being held tight around the shoulders by Ma.

"Look, Sally," she says.

I'm scared to. But when I open my eyes, all I see is the old lady in a chair across from me, holding the jar in her lap.

"This is Greek test—oil and water, the water has floated to the top," Ma says in her storytelling voice. "Mei Shie says that someone has put a curse on you."

Then they are jabbering away in Chinese again, and Mei Shie gives my mother several little plastic bags. On the train ride home Ma closes her eyes and starts to snore. I take one of the plastic bags out of her carryall and examine the rust-colored powder. I know what it is even before I ask, later, at home—it's dried blood. I don't know how I know this. Ma will boil it in water for me to sip from a mug. It will turn my breath and sweat bitter so that the kids at school will say pee-yeww! and no one will want to stand next to me in line.

The first night I take the potion I can still taste it in my mouth after I brush my teeth. In bed I fall asleep instantly, before my sister even, because the last thing I remember is her voice in the dark.

It works. Monkey King never comes to my bed again.

12

Downstairs my parents are fighting in Chinese but the different way they talk makes it sound as if they're speaking different languages. Ma is fast, slippery, slurry. Daddy is choppy and whiny like a baby. Marty and I listen from our bedroom. She is six and I am seven. My sister claims she understands.

"No way," I say.

"He's saying he never had a father, so he doesn't know how to behave."

This is what he says to Ma after he spanks us, which he has been doing a lot lately. We are evil girls. Marty talks back and gets into fights. My trouble is what I don't do, like going up to my room before helping Ma with the dinner dishes. Plus my sister and I are both stupid in school, Bs instead of As, Marty worse than me because she never does her homework.

Ma scolds Daddy. "Bad for character," she says in English. "My father hit me and it didn't make me study more."

No matter how hard our father hits us, though, he can't make us cry. I can tell by his face just how much he hates that I can get to my feet, pull my skirt down, and walk upstairs like nothing happened. Marty used to cry, but I have taught her not to. Now my sister and I show each other our bruises and agree that he is a weakling.

I know what they are fighting about now. My hair. Ma wants to cut it, Daddy says no.

My father's voice gets higher, louder, filling my head no matter how hard I press my palms against my ears. He is cursing in

Chinese, peasant curses. Marty and I call it his murder voice.

Ma's voice stays low and cool, like he could shout all night and she wouldn't care. Still, Daddy will win the argument, like he always does. I will have two long braids until I die.

Our parents teach Chinese to Yale students but not to us, so although we understand a little we can't speak it. For a couple of months we have to take lessons on Saturday mornings in the living room behind the Sung Trading Company. Aunty Lilah—she and Uncle Frank own the store—is our teacher. She holds up cards with magazine pictures pasted on them: chair, table, cat. *Yizhi, zhuozi, mau.*

After our lesson we go out to the store to wait for Ma. We are supposed to be nice to Mimi Sung, who is our age, but I can never think of a thing to say to that round, beaming face behind the cash register.

"Ah, how's it going?"

"Just fine, thank you," she replies in her prissy way. She's a whiz at making change, can practically figure out what Ma is going to give her before she opens her purse. I watch her plump little hands riffle confidently through the stacks of bills, scoop the coins out of the cash drawer without her having to look down.

"Such a *pleasant* girl," Ma says in the car. "So helpful to her parents."

But the Oriental kid we really hate is Xiao Lu, who is the reason we get into trouble and can't play with the Katzes for an entire year.

Xiao Lu's father is a math professor, his mother stays at home and does nothing. "Very old world," Ma says. When he was little that strange mother let his hair grow long and put him in dresses to fool the gods into thinking he was a girl so they wouldn't steal him. He's skinny and yellow-colored because he's rarely allowed to play outdoors.

Marty and I call him Pointy Head and Flat Face.

"He looks like he was run over by a truck."

"How can he even *see* out of those eyes?"

When he really gets on our nerves we call him Girl. "Get the ball, Girl." "Bring us some lemonade, Girl."

At the dinner table Aunty Winnie says something to him in Chinese, like "Go do your homework," and he obeys instantly, ducking his head and clambering down from his chair.

Our parents can't tame us. Once a month we drive into New York City to have dinner in Chinatown, where the narrow, winding streets are jammed with short people and funny smells and whose stores I try not to look into when we pass, for fear of seeing pressed duck like hanged men in the window. "Shanghai much worse," Ma assures us. In the restaurant Daddy speaks in Mandarin, stroking characters on his napkin with his Parker fountain pen when the waiter doesn't understand. But the language on the street is Cantonese, where people sound like they're fighting, even when they're not. In the car on the way home my sister and I imitate it, breaking ourselves up. "*LO LEE LO GOO*," I shout, exaggerating the up and down tones. "*GUM GO JEE WOK NA NA NA*," Marty gasps back.

"They don't study in Chinese class, so what is this?" Ma asks Daddy.

But we never get scolded: my parents are in too good a mood after going to Chinatown. Daddy has a pile of Chinese newspapers to read in his armchair after dinner, and Ma has stocked up on her movie-star magazines.

It's Chinese New Year and we are going to be on TV. The kids—Mimi, Xiao Lu, Marty, and I—plus the crew, are crammed into the tiny living room behind the Sung Trading Company where we have Chinese lessons. Our parents are outside in the shop—I can hear them gabbing to each other in Chinese.

We are going to perform the Dragon Dance. The dragon looks like the one we saw in the Chinese New Year parade in

Chinatown—an enormous wooden head painted mostly green and red and bulging golden eyes without pupils. It has a mane like a lion's, although it doesn't look like a lion because the head is square. The body is made of cloth, long, with multicolored scales. One kid will get to put on the head and wag it around ferociously; two more will prance behind, draped in the body. One will be the teaser, who stands in front of the dragon and beckons it to chase them.

"I want to be the teaser," Marty announces. Because we are going to be on TV my sister is wearing her red pullover sweater and red-and-blue-plaid pedal pushers.

The man in charge frowns at her.

The other TV person, a woman, says to the man, "She really is a beautiful child."

"Too short," he says. "We need her for the tail."

Mimi's just smiling in her silly way, like the big-headed wooden dolls they have in the window of the store, and of course Xiao Lu doesn't say a word. I know his mother is standing right outside; from time to time I hear the curtain of wooden beads clicking as Aunty Winnie peeks in.

The way it ends up is this: I am the teaser, Xiao Lu the head, Mimi the front of the body, my sister the back.

The TV man yells, "Ready!" and Uncle Frank, Mimi's father, comes in with his giant tape recorder. He switches it on: *bong! bong! bong!* Chinese cymbals and some other kind of high-pitched boingy instruments. It sounds as bad as the Cantonese ladies arguing in Chinatown.

"Okay, tease the dragon, honey," the woman tells me, and I hear the camera start to whir.

I begin to walk backward, staring into the glaring golden eyes, reminding myself that it's only old Flat Face behind them. I insert my thumbs into my ears and wiggle my fingers.

"More," says the man.

I stick out my tongue. I know I look ugly.

"That's good," says the man, "but you, the head, let's see some more action. Jump up and down. All of you."

The gaudy head inclines toward me slightly, and the floor quivers from the thumping of three pairs of sneakered feet.

At six o'clock that night our family crowds around the television set in the living room. They do all the other news first—national, local, until it's nearly six-thirty. Finally: "And tonight marks a special celebration for some members of our community. This is the beginning of the year of the horse according to the Chinese calendar." And there we all are, in black and white. All you can see of me is my back, braids flopping up and down. The camera pans onto the dragon's head, which is wagging ponderously with Xiao Lu's corduroys baggy beneath, and then down the length of the body. It lingers a moment on the tail, which gives a mischievous little wiggle. Through the Chinese music, we can hear people laughing. And that's it, it's the end of the newscast.

"I was *great*," says Marty. "Ma, wasn't I great?"

"Very realistic. Just like dragon."

Daddy doesn't say anything at all, although I can tell he is pleased we have done something Chinese.

One Saturday afternoon a month Xiao Lu comes over to our house while his mother goes to her mah-jongg club. Our mother doesn't play mah-jongg. "Gambling's waste of time," she says. "Just look at your aunt and uncle."

"What about them?" I ask.

"They don't even own their own house. Track, sports, you name it. Your uncle has no control."

Daddy quizzes Xiao Lu in Chinese. Xiao Lu answers with his head hanging.

"Hah," our father says, pleased. He says to us: "You treat him like an elder brother. With respect."

This one afternoon, the afternoon we get into trouble, the three of us are out in the backyard performing a play. It's our own version of Captain Hook, where I'm the evil captain and Marty the princess, and Xiao Lu the good captain who's supposed to come and save her. Xiao Lu is just standing there looking miserable, not saying his lines.

"Whatcha doin'?"

I look up to see David Katz lounging up against the outside of our fence. I'm surprised to see him, he usually ignores us when Xiao Lu is around. He says: "Hey, I got some cherry bombs. Let's set them off on Witch Dugan's front porch. It'll scare her something wicked."

"Why don't you just do it yourself?" I ask.

"Stupid. There has to be a lookout."

My sister, lashed with clothesline to the dogwood tree, rolls her eyes. "You're the one who's stupid. All she's gonna do is call your parents anyway. She'll know it's you."

"It's him, isn't it?" David glares at Xiao Lu. Then he presses his palms together like he's praying and gives a little bow. *"Ah so."* He walks backward down his driveway and around the corner of the garage till he's out of sight, bowing with every step. The fact that it's David doing it makes me queasy in a way it never has before.

Xiao Lu gazes after David, cowering to the ends of his hair, which stands up softly on his long head. Then he puts his plastic silver sword down on the picnic table and hunches his shoulders. I feel like strangling him.

"Now what's the matter?"

"I don't feel like playing anymore."

"You want to watch TV?"

"Okay," he whispers into the collar of his oxford shirt. It's the kind everybody at school makes fun of, with a strip sewn to the back. Fruit loops, the kids say, and pull till it rips.

"Go inside," I tell him. "My mother will give you tea and plum candy."

I untie Marty and we go to find David, who is pitching pebbles into the goldfish pond. "Let's go to Kramer's," he says, a little too casually. I know right away what he means. Kramer's Pharmacy on Whitney Avenue is David's favorite shoplifting target.

The three of us saunter down Coram Drive and make a left onto Whitney Avenue, past St. Cecilia's, which has open doors for Saturday mass. The bad boys are all Catholic. I wonder if making Chinese eyes at someone is a sin, and if they have to confess it to the priest in his screened box.

In the drugstore we wander around, waiting for old man Kramer to get busy with someone's prescription in the back of the store. David is a pro. Once he even stole a steak from the supermarket. He goes first, a Mars bar in his sock, and then watches Marty and me from a nearby aisle. I grab blindly, but my sister's brow wrinkles, choosing. Afterward, I go to loiter in front of the birthday cards until Marty comes up and pinches the skin under my arm. Mr. Kramer is back in his regular place, by the front cash register. As we come up, he asks us what we would like.

"Just these Neccos, please," I say in my politest voice.

"Remember to count your money," Mr. Kramer quavers, as he always does.

My knees are shaking, I hope he can't see. I tell myself that people think that Oriental kids, especially girls, never do anything bad.

"Piece a cake," David says, his mouth full of caramel goo, as we walk home.

I'm still worried. "Do you think he saw us?"

"Nah. Kramer's blind as a bat." Marty offers me half a Nestle's Crunch bar. I eat it, along with some Neccos, although I'm not hungry.

When we get past the L-bend, the Lus' old beige Rambler is pulling away from the curb in front of our house. Daddy is standing on the front porch.

"YOU BOTH COME HERE."

"Oh-oh," David says cheerfully, his mouth still full. "See you later."

In the living room Daddy begins to pace, hands clasped behind his back. I'm trying, unsuccessfully, to think of convincing reasons we would have left Xiao Lu by himself.

"So what you have in your pockets?"

"Candy." I am not a good liar, and worse when surprised into it.

"Let's see!" Daddy's eyes have stretched into menacing slits like the Peking opera masks he gave me for my birthday. I reach into my pocket and put everything on the coffee table: the half-eaten roll of Necco wafers, the three packs of Juicy Fruit I stole.

Our father turns to Marty. "Now you."

My sister gives me a pained look and then jerks her T-shirt out of her jeans and two Hershey's almond bars and one strawberry Bonomo Turkish taffy come flying out to skid over the carpet.

"You pick it up and put on table!"

My sister sighs and as slowly as possible does what she has been told.

Daddy's face has turned purple. He points at me. "How did you get this candy?"

I'm unable to speak.

He looks at Marty. "How did you get?"

My sister articulates each word: "It's none of your beeswax."

Daddy is stumped, I can see that, but he knows one thing: she's being disrespectful. "You don't talk to your elders like that. You never, never talk to your elders like that." He reaches up and strikes my sister across the face with the flat of his hand. Marty topples backward and lands on the floor.

That she falls surprises me; I want to tell her to get up, he's a weakling, he's nothing. But my sister keeps lying there and begins to shriek. Ma comes flying out of the kitchen, sprinkling water drops, and bends down over Marty, who has suddenly quit screaming and is beginning to gag. All the candy she has eaten comes up onto the carpet in a yellowish brown puddle. I think I might vomit too.

"Mau-mau, it's all right." Ma holds my sister's hair away from her face and glares up at my father. "I tell you not to hit!"

Daddy has already turned away, heading toward the stairs, stiff-legged, as if he has no knees.

Later we learn that it was old man Kramer himself who witnessed our crime in the convex security mirror hanging in the corner behind the pharmacy counter. After we left, boldly jangling the chimes, he phoned both our houses.

My sister is put to bed and after dinner I have to go alone with Daddy back to Kramer's. My father is quiet all through the meal, but as soon as the front door closes behind us he begins to talk. Daddy talk.

"Your mother tell you about the park sign in Shanghai?"

I shake my head.

"No Chinese and no dogs. You hear that? No Chinese and no dogs. You know what that means?"

I say nothing, kick at a pile of maple helicopters on the sidewalk.

"DISCRIMINATION!" He thunders out the word as if he has just invented it. "In China, in our own country! Your mother and I try for one month to find apartment in California. Look all over town. No room, everyone says. No Orientals allowed. This is what Americans think of us. This is why you have to be twice as good as anybody else."

We walk the rest of the way in silence. Marty and I have been told we cannot watch TV for a month. I wonder what David's punishment will be. His parents must be running out of things to do to him.

In the pharmacy I hand Mr. Kramer the candy we stole in the Baggie that Ma has insisted on so "it still looks new." I have exact change from our allowances to pay for what we ate, and I stack the coins carefully on the counter.

"I'm sorry," I say to Mr. Kramer. That is an American thing, something I learned from TV. No one in our family ever says they are sorry.

My father makes a speech: "I have no explanation for my daughters' behavior. We are not a wealthy family, but there are no thieves." Mr. Kramer peers at me through his bifocals, and I know that I am never going to set foot in that store again.

When we are outside, Daddy says, "If we were in China, maybe your mother and I would not talk to you for a year."

I look at my father, who although he is much younger, walks with his shoulders hunched over like old man Kramer. I picture sticking a leg out and tripping him so he'd crash face-first onto the sidewalk and break his nose. I know it's possible—I once saw David do it to one of the younger bad boys.

"We're not in China," I say.

"But you are a Chinese daughter."

We are passing the Cuddys by then, and I imagine the kids with their faces pressed to the porch screen, listening to everything we're saying. Good. They just might learn something.

"You are a Chinese daughter," Daddy repeats. His eyes are as dark as snake holes. "You have shamed me and all my ancestors."

"I wish you would have a stroke and die," I say. I expect my father to turn purple again, I almost want him to, but in the dusk his face tightens and grows very white and he stops walking. I stop too.

He is staring straight ahead, at our little green house, as if he can see through the walls, to Ma washing the dinner dishes and humming along to the radio, to my sister upstairs in bed, her hair spiked on the pillow as she jerks her head from side to side in a half sleep. My father finally turns to me.

"I name you Delicate, because you are a girl. Virtue, so you will be good. But in all your life, you never give me one moment of happiness."

*   *   *

The next day my sister's eye looks like a plum. We tell the kids at school she fell off the swings. At recess I see her out playing softball, running around screaming and happy like nothing happened.

At home, though, things are different. When Daddy comes into the kitchen to get his tea Ma stays at the stove with her back turned and he has to find his glass and the tea can and pour the water himself. At dinner my mother still serves my father first, but she doesn't look at him. During the meal I notice her sneaking things into Marty's rice bowl—extra Chinese pickles, a big piece of sweet fish.

Then my mother decides she doesn't want her permanent anymore and gets her hair cut short like Twiggy. I know Daddy hates this because the day she does it he says to me: "Look at your mother. You want to be ugly like that?"

I want to say I do, that it's not fair that Ma can have any hairstyle she wants. She looks good with short hair, although not like my mother. When she and Marty and I go out people start asking if the three of us are sisters.

My father no longer spanks us.

At night it's quiet downstairs except for the TV.

13

The first year we live on Coram Drive, our family goes down to Florida to visit my Aunty Mabel who has just moved there with her new husband. On the drive down we stay in a motel that has a monkey in a cage in the parking lot. When we get to their house Aunty Mabel gives us Coke in glasses with the Flintstones on them. Everyone wears shorts, even Daddy, with his rickety white legs. Uncle Richard has a belly like a bag over his belt and smokes Camel cigarettes. I'd walk a mile, he says. There are grapefruit trees in the backyard and in the morning Uncle Richard goes out to pick some for breakfast. They are bulging and heavy and squirt out when Ma cuts them. She wipes the juice off her cheek like a tear. Ma and Aunty Mabel stand at the kitchen counter, both wearing the same apron, white with an orange flower like the sun in the corner. Uncle Richard points at them with his cigarette and says in a loud voice: "Sisters! Can you tell?"

Marty makes a mistake once, grabbing Aunty Mabel's knees from behind. Aunty Mabel is taller than our mother, with a long face and one front tooth that crosses over the other, and there are little brown spots on her cheeks. But she and Ma have the same hair, and when they go out they both wear red sunglasses that point up at the corners.

When Uncle Richard makes his sisters joke, I know he's talking to Daddy. "Pau-yu, eh?" he shouts. Aunty Mabel gets red and Ma pretends not to notice. Daddy looks straight ahead at nothing. "Ai-yah," he mumbles.

At breakfast Lili the white cat climbs onto my lap and I keep as still as possible. When no one is looking I feed her bacon. Her sharp teeth scrape my fingers. We can't have pets at home.

"She's a stray," Uncle Richard tells us. "But your Aunty Mabel thinks she's family. And you know Chinese—they have to feed family."

"I know," I say.

My uncle winks at me. "Hey, Pau-yu, your elder, she's a clever one, understand grown-up talk."

Daddy doesn't like Florida during the day. After lunch he takes a long nap and we have to be quiet or play outside. But at night, when we're supposed to be asleep, I can hear his voice in the living room and then all the grown-ups laughing, even Ma. I hear him say my Chinese name and I know he's telling about how when we first moved to Connecticut and I heard footsteps in the attic. In the morning Ma made me go up the stairs ahead of her and I wouldn't stop screaming not even when she showed me there were just suitcases and old magazines. My father has told this story to all my parents' Chinese friends: Mr. Lin, the Sungs, the Lus.

"My elder daughter hears ghosts," Daddy says. "She has special power." I can't tell whether he's making fun of me.

Sometimes at night Lili jumps up on the bed and sleeps on my feet but in the morning she is gone. There are twin beds, just like at home. Only here I sleep by the window, and my sister sleeps by the door, because Ma is afraid she'll be sick in the night, like she was in the hotel with the monkey scream-ing. Marty is the real baby. Why doesn't my father tell stories about her?

The curtains at the window are thin like wedding dress material, and there are no shades. In the morning the sun comes in and I know right away I'm not at home. There is a funny smell in the air, dusty and sharp, that stays in your nose. The first day we got here Ma leaned over Marty's bedspread and sniffed it. "Mil-dew," she said, and Marty and I laughed because it sounded like doo-doo.

My parents sleep in the fold-out sofa bed in the living room, and my aunty and uncle are in the room across the hall from us. In the middle of the night Uncle Richard has coughing fits. Over and over, like he's going to die. Aunty Mabel never makes a sound. I picture her lying there in the dark listening, the same as me, until it's over.

We go to the beach. "Just the girls," Aunty Mabel says. Daddy wants to sit at home on the patio and read and Uncle Richard doesn't come with us because he has to work. Aunty Mabel has a dark blue bathing suit made of thick material like a winter coat. Ma's is green with flowers. They are wearing their matching sunglasses. I watch Marty walk over the sand to where the waves are and just stand there.

"Sally, you remember California?" my aunt asks me.

"No, no, too long ago," Ma says.

Aunty Mabel says something in Chinese.

My mother translates: "Your aunt says you girls both look very healthy. Must be that American food."

Marty is stooping down now, looking at something around her ankles. She puts her hand into the water, then snatches it back.

Back at the blanket she tells us, "I saw a crab." She has her fingers in her mouth.

"Baby," I say.

"He bit me." Marty's face crinkles up and she starts to cry.

I collect lots of shells, tiny oval white ones with pink insides, like ears. Ma gives me a Kleenex so I can wrap them up and put them in the pocket of my shorts.

When it's time for lunch we pack up the beach things and drive to the mall for hamburgers deluxe—with lettuce and tomato. Ma lets us have orange soda but she calls it orange juice so the waitress gets confused. After lunch we get ice cream cones. Marty picks pistachio because she likes the color, but it tastes so awful she spits it out in the parking lot. Ma lets her have the rest of hers, raspberry sherbet. I have chocolate, as I always do, licking it slowly into a point like a Hershey's kiss.

I sit at the kitchen table gluing my shells to a piece of shirt cardboard. When I am done I want to draw on it, so I go looking for crayons or a pen. In the living room Aunty Mabel is sitting on the sofa with the shades pulled down, a washcloth over her face. At first I think she's asleep, but all of a sudden she says in a creaky voice: "Who's there?"

"Sally."

"Oh." She lifts up the towel and looks at me. "You having a good time?"

"Yes, Aunty Mabel."

"You so much like your father," she says in a soft voice, and then lays the towel over her face again.

My sister is sitting on the front steps, scratching the back of her legs. She can't find Lili, she says.

Uncle Richard saw Lili when he was driving home from work. That's all he says, but Marty and I know she was run over, like the animals on the side of the highway when we drove down. "Too bad," says Ma. Aunty Mabel just looks tired, like her headache came back.

Daddy wants to know why I'm not eating anything. When Ma says it's because of Lili he laughs. "She so upset about an animal?"

"This cat was like family," Uncle Richard reminds him.

"I hope she's half as sad when I die," says Daddy.

Everyone laughs except me. I am picturing Lili at the edge of the road, waiting to cross, but the cars won't stop coming, so she finally runs out anyway. It's the only way she knows to get home.

*   *   *

In the morning I go out to the patio to give my father the shell picture.

"What's this? For me? So beautiful! Thank you, Sealy."

I don't say anything.

"What's the matter? You miss home?"

I shake my head. He opens his arms so I can climb onto his lap like I used to do in California. "*Ai-yah!*" he says like I'm too heavy for him and it's true that I'm the biggest girl in kindergarten. He holds me stiff, too tight, and I want to get back down again.

The sliding door opens and there is my sister. "I got bit by a crab," she announces.

"*Ai-yah,*" my father says again. He lets me go. "You girls be good now. Go eat your breakfast."

The next day, when we are getting ready to go, I see the shell picture out on the patio. It's caught under a chair leg, already ruined by rain.

Back in Connecticut all I can think about is Florida. The ocean, the little palm tree in the backyard, every meal we ate at the yellow kitchen table. The way the air smelled, heavy and sweet. Uncle Richard saying to Daddy, "Clever, she's clever, eh?" about me. Daddy nodding.

I think about it at night while Marty and I wait for Ma to come in and read us to sleep. We lie there stretching our legs down as far as we can.

"I will NEVER fill up this bed," I say, and my sister laughs, kicking up the covers. I arrange all my stuffed animals with my big golden giraffe, Charlie, at my feet to protect me, and Piggy by the pillow.

Ma is reading to us from a book of Chinese folktales. It's in Chinese, so she translates as she goes, holding up the book so we can see the pictures before she turns the page. We don't mind her slowness, it just adds to the suspense. She sits in one of the baby rocking chairs Nai-nai gave us when we were born.

One of the stories is called Monkey King. The Monkey King is a god and he doesn't look like a monkey at all. His head is painted blue and red and yellow and he has the body of a man and a long curly tail. He has a pole that he can make small to carry, big to hit people with. Even though he has eternal life, he's not happy, and is always making trouble in heaven. When he's assigned to guard the Queen Mother's magic peach garden, he ends up gobbling up all the peaches himself.

"Such a greedy, greedy monkey," Ma says, looking at us like we're greedy too.

Marty looks scared. I know she's remembering the hotel monkey.

"He's just make-believe," I say.

"I saw him once," Ma says. "When I was a little girl, my family went on a cruise down the Yangtze River. My father say, 'Around this bend you look up at the cliff and see the Monkey King.' Sure enough, we see him standing on the rock looking out with mischievous face."

"Did he talk to you?" Marty asks.

Ma shakes her head. "Of course not. I tell you, he's not interested in humans, in a small boat like that. He just watches us."

After we're finished with the book of folktales Ma tells us stories we remember from Monterey.

"Tell us about Nai-nai falling off the stage in Vienna."

"Tell us how the servants used to put your toothpaste on the toothbrush for you."

Ma sets her lips together before she speaks, and the words come out like a dream from her head:

"When I was a little girl, our whole family love steamed chestnuts, you know, like we have in the stuffing at Thanksgiving . . ."

On those nights she sits later, sometimes turning the lights out and continuing into the dark. Beyond the sound of her sleepy words, piling like snow, I can hear the faint TV from downstairs.

                    *   *   *

For Christmas we get Great Illustrated Classics: *Little Women*
and *Tom Sawyer,* which my mother had when she was a little
girl in China. "You read by yourselves now," Daddy says.
These books are way too hard for Marty. At bedtime I drag out
The Cat in the Hat and *Curious George Rides a Bike* and pretend I am Ma, reading out loud to my sister.

Where Daddy can see me, though, I read the grown-up
books. "Good, good," he says. "This is the way you get into
Yale."

"Yale only has boys," I say.

"Well, you be the first girl."

One day when we get home from school someone has
removed all the stuffed animals except for Piggy on Marty's
pillow and Raggedy Ann on mine. The first thing I do is switch
them and then I go running down to the kitchen, where Ma is
cooking dinner. She takes us up to the attic and shows us
where the animals are, piled in an old plastic laundry basket
in the corner. I pick up Charlie the giraffe and hug him.

"Your daddy says you are grown up now, you don't need
anymore. You save for your children. I don't throw away."

"Can we get a cat?" my sister asks.

"Mau-mau, you are my little cat," Ma says, stroking Marty's
hair.

That night I don't read. In the dark I tell Marty I'm going to
run away to Florida.

14

And finally this: Disneyland. It was the last summer we lived in California, my parents had accepted teaching posts at Yale, and Nai-nai had already returned to San Diego.

I've never seen so many people in all my life, people in shorts and T-shirts, with sunglasses on. Mothers with fat arms pushing strollers. Fathers carrying kids on shoulders, like a parade. It looks like a town, with streets and signs but there aren't any cars, people are stepping off the curb, walking right in the middle of the street. Daddy has a map like all the other fathers. He has on a white shirt with black and red swirls and black pants and a maroon baseball hat—what he wears when he takes me to the beach on Sunday afternoons when Ma is cleaning the house and Marty's having her nap.

My sister wants to go on the teacups, but when we get there the line is way too long.

"Come back later," Daddy says.

We keep walking until we get to a little house with a green-and-white-striped awning. Ma buys four big glasses of orangeade. While I'm drinking, a bee floats into my cup and buzzes there right in front of my face, trapped.

"Sealy, don't move," Daddy's voice says, quiet. I close my eyes. I feel the cup being pulled away gently, slowly.

He shows me the bee floating dead and then takes the cup to the trash can. Then he walks off, in the other direction.

"Sally almost got stung!" Marty says, like she's disappointed I didn't.

I ask Ma where Daddy went.

My mother frowns. "He'll be back."

There are cartoon characters everywhere: Pluto, Goofy, and Marty's favorite, Donald Duck. "Dono," she calls him. I can tell Donald Duck likes my sister, because he comes over so Ma can take a picture of them together. He has real feathers, a soft little white tail that sticks up. But I am holding out for Mickey and Minnie, especially Minnie. At home I have a Mickey Mouse Club T-shirt and ears, and a pen with Minnie Mouse on it that shows her winking if you move it from side to side. I love Minnie's white gloves, her polka-dot princess dress, her big red high heels, and most of all that enormous smile that takes up half her face. Along with flowers and snails and houses, that's what I draw the most, Minnie Mouse, on the backs of the old flash cards my parents bring home from work. Sometimes I draw her dressed in my own clothes: shorts and T-shirts, my favorite aqua overalls, PJs.

Ma is sitting on a bench, humming "It's a Small World After All." That's a ride we've already been on, where you get in a boat and go through a dark tunnel and miniature people from different countries pop out at you. Ma and Daddy laughed really hard when they found out we had to go on a boat. When Marty asked what was so funny Ma said: "Your father is not a good sailor."

"Watch your sister," Ma says to me. Marty is standing off to the other side of the bench watching this little lake that has a stone bridge over it. It must be a famous bridge—people keep stopping to get their pictures taken on it.

"Dono," she says.

"No, silly, he isn't there."

The next time I look my sister has disappeared. I glance back at Ma, but she has her red pointy sunglasses on and isn't looking in my direction. The bridge isn't very far, only about ten people away, so I edge my way over and sure enough, there's Marty, crouched by the railing, staring into the water.

"He's not THERE!" I yell at her, and when she sees me she gets up and runs farther away, over the bridge and onto the other side of the lake. Luckily she is wearing red—a red T-shirt with white snowflakes and red shorts and sneaks—so I can follow her easily through the crowd.

"Dummy," I say when I catch up with her. I take her hand and look back over the bridge to the bench where Ma is sitting, but I can't see the bench. Marty looks too. I tell her: "We better go back."

"Where's Ma?" my sister whines.

"She's there."

But when we cross the bridge the bench where Ma was sitting is taken up by another family, a big Negro woman with a newborn baby and two boys who just stare at us.

There is a low concrete wall behind the bench, and I take Marty over and lean her up against it. "Don't move," I tell her before climbing up. My sister's face is scrunched up but she obeys. I know what to look for—Ma's puffy black hairdo, Daddy's maroon baseball cap. But all the colors in the crowd—except for the family sitting on the bench below—are pale—pinks and light blues and yellows.

Marty starts to cry. "We'll *find* them," I tell her. It doesn't occur to me that they'll find us. People are noticing us, alone together, and this makes me nervous. There's big old Goofy in the distance, and I consider asking him what to do, but Ma says none of the cartoon characters can talk. Anyhow he's kind of scary-looking. Who ever heard of a purple dog? He doesn't even look like a dog.

My sister has stopped sobbing, although tears are still sliding down her face. "Don't worry, Mar-Mar," I say, hugging her. Though we are only about a year apart I am so much taller, and sometimes we pretend that she is my baby. She's small enough to still fit in the buggy and I used to wheel her around the backyard until Ma told me to stop. My sister sticks her hand into mine again, and we continue walking, away from the bridge, which seems the right thing to do.

Suddenly we're at the teacups again—I recognize the little pink house where you get your tickets. There's still a line of people in front, but I just keep walking and no one stops us. At the window there's a lady with curly blond hair and a diagonal band across her body, like Girl Scouts. She leans down.

"What? I can't hear you, little girl."

I repeat: "We're looking for our parents."

This causes a commotion. The lady in the booth speaks to someone behind her and then tells us to stay put. Now the people in the front of the line are paying attention to us. One of the mothers with fat arms is saying she's surprised this doesn't happen more often here, kids getting lost. A man in a flowered shirt squats down in front of Marty to offer her a Tootsie Pop. She shakes her head, which I am glad of. The man tells his wife: "Looks just like one of them Japanese dolls, doncha think?"

The lady in the booth comes out and says we should come inside to wait. She puts her fingers, with their long purple nails, on our shoulders, to pull us in.

The booth is dark, with lots of shelves and a table with a big roll of green tickets and some paper napkins and empty paper cups. The other person in the booth, a man with a brown face and a black mustache, points to a couple of stools in the corner and says, "Take a load off!" As we sit down, Marty is still clutching my hand. I shake my own hand until she lets go.

"Don't be a baby," I whisper.

"Okay," says the lady. "Tell me your last name again."

"Wang," I say.

She wrinkles her forehead. "Won? Your name is Won?"

"WANG. Sarah and Martha Wang."

"Okay, Denny, you hear that?"

"Yeah. Don't worry, hons, we'll find who you belong to." The man adjusts his microphone, which I notice for the first time, and leans into it. "ATTENTION ALL PARENTS. WE HAVE TWO LITTLE LOST ORIENTAL GIRLS AT THE TEACUP RIDE. I REPEAT, TWO LITTLE LOST ORIENTAL GIRLS AT THE TEACUP RIDE."

He doesn't say our names. How are Ma and Daddy going to know, unless they hear our names? I look over at my sister. Although she has finally stopped crying, I can tell from the expression on her face that something bad is about to happen.

"That should do it," the man says.

Marty is peeing in her pants, right on the stool, and it's spilling onto the floor.

It's my fault. I forgot to ask her if she needed to go.

The man and the lady both turn around. The man says a bad word.

"You poor little thing," the lady says to Marty. "Don't worry, your mama and papa will come to get you soon." She scrunches up some napkins and walks over to my sister. Marty leans away from her, almost falling off the stool.

"I'm not going to hurt you," the lady says. She looks at the man, who shrugs his shoulders. Then she just tosses the napkins on the floor around my sister's stool, to soak up the pee.

The man leans into the microphone again. "ATTENTION PARENTS. TWO LITTLE LOST ORIENTAL GIRLS AT THE TEACUP RIDE."

The lady goes over to stand at the window and the man ignores us. I think he's just hoping neither of us is going to do anything disgusting again.

Then I hear the lady say: "Hallelujah, I think it's them."

Our parents look very hot. I am surprised to see them. Right away Ma reaches for Marty, who's crying her head off again. "She wet herself?" Ma asks me, like anyone couldn't tell.

"Sealy," Daddy says. He has a funny expression on his face.

"Okay, okay," says Ma. She says to the lady and man: "Thank you for taking care of them."

"No big deal, I got nieces and nephews," says the lady.

The man makes a grunting noise.

Ma points at me. "I told you watch your sister. Can't you hear? Something wrong with your brain, Sal-lee?"

She takes Marty to the ladies' room to wash her off, and Daddy and I sit down to wait for them on the concrete wall. I'm so thirsty I think I am going to die. I remember I didn't get to finish my orangeade.

Daddy touches the top of my hair and says: "Ouch! What a hothead!" He takes off his baseball cap and puts it on my head. It's sweaty and smelly and way too big but immediately I feel better.

And then I see her.

"Daddy!"

"*Ai-yah*, what's this?"

"Minnie Mouse. Look, Daddy, right there."

"Mickey Mouse?"

"No, *Minnie* Mouse. See, in the red dress."

"She's the one you like, huh, Sealy?"

"Yes."

He looks at me and then before I know what's happening my father has lifted me up and I'm sitting on his shoulders, just like the other kids. But Daddy is so tall that together we're taller than anybody else. We march through the crowd to Minnie and then he sets me down, exactly in front of her, so she can't help noticing me. I can't believe it. I stare at her white gloves—so clean, like Nai-nai's—her white stockings in their slender lady legs, and then finally at her big smiling white and black head with its red and white polka-dot bow that matches her dress.

"You're more beautiful than Miss America," I say.

The head tilts toward me like she's going to say something, but then I remember that of course the cartoon characters don't talk. Instead, she bends down—she's wearing a petti-coat, I can hear it rustle—takes my hand in her gloved one and gently shakes it, as if I were already grown up and we were meeting at a party.

Behind me Daddy makes a sound. It's only many years later that I recognize it—my father is crying.

Part
Three

15

In the end Ma never carried out her threat and I went to St. Petersburg as planned, two days after my discharge from Willowridge.

During those two days I wandered around the house on Woodside Avenue, trying to convince myself I was normal now, fit to be a citizen of the outside world, although normal was the last thing I felt. Jury-rigged was more like it. The pieces reassembled, and, as Sylvia P. would say, stuck together with glue. A month and a half of medication and group therapy had made me more talkative, but it was an uncensored kind of talkative, the kind that wouldn't wash at a cocktail party, for instance. Still everyone—Valerie, my group, the MHs—had agreed that I was ready. And it was true that there were things I could do again, like sit down and read the *New Haven Register* from front to back, or call Fran in Cambridge—I thought she sounded a little off, but maybe it was because she was finally sick of my angst.

The house was too damn quiet. My sister was gone again—this time to Vermont, where an old boyfriend of hers had dropped out of Wall Street to become a carpenter. I avoided my bedroom with all its heavy furniture that was familiar but wrongly placed, like objects in a nightmare. The pink runner on the floor by the bed, which used to lie in the front hall of the house on Coram Drive, was stained forever by my vomit. Our old baroque telephone stand, with its one latticed shelf, was my bed table, mismatched to the simple blond lines of the twin bed that had lost its twin. Most disturbing of all was the wallpaper—enormous abstract brown and beige daisies that had looked to me like deformed children, all those long days I'd lain staring at it. Almost as bad as the apple blossoms on Coram Drive.

I did check the top drawer of the bureau, and the empty vials—Valium and Elavil—were still there. I'd taken thirty-six pills in all, for the thirty-six hours my mother had been in labor with me. Kind of a last private joke. And I noticed that some-one—Ma, of course—had removed the envelope containing my will, which I'd anchored under the prancing wooden horse.

My first session with Valerie, I'd asked her what was wrong with me.

"You're acutely depressed."

"That's all?"

It had sounded too minor, like the flu. I was sure that what-ever I had was causing my internal organs to rot—I could smell it on my breath.

Understand this: at first death had been a mere flirtation, for instance, catching my foot lying hard on the gas pedal at the curve around Lake Whitney, the one that had killed Darcy and her boyfriend.

But then it became a true love affair, my heart was swollen for it, it lay down with me in bed and seeped into my pores while I slept.

I knew it was a sin. I knew that in the West human life was valued above all else, that it would be considered a virtuous act to keep this body of mine alive, no matter how stupid I got. Valerie had already begun talking about a hospital. Facil-ity, she called it. Nothing facile about it, if you'd asked me, except for the people who wouldn't have to deal with you any-more.

I was sorry thinking that Ma would be the one to discover me. She had found her own father's body, face twisted, pillow soaked with the life blood he'd coughed out in his sleep. His favorite, my mother had run into his room every morning, even before the servants came with hot water.

You'd think, given my history, I would have chosen to cut. And I admit I did consider it, standing in front of the mirror in my parents' bathroom, that ghastly fluorescent light illuminating the blue veins in my already scarred left forearm. There was even a package of Daddy's razor blades left in the medicine cabinet. But in the end I chickened out. Although I could imagine the kind of pain from a vein rent clear through, could even imagine existing through it, I simply did not want to die in that kind of agony.

It would have to be sleep.

I chose the day, a Saturday, when my mother would be away at a Smith luncheon in New York City. The night before I made my will, which was simple. When I was finished I saw that my handwriting was illegible so I did it all over again in big block letters, simplifying as much as possible.

FRAN—ART. MARTY—EVERYTHING ELSE. CREMATE.

They'd figure it out.

Then I opened the bottles and spilled the pills onto the scarf Aunty Mabel had embroidered for my sixteenth birthday. Fuchsia satin, with clumps of white kittens in the corners. Counting, I had trouble focusing, the color contrast was so vibrant, the tablets so tiny. I pushed the pills into the middle of the scarf and knotted it up into a bundle. Someone long ago had taught me to do that, I didn't remember who.

That night I was too keyed up to sleep, still staring at the ceiling when Ma leaned into my bedroom. She had on a brown tweed suit with a yellow and red scarf wrapped around her throat and her favorite earrings, Nai-nai's black pearls.

"Sure you don't want to come to New York with me?" she asked. "You can go to museum. Or I give you my Bloomingdale's charge card."

"No."

"I'll be back before six. If you need money it's on top of the radio in the kitchen."

I waited for the front door to slam, the gust of the taxi making the turn down the hill. Then I lay for a while more, listening to the silence of the house, punctuated by random bird and squirrel noise from the backyard. From a crack under the window shade, I could see that the day was overcast, and for this I was thankful.

I took a shower, out of habit I guess, and afterward went into Marty's room. Over the bedpost was flung a crimson feather boa. Somewhere there was a Polaroid of my sister in costume: gold-painted eyelids, black unitard, spike heels, and that boa draped across her breasts. I got into the bed and reached up and pulled it down, wrapping the ends of it around my face, inhaling that scent of my sister, a smell that I could distinguish from a thousand other people's in the dark.

Then I went downstairs, only glancing into the half-open door of my parents' bedroom, the double bed immaculately made with its blue-and-white-striped spread, the low bureau cluttered with straw trays of cosmetics and jewelry and a couple of the Chinese movie star magazines my mother still read. My parents' wedding picture in its silver frame was propped in the corner.

In the kitchen, Ma's tea mug filled with swollen green leaves sat on the table, still warm to the touch. There was one more thing I needed to do. I slipped my feet into the old sneakers my mother kept by the back door for gardening— they were so small my heels hung over the backs—and then went out and climbed onto the curb of the driveway. Standing there I could see my breath, but the cold seemed to just lie on my skin, like snow on the ground, without penetrating it.

I'd come out to say good-bye to my favorite tree, the black walnut. It stood stark and plain at the bottom of the hill, the dark brown trunk rising straight for fifteen feet until the limbs began reaching upward.

I'd wanted that image to be the last thing branded into my

brain in this world, but now, seven weeks later, I was standing at the top of the hill again, watching the shadow play of pale green flower and unfolding leaf in an angle of sun. In the tortured narcissism of my attempted suicide and its aftermath it had not occurred to me that this tree would bud and bloom, that in fact things would simply continue.

16

Right before takeoff I had this sudden urge to stand up in the aisle and announce that I was fresh out of the loony bin, what did everyone think about that?

But how perfectly easy it was, after all, to appear normal: just stay in your seat and keep your mouth shut. I thought that if Mel had been in my place he'd have been practicing his charm on the flight attendant, trying to cadge a drink out of her.

We'd said our good-byes out by the lake, after breakfast on the day my mother came to pick me up. He gave me his poetry anthology and told me he'd marked certain poems for me.

"But you're always reading that book."

"Consider it a loan. That way I'll be sure of seeing you again."

The sun was tipping the wavelets gold, too dazzling to focus on. The ducks, who didn't seem to care that this was a mental hospital, had glided hopefully to shore as they did anytime anyone passed. I dug into the pocket of my jacket and found the remains of a packet of oyster crackers, which I tossed out onto the water.

"Ciao, Club Willowridge," Mel said. I laughed.

"We never got to play tennis."

"You'll play in Florida." He studied me, as if searching for something in particular. "You get better down there, you hear? At least get a tan."

"Visit me," I said impulsively.

He scrubbed at the wet grass with the tip of his sneaker. "I don't have the dough."

"We'll talk about it."

"Sure."

"I don't have the number with me, but they're listed. Richard Ding. I'm sure they're the only Ding in St. Petersburg."

"Okay." Mel smiled and reached behind me to slide the elastic out of my ponytail so that my hair fell down around my face. Then he leaned forward and gave me the lightest of kisses on the mouth.

The book of poems was in Daddy's black leather bag, along with warm-weather clothes I'd scrounged from my sister's bureau: gym shorts and a couple of giant T-shirts, all of which I was sure were originally Schuyler's. The pickings had been pretty slim. This was the story in our family: when Marty and I weren't looking, our mother would give our clothes away. There was always someone in need: a distant relative or a friend who had just arrived in America. Or someone who, although not exactly in need, was more deserving than my sister or me. My camel hair jacket went this route. Ma donated it to Aunty Winnie, Xiao Lu's mother. It was true that I'd left it hanging in the front hall closet, deciding it wasn't cool enough for sophomore year, when everyone was wearing distressed denim. But it had after all been mine.

"You never wear," Ma said. "*She* thinks it's chic."

Marty would fly into a rage. I remember her hollering down the stairs, demanding to know what my mother had done with her purple sweater, black jeans, gold scarf.

A few months after Daddy died, Carey and I came up to New Haven and found Ma in the midst of sorting clothes to give away. She was very organized about it, having lugged several moving boxes from the attic and labeled them: THROW OUT, GOODWILL, NEARLY NEW SALE, FLORIDA.

"What's 'Florida'?" I asked.

"I send to Uncle Richard, maybe he can use." Uncle Richard was considerably shorter than my father but easily weighed twice as much. I looked in the box and saw that it was full of ties—brightly colored, bold patterns. Daddy had grown conservative in dress, but always favored loud ties.

In the GOODWILL box were piled dress shirts. Even though they'd been washed, I thought I could still detect his smell on them. A dry, slightly stale odor.

"Why don't you take?" Ma asked. "They fit you perfectly."

She was right; I was broad enough through the shoulders. But I shook my head.

Ma picked up a tan V-necked sweater and held it up for us to inspect. "Definitely too small for Uncle Richard. Carey, you like this? Such nice cashmere, feel."

I said quickly: "It's not his color."

My mother frowned at it, then refolded it and put it aside. "Maybe I wear for around the house."

All the trousers were cut baggy. Ma laughed suddenly. "Look at this." She laid out two pairs on the bed side by side. We could see that one was much larger than the other.

"Your daddy got very fat right after we married. Everyone says it's my good cooking."

"I can believe that," Carey said, and I rolled my eyes at him. My mother was a terrible cook.

"It was your daddy who liked to cook," Ma said to me. "Every night, he made a feast, six courses at least. He used up every knife and pot and pan we had." She sat back on her heels with a dreamy look. "When I was pregnant with you, Sally, I have to tell him to stop, I was too tired to do the dishes."

"So did you cook?" I asked.

"No one cook. We go into Monterey for spaghetti with clam sauce." I could see my parents sitting in front of their enormous plates of pasta, looking daunted. "This American food,"

Ma would have sighed. Daddy would have pointed out that spaghetti was invented by the Chinese.

"I thought you were so sick you couldn't eat," I said.

"Who said that?" My mother folded each pair of trousers over her arm, pulling the legs out so that the creases lay perfectly. She handles clothes meticulously. So did Nai-nai. But there was a difference in attitude. To my grandmother, clothes held a kind of magic—they could change your destiny one way or the other. To my mother, they were servile, like farm animals in China. Treat them well and they'll perform their function.

Marty and I, American girls, were frivolous. My sister's clothes lay heaped on chairs and strewn on the floor, forgotten until she needed something in particular. I bought things for the color, and liked to see them hanging arrayed in my closet—whites, blacks, warms, cools—almost more than I enjoyed wearing them.

"You want me to help you sort?" I asked my mother.

"No, easier if one person does."

Her answer made me feel guilty. She knew I hadn't loved my father enough to go through his clothes when he was dead.

As the plane taxied down the runway, I noticed that almost everyone was reading, or pretending to read. Not me. I sat straight up, waiting for that moment, exactly the space of a slow intake of breath, when we lifted off and began to climb steeply into the sky.

Those couple of days I'd spent at the house on Woodside Avenue, my mother and I had treated each other neutrally. We cooked meals, ate, cleaned up, watched the news, and it was as if I were just home for the weekend, had never tried to off myself, or been in the hospital. That last family therapy session might have never taken place.

The last thing Ma said, when she dropped me off at Connecticut Limousine, was that I'd probably have to take a taxi from the airport because Uncle Richard didn't have a license anymore, his eyesight had gotten so bad, and Aunty Mabel hated to drive.

But there my aunt was, waiting behind the rope, in a pink-and-white-flowered shirtdress and big sunglasses. Thinner in some places, fatter in others. She waved so wildly when she saw me that everyone looked to see who it was. I felt like a movie star.

"*Wo lai na, wo lai na,*" she insisted, holding out her arms for the bag.

"No, I'm okay. It's really light."

She regarded me critically. "Too thin. Come, I'm right outside."

I barely had time to register the heat before we got to the car, an old maroon Tercel. My aunt switched on the radio to Muzak. "Eleanor Rigby." "I thought you didn't like to drive," I said.

"In Florida you have to drive." My aunt's voice had a lilt, a trace of southern. Her lips and fingernails were painted coral. I could tell right away I wasn't going to blend in here. Florida was surreal, I couldn't take seriously anyplace that had palm trees. And it was stunningly flat, the bay itself a vast plain, stretching out light blue and gleaming on both sides of us as we skimmed across toward St. Petersburg, which shimmered ahead of us through a fog of heat.

"You know, Sal-lee, my friend from the library has a pool, she says you can use. Or you can go to the beach. We have ninety-five degrees every day this week."

"I didn't bring a bathing suit."

"No problem, we buy at the mall."

"What's this about a library, Aunty Mabel?"

"I have part-time volunteer job at public library. Shelve books, catalog, things like that. Once in a while there's a kids' art exhibit, I help organize."

Despite myself, I began to relax. It was soothing to be driven like this, into a strange pale metropolis that whatever surprises it might hold, could never be as jangling as New York. When we got into the city proper, on the left, through the buildings, I could still catch glimpses of the bay. And even here, downtown, was that Florida light, with its peculiar empty quality, as if it were reflecting only ocean, like at the beginning of time.

Aunty Mabel said: "You know, your Uncle Richard isn't so good."

"What's the matter?"

"Since he retired. I think he lose his spirit. Maybe you can cheer him up."

"Me?"

"All the time he's in front of the TV. Maybe you can do some project together."

"Okay."

"He always want daughter, you know. Never son, like most men. He's so looking forward to your visit."

Ma had once told me that my aunt and uncle couldn't have children because when Aunty Mabel was young, she had been cursed by a beggar on the streets of Shanghai.

The street they lived on was all ranch houses, each with its own tiny backyard. Uncle Richard opened the door for us, wheezing. "Welcome, Niece." He was fatter than ever, thinning gray wisps combed back from his forehead, eyelids so heavy with wrinkles it made him look sleepy. "Typical Cantonese," Ma always said about him. "You know, that round face."

"You bring your pretty sister with you?"

"Not this time."

I followed my aunt down the narrow hallway. The guest room was practically unrecognizable from when Marty and I had visited as children. Then it had been all white—gauze curtains, flimsy spreads, like in a beach house. Now it was filled with heavy, bright embroidery: the spreads peach-colored satin with intricate scarlet rose borders, matching curtains with valances, a footstool plump like a pincushion. On one bed was a large pillow in the shape of a ladybug and on the other a toy cat, white and fluffy, like the ones on my bureau scarf, like Lili, who had gotten run over. Aunty Mabel had a lot of time on her hands.

After I'd unpacked—even the satin hangers had little daisies embroidered on them—I went back into the living room. The TV on a rolling cart was blasting a basketball game. On the sofa beside my uncle, Niu-niu, whom I'd only seen in a snapshot as a kitten, was sprawled out arthritically. There were flecks of white in her black coat. Uncle Richard stroked the cat absentmindedly as he watched the game. When the action got exciting he'd heave her up by her shoulders and point her at the screen. "See that breakaway? Good for three points. I knew it!"

"Who's playing?"

"Wildcats versus Hoosiers. I have one hundred smackers on this game. You don't tell your aunt."

I settled myself into a rocking chair with gingham frills over the arms. "Who are you betting on?"

"Wildcats, of course. You play basketball?"

"No."

"Too bad, you're tall and slim. Like your aunt, but she's also not sports-minded."

I remembered our Willowridge rec therapy games, where the therapist would keep switching the rules. "Okay, now both teams go for the same basket!" "Men against women!" "No dribbling for the next five minutes!" This last call usually got a laugh. Lillith, for some reason, would always pass to me, underhanded, arms flailing, as if the ball were way too heavy for her. It got so I would expect it.

It was too sad to think about.

Mel and I had tried calling her a couple of times at State, leaving messages she'd never returned. We did find out that she'd been transferred from Medical to a regular ward.

The Wildcats were down by ten when Aunty Mabel came in with a tray holding a pitcher and three glasses. "Turn down

TV," she said to Uncle Richard. He obeyed, winking at me, and then began clearing a place on the coffee table by shoving aside a pile of magazines and newspapers, including, I noticed, an old *Racing Form.*

"So you were in the hospital." Uncle Richard took a big sucking sip of his lemonade. "They call it a mental break-down, huh?"

"Something like that."

"Your mother tells us you try and kill yourself."

"Ding-ah!" my aunt said.

"You are Chinese, not Japanese. Japanese like hari-kari, honor, all that. Chinese have other way out of troubles. Chinese know it's all luck. So they try to change luck."

"Sally's luck is changed," Aunty Mabel said. "She comes to visit us."

"That means *our* luck is changed. You come to cheer old man up." Uncle Richard poked at Niu-niu, who didn't budge. "See this cat? I'm like this cat now. Decrepit."

"Come on," I said.

"Good for nothing. They should mercy kill me."

"See how he talks?" my aunt said to me.

"Every time I go to doctor, he gives me more medicine to take. Now it's my heart. Like a rusty valve, Mr. Ding, he says. You get older, things start fall apart."

"You smoke too much," Aunty Mabel said.

Indeed, I'd noticed that on the ceiling over where my uncle was sitting was a distinct brown stain, spreading out from the middle like an aura.

When I offered to help with dinner my aunt shook her head and pointed through the glass doors at the back patio. The red-and-white-webbed lounge chairs that had been there when I was a child had been replaced by ones cushioned in lengths of squishy lime green tubing. "*Xiuxi.*"

The grass in the backyard was overgrown and weedy. From

where I lay I could see that the grapefruit trees hadn't been kept up, but here and there among the glossy dark leaves a patch of yellow showed through. A palmetto plant made a sagging fountain in the middle of the yard. There was even a full-fledged palm tree, a short one whose trunk was the shape and pattern of a pineapple. Honeysuckle draped from the eaves of the garage, entwined with a vine that shot out trumpet flowers the color of blood oranges. The flowers were so beautiful I knew they must be poisonous. And the air was brimming. It wasn't just honeysuckle I smelled, there was something even more heady, a fragrant rush that was almost decadent.

The South pulled no punches when it came to decadence.

I fell asleep and dreamed I was five years old again and very sick. Pneumonia with complications. It was our first winter on Coram Drive. There were ghosts in the room, hiding in the pattern of the apple blossom wallpaper, in my clothes. I was staring at my favorite T-shirt folded on top of the bureau. It was red and blue stripes, with very thin black stripes between. Ma came in and I pointed to the shirt. "What?" she said. I pointed again. She picked it up and shook it and a ghost flew out and into the open door of the closet.

I opened my eyes and was back in Florida. In the yard to my right a sprinkler was going. What had awakened me was the sound of a car pulling into the gravel driveway. A middle-aged women in a pink top and mint green denim shorts carried grocery bags into the house. She gave a friendly nod as she passed. "We have such nice neighbors, this quiet old Oriental couple," I imagined her telling people. "And now their sweet young niece has come down from Connecticut to keep them company."

A heavy, slow breeze stirred against my pale chill northern skin, teasing the blood to the surface. I enjoyed the caress, not moving until my aunt called me for dinner.

She told me the smell was confederate jasmine. "Behind the garage, you see. All yellow."

"Watch out for armadillo," Uncle Richard added.

"Armadillo?"

"What do you think makes all those tunnels in the lawn? Big Mama Armadillo. Your aunt is out by the garage the other day and she sees one of the babies. Usually they don't come out in daytime. She jumps and says, *'Ai-yah!'* Armadillo jumps even higher than she does!"

As easygoing as my aunt and uncle were, conversation with them was exhausting. After dinner I excused myself as soon as was tactfully possible, and retreated back to the guest room. I took out Mel's book and propped myself up in the twin bed farthest from the door, near the window, where I'd slept so many years ago. On the sill was a parade of little glass animals, starting with the rat. The signs of the Chinese zodiac. I picked up my year, the dog. It looked like some kind of spaniel. Strong and reliable. Last in line was pig, Marty's year. Lazy but lucky.

I set the dog back in its place and let the book fall open to the page that had been read the most. It was Gerard Manley Hopkins.

Margaret, are you grieving
Over Goldengrove unleaving?

I knew it by heart. It was one of the poems Fran had recited to me over and over on the banks of the Sudbury River. I saw that Mel had marked the last two lines:

It is the blight man was born for,
It is Margaret you mourn for.

17

Next morning was overcast and cooler, the house perfectly silent as I checked my watch. I'd thrown my wedding ring into the East River, given the pear diamond back to Carey (it had been his grandmother's), but this token of my marriage I kept because it was from Ma, the most expensive present I'd ever gotten from her. Six-thirty. I was still on hospital time. I got out of bed and, still wearing the T-shirt I'd slept in, pulled on my corduroys. In the kitchen, my aunt and uncle's other cat, a little tiger, rubbed against my ankles and then shot through my legs when I slid open the glass doors to the patio.

I went out barefoot into the backyard and made my way through the tall grass, cold and heavy with dew, leaned against the back fence, and lit up a cigarette. That was a terrible habit I'd picked up in the hospital, smoking first thing in the morning on an empty stomach, but there was something divine about it too, the buzz so strong it was sick-making. I noticed the grapefruit lying scattered beneath the trees like bocce balls. They were rotting, riddled with insect holes. The grapefruit still in the trees didn't look much better. The ones Ma had brought to me at the hospital were obviously not from this yard. For a moment I entertained the urge to paint them, and then I stubbed out my cigarette and put the butt in my pocket and began picking up the decaying fruit, making a heap in the corner by the fence.

If only it could always be early morning or night. It was the day that killed me.

I heard the shrill of the teakettle from the kitchen and when I went back inside Aunty Mabel was pouring hot water into mugs filled with leaves. On the stove something acrid-smelling simmered in a clay pot. In the cool morning light I could see how my aunt's face was a reflection of my mother's. But where high cheekbones made Ma regal, in my aunt they were exaggerated, giving her the melancholy air of a Modigliani. My aunt's eyes were long and narrow, like those in Chinese fairy-tale books. Like mine.

"Too cold out there without sweater."

"I'm fine, really."

I could hear my uncle coughing in the bathroom. He'd lost his basketball bet last night.

Aunty Mabel set two mugs on the table. "Who would think Pau-yu be the first to go," she said as we sat there sipping. "I always think it's your uncle."

"Daddy was older."

"Your Uncle Richard, six different doctors he has, for all his disease. Lucky we still have insurance and disability from his job." My aunt got up to turn off the burner under the earthenware pot.

"What is that?" I asked.

"Special Chinese medicine for his heart. We have a friend sends it from Queens."

I remembered the potion I'd taken the year I was eight, which I'd believed to be dried blood. I never did find out what it actually was.

After breakfast my aunt drove my uncle to the cardiologist and I sat out on the patio in the sun, which had finally come out, until I felt too much like a bum. I decided to gather the rest of the grapefruit, filling two giant trash bags. Insects had begun to hum in the jungly grass. *Savannah* was the word that came to mind as I stood there surveying the yard for any strays I'd missed.

The next task I set for myself was to clip the grass with hedge trimmers, wearing an old sun hat I found in the garage hanging beside the tools. When I was done I went in for lemonade and the last half of the Sally Jessy Raphael show—bulimic boys, not as entertaining as you'd think, or maybe I was finally losing my taste for talk shows. By then it was around eleven-thirty and my aunt and uncle still hadn't returned, so I went out to the garage again and got out their old rusty rotary mower, which kept jamming on me. The ground was even more hummocky than it looked. I kept a hopeful lookout for armadillos, never having seen one before, but all I came across were lots of fat flying bugs and a tortoise, which I carefully picked up and put by the back fence, behind the grapefruit trees. The pastel lady from next door was hanging out her wash and waved to me.

Physical work doesn't keep you from thinking. In fact, sometimes it stimulates it. My aunt and uncle were as good as could be, but I was still in my life, I still had to return to New York City. As I struggled with the clackety mower I calculated my savings: I could survive for about a month and a half on what I had and then I'd have to find a steady income. One possibility was freelance from my old boss, if she still trusted me. My last assignments had been delivered late and barely acceptable. I'd told her I was going to Connecticut to live with my mother for a while, and then with all the mess, going into the hospital and all, I had completely lost touch.

It was hard to believe now, but at the agency I'd handled all the biggest projects. I was known to be great under pressure. Crank up the Vivaldi, order out pizza, and I could work through the night, meet the toughest deadline with panache. Where I worked, the darker the circles under your eyes, the more promising your career. Sally Wang-Acheson, senior art director. So chic, that hyphenated name, and so chic was I, my long hair done up in all sorts of intricately casual styles—I had finally begun to accept my looks for what they were, not beautiful but something else—with all those flowing tropical-colored outfits, dangly bronze and silver earrings Carey had given me every birthday and Christmas. A woman with style. A woman on her way up.

And then—catastrophe. A foot over on the other side, and it had affected me permanently, down to my brain cells. After degenerating to idiocy, I had to learn to be smart again, an adult in this world. How was it possible? Since I'd been sick I had taken to wearing the kind of asexual outfits I'd favored at boarding school—T-shirts, corduroys, sneakers. No makeup, no particular hairstyle. My reflection in the mirror was disturbing to me, the face thinner, childish, with a stripped expression I remembered from working with the mentally handicapped. Pure shock that you had to be out in the world at all.

I was almost done when I heard the car pull in. My aunt stood on the patio shading her eyes with her hands.

"Next year we spray the trees again."

"Aunty Mabel, there's some kind of other fruit out here. Little orange things on bushes."

"Calamondin. Too sour to eat. You can make marmalade from."

Unexpected treasures in your own backyard. I thought of the patch of lily of the valley behind the swing set on Coram Drive. Fortunately the bad boys missed it in their rampage. Once in a while Ma would pick a handful to keep in a glass in the kitchen. "This is what I have in my wedding corsage," she told Marty and me, although she didn't know the name in English. We didn't know that they were so rare that it was actually against the law in Connecticut to pick them.

"Sal-lee, you come in now," Aunty Mabel said. "After lunch we go shopping."

In Montgomery Ward I selected the most conservative bathing suit I could find—a red one-piece with white polka dots and low-cut leg holes. I changed into and out of it as fast as possible, stopping long enough only to check that it was serviceable. Department store lighting was so cruel. "Let's see!" my aunt called from the other side of the curtain and I said, "It's fine, it's fine."

On the way to the cash register Aunty Mabel stopped at a rack full of tropical flowered sundresses, her coral nails fluttering over the hangers. "Sal-lee! *Ni kan!* This style become you very much."

To please her, I tried one on. It had a full skirt—not my taste—with purple hibiscus on a green and white background that vaguely resembled leaves. But the bodice was cut in a sophisticated way, as snugly as an evening gown, with a graceful scoop neck and deep armholes. I wished the bones of my chest didn't show, but they always had, as long as I could remember. This time I gave in to my aunt and stepped outside to model.

"Huh," she said, drawing her eyebrows together in a delicate frown. I was barefoot and my ankles were raw from the sandspurs I'd picked up from working in the yard, but I could see that what she was looking at was the inside of my left arm where the tiger stripes overlapped delicately but distinctly from wrist to elbow.

"It's gorgeous," Aunty Mabel said, finally deciding she wasn't going to ask. "I buy for you."

For dinner my second night in Florida we had *jiao zi.* My aunt rolled out the dough and pressed circles into it with the rim of a teacup to make the wrappers. I spooned the pork and cabbage filling in and pinched the dumplings shut. Thanks to Nai-nai I'd perfected my technique at making them dainty, evenly scalloped at the edges. My sister's had too much filling and spilled out the sides. You could always tell which ones were whose when they came out of the pot.

"I'm not eating any of Marty's," I'd announce.

"Mine are better, they have more meat," my sister would shoot back.

"No fight," my father would say in his high-pitched starting-to-be-mad voice. But I noticed that Daddy ate more of mine than my sister's.

Aunty Mabel asked how Marty was.

"She has an apartment in New York now."

"How does she support herself?"

My sister lived off men, but I didn't think my aunt needed to know this.

"When she's in the city she works as a clown at South Street Seaport. Now she's up in Vermont with a college friend of hers."

"So she moves to the country?"

"No, no, this is just temporary. She still wants to be an actress in New York."

"Actress." Aunty Mabel sighed. "Your sister, she's always so active." She slid a pile of dough circles across the table to me. "And you! When you were little, you send us such beautiful cards. All kinds of animals, horses, dogs, cats. I still keep. You remember? And your ma-ma told us you won so many prizes in high school, for painting pictures."

"She told you?"

"Of course she told us. I think this is a very difficult school you attend, lots of talented girls."

"That's what it was like."

"So much talent, though, doesn't help find a husband."

"I did find a husband, Aunty Mabel."

"You found *wai guo ren*. Maybe it's better you find Chinese."

"You mean like Xiao Lu?"

My aunt considered. "Those New York Chinese too small and pale. Maybe Hawaiian, or some big, strong California one. You ever think about moving out to California? We still have relatives there, you know."

"Your ba-ba so handsome." In the living room after dinner, my aunt and I were looking through old photograph albums. I remembered that she had once been interested in my father. We had come to a photograph of my parents just before they got married. They were leaning against the railing of a ship, hand in hand, hair blowing every which way, eyes only for each other. Daddy's face was angled a little away from the camera, smiling and shadowed. Even in that casual pose, you could see the intensity in the twist of his neck. Ma, dimpled in a big-shouldered dress, looked fragile beside him.

"Bau-yu and Pau-yu," my aunt said. "Similar and not similar."

We had the same picture in an album at home; I knew the story that went with it. After the ship photographer snapped their photo, they'd set out on a cruise around San Francisco Bay. Although it wasn't particularly rough, in ten minutes my father had completely ruined his fancy seersucker jacket. "I never saw anyone so sick in my life," Ma told us. "I had to take it to the cleaners three times." Back on land, Daddy told her how he'd suffered on his voyage from China. He'd lost eighteen pounds on the way.

I studied the face in the photo, noticed how the young man's side-parted hair fell in a way that reminded me of Marty's. Daredevilish.

Then came my parents' wedding. What touched me most was Aunty Mabel standing alone, her big, good-natured face framed by a bad perm, wearing a light-colored dress with petal sleeves and a straight skirt too tight around the hips. When she smiled her eyes disappeared into half-moons and you could see her crooked top teeth. Ma said that Aunty Mabel did better than anyone expected. She moved to New York and six months later started dating Uncle Richard, who was an accountant at Grumman, where she worked as a secretary.

No photos of their wedding, they'd gone modestly to City Hall. The next series showed my aunt and uncle standing in front of a two-family brick house in Flushing—they'd lived there only three months before my uncle got a job with Martin

Marietta in St. Pete. Uncle Richard was chunky and broad-faced and beaming, a heaviness around his chin foretelling the jowls to come. My aunt looked dazed in her heavy jewelry and unbecoming dresses.

"Ding-ah!" she called to my uncle, but he had fallen asleep on the couch across the room.

Me as a lumpy infant, a cowlick I still have springing from the left side of my head. Marty, smaller in every way, and more self-contained. The album chronicled the two of us growing up into our late teens. Between us, often, stood my mother. Seeing Ma and Marty together over and over made me note the difference in their beauty. My mother had a portrait prettiness, with her styled hair and regular features, while my sister's face was narrower, feline, a little dangerous. It wasn't just the generation gap—my sister was born knowing something my mother never learned.

At first Ma's look changed dramatically from scene to scene, her hairstyle and clothing reflecting each passing fashion. You could practically pinpoint the year by looking at her. There we were at Disneyland, in front of Cinderella's castle, my mother in a modified beehive and Bermuda shorts, me in stripes, my sister in snowflakes. In front of the White House: Ma in a boldly patterned sleeveless shift and the Twiggy crop Daddy had hated so much, Marty and I on either side of her with our arms clutching the crosspiece of the fence, pretending we were being strung up.

Then suddenly my mother's fashion sense seemed to regress until finally it froze. The pixie haircut, the school-marm outfits, the tight mouth. She remained static, only growing older, while my sister and I blossomed.

Daddy, usually the photographer, was in few of the pictures. I watched him age, hair whitening first at the temples and then clouding through. His eyes got smaller, darker, and more brilliant. His body shrank to bones inside the endless similar sets of loose shirts and trousers that he wore year after year. The ties got more and more excessive. The rare smile become nonexistent. How bitter the lines framing his mouth, how resentful the hunch of his shoulders, how desperately his long hands groped the air by his sides.

For the first time I saw my parents' marriage as a love story gone terribly awry.

"Your ba-ba ever tell you he want to be pilot?" Aunty Mabel reached down into her wicker workbasket, fished out a card of bright orange embroidery floss, unwound it, and licked the end into a point, which she threaded through a darning needle.

"No, really?"

"He want to join the Chinese air force. You think he's so healthy, a tall man like that. But he failed the physical. All those childhood diseases make his constitution weak."

"I thought he wanted to be a physicist."

"That too. Afterward. Pilot was childhood dream." My aunt shook her head. "Your father was a genius, you should hear him talk! So clever, all those stories. His sisters would be so proud of him. Too bad he was stuck in the United States. All the time he hopes China opens up again so he can go back. He is almost thirty years old when he comes. You come to a new country too late, you are always stranger. Your mother and me, we go to school here, we make friends. Not so your ba-ba. He is incurable Chinese."

"He did go back. To Taiwan."

"When a Chinese returns to China, he goes to *lao jia*."

In the early 1970s, when it was beginning to be possible to do so, my parents had written to their respective families. Ma had received several letters back: her oldest sister had died (one of those aunts whose blurry heads Marty and I had scrutinized in Nai-nai's ancient sepia family portraits), such and such a cousin was professor of German at the foreign language institute in Shanghai. Since it was impossible for those in China to obtain visas to the United States, would Nai-nai and Ma and Aunty Mabel please come back to visit them as soon as possible. Nai-nai had wanted to, had made plans, but the cancer had gotten to her bones by then. Her daughters had never gone.

My father had received only one letter back, on onionskin paper, the characters drawn with blue fountain pen ink in an uncertain hand. It was from a stranger, a primary school teacher in the town where he'd grown up. So sorry to have to be the one to convey such news to his illustrious American colleague, etc., etc., but Wang Pau-yu's younger sister had passed away several years ago from the sugar sickness. Diabetes, Daddy explained. She'd been a laborer, a farmhand, unmarried. No one knew what had become of the older sister. She'd held a local government post, and then joined the Communist Party and moved to Beijing during the Cultural Revolution. She'd changed her name and was impossible to trace.

I asked my aunt: "Do you think Ma should have married someone else? Someone more her class?" I remembered Uncle Richard and hoped Aunty Mabel wouldn't take offense.

She didn't. "More than difference in class. Difference in character. Your father had a very bad childhood. So insecure, always afraid. Your mother—well, you know, she's the baby. A little spoiled, like your sister. She doesn't understand this kind of fear."

I was flipping the pages of the album fast now, until a large group photograph made me stop. There was our whole family, La Guardia Airport, Christmas, my sophomore year of boarding school. My parents still the perfect couple for the camera: Daddy, his hair almost completely white now, my mother close beside him with her dutiful, distant smile. Uncle Richard in a Russian fur hat, which he must have kept mainly in mothballs, for who would need such a thing in Florida, his arm raised in a bon voyage salute—his other arm around my aunt, who looked caught off-guard. Me in an army jacket and ragged-hem jeans, my sister with heavy mascara and a bad layered haircut. Between the two of us my Nai-nai, wearing the long beige cashmere coat my mother and aunt had given her for Christmas. I could see in the photograph how it hung off her shoulder blades, she had gotten so thin. By that time she was wearing turtlenecks rather than high-collared blouses to hide her mole because she couldn't manage buttons. A couple of years before, she had broken her hip, and still sported an ivory-handled cane.

"Your Nai-nai look distinguished, eh?" she said to me. "Not just like any old lady." When I walked her to the boarding gate she leaned against me, clutching my arm, and I could feel the brittle bones of her fingers through her soft leather gloves. It was the last time I ever saw her, touched her.

My mother was fussing, asking if Nai-nai was sure she had her ticket. My grandmother ignored her. "You much taller," she said to me. "It's good to be tall. Tall girl stands out."

And I remembered how I had felt comforted, although I had heard it a hundred times before.

The phone rang and my uncle started, in the middle of a snore. "Hello?" Aunty Mabel said. Then she handed the receiver to me. "For you."

"Ma?" I asked, but my aunt shook her head.

"Sally? It's Mel."

"Oh my God, how are you?" His voice was like elixir, cool, filling, impossible to describe how glad it made me feel. "Where are you calling from?"

"My parents' house."

"Are you on pass?"

"I'm out, Sal. They sprung me."

"That's great! What are you up to?"

"Well, for starters, I thought I'd come down and see you."

"I thought you said you were broke."

"There are ways, darling, there are ways. I think I can borrow some wheels."

"It's a little crowded here—"

"Oh, don't worry about that, Sal, I wouldn't impose on your family. I have a place to stay."

"When?"

"Not sure yet. I'll call you in a couple of days. Is it hot down there?"

"Ninety-five in the shade."

"Beautiful. We'll go sailing. I have to go, hon. Just sit tight, I promise I'll call you. Bye."

Aunty Mabel was bowed over her embroidery, but my uncle, now fully awake, leaned forward on the couch, rubbing his pudgy palms together. "Boyfriend, eh?"

"No. Just friend."

"Just friend. *Ni kan*," he said to my aunt, "see how she blushes."

18

Aunty Mabel was in the kitchen, answering questions: Is she eating enough, is she sleeping, is she being a help to you. My aunt's Shanghainese was so quick the sibilant syllables seemed to trip over each other.

I was summoned to the phone. Before she handed it to me, my aunt whispered: "Your sister's in an accident."

When I asked, Ma said: "No, no, nothing serious. Marty's rental car, it went into a ditch. Insurance covers everything. She has a broken arm, that's all."

"Where is she?"

"Still up in Vermont now, but she's coming back down. Her friend drives her this weekend."

"Are you sure she's all right?"

"Of course, of course. I think she's getting tired of there anyway. I think it's time for her to come home."

While my aunt was out of the house at her library job, Uncle Richard and I played gin rummy, a penny a point. The cards were special ones, with giant print, for people with bad vision. My uncle leaned back on the sofa, his eyes sly over his half glasses. On the table in front of him was a pair of silver globes, the kind you see for sale in Chinatown in satin boxes, that he picked up and clacked together when he was thinking. It drove me crazy.

"You're just like Captain Queeg."

"Hah hah. Humphrey Bogart." My uncle had four cards

left. His eyes narrowed and he threw down the queen of hearts into the discard pile. I reached for it, hesitated, and then pulled my hand back. He laughed. "That's right, Niece. You have to weigh things, think them out. You think it looks like a treasure, it might be a poison."

"I need a cigarette."

Without taking his eyes off his cards, Uncle Richard reached behind him into the crack between the cushion and the back of the sofa and pulled out a battered pack of Camel nonfilters. He shook them expertly so that one slid out toward me. "Be my guest." With his slippered toe he poked under the sofa fringe and nudged out an old tuna can full of butts.

"Looks like you've got it all set up."

"That's right." He took a gold lighter out of his shirt pocket and lit my cigarette, then his, and set the can on the coffee table.

"Doesn't she smell it?"

"Nah. She too busy worry about other things." He frowned down at his hand.

"Uncle Richard, what did you think of my father?"

"What's this, you studying your roots?"

"No, I'm just curious."

"Pau-yu was a very intelligent man. And he has charisma, like movie star. Not like your old uncle."

"Do you think he loved my mother?"

"Why you ask all these questions, Niece? He cherish your ma-ma. She is very able woman. Your turn."

I picked up the king of spades, one of my favorite cards, but I couldn't use it, since all I was holding was low clubs, so I laid it down. I remembered, sinkingly, that I hadn't seen a lot of high spades in this game. "Ah," my uncle said. His hand hovered over the facedown pile, teasing me, then swooped down for the king I'd just discarded. "Gin. Forty-five points." Jack, queen, king, ace. Royal flush.

"Luck," I said.

"I tell you, Niece, that's what it is. Luck. Everything is luck."

"Someone else's good luck is your bad."

"In cards, maybe. Not in other things. You know *feng shui?*" He pronounced it the Cantonese way, "shwee."

"Wind water."

"Very good. I have friend in Queens, expert in this. He came down, look at our house, make recommendations. You gotta bad angle on your door, he says, no money can come in, you put a mirror here to fix. Energy trapped behind this window, you put something glass to catch it. Then what happened? We get a six-thousand-dollar refund from IRS. What do you think?"

"I think you had something to do with that refund."

"See these bells and chime hanging here? That's for *chi* to play. You give it toy, good luck wants to come in. Hah, I can see you don't believe. I tell you what. We go see some real luck in action. The puppies. You ever see greyhound race?"

"Once. A documentary on TV."

Uncle Richard laughed raucously. "Forget TV." He counted his cards quickly, swept them together. "One hundred thirty points. You owe me seven dollars."

"What's the matter, Niece? This old car is too much for you? Japanese-made, very good, we got it secondhand."

"No, no, everything's fine." It was a good thing my uncle was nearly blind, he wouldn't be able to pick up details like the fact that my palms were sweating all over the steering wheel. It was the first time I'd been in the driver's seat since I'd gotten sideswiped in Ma's Honda. I put on my sunglasses and adjusted the rearview mirror, casual, like I did it all the time, like I was born driving.

"So what we say to your aunt?" Uncle Richard tested me.

"We saw *Cousin Cousine.*" Aunty Mabel had come home with one of her migraines and had gone to lie down after lunch. I'd scrawled the note we left on the kitchen table: *Going to the movies. Be back for dinner.*

"Good. You tell me the story."

I glanced behind me and in front of me and when I was surer than sure it was absolutely safe pulled out of the drive-way. I was usually bad at recalling the plots of movies, but this one I remembered, because it was the one Carey and I had seen on our first date and we'd argued about it afterward. He'd thought it was immoral.

"They're these two couples, the man in one couple is the cousin of the woman in the other couple. Anyway, the man cousin is a real jerk, always having affairs, and the wife is good, the actress's name is Marie-Christine Something."

"Make a left at this light. What does this Marie look like?"

"Oh, I don't know, long blond hair, not pretty pretty but very attractive. And in the other couple, it's the wife cousin who's the jerk. She's extremely beautiful, dark hair, neurotic as hell, always threatening to commit suicide. For attention. You know she's never going to do it. You following this, Uncle Richard?"

"Ummhmm."

"Her husband's totally easygoing, totally sweet. A doll. So guess what happens."

"Either the good and the good or the bad and the bad get together."

"But the bad and the bad are related by blood."

"When I was growing up cousin could marry cousin. You make a right at this intersection. Watch out for trucks. *Right,* Niece."

"Sorry." It seemed as if my uncle's eyesight was improving geometrically the farther away we got from the house. We'd been following the Gulf shore a ways, and now we were head-ing toward downtown St. Pete. We passed a low-slung stucco hospital with a row of those tall gangly palms, the kind where the trunks were skinny at the bottom and widened toward the top. "Bends in hurricane," Aunty Mabel had explained to me when I'd pointed this out.

"You ever miss New York?" I asked my uncle.

"Of course. Chinese food. You think you can get decent here? Seafood is okay, but has American taste."

"How about your friends?"

"All retiring now, and they come down here, you know, or to Miami. Miami, Miami. Big deal. Sometimes your aunt and me, we think Hawaii."

"Hawaii! That would be great."

"Yeah. Honolulu. You come visit us there, eh?"

"Of course."

Now we were in a particularly seedy section, auto repair shops and bars and very few people on the street. I found the automatic door lock button and pressed it. Per capita, there was much more crime here than in New York. I remembered what Lillith had told me about the town of Starke, near Gainesville. "You want to hold your breath when you pass that," she'd warned.

"Why?"

"'Cause that's where all the worst serial murderers are penned up. And that's where they keep Ole Sparky."

"What?"

"The electric chair."

"I thought they didn't use that anymore."

"They do in Florida."

How did she even *know* things like that?

"So how much money you bring, Niece?" My uncle's jovial tone brought me back into the present.

"Not much. I'm living on a shoestring, Uncle Richard. I haven't worked since January."

"Your luck will change. Don't worry." On the *worry* my uncle started to cough, until he was hacking away like he did mornings in the bathroom. He whipped out a handkerchief, hawked, and spat. It turned my stomach and I tried not to let him see.

"Are you okay?"

"Fine, fine. Okay, make a left here on Gandy Boulevard and go two blocks and you see a parking lot."

You couldn't miss it, it was so enormous, with DERBY LANE in ten-foot-tall letters over the main entrance. Fortunately the lot wasn't very full, so I didn't have to pull any fancy parking stunts. As we got out of the car I could hear a band playing and a loudspeaker announcing something over it. The other people going in looked fairly normal, plump blond tourists in shorts and T-shirts. My uncle was by far the most nattily dressed, in a yellow linen suit and white bucks.

As we walked toward the entrance he nudged me. "You like this tie?" he asked, holding it out for my inspection. It was unfashionably wide and had tiny brightly colored parrot heads on a black background.

"That's Daddy's." Now I knew why it had bothered me. Ma and I had picked it out for his birthday and I remembered the last time I'd seen him wear it, at the eighth grade Christmas play where my sister had been the Madonna.

"I wear it for you, Niece. Plus, it happens to be my lucky tie."

I wondered what Daddy would have thought about this, whether anything of his could ever bring luck to anyone. I wondered what he would have thought of Uncle Richard and me going to the greyhound track. I myself was afraid I'd hate the track, I didn't know why I was there, except I was bored and humoring Uncle Richard. I was afraid the dogs would make me sad.

My uncle paid for the dollar apiece tokens to get us through the turnstiles, bought a program, and then led me through the infield over to a building he called the benching area, where the dogs were penned, ready to go, or cooling down. I wasn't prepared for what it would sound like, that greyhounds were after all hounds, all that howling and yelping. They weren't show dogs and didn't have to be beautiful, although some of them were. Bred strictly for speed, their spare lines were not unlike horses' and they weren't just gray. White, some of them, one even pure black, blue-black, a whole range of tans, pintos, dappled. Uncle Richard was friends with a handler, who flipped back the ear of one of the dogs and showed me the tattoo. The hound stood lean and quiet beneath his hands. Her name was Shady Lady and she was scrawny, light gray with little black spots. Her face markings resembled a raccoon mask.

The dogs were barking, the announcer was barking, my uncle and I left the benching area and went back through the infield to the betting windows. As we walked he was scribbling notes in his program. Opposite the windows hung a row of television sets before which stood a shoulder-to-shoulder crowd. I thought it must be closed circuit and then I saw that one screen was showing a horse race while the one beside it was displaying jai alai.

Uncle Richard placed several bets, talking and flinging down bills so fast that I had no idea what he was doing. "Tenth race, quiniela box," I heard him say. Then he turned to me. "Okay. You pick a race, pick a number. We make it simple, your first time. You pick which one to win, place, or show. You know what that means?"

"Yes."

I made my choice by name: Khartoum (named for a famous horse, I knew), Hotsplit, Greyghost the Fourth, and Shady Lady, a long shot in the seventh race, ridiculously long, twenty-five to one. Those were my kind of odds. I bet all my dogs to win and handed over thirty dollars in all. My uncle bought a plastic glass of beer and we went to lean against the fence. Across from us the odds flickered on the big board and a brass band played "The Girl from Ipanema." In the center of the track was a carefully styled oasis, complete with pond and playing fountain. The whole scene wavered in the blazing, unforgiving savannah heat. I put my sunglasses on again.

Uncle Richard sipped his beer and pulled out his cigarettes and we smoked and waited.

I studied the program. "SHADY LADY, number 7 Green and White. Night Shade—Lady Godiva. Rl Erly-Crwdd 1st Tn. Weaknd in Stretch. Sought Rl 1st—Bmpd. Led Briefly-Weaknd." My uncle was watching the odds flip with the calm concentration of someone who could do intricate calculations in his head. A snowy egret wafted onto the oasis and stood, as if posing in the brilliant green by the fountain, then took off as the band began playing a march. The dogs were being led out.

Saddled by their colors, muzzled, they paraded before us from right to left to the starting gates, in order of number. They each had distinctive strides, held their heads differently. I saw right away that Number 6, tan and husky but with an extremely narrow pelvis, straining at the leash, was going to win. I told my uncle.

"You wanna change your bet, Niece?"

"No, I'm just telling you, I'm positive he's going to win."

At some signal the dogs were crammed one by one into the starting gates and the handlers, dressed identically in white polo shirts, khaki shorts, and running shoes, sprinted down the track to the grass by the first turn. And then, for the first time I heard the dogs, whining, barking, all their various impatient voices. "Here's *Rusty*," someone said, and somewhere a clattering bell, like an old fire alarm, shrilled. The sun caught a gleam off the little device on wheels that ran along the inside railing and suspended the bouncing white stuffed rabbit over the packed dirt. When the rabbit had just cleared the corner by the starting gates it tripped some wire and the gates lifted and the dogs were off, silently shooting out from their little gates like the professionals they were, eating up ground in giant gallops, those lean legs that were entirely muscle, the trim-hipped torsos, the tiny aerodynamic heads that contained just enough brain matter for survival and the knowledge to run. The human beings were the unruly ones, leaning forward with their tickets grasped in their fists, screaming numbers as if they were the names of drowning lovers. I followed the dog I'd bet on, Khartoum, Number 5, for about ten seconds, and then I lost him. "Shit!" my uncle yelled. "Watch that turn, just edge over, that's right, beautiful." As far as I could tell, his vision at that moment was about twenty-twenty. They ran around one and a half times and it was over.

Number 6, the robust tan I'd picked at the last moment but not bet on, won.

"Huh," Uncle Richard said. He'd thrown his ticket to the ground in disgust the instant the dogs came in. "Well," he said to me. "You were right. You should have changed your bet."

My dog for the next race, Hotsplit, was scratched. "You could get your money back right now," my uncle urged, poking me, but I didn't want to bother. Again we watched the dogs parade by. "This time it's Number One," I said. Number 1 was jet black and although far from the largest had a confident step I liked.

"Okay, okay, you go put money on," said Uncle Richard.

"Nope. I just want to watch."

Number 1 came in an easy first. "Bad race," my uncle muttered.

"Why was it bad?"

"Dirty. You see that first turn, that one big white dog, you see how he goes sideways like that, cheats all the others, not fair."

"But dogs don't know to cheat."

"You think they can't be trained?"

"Maybe."

"I'm surprised the judge didn't call. No, it was a cheat. But I tell you, Niece, you're something. Two for two."

Once Carey and I had gone to Saratoga Springs and I had won two hundred dollars on a long shot who looked good in the paddock. I don't know how I did it. It's like falling in love, your eye automatically picks out one in a crowd, you can't explain why.

In the next race my uncle won seventy-two dollars. To celebrate he bought another beer and a Coke and a sun hat with a visor for me. After that he began to lose steadily. I didn't even bother to check my tickets. I hadn't bet on a single winner, although I managed to call them all, four more in a row. I admit, it was some kind of a thrill.

"Jeez Louise, Niece," Uncle Richard said. "Next time we place our bets right before post time. But you gotta pick second and third too. You practice, we can do superfectas." My uncle's face was distinctly gray in the sunlight and noticing this gave me a shock.

"Uncle Richard, maybe we better go home now."

"One more race, Niece. You like this one, it's that dog you met."

So we watched, although I was distracted and didn't even bother to pick a winner this time. I tried to focus on Shady Lady instead. She didn't cut a very promising figure, slightly splay-legged, her head bowed down in a deferential manner. Beside her the competition looked like Arnold Schwarzenegger dogs. By the time the starting bell sounded the odds against her had climbed to twenty-seven to one. I was afraid to look, but when I did, she was right in the middle of the pack. At the first curve she slid into third place. I imagined I could see her ribs heaving under her colors, and I wondered what the hell was driving her on, didn't she know how outclassed she was? As the leaders bounded toward us, it looked like the second-place dog was losing ground. Shady Lady had taken his place when they whipped past. The crowd was on its feet. Someone was screaming louder than anyone else, right in my ear, and I realized, later, that it was me.

She stayed a close second right to the finish. It cut me to the quick, I don't know why. It wasn't like I had a lot riding on it. My uncle put his hand on my shoulder. I had completely forgotten that he was there.

"She had the most heart, that's for sure. Good race." He

coughed and reached up to unbutton the pocket of his shirt. "Hey, Niece, maybe you could help." I reached in to his pocket and found the vial and unscrewed the top. My uncle opened his mouth and I tried not to breathe in the blast of his breath—cigarettes, beer, Chinese heart medicine, old-man decay—as I slipped the pill under his tongue.

The band was playing "Blue Moon of Kentucky."

"So much excitement." Uncle Richard's color was still off but he was smiling. He took off his glasses and rubbed the bridge of his nose, trying to be casual. The gesture reminded me of Carey. "Next time we sit upstairs in the air-conditioned part. I take you to the infield because it's your first time, you want to see the dogs close up."

"I really think we should go home now."

"What if I really have a heart attack? Can you drive fast to the hospital? How fast can you drive? Can you break speed limit?"

"Not funny. Remember the boy who cried wolf."

"I don't fake, Niece." Uncle Richard put on his glasses and leaned forward in the plastic seat to scrutinize yet another batch of racers. "Who do you pick this time?"

"I don't want to play anymore."

"You with this power, you don't want to use. Okay, okay. We go home now." He got up, brushed off the seat of his pants. "How much money you lose?"

I told him.

"Not too bad. You are cautious, like a crab."

"What about you?"

"I net about what you lose, so we just break even."

"It was fun."

"Yeah. More fun make money."

"Better than losing."

"You are funny, Niece. You expect to lose. No gambler's spirit."

We collected my uncle's winnings at the window and went

back to say good-bye to his friend, who was in a good mood because Shady Lady had performed so well. He let me give her a Milk-Bone and she licked my hand. She was just a normal dog, way too normal to be racing.

In the car I was already beginning to feel like an old hand, easing us around the lot to the arrowed exit. The little Toyota had its quirks, like the way it would slip out of gear between first and second, but I was learning to put that little extra pressure on the heel of my hand while pulling back. At the exit, as I waited for a window in the traffic I told myself, Watch it, Sally. You're not totally yourself yet. Your reflexes aren't up to snuff.

As if contradicting my thoughts, Uncle Richard said: "Good driver," and I looked at him and saw that his eyes were beginning to blur over again. He manipulated his seat back, loosened the parrot tie. "Okay, back to the movie. What happens to the good couple?"

I made the turn out of the parking lot and we were on our way back to town. "Well, they get together, you know, and it's obvious they're having an affair and their spouses are furious, but they don't care, they're happy. They deserve each other. She cuts his toenails in bed."

"What?"

"They meet in a hotel room and she loves him so much she says she wants to trim his toenails."

"Boy-oh-boy."

"What?"

"So French." The traffic was getting sluggish, it was four o'clock already, the start of rush hour. "Could you turn up AC, Niece?"

I fumbled around the dashboard. "It's already cranked up to high. Are you sure you're okay? I'll take you to the emergency room. Or we can stop somewhere and I can phone your doctor."

"I tell you, Niece, I'm fine now. And don't mention to your aunt, you hear me?"

"Uncle Richard, she's worried about you."

"Yeah, yeah, you just see, she die before me, she kill herself with worry."

I flicked on the radio. Warmer tomorrow, less humidity, and then some news about a guy who had set his girlfriend on fire and stuffed her charred body into the trunk of his car. He was being arraigned on charges of first-degree murder. I turned the radio off and we drove in silence. I thought my uncle had fallen asleep when he suddenly said: "It's funny, Niece, how you two, you and your sister, both turn out to be artistic type. Everyone always think one of you be a scientist, like your father."

"I know."

"You hear what they tried to do in PRC," Uncle Richard continued. "Remember the Four Modernizations! Everyone in the country is gonna be scientist at the turn of the century. Or businessman."

"Well, that's kind of sad. What about the artists and intellectuals?"

"You know your ma-ma always say you're made to be a surgeon. Because of your hands."

"Uh-huh."

"Whatever it was, we knew you were gonna be something special." My uncle cleared his throat and then he said, "You want to know about your father. I tell you this: if his luck is better he'd be very famous. You should be proud of an ancestor like that. You should live up to inheritance."

"Uncle Richard, I don't even like science."

"That's not what I mean. You have good genes. Brilliance of your father, tough character of your mother. No reason in the world to waste."

"Last chance," I said. We were passing the hospital with the palm trees.

My uncle ignored me. "I waste my life. You see me? I end up in Florida, who knows where this is, live on pension and disability, gamble away my money. But you, you could do anything. What an education you have. What connection. All this American stuff."

"Okay, okay."

We drove in silence for a while and then Uncle Richard sighed. "You are a good girl. Your aunt always tells me this, what a good girl you are. No more old-uncle lectures."

When we got back to the house I realized that there was no point in even trying out our movie story. We hadn't fooled Aunty Mabel at all. "Ding-ah!" she said, and gave me, what was for her, a dirty look. She made him go to bed immediately. There was already a pot of medicine bubbling on the stove.

19

Dear Fran:

Yep, this is the year we hit twenty-eight, two years till the big three-oh. Thanks for the birthday card. Still vegging away in the sun but I am drawing a little. My uncle has to go for some tests, but they think he's going to be okay. Talk to you when I get back.

Love,
Sally

While Aunty Mabel took Uncle Richard over to the hospital every day for a week, I ran what errands I could for her on foot: grocery shopping, bank, dry cleaning—kind of like I'd planned to do for Ma in New Haven before I got sicker. Suburban therapy. I trimmed the hedges in front of the house using giant power clippers borrowed from the pastel lady next door. Lally Escobar would have been proud. But my pièce de résistance was the garage. I covered it with a fresh coat of Antique Blue and even did a little scallop design on the eaves in off-white.

Aunty Mabel was impressed. "Like professional!" She'd finally forgiven me for the greyhound expedition.

I contemplated quitting New York City and becoming a house painter. It wouldn't be the worst of fates. I'd be a nice dumb girl with muscles.

Mornings, before the humidity got too mind-numbing, I

went out into the backyard with my sketch pad, like I had on Woodside Drive as a teenager. Only now I was doing automatic drawing, something I'd learned way back at RISD and never appreciated until recently. A trick to plumb the depths, like stream-of-consciousness writing. I'd started keeping the pad on my nightstand in the hospital, and more mornings than not, as soon as I'd wake up I'd start to scribble. These drawings were completely abstract, full of floaty pieces and jagged, broken-off lines. I had no idea what they were about.

Later in the day I drew from life. The vegetation in Florida had a wildness to it, things would grow rampant the minute you turned your back.

In the house I drew my uncle asleep on the sofa under the violet and kelly green afghan, the black cat a ragged splotch at his feet, his wire-framed half glasses splayed on the teeming coffee table before him. I drew my aunt, a tall thin shadow with no features, standing out on the patio shading her eyes and gazing out onto the back lawn, which was already beginning to look unruly again.

One lazy afternoon after lunch I was out on the patio, having given up on the St. Pete *Times* and wondering what was up with Mel, since I hadn't heard from him. My uncle's tests were finally over and I could hear him in the house on the phone to his bookie while my aunt was out grocery shopping. A few minutes later the sliding doors scraped open.

"Hey, Niece!" Uncle Richard was carrying a tray. He had made us iced tea in plastic glasses with watermelons on them, and there were plum candies in a cereal bowl. "I know your aunt uses special dish, but I can't find." He set the tray down on the frosted glass tabletop and pulled up the second chaise alongside mine. "Look at us, the two invalids! Not such a bad life, eh?"

I plucked a candy and undid the waxy wrapping. Most of

my American friends hated these. Who wanted salt and a hint of bitter when they expected sweet?

"I've only gained about ten pounds since I've been here," I said.

"Good, good! Men don't like too skinny, you know."

"I'm not looking for a man, Uncle Richard."

"Sometimes you don't look, you find." He sipped his tea and smacked his lips. "Lipton's mix. You don't tell your aunt. So what's wrong with that husband of yours? Why you get divorce?"

"It was time, Uncle Richard. We both changed too much."

Uncle Richard frowned. He knew this was bullshit.

The truth was, I'd run away.

Safety was what I was looking for, and safety was what I thought I'd found. Carey Acheson. The name had the comforting resonance of old money. Bourbon money, I found out later. We met at a lounge party at Brown when I was a freshman, dragged up the hill by a RISD roommate. My father had just died, I was listless in my classes, dreaming of I don't know what. Carey was a junior, a gangly slow-talking molecular biologist from Cincinnati, prep school all the way. That he was even attracted to me was amazing, given my own boarding school experience, although that summer on the Cape Fran and I had perfected our slumming in local bars, flashing the IDs that proclaimed that we were newly eighteen and of drinking age. That was back when eighteen *was* the drinking age.

The first time we made love Carey whispered in my ear: "I want to be where you've been." Goat's Head Soup was blasting to cover up the noise from his apartment mate's room next door, to cover up what we were about to do. I thought of Marty and Schuyler.

"You don't know where I've been."

Starfucker starfucker starfucker star.

He began unbuttoning my shirt.

Of course it was different from Monkey King. First, I knew what was going on. Mutual consent. And I liked it, a little. Although I wasn't lying when I said it hurt, much more than I'd expected.

At one point Carey asked: "Are you sure you're a virgin?"

I stared at the green light of the stereo. The music had gone off. "Of course I'm sure."

"It doesn't seem like it."

It's Carey, I told myself. A boy you know.

I shut my eyes and pretended I was my sister.

When it began to get light I put my clothes back on and walked back down the hill to my dorm. I was exhausted and queasy, but I had done it, taken the first step to breaking the spell.

My mother looked Carey in the eye and loved him. We drove down from Providence one Saturday night to have dinner with her. It was just the three of us, since Marty was away for the weekend. Ma and I were in the kitchen clearing up while Carey, seated at my father's place in the dining room, was smugly polishing off the Burgundy we'd brought. He knew he'd been a hit.

"It's a good thing he's *scientist*," said Ma. Then she turned on the tap full force so I couldn't say anything. It reminded me of when I was small and she'd be lecturing me about something in the car. Just as I was about to answer she'd say, "Not now, Sal-lee, I have to concentrate on this turn."

But this time I continued covering bowls of leftovers with plastic wrap until she turned off the water, and then I asked, "What does that mean, it's a good thing he's a scientist?"

"You are a dreamy artist," Ma said, pointing at me with a wet finger. She was wearing a navy-and-brown-checked dress for the occasion, and her cheeks were slightly flushed from the wine. I hadn't seen her look so good since Daddy's death. "Scientist is down-to-earth. This is a good match."

It was true that on the outside Carey was perfect—intelligent, well-bred, and much more handsome than I deserved. He'd sung in the church choir when he was little, attended two boarding schools (he'd gotten kicked out of the first one for growing pot in his closet, but I didn't tell Ma that). His parents were social register.

"Carey's so dignified," Ma told me. "I think your daddy would have liked him."

True to character, Carey got into every grad program he'd applied to but decided on Columbia because it was in New York City. We'd been going out a little over a year, and I knew this was the best shot I'd ever have. It was I who proposed to him, over a late breakfast between classes at a greasy spoon on Thayer Street, although he'd first put the idea into my head by implying that I'd like sex better if we were married. When he asked me about my own plans for school I said I didn't mind dropping out of RISD, I was sure I could get into Parsons.

"Well," he said. He shook his head and smiled. "I guess I could picture us." He put his fingertips on either side of my chin and brought my face close to his. "For the rest of my life, every morning waking up to this. Yes, I can see it."

That was about as romantic as Carey got. I remember that the waitress was clearing the table next to ours, making a huge clatter, and I felt like telling her to get lost, but that would have made things worse.

I never got around to applying to Parsons, I guess I was sick of school. I got hired as a pasteup artist at the first place I interviewed, a small advertising agency whose specialty was toy accounts. My first big break came when they gave me a brochure for a new game, something to do with the alphabet and the names of different dinosaurs. I stayed late every night for a week, rifling through everyone's type books, deconstructing letters into reptilian shapes. The result was a collage that got me promoted out of the pool to assistant designer.

Carey and I lived cozily in one of those rambling university housing apartments between Broadway and Riverside. After dinner, if he didn't have a night lab, he'd take me into his lap and surprise me with presents from gift shops in the neighborhood, odd and mysterious things, like a bowl made of lava, or brass earrings crafted by an Italian monk.

The sex got better, but what I loved most about Carey, what I missed about him after the divorce, was simply his physical presence. Nights, I'd wait for him. Even if I fell asleep, some part of me would still be waiting, anticipating the dip of the mattress, the heat of his body. I knew this always, even through my dreams.

The second phase of our marriage, what I later thought of as the yuppie phase, was marked by Carey receiving his doctorate and a tenure-track teaching position at Columbia. By that time my agency had expanded and merged with a Madison Avenue one, and I'd been promoted from designer to director. It's only now that I understand I was throwing myself into my job the way I'd thrown myself into painting at boarding school. I did it in order to numb the monster inside me, the one who wanted to murder Monkey King but instead ended up trying to murder herself.

We moved ten blocks downtown and over to Riverside into a fifteenth-floor co-op. One Saturday I started looking through my old boxes and found brushes and paints, which prompted me to set up a skeleton studio in the spare room that was supposed to be the nursery for our future progeny.

It's funny how all the big decisions I'd ever made were about escape. Maybe that's why I was able to make them so quickly—they were all basically the same decision. While Carey was away at a conference I went down to Charlottesville to visit Marty. God knows how she'd ended up there, something to do with an old boyfriend, like all her expeditions. I hung around in the old blues club where she was tending bar, Miss Exotic, the sleek mink in a pen full of mice. "What about your acting?" I asked.

"They let me sing here, sometimes. It's worth it. It's experience." She was smoking a lot, to roughen her voice. Give it character, she said. I remember this: she had an Ace bandage wrapped around her left wrist.

"What's that?" I asked.

"Coffee burn."

She was lying, but I didn't call her on it.

I returned to the city, dropped my bags in the living room, and stood there in the dark looking out at our spectacular view: the midnight blue Hudson with the George Washington Bridge stretching jeweled and serene to the north into New Jersey. But when I turned on the light I was surrounded by the oppressive furniture of my life: the dining room table with its six walnut chairs whose flowered upholstery took Carey's great-aunt twelve years to embroider, an elaborate teak sideboard with baroque scrollwork, ancient pale Oriental rugs, and four extremely ugly table lamps in the shape of bucking horses which Carey adored. The shelves were crammed with textbooks, lab notebooks, and boxes upon boxes of slides my husband had shot of the new kind of bacteria that had been the subject of his thesis. There was not a whisper of me in this room. I might as well have not been living there at all.

I played back the answering machine tape. There was a message from Carey, which I buzzed past. I changed into my painting clothes and went into my studio and started scraping away at an old canvas so I could start again. I was twenty-six years old and I wanted to start again.

You don't know how to give in. You don't know how to love like a wife has to love.

Maybe Ma had been right.

I came home from work the next day and saw my husband's suit bag draped over the sofa and his shoes side by side on the carpet, heard the shower running. I sat down in the living room and waited till he was on the way to the bedroom, towel wrapped around his waist.

"Christ! I didn't hear you come in." He padded toward me making wet footprints, and I thought he looked just like a dog, all brown-eyed and hopeful.

"We have to talk," I said.

"Okay, okay, let me put on a robe and my glasses. Did you get my message?"

"Uh-uh." He looked perplexed and then went to the bedroom while I steeled myself. When he came back I said, "I think we should try living separately for a while."

He looked absolutely floored and I felt cruel but continued.

"I've been thinking things over. I'm not happy, Carey. I don't know whether it's us or what. I think I need some time away so I can think things out."

"Sally. Dear." That was his only endearment, and a rare one. He sat down on the sofa beside me. "Being alone is going to let you think more clearly? I don't understand that."

"Well, it's true. Maybe not for you, but for me."

"We can see a marriage counselor. There's no need for hasty decisions."

"We can see a counselor, but I still want my own apartment. I just need to be by myself for a while. Is that so much to ask?"

"Look, I told you anytime you want, you can just quit working. Don't you want a baby? I thought you wanted a baby."

He sounded simpleminded. I gripped my hands into fists. "I'm not talking about ending anything, Carey. I'm talking about a break."

My husband looked down at the floor, noticed that his wing tips were out of alignment, straightened them, and then said, "Okay, Sally. If that's what you really want. We'll try it. How long were you thinking of?"

"Six months."

He folded his arms across his chest. "Do you think you can find a place to rent for six months?"

"I don't mind breaking a lease."

"You're sure of this now?"

"Yes."

"All right." He was being so reasonable I wanted to scream, pick up one of his damn shoes, hurl it across the room, and shatter a horse lamp. But I didn't. We just sat there in silence for a while and then he leaned over and said softly: "Sally." My stomach clenched.

"How can you want that now?" I asked him. "How can you even think it?"

"If we're going to be living apart—"

"No," I said. And it was as simple as that.

I was happy, at first. I went out with people in my office, who said, "God, Sally, we always thought of you as such the perfect little wife, and now here you are acting crazy like the rest of us." I played pool, started wearing my skirts a little shorter, but not too short. I was not the one with great legs. Ma called every night. Carey had been talking to her, he was such a responsible, generous husband, he loved me so much. After I hung up with Ma, I'd call Fran. "I feel so free," I said.

"Then stay free."

"I want rapture."

"Then hold out for it, honey."

My husband did not let me alone. He sent me roses, took me out to every new restaurant that opened in town. It was the courtship we'd never had. I gained weight, from those dinners and from all the beer I was drinking on pool nights. Carey said I looked terrific. "Could you be, maybe you're . . . ?" he asked me once.

"I'm not pregnant," I told him.

Six months turned into eight. Neither of us had done anything about counseling.

"I want you home," he said. We were at a Tex-Mex place in Chelsea, where the food was so beautiful, blue corn everything and every color pepper you could think of, that it seemed a pity to eat it.

"I can't," I said. "I need more time."

"I need a wife," he said. Nothing more. I should have known. I didn't hear from him for three weeks and then he called me at the office. "My lawyer will be in touch with you."

"Why?" Panic did not begin to describe how I felt.

"I want a divorce."

"Have you met someone?"

"I want a divorce," he repeated.

I thought: so it begins, you asked for it, Sally, here it is.

It never occurred to me to try to win him back.

When I told this to Uncle Richard, naturally I left out the sex parts. He kept saying, "Mmmhmm, mmmhmm" until I realized that he hadn't said it for a while. When I looked over he was fast asleep, his mouth open, the big belly rising and falling gently, one hand dangling childishly over the chaise as if he had dropped off in the middle of reaching for his glass of iced tea.

20

The calamondin was ripe, practically falling off the bush, and the day after my tête-à-tête with Uncle Richard I decided to pick them. In terms of worms and insects they had fared better than the grapefruit—every third one or so was salvageable. Aunty Mabel saw what I was doing and came out to help. It was around three o'clock, nearly one hundred degrees, and I was wearing Schuyler's T-shirt and shorts, now paint stained, my hair tucked up into a bun under the Derby Lane hat. As we were stooped there, working, we heard a car zoom by the house, stop, back up, and then the spray of gravel as it slid into our driveway.

"Plumber not supposed to come till tomorrow," Aunty Mabel said.

I didn't recognize the car, an old teal Oldsmobile, but why would I, I'd never seen Mel out of the hospital, I didn't know what he drove.

"Christ! You never called, you said you would call."

"Good to see you, too, honey." He was slightly smaller than I'd remembered, leaner, and as he removed his Ray-Bans I saw faint laugh lines that surprised me. The gold stud in his left lobe had been replaced by a pale sapphire that seemed especially picked for the Florida light. So neat, everything about him just so. A sight for sore eyes. He leaned to kiss me on the cheek and then he held out his hand to my aunt, who had come up, frowning, fruit gathered in the corner of her apron.

"Mel LaMonte. Mrs. Ding, it's a pleasure to meet you. Sally's told me so much about you."

My aunt fussed with her hair a little, pushed her own sunglasses up on top of her head, shook his hand. How could I have forgotten the pure charm of him, those manners that would have put any of the snide New York boys I'd hankered after as a teenager to shame.

I said, "We'd invite you in, but my uncle's resting."

"No problem. We'll go to the beach. Get your bathing suit."

I turned back to my aunt, who flapped her hand at us. "*Qu, qu, qu.*"

"But what about the fruit?"

"One more teeny-weeny bush, big deal, I can do."

He'd driven two days, stopping the night in North Carolina where a friend of his lived. He had a billion friends, something else I'd forgotten about him.

"How'd you know I was still here?" I asked him. "Why'd you take the chance and come all the way down without calling?"

"You're never going to believe this, but I ran into your sister."

"Marty?"

"On Chapel Street, in New Haven. She's kind of hard to miss, with that sling and everything. She was awfully friendly."

"I'll bet."

"I told you, honey, with her it's so much surface. With you, on the other hand—"

"Make a left here."

"Where are we going?"

"My favorite beach. But we kind of have to sneak in."

"I love it."

Mel was a graceful driver, maneuvering the tanklike Olds as adroitly as if it were my aunt and uncle's Toyota. This was his dad's car, he explained, he was sorry it didn't have air-conditioning. I didn't care. It was romantic with the windows rolled all the way down. He had his arm along the back of the seat, right behind my neck, and I could feel all the little hairs there rise in response. I felt like the kind of teenager I'd always wanted to be, the kind that Marty and Darcy had been. The radio was on, a song that was popular that spring, about a girl being the captain of a guy's heart. Mel hummed along and then he laughed. "I think I've heard this idiotic tune two thousand times since I left Connecticut. Why so quiet, Sal?"

"It's just so strange to see you out of the hospital. Like two worlds colliding or something."

"You look great," he said. "Like a Tahitian princess. Like that French artist, what's his name."

"Gauguin."

"Yeah. Gauguin."

"So how is everyone at Willowridge?"

"Well, the MHs are the same. There's this new guy, Colin, from England, who's into Gestalt and makes everyone play these games where you have to say stuff like: I am this Coke bottle and I feel empty. Everyone in our group is gone except for old Doug."

"What's up with him?"

"They want to discharge him, but he obviously can't live with his mom, and his father won't take him. And you know how he feels about halfway houses."

"So what's going to happen?"

"I have no idea. He's going to have trouble finding a job, that's for sure, with the way he looks now."

"How about Rachel?"

"Her parents packed her off to some spa in Germany."

"I can see it. She'll probably meet a rich Italian count there and live happily ever after. What about Lillith? Has anyone heard from Lillith?"

"Didn't you get the postcard?"

"What postcard?"

"She sent you a p.c. at Willowridge, I thought they'd forwarded it. She's out, honey, back at that place she was living before."

"That's good, I suppose."

"I thought about stopping by on my way down here, but I wanted to make good time. I guess I'll go see how she's doing when I get back."

We parked in the lot across from the Don Ce Sar. I'd asked Aunty Mabel which beach we had gone to the time we came down to visit as kids, and she told me that it had been turned into a resort on Gulf Boulevard. Private, for guests only. A couple of days ago I'd cased it out for myself. The main building was huge, sprawling, and pink, in a kind of faux–mission style, like something out of Disneyland. I'd parked on the street and peeked into the glass doors of the lobby. It had seemed almost deserted.

"You better lose those earrings," Mel said to me, so I took them off and put them in the glove compartment. I'd already changed into my Montgomery Ward bathing suit back at the house. When we strolled through the air-conditioned lobby in our ratty outfits, we got looks from the personnel, but I didn't care because I was with Mel. Somehow he inspired me to bend the rules. Out back, we took off our shoes and strolled along the water, digging our toes into the talcum white sand I remembered. Seagulls, smaller and scruffier and darker than their northern counterparts, stalked along the waves as we passed.

I could have walked all afternoon, but Mel had the sailing bug. We found a concession stand with boats for hire. He bargained with the guy. A Sunfish was too small, but it was late in the day, how about a Hobie Cat for half price? We would stay in sight, the guy didn't have to worry. The boat Mel picked was fancy with a striped sail—blue, red, yellow—and as we dragged it over the sand to the water he explained to me that what looked like skis on it were pontoons, for speed.

"How fast are we going to go, anyway?"

"Live a little, Sal. This isn't the real ocean, anyway, no one's going to be racing."

We cast off on a little foamy wave, and there was so much to do, Mel yelling orders and me trying not to get creamed by the boom, that by the time I looked back to shore the red and white umbrellas in front of the resort were the size of mushrooms. I could barely make out the people sitting sipping their drinks. The sea sped by us on both sides with a rushing noise. Mel peeled off his T-shirt and tied it around his waist, and I did the same, since there was nowhere to put anything, no little hooks or holes. He was right, this was a boat built for speed and nothing else, like the greyhounds with their stylized proportions.

"Isn't this fun?" Mel yelled.

"Are you going to be able to steer us back to shore?"

"What do you think this is?" He had his hand on the rudder. "C'mon, take the helm for a while." He pointed out the telltale flag, showed me how to gauge wind direction. I steered watching the tip of the mainsail, and he said, "No, no, keep an eye on the coast. That's the only way to really tell how you're doing. Wanna see something cool?" He handed me his sunglasses and then clambered over to the prow. I watched him ease himself over the right pontoon and, leading with his chest, grip onto it with both arms and then both legs, making himself an extension of the boat. The catamaran listed violently and I instinctively leaned back hard, to correct it. The waves washed over Mel's head, drenching his hair, and he blinked saltwater at me, grinning. The drops made his lashes starry. "Now you try it," he called.

"Are you crazy?"

"C'mon, darling."

"No way."

"I saw those biceps, honey. I know you're strong enough. I dare you."

He wriggled back onto the body of the boat and made his

way back to the tiller. I gulped a deep breath and went forward and tried to do exactly as he had done. Once I got my arms in the water I was nearly swept away by the force of it, and then and only then did I realize how fast we were actually going. I kept on, sliding inch by inch over the slick surface. I could see the headline in the St. Pete *Times:* "Ex-Crazy-House Inmate Drowns in Freak Gulf Accident." There was spray in my mouth, in my eyes. The muscles on the insides of my thighs, my forearms, had a life of their own, they were in a state of permanent contraction.

"You look like a figurehead."

"I don't give a shit what I look like." My Derby Lane cap spun off my head and was lost forever, and then I could feel the knot of hair at my nape loosening. I was damned if I'd let go to do anything about it. "Can you slow this thing down so I can get off?"

I heard him laughing, as if that were the funniest thing I had said so far. "Okay, now one arm and one leg."

"I'd like to live, if that's okay with you."

"Oh, Sal," he said, still laughing. "Oh, honey."

The boat guy reneged and charged us the price of a full afternoon.

"What the fuck?" Mel asked him.

"It's the stannard rate," the boat guy said, not looking at us. He was chewing gum, a kid, about the same height as Mel but thinner.

"We had an agreement," Mel said reasonably, but with a trace of threat, a tone I'd noticed that men used often and women almost never.

"You took out a Hobie Cat. That's thirty-five."

"You said eighteen, you little prick."

I was digging in the pocket of my shorts. "Just pay him," I whispered. "He's a jerk, but what can we do? We're not even supposed to be on this beach anyway." I passed him a ten and at first I thought he was going to bat it away but then, with an effort it seemed, he opened up his fist.

"Thanks, honey."

The boat guy smirked. Mel threw the money at him.

"You're still seven dollars short."

"So sue me."

As we walked away toward the Don Ce Sar I could hear the boat guy swearing at us and I had to exert pressure on Mel's arm so he wouldn't run back and pummel the punk's head into the sand.

Before we hit the road we stopped at a Dairy Queen and bought synthetic-looking sundaes in plastic cups. I offered Mel a taste of mine, which was chocolate on chocolate. He took a bite from my spoon and winced. "Jesus, that's sweet."

"Something I think you might need," I said. He was still mad at the boat guy.

"I hate that you had to pay."

"You don't have to be so macho. You paid for the ice cream."

"Uh-huh," he said, sounding crabby, but when I looked at him he was grinning.

It turned out he was staying at a friend of his mother's, who was away visiting her family up north. Her place was more than an hour away—actually closer to Ft. Myers than to St. Pete. Mel kept punching the radio buttons impatiently. "Christ. What do people listen to here? Isn't there a college station or something?" Finally we settled on classical: Aaron Copland, *Appalachian Spring*, which suited me fine. In fact, I was so warm and relaxed I slept most of the way.

The friend lived in a development of condominiums with an old glassy lagoon out front where canoes and little power boats were moored. It seemed no one was around but us. It was stuffy inside the house, and Mel went around opening windows. "Sorry about the mess. I just dumped my stuff here and headed up to your relatives'. I didn't even stop to take a shower."

Sitting on the sofa, we drank the Cokes in glass bottles we'd bought for an unheard-of fifteen cents each from a rattling machine at the gas station down the road. The Cokes were so small that we'd gotten three apiece. Mel propped his bony shins up on the coffee table. His legs were impossibly lean, the mahogany color of sunburned skin beginning to tan, covered with dark hairs, darker than Carey's. I couldn't stop staring at them. He had his arm around me and I didn't dare look at his face: the sharp angles, the narrow chin, the deep-set watchful eyes. A face that was hard to memorize, probably excruciating to draw, because it changed drastically with every passing mood. Of course I knew what was going to happen, had known the moment he got out of the car in my aunt's driveway.

I felt his fingers tickling the back of my neck, undoing the few bobby pins that were left. My hair fell down in a damp salt-smelling mass, and he pushed it back over my shoulders and away from my face. Then he slipped off my earrings one at a time and studied them cupped in his palm. They were my favorite, silver dangling fans from Carey, each pleat carved with a character in Persian. "Beautiful," he whispered, and laid them carefully on the coffee table, where they made a sweet little clack.

When he started to kiss me I thought: this is what's responsible for the propagation of the species, there's no way in hell of resisting this. He felt for my tongue with his, but slowly, without urgency. Then he stopped, pulled back, looked in my eyes.

"You like that, honey?"

"What do you think?"

"I like to hear it."

He slid his hand up my T-shirt and encountered my bathing suit, but that didn't faze him, he didn't rush, just stroked my nipples through the damp fabric. I shivered, although it was about 110 degrees in there. It had been way too long and I was feeling clumsy, like I might make a mistake, but we proceeded so slowly this was not a possibility. Every time he did anything new he'd ask, "Is this okay?" "Does this feel good, Sally?" It wasn't only the way his breath smelled, it was his skin, pungent and sweet, still adolescent.

When I reached down to touch him he trapped my wrist against his thigh, the most erotic gesture of the afternoon so far. "No. Not this time."

I was naked before he was. "You're lovely," he said. What did that mean? Was it part of his routine, what he said to all his girls the first time?

His fingertips brushed up on the inside of my thigh and then he slid himself down. I'd heard that there were some men who preferred this beyond all other acts of the flesh, and I was sure Mel was one of them, the way he slipped his hands under my ass and pressed his lips, his tongue to my other mouth with such expertise but also with an unexpected gentleness, almost a politeness. Getting to know you. Carey had done this rarely, and I didn't know enough to ask.

So much pleasure, like so much pain, is hard to bear. My mind did a little hop-skip, like someone was changing the reels, and I began noticing outside things, like how the couch smelled of decrepit dog, the dust motes swirling like atoms in the tunnel of late-afternoon sun coming in through a small window at the end of the room.

"Sally, are you still with me? Say something."

"Mmmhmm."

"Come on."

"I can't talk."

"I want you to talk. Tell me what you're feeling. At least if you like what I'm doing."

"You know I like it."

"Yeah"—working me harder with his tongue—"but I want to hear it. Say it, Sally. Do you like this?"

"Yes."

This is what I was thinking: never in a million years would I have believed him capable of such patience, restless old Mel, pacing the dayroom, jumping up and down on the sidelines in rec therapy when the therapist wouldn't let him play because he showed off.

"Okay," he said. "Now what do you want?"

"You know."

"Say it."

"I can't."

He pressed into me, so I could feel everything.

I was swimming with the seals, I was a seal, no one could see me.

"I want you inside," I said.

Still on top of me, he struggled out of his trunks, shimmied them down, kicked them off. And then there I was, lying back on the scratchy cushions, the insides of my thighs already aching from clutching the pontoon and now from holding him. I was making noise, I couldn't remember ever having made noise before. He was opening me up, more and more.

"What are you thinking of, honey?"

"You," I said.

"If you knew how much I *wanted*—" he said. "How I *waited*—" He pushed all those tangled strands of seaweedy hair back from my forehead.

I was gagging, trying not to.

"What's the matter?"

I couldn't answer.

"You're scaring me," he said. "Don't—" And then he began to come.

I am swimming with the seals, I thought, and just let it happen.

21

And after. The room was still, golden, each object stood out with great clarity. The late-afternoon sun through the blinds striping the green and brown rag rug, a purple and white yarn god's eye on the wall, framed photographs of babies and children propped in the bookcases. Mel beside me, eyes closed. His head was turned so that the sapphire caught a gleam. I could barely see his chest move.

"You asleep?"

"Nah," he whispered. He opened his eyes and pulled me to him. "You're a wild one. My wild wild baby."

"We sure made a mess of this sofa. I hope your mother's friend doesn't have a cow."

"She's an old hippie, it's cool. Say, honey, are you okay? What was that, anyway, at the end?"

"I don't know. It's never happened before. I guess I'm retarded, or something."

His eyes narrowed. "You're not retarded." Then, more gently, "Did you come?"

"Yes."

The hair under his arms was sparse and ginger colored and I touched there, lightly, to see if he was ticklish. He wasn't. In response, he picked up my left arm and slowly licked every single stripe, one by one. "Connect-the-dots," he said. "I shouldn't encourage you, but I've always found these awfully sexy."

"You wanted me at Willowridge?" I asked.

"Are you kidding?"

"Where could we have done it?"

"In the upstairs bathroom, you know, the one with the rug."

"Mmmhmm. Where else?"

"By the lake."

"I like by the lake."

"I knew you'd have beautiful skin."

"Why didn't you do anything?" I asked him. "Say anything?"

"I thought maybe you had a thing with Lillith. I wasn't sure."

"I wasn't sure either." Then I asked, "Am I your first Asian woman?"

"As a matter of fact, yes."

"You've just had white?"

"There was a black girl for a while, before Bethie."

"I always had white guys." Like two counted as always. Plus Daddy, but did he count? I didn't know.

When Mel dropped me off a little before midnight my aunt was waiting up. She said Uncle Richard had had chest pains all evening and the doctor had told him to take it very easy.

For the next four days, this was the routine: mornings, I kept my uncle company. We played gin rummy, watched TV, or I just sat in the rocking chair and read while he nodded off on the couch. Sometimes, asleep, he'd cry out, single syllables in Cantonese, startling me. "What were you dreaming?" I asked him later, and he shook his head. "Who knows? You remember your dreams, Niece?"

At lunchtime my aunt would take over. I'd pack a beach bag and go sit on the front curb to wait for Mel. The second time we'd snuck into the Don Ce Sar they'd really given us the hairy eyeball, so we'd started going to the public beach farther down the coast. We'd sun for an hour or two and then hightail it to the condo, grabbing a bite on the way—Denny's, McDonald's, Taco Bell, it didn't matter to us—and spend the afternoon in bed. Each time I came it was like a little of Monkey King was blotted away. Something that had never happened with Carey. "What was it like with your husband?" Mel asked me, and I had to answer: "He was rough."

"No wonder," Mel said.

"I wasn't really there," I said.

Mel was very good at me, but I did my own studying. The first time I made him come in my mouth his fingernails on my wrist drew blood. The feeling of power this gave me was unexpected, and I was careful with it, as I would have been with any new responsibility.

At dusk we'd get up to take the friend's canoe out on the lagoon. There were alligator warnings posted, and though it seemed to me that they must be more day creatures than night, I avoided trailing my fingers in the still water. Worse than possible alligators was the real presence of gnats and mosquitoes, which had mutated to monster proportions in this climate, as well as those strange squishy bugs I'd noticed when I was mowing the lawn. At the Cumberland Farms next to the gas station we purchased Deep Woods Off! and rubbed it all over each other's exposed parts.

Mel and I took turns steering. It was easy to catch a paddle in the murky weeds, or run aground in unexpected shallows, especially when dark had fallen completely and we were traveling only by starlight and moonlight, but we weren't headed anywhere in particular, and since there was no current, there was no danger. Mostly we just drifted, drinking the bottled Cokes we'd gotten addicted to—I could swear Coke was sweeter in the South—and talk and smoke. Sometimes we'd mix rum in with the Coke.

"You have the sexiest fingers," Mel said once, when we were passing the bottle.

"My piano teacher used to say I had the widest hand span of any child she'd ever taught."

"I didn't know you played the piano."

"Badly."

I told him about the after-dinner recitals where Mimi sang Chinese love songs in a piercing falsetto. Xiao Lu, who was studying the violin, had a repertoire of fancy pieces, starting with "The Flight of the Bumblebee," which I suspected he played much more slowly than he was supposed to, so he would be sure not to make any mistakes. A lot of the music was modern, so that it was hard to tell if he was making a mistake at all if you didn't watch Aunty Winnie's face.

I never played as well as I did when I was alone, and I didn't dare look up for fear of meeting the frozen polite expressions of the guests. What were they really thinking? Unlike Xiao Lu, I played faster than I was supposed to, to get it over with. Afterward there was always a surprised silence, as if the audience hadn't really expected it to end. "So good, so good," the grown-ups would murmur, and my mother's voice would rise over them all—"Oh, no, she's terrible, really."

After me came my sister, the comic relief. She'd announce her piece—"Indian War Dance"—and then pound it out as forcefully as possible. The applause for her was more enthusiastic. "She doesn't practice" was my mother's only comment on Marty, as if that were the only reason she wasn't a musical genius.

The only guest who seemed to prefer my playing to Marty's was Mr. Lin, a friend of Daddy's who lived by himself in the top floor of a rickety house in a bad neighborhood downtown. Mr. Lin was an artist who had been chased out by the Communists. Ma said he was too sad to paint anymore.

Once Mr. Lin took our family to an exhibition of contemporary Chinese painting at Yale. "Which one you like best?" he asked my sister and me. Marty chose a cat chasing a butterfly. I looked awhile, and then selected a very long horizontal painting of grasses bent by the wind. "Why you like?" he asked me.

"It looks like writing."

"Pau-yu, your elder daughter has the heart of the philosophers," Mr. Lin said.

One afternoon Mel said he was going to make me lasagna with white sauce. "White?" I asked.

"Northern," he told me. "At my dad's restaurant they don't serve anything else."

We went to the Winn-Dixie and Mel fretted over their selection of olive oils and ricotta. Then he banned me from the kitchen and I curled up on the brown dog-smelling couch to sip Chianti and watch the six o'clock local news, which had replaced talk shows as my new addiction.

"God, that's so much food," I said when it was all laid out.

"Well, you ought to eat. My mom would faint if she saw you."

Besides lasagna, there was pompano fried in beautiful little crisps and risotto and a salad with three kinds of lettuce and, of course, garlic bread. Zabaglione for dessert. Espresso, black and unnervingly strong.

Mel came over to my side of the table, knelt down, and lifted up my shirt. "Hmm. Looks like an expansion of at least three belt holes."

"That tickles."

"What are the chances of your staying the night?"

"I don't know. I think I better go back."

"You sure?"

"Don't you think we should do the dishes? Or maybe I should, since you cooked."

"Should you?" He slid his hand up the leg of my shorts and stroked. "Did you know that garlic is considered an aphrodisiac?"

On the stereo Eric Clapton was playing the blues.

I thought of plausible lies to tell Aunty Mabel.

*   *   *

We stuck one of the candles we'd bought at the Winn-Dixie into the empty Chianti bottle. It was a cliché, but like many clichés I'd never had a chance to try it.

"It isn't going to work, you know," I said to Mel. He was inside me but we weren't moving, he was blowing on the little hairs that grew along my temples, the ones Marty used to call sideburns when she was making fun of me.

"Who said anything about work? We're screwing, honey."

"You know what I mean."

"Yeah, okay, I know what you mean."

"What about your girlfriend? The one with the rabbit coat?"

"Bethie? She's history."

"But there must be others."

"Christ, Sally, you really know how to kill a mood."

"Sorry."

"And you're not concentrating. Concentrate on this." He began again, and I forgot what more I was going to say.

Afterward he whispered, "I'll miss you, you know."

"That's what you said at Willowridge. That time in the kitchen."

"Well it was true then. And it's true now."

I didn't tell him that what had kicked me into coming this time was my father's face above me in the dark, his straining Monkey King scowl. And he stayed, that ghost, in the bed with us. As Mel twitched into sleep I lay there counting each breath in, each breath out.

I was awake at dawn and drawing. I hadn't brought my pad with me but managed to find an old composition book in a desk drawer and took the liberty of ripping out several blank pages. Mel found me at the kitchen table bearing down so hard I'd torn holes in the paper.

"Hey, hey," he said, his voice husky with sleep.

I stopped and looked down at what I was doing. It was stupid and crude. "Okay," I said and ripped the page up into the smallest pieces I could and brushed them off the table so they snowed onto the linoleum. The gesture was familiar but I couldn't remember why.

"Whadja do that for?"

I didn't answer but picked up the other drawings and tore them up too. I could feel Mel standing in the doorway, waking up, watching me.

"You feel like explaining or are you just going to sulk?"

"It's my pathetic attempt to make myself feel better."

"Feel better about what?"

"The fact that I can't paint anymore. Or draw, for that matter."

"I've seen your stuff."

"What you saw was shit. Art therapy shit. Anybody can be a star in a loony bin."

"What I think is pathetic is you feeling so sorry for yourself." He turned away. "I'm going back to bed."

I made tea and drank it sitting out on the dock. Behind me I could hear doors opening, cars starting, people going to work, beginning their normal day.

It was amazing how up until now I had almost been able to fool myself that if I worked hard enough, I could become an artist again. But it took something I didn't have anymore. Going through the motions was a futile exercise. I had lost that peculiar quality of concentration needed to tap into the soul. That was the price for being allowed to live after having swallowed thirty-six tranquilizers. Or perhaps the truth was I had lost it way before that, at RISD, and I had known it then. That was the real reason I'd dropped out, gotten married.

I had my Swiss Army knife with me, but it was back in the bedroom with Mel. There was a paint scraper lying in the bottom of one of the rowboats, and I retrieved it, wiped the blade off on my shirt, and tested it on the inside of my wrist, where the impressions of Mel's nails were still printed from last night like sickle moons. Then I moved higher until I found an open spot, closed my eyes, and flicked.

"When was your last tetanus shot?" Mel asked. He was furious, I could tell, although his voice was even. We were in the car, driving down the coast to a place where we'd heard brown pelicans congregated.

"I'm fine, I promise. It's just a scratch. Anyway, I thought you liked my scars."

"If this is a game, I'm not playing, Sally."

"Don't flatter yourself. I've been doing it since I was fourteen."

"You sound proud of yourself."

"I'm not. Why're you being such a pill? You're the one who brought it up. I wasn't even going to mention it."

"I think you're mixing me up with someone, Sally."

"Oh, so now we're going to play group therapy. Who might that be? My father?"

"You said it, not me."

"Maybe you should drive me home. I'm worried about my uncle, anyway."

"We can turn around anytime you want."

I didn't say anything.

When we were almost to the beach he said: "Did you know that Catholic suicides can't be buried in consecrated ground?"

"Are you trying to make me feel worse?"

"I'm trying to tell you a story. A cousin of mine blew his brains out. My aunt asked around at various Protestant churches to see if they'd take him as a member posthumously. No luck."

"I want to be cremated."

"Well, that's what they did with Joey. His mom and dad flew to Italy and threw his ashes into the Mediterranean."

Strewing ashes was what I was thinking about as we fed the

birds. The pelicans ate only fresh fish, but you could buy plastic bags of meal at a shack by the road for the gulls and terns. A very touristy thing to do, I saw other people with bags, but I didn't care. Not only did I want to be a regular tourist, I also wanted to be faceless, anonymous, not special. I was sick of being special.

The birds liked Mel. It was the way he flung the meal, so that it fell in an ostentatious arc, easily visible.

"They're so ugly," I said.

He pulled me so that my face was in his shoulder, so that no one could see me crying.

"Yes," he said. "I guess they are."

"Do you really want to know what I think about in bed?" I asked

It was our last night on the lagoon. Mel was steering and I was resting, slouched in the front of the canoe, knees up and my own paddle balanced on top of them. His voice came from behind me: "You know that stuff I talked about in the hospital, about my older cousins in the garage?"

"Uh-huh."

"Well, there's a part I left out. They jerked off on me while they were sticking the pins in."

"Jesus. Are you sure?"

"Of course I'm sure. I didn't realize what was going on until I was older. I used to think they were peeing. That was bad enough. The point is, I used to think about it during sex. In this very fucked-up way, it used to turn me on."

"Why didn't you tell that to the group?"

"I bet they're some things you didn't tell the group."

"So do you still think about it?"

"Sometimes. Does that upset you?"

"No," I said. "I guess you know what I think about then."

"Yes." The way he said it made me realize that not only did it not upset him, he got off on it a little.

"The trouble with us is that we know too much about each other." I leaned over into the swamp, slid my arm in right up to the elbow. We were in a relatively deep passage and I could feel the variation in temperature, from body to lukewarm to a hint of chill. Mel made a crunching noise but I ignored him. I was remembering that dream I'd had at Willowridge, of the black water that was going to reflect something unspeakable back at me.

It was quiet, too quiet. Mel tapped the bottle of rum and Coke on my back. I knocked back a long swig and felt it almost immediately.

I said: "You know all I can pay attention to in the news are crime stories. Violent crime. The more violent, the better. Is there something wrong with me?"

"No, honey. It's drama you miss."

"What do you mean?"

"Willowridge was one big soap opera. You're going to have to get used to the mundanity of daily life."

"I'll show you dramatic." Without thinking about what I was going to do I began stripping, pulling off my T-shirt—I wasn't wearing a bra—and then my shorts and underpants. Then I stood up in the prow, the boat jerking abruptly with the movement. Mel watched me, smiling, until I took a breath, and jumped.

Despite its murkiness, the water was surprisingly clean feeling, although as I surfaced I could feel my toes dragging a bit of seaweed. Or was it an alligator? *Live body overboard.* Let them get me, I thought.

Mel was leaning right above me. "Are you *nuts?*"

"Yes," I said, and moved several feet away from the canoe. It was like I couldn't stop myself. Treading water, I threw back my head and screamed up into the dark gray-green sky fringed with overhanging trees. Screamed once, got the echo, and screamed again. And again.

"Get back in here, Sally." Mel sounded a million miles

away, or maybe it was just the water in my ears. I swam over and he helped me aboard, a precarious and clumsy process which slopped a lot of water into the canoe. "You were afraid of drowning in the Gulf, but you don't give a shit about being Jaws bait," he said.

"I don't know why I did that."

"Sshhh." He put his arms around me from behind, and we sat there like that until I stopped shivering.

"Feel better?"

"Guess so."

"You probably needed to do that, although I wish you hadn't picked alligator swamp." He took off his own shirt, patted me dry, helped me get dressed.

I said: "I'm sorry about the other morning."

"You don't have to apologize to me."

"I haven't slipped up since I left Willowridge. D'ya think there's a support group for that kind of thing?"

"You mean like Self-Mutilators Anonymous?"

"I guess not. Wouldn't be a pretty sight, anyway. The meetings, I mean." I thought of Douglas.

We headed back, neither of us talking, although we kept passing the bottle. I knew I was getting drunk and I didn't care. I could smell and feel the swamp drying on my skin and hair, that high stagnant odor like the Katzes' goldfish pond. When we tied up at the dock Mel said we'd better bail out the canoe, so we found a couple of old paint cans and scooped methodically until he laid his hand on my arm.

"Look."

The sky above the trees where we'd just emerged was alive with silver streaks.

"Meteor shower," Mel said.

"Wrong time of year."

"Nonetheless."

In a minute it was over. The regular stars shimmered demurely in the dense black.

"Did you make a wish?" Mel asked me.

"No. I didn't have time to think."

He put his arm around me and we stood there on the dock watching the sky for a while, waiting for something else to happen.

22

The restaurant was dim and for once just the right coolness, not the usual bone-chilling freeze I'd come to expect in Florida. Amber cut-glass tumblers clinked discreetly as ice water was poured into them from a silver pitcher, a relief compared to New York City restaurants, where you felt as if you were at a very loud nerve-racking party with everyone else in the room. Our waitress's name was Slim, which I thought was a strange name for a woman until my uncle explained that Slim was what you called anyone who was tall. Like Red, for redheads. Down South, nicknames stuck. In my class at RISD there had been a girl from Alabama named Shug Maloney, Shug short for Sugar.

It was my last night in Florida, which also happened to be my birthday. I was wearing the hibiscus print dress Aunty Mabel had bought for me although I had a cardigan on over it because I was self-conscious about my newest scar. My hair was up in a bun like Nai-nai's. The trick, I'd found, was to do it right after you got out of the shower when your hair was still wet. I could feel the chill of the jade point on my nape.

"I'm a lucky man," Uncle Richard pronounced. "Out on the town with the two handsomest women in St. Pete." He was looking the healthiest he had in days and dressed like a real high roller—gleaming black oxfords, gold cuff links, but not, I was relieved to see, the parrot tie. It made me feel less guilty about the mornings I'd missed with him. He squinted at me behind his glasses. "So who you think she looks like?" he asked my aunt.

Aunty Mabel considered. "She used to look like her ba-ba. Now she looks a little like her Aunty Ching-yu." She explained to me: "My second-to-oldest sister. Serious face, always thinking." I tried, unsuccessfully, to remember which face that was from Nai-nai's old albums.

"And what happen to this sister?" My uncle picked up a roll and reached for the butter dish as my aunt deftly slid it away from him.

"She married a merchant's son. Three children."

"Merchant's son," said my uncle. "That means rich. We gotta find a rich man for Sally, support her be an artist. That Mel, is he rich?"

"Not exactly."

"He's a good boy, though."

My uncle had met Mel only once, when he'd come by to pick me up and Aunty Mabel had persuaded him to come in for lemonade. They'd talked basketball. Everyone was polite. I knew Ma would hear every detail of my bad behavior, how I hadn't even come home for the last two nights.

That morning I'd watched Mel shaving naked, angling into the bathroom mirror, one foot up on the edge of the bathtub, as classical a stance as any marble Greek warrior. "You could drive back with me, you know," he said.

"My plane ticket's nonrefundable."

"Maybe I'll just have to make a pit stop then."

"What are you talking about?"

"Well, there was this gas station attendant in Savannah."

"How old is she?"

"You're jealous," he said, reaching behind to wrap his arm around me. "I like that."

On this, our last morning together, we drove into St. Pete to a consignment shop and he bought me a birthday present, the cardigan I was wearing, black with pearl buttons in the 1930s style I liked. Then we got some postcards and sat in a coffee shop to write them.

"Which should we send to Doug?" Mel asked me. "The manatees?"

"How about the alligator wrestling one?"

"Excellent choice."

"The manatees go to Lillith."

"You wanna do it?"

"Sure."

I wrote: "This is how Mel and Sally spend their time in Florida, swimming and getting fat. We hope you are too."

Mel was hunched over, scrawling something complicated to Douglas. The errant hair like an exclamation point was standing up. I reached over and brushed it down. "Your gas station lady won't recognize you, you're so dark."

"Nothing compared to you."

"I could stay here forever."

"I know what you mean, honey."

"What's going to happen? I mean, when we get back."

"I'm going to summer school and you're going back to New York City to your advertising job."

"What about us?"

"We'll talk."

I knew, then, for certain, that it was over. Something was over.

After a while I asked: "What are you telling people? About the hospital, I mean."

"The truth. It's kind of hip to have a screw loose, don't you think? Especially if you're an artist."

"Not if you're a graphic designer."

"Yeah, yeah." He grinned and then leaned over and whispered: "You know what I'm going to be thinking about every single second I'm on the road?"

"Yeah, right."

"Swear on my mother's honor. You are unquestionably the sexiest woman I have ever known."

"Out of how many? You are so full of it."

"Admit it, Sally. You know we're a match."

And it was true, driving back to my uncle and aunt's, I wasn't sure whether I could let him go. I had an image of us pulling up in front of the house and him asking one last time if I wanted a ride up and I'd say yes and run in and pack in two minutes and we'd be off, speeding up I-95 where it would grow cooler and cooler, back into early spring like a time warp. Somewhere in the Carolinas we'd pick up a six-pack and check into a No-Tel motel and mess up the sheets. But he didn't ask, and after we'd kissed good-bye he let me off at the corner and said, "I'll miss you, honey." As he pulled away, honking the horn wildly, I felt something extreme lift from me, and I was almost relieved, as if this were a signal that I could go on with my life, although I knew I was going to be sad later.

Uncle Richard wanted lobster, but my aunt took the menu from him and gave the waiter directions: scrod, broiled, margarine, no sauce. Uncle Richard pointed at me. "Niece, you order anything you want. Shrimp, huh? They have them delicious here, jumbo prawns, you'll like."

"I think I'll have the lobster."

My uncle leaned back, unbuttoning his vest. "So how old are you, Niece? Twenny-eight? What was I doing when I was twenny-eight? I got my accountant's degree, thought I was a big shot. Impress your aunt, huh?"

"Ding-ah!"

"Work extra hard to impress this lady. She's so sophisticated, from good family. I wear flashy clothes, doesn't impress her. She wants to know how much money I have in the bank." My uncle hoisted his glass of Perrier. "To my niece on her twenny-eighth birthday. Prosperity, long life, and good fortune."

When our entrées came I broke off a claw of my lobster and put it on my uncle's plate. Vertical lines appeared in Aunty Mabel's forehead but then she said: "Okay, it's special occasion."

Daddy hadn't believed in birthdays. New Year's is everyone's birthday, he always said. In fact we never did anything for his, which was sometime in September, I don't even know the date. On hers Ma would get a call from Aunty Mabel. For her daughters she'd buy bakery cake, devil's food with chocolate frosting for me, and two weeks later, strawberry cream for Marty. Every year Daddy would say the same thing: "Remember, this is not a day to celebrate yourself. This is a day to remember your mother's pain and your father's sacrifice."

Ma had called just before we left the house. She wanted to know what time my flight was arriving, when she should pick me up at Connecticut Limousine. I told her I was going straight to my apartment in New York.

"Oh," she said. "Well, happy birthday. You think I forget?"

"Thanks," I said.

"With your sister home, maybe we can have double celebration when you get back."

There were gifts. A package from my mother, fancy stationery, cream-colored with my name embossed: Sarah Collisson Wang, I guess to replace the dozen boxes of Sarah Wang-Acheson stationery she'd ordered for me when I got married. From my aunt and uncle, a set of Chinese calligraphy brushes in a satin box. I fingered the bristle: fox, sheep, goat. The sheep was the softest. Good for ink, of course, or watercolor.

"*San zhi mao bi*," I said.

"Three Chinese brush." Uncle Richard chuckled. "Very good."

Nothing from my sister, but it had been years since we'd exchanged presents.

After dinner we drove into Tampa to play bingo at the Seminole reservation. Over a thousand people, mostly over the age of sixty, were seated in numbered plastic chairs at long tables with cards and good-luck charms lined up in front of them. They used monster highlighters to daub each number as it was called out. Except for the caller, it was as still as an examination room. When someone won they'd raise their hand or say "bingo" very quietly, and the whole room would go up in a sigh.

Was anyone even having fun?

Bingo at the slot machines was depressing in another way, because you could lose so much hard cash so fast. "Not your game, Niece," Uncle Richard said finally. "Like basketball not my game. Too bad we never go back see the puppies run."

"Next time, Uncle Richard, I promise."

What I couldn't tell him was that my power wouldn't work if I tried to do it on purpose. Luck could be chased away if you took it too seriously, like those silent bingo players. The trick was to concentrate without focusing, to let yourself feel without understanding.

When we returned to the house I went out to the patio to smoke. Before lighting up I just sat there, staring into the dark, breathing the now familiar mix of jasmine and honeysuckle. Then I saw the mother armadillo. She came lumbering through the grass to the edge of the pool of kitchen light, a homely plump hunkering shape like one of those old-fashioned rag dolls where limbs, head, and torso are each a separate stuffed piece. Her tiny black elephant eyes caught the light and she squinted. I don't think she saw me, but she must have sensed something alien because she froze before backing off into the darkness.

When I went back into my room to pack, the tiger kitten appeared out of nowhere like cats do and followed me, jumping up onto the unused bed next to the stuffed white cat. Aunty Mabel knocked at the open door. She was carrying six gemlike jars, sealed with wax and labeled. It was the calamondin made into jam.

"Here, you take. Give some to your ma-ma, too. She like sour thing." She set the jars in a row on the bed next to the kitten, who matched them in color. I imagined my aunt bent over the stove stewing the fruit on one of those sultry after-noons Mel and I had spent in bed.

"I'm sorry I haven't been home much lately, Aunty Mabel."

She waved her hand. "You marry too young," she said, as if that explained it in some way. She watched in approval as I wrapped each marmalade jar in an article of clothing as care-fully as I had packed Lillith's food sculptures in her socks. "You know, back when your ba-ba died I was so worry about you."

"I was okay," I said. "I had friends."

"Friends not like family. Your ma-ma and I discuss this. What if we were in China? What if you grow up surrounded with relatives, like you're supposed to? Maybe you both be happier, you and Marty. And your ba-ba is such a sad man. You know how his father die?"

"No."

"He commit suicide."

"I didn't know that."

My aunt was silent for a moment, and I saw from her face how difficult it was for her to say what she was about to say. "I know about this thing your ba-ba did when you were small. I know what he did, Sal-lee. Terrible."

For a moment I couldn't speak and then I said, "Incest." I said it to hear the word out loud, and to make sure we were talking about the same thing.

"This is rare in China. Chinese adore their children."

"Ma told you."

"She call me before you come down."

"She doesn't believe me."

"Don't be so sure." My aunt lowered herself onto the unused bed, carefully, as if her joints ached. "If I know then, I would tell your ma-ma send you girls come stay with us."

"I wish you had."

"You know I can't have children," my aunt said. "In China that's a big big tragedy, my husband can divorce. Well, you know your uncle, when we find out he says we can get cats. Always joking. And he says I have you and Mar-tee, I shouldn't be sad." My aunt began running her fingers over the satin spread, smoothing it out. "I remember when you were born. I was there."

"I thought you were in New York."

"No, no. Yes, I was still at Grumman, your uncle and I just start to date. One day at work I get a call from your ba-ba— 'Your sister says she wants you. I pay your airfare roundtrip.'"

"Was she in labor?"

"Not yet. You were two weeks late. He call me the day you were due. I lie to my boss. I tell him my mother is dying. It's bad luck, I know, but I can't think of anything else. All the way, on the plane, I worry that I'm too late, she's going to have baby without me. And then your mother came to meet me at the airport. Can you believe? So big, like this, all by herself she drives the car."

There were pictures in the album. Ma like a beach ball, dark lipstick, her hair perfect.

"I sleep in the nursery, where they were going to put you, yellow and pink and blue, all the little diapers folded on the bureau. And so many stuffed animals, I guess they already know you liked stuffed animals."

I buckled my bag shut and sat down on my bed, across from my aunt.

"Your ma-ma and I go to the movies every day. Fifty cents, can you imagine. We both like James Dean, Natalie Wood. You like Natalie Wood too, I remember. Sometimes we see the same movie three times. Always, people stare at your mother. Not many pregnant Oriental women in Monterey. She has only one outfit that fit her, a blue jumper. You remember May in Monterey, how beautiful. We are walking on the beach when the pains come. Your ma-ma is so stubborn, she sits down and doesn't move. I'm so scared, I leave her on the rocks and run to the house and call your father at school. He comes and takes us to the hospital. The doctor says she's slow, it's going to take a long time, he wants to give her this medicine and that medicine." My aunt's eyes were shiny. I could see that she would have gladly undergone that kind of pain, and much worse. "Your ma-ma says no, she doesn't want any drugs, but then she cries and cries and I say *Mei* you must be brave and she says you don't know what it's like, this *yang gui* doctor is going to let me die. This scares me so much, you know your ma-ma is always the cool one, always knows what to do. She wants Chinese remedy, so I go to grocery store and buy brown sugar and stir it in hot water. At the end, when it's the worst, she curses your father, calls him disgusting peasant, even worse names. In Chinese, lucky, so the doctor doesn't understand.

"You were a long baby, twenty-three inches. Your ma-ma has a private room, third floor, overlook the ocean. She has you in the bassinet by the bed. 'Look, *Jie*, such a pretty room they gave me!' She can see the cliffs from her windows, all the flowers. She can hear the seals. And I think, What a lucky mother. What a lucky baby."

"I'm sorry, Aunty Mabel."

"Sorry? Why be sorry? True, she's not like my baby sister anymore. Doesn't need me now. Your Nai-nai comes up from San Diego on the bus. A lot of hair, she says. It's a good sign. But I am so stupid, I almost lost my job. I got back to the house and remember I must call New York, my boss. So I do. My boss asks me, How is your mother? and I say everything is all right, my mother is going to live, we are all very happy."

Uncle Richard came to the airport to see me off, sitting by himself in the backseat like the wooden laughing Buddha my parents had brought back from Taiwan, making comments on the roads, how all the repair work they'd been doing hadn't helped the traffic any. We were barely in time, and as we rushed toward the boarding gate, my uncle pressed something folded into my palm. "For good luck, eh? No, no, don't open now." I tucked it into the pocket of my jeans, having already caught a glimpse of Ben Franklin.

"G'bye, Slim," my uncle said, laughing at his own joke. "I think I start calling your aunt that too."

All of a sudden I couldn't think of anything to say, and there was no more time. "*Xie xie*," I said. "*Zai jen.*" Not *adieu*, but *au revoir*, see you again. All languages make that distinction.

"You hear," Uncle Richard said to my aunt. "She has northern accent, just like her ba-ba."

Part
Four

23

At La Guardia I decided to treat myself to a cab, although I had hardly any luggage, just the black bag. I contemplated what I was returning to: clustering traffic, glowering skyline, the nervy discontented hum of the city and its denizens. How had my Aunty Mabel felt, landing here alone for the first time, the phone number of a friend of Nai-nai's tucked into the flap of her purse, on her way to Penn Station to take the train to Long Island for her job interview? I could feel my own adrenaline as we pulled onto the FDR Drive.

My street was deserted and creepy, I'd forgotten the cracked sidewalks, the stairwell of my building shabbier than I'd remembered, with its worn marble steps and peeling black-and-white honeycomb wallpaper. I could smell acrylic fumes from the loft of the other artist, a sculptor, who lived on the first floor. When I'd undone all three of my locks, including the police one, and swung open the heavy steel door, I saw a space that was plain, even homely, smaller than I'd remembered, but in some ineffable way soothing to my soul. I'd painted the walls of my studio stark white and hung them with only Japanese prints and a blotchy green and violet painting I'd been working on before I left. Somewhere in the still, stale air, beyond the first whiff, I could smell that blend of turpentine and linseed oil that used to intoxicate me.

I walked over to the north bank of windows, lifted away the dusty sheet, and looped it around the nail I'd fixed to the wall for that purpose. Across the street two men were in a huddle in front of the candy store. A young Hispanic woman strolled by in heels and purple spandex, walking an old English sheepdog, and they both turned to look. I shoved one of the windows up as far as it would go and New York blew in. Exhaust, warm pavement, and weeds from Tompkins Square Park.

There were three phone messages. The first one was from my old boss—"Sally, please call me as soon as possible, I have an offer I think you'd be interested in." The second was from my sister. "Sa, are you there? Call me, I'm at home." The tinny girl voice on the last message I didn't recognize right away. "Hey there. Thought I'd give you a try. I'm out in the real world, sort of, at the place I was last winter. Things are going okay, though I wouldn't wish my last stay at State on my worst enemy. Although I'm the first to admit that I might be my own worst enemy. Okay, guess you're not there. I'll try you again sometime." She didn't leave a number. I wonder if Mel had beat me up north, as he'd boasted he would, whether he had dropped by to see her on his way home. On the tape Lillith sounded almost normal, as she had on her best days in the hospital.

I took one of the jam jars out of my bag and went downstairs and knocked on the door of the sculptor, whom I'd asked to collect my mail while I was gone. "You been to the Caribbean or something?" he asked, referring to my tan. I told him Florida. "Well, your timing was good," he said. "At the end of March they turned the heat off for two weeks and of course we had that record cold spell. And the water pressure's been completely fucked up, although at least it's hot now." I could tell he wanted to get back to work and I didn't exactly feel like having a long conversation so I asked him for my mail. He handed me a shopping bag of what looked like mostly junk. I gave him the jam as a thank-you and went back upstairs.

The water pressure, as the sculptor had warned me, was not what it used to be, and while I waited for the rust to run out of the kitchen tap I put on a tape of Chopin scherzos. Fran used to say that the scherzos reminded her of cats chasing each other over a bare floor. She wasn't too fond of the recording I had, according to her the pianist was a little too showy, but I had always loved it. I put on water for tea and lay down on my floor mattress and listened until the kettle shrilled.

I'd left when it was bitter cold, and now I needed to figure out where I'd stored my fans. As I drank my tea without honey I noticed a sheet of memo paper taped to the refrigerator. I had to squint to make out my tiny sick scrawl:

> join gym
> eat better
> find out specs for group show
> call Reik center and get therapist?

I had accomplished none of these things. I ripped the paper off the fridge, turned it over, and made a new list in bold handwriting:

> call people
> call work
> groceries
> drugstore

My mail contained threatening notices from Con Ed and the phone company, but nothing from my landlord—I'd kept up with my rent at least. There was an enormous square envelope of heavy stationery that looked like a valentine—I could see that the card inside was red. It was, of all things, a wedding invitation. Silver curlicues on crimson:

> *Mr. and Mrs. Winston Woo request the honor of your presence at the marriage of their daughter Grace Loo-yi to Mr. Jian Lu.*

Good God, Xiao Lu was getting married. Wimpy Xiao Lu who had once eaten an inchworm and two ants under the threat of being hung upside down by his ankles from the top bar of our swing set. Who was this girl who was willing to spend the rest of her life with him? A sweet one, for sure. Sweet as pie. One who wouldn't laugh when he screwed up his face before bursting into tears, that is, if he still burst into tears.

I felt a pang of jealousy.

Marty wasn't home. "She go back to New York for a couple of days," Ma told me, but when I called the old number, there was no answer. "When you coming to New Haven?" my mother asked, and I told her I'd be there for my appointment with Valerie the day after tomorrow. "Good," Ma said. "You come over afterward. I make special birthday dinner for you and your sister."

On the phone I told my boss a little about what had happened, using the term nervous breakdown, although I didn't mention Willowridge. She asked me how I felt now.

"Better," I said.

"Well, since you left things have been exploding around here."

"What do you mean?"

"I can't talk. Let's meet for lunch."

At O'Neal's, two blocks from the office and exactly the kind of cavernous noisy New York restaurant I hated, she told me that the agency was in the process of being acquired yet again. She had decided to leave and start her own company. "I found a space in SoHo. Two thousand square feet, northeastern light, all the fixtures in. I already have a couple of accounts lined up." She told me what they were and I knew I was meant to be impressed, so I said I was. The truth was I felt distanced from all that shop talk. Why was she persisting in treating me as if I were still Sally Wang-Acheson, senior art director? That person she thinks she's talking to must have been good, I thought. She must have been something.

Finally my boss leaned over, laying her hand over mine, looking at me shrewdly. "Okay, I can see you're not into this. The reason I called was I thought maybe you'd be interested in coming aboard as full-time staff. But only if you're completely okay."

"I'm a little distracted," I said. "I'm sorry. How about part-time? Is that out of the question?"

"I'll be straight with you, Sally," my boss said. "You're the most talented designer I've ever worked with. You're my first choice."

"Thanks."

"Part-time is a possibility. When do you think you can start?"

"I don't know," I said. "Maybe in a couple of weeks."

"Okay," she said. "You call me when you're ready."

This was a second chance, but I couldn't bear to think about it. It was too soon for me to be in the outside world. I couldn't wait to return to the safety of my apartment.

In Valerie's office there was a framed poster from an exhibition at the Met, an Indian tapestry of elephants crossing a river. It was all I'd been able to focus on, those last afternoons when I was trying desperately to keep a grip on my mind. The elephants were flat and brilliant, with intricate blue and gold trappings. I remember thinking that they resembled tropical fish and that if I were half as good an artist as that ancient court weaver I wouldn't be in this fix.

"Welcome back," Valerie said in her husky voice. There had been a time when I hadn't liked the way she looked, when her lankiness seemed gawky, when I believed her to be cold and harsh. Now I thought of her as a warrior, someone who'd fight to the death to protect another soul. A fresh legal pad was balanced on her knee. "How've you been sleeping?"

"Not so well."

"Oh? How is that?"

In Florida I'd slept long and drugged, at my aunt and uncle's, in the condo with Mel. Now that I was back in my life I'd awaken in the night with a start, heart pounding, tensed as if ready to spring out of bed. Three A.M. on the dot, it got so I didn't even have to look. I'd get out of bed and turn on the lights and it was a shock to see all the details of my apartment, not at all like I'd been imagining them in my uneasy doze. Sometimes a siren would be shrieking or a drunk yelling in the street below, adding to the surreal effect. The only thing that helped was food. Take-out leftovers or I'd make popcorn and bring it into bed with me, greasing up the sheets with butter. Then I'd smoke, even if I had managed not to all day— sometimes it was the only way to get through the night.

Mornings were another kind of torture. Walking around my apartment I got light-headed—or maybe it was more like light-bodied. I simply felt way too much: the blood pulsing through the veins in my wrists—Lillith said that it would be easy for me, had showed me the precise vertical cut to use if I really wanted out—the air tickling the hairs in my nostrils, the smooth warm dusty floorboards against the soles of my feet. It was like I had no skin.

I told Valerie about the conversation with my boss. She nodded. "Sounds promising."

"But I'm too fucked up, I can't go back."

"How about part-time? Didn't you just tell me she'd agreed you'd both think about that?"

"Maybe. If I can concentrate."

"What's that on your arm?"

"I had a relapse."

"You could have picked up the phone."

"I know. I didn't think."

"What happened in Florida?"

"I had a fling with Mel."

Nothing surprised her. She nodded again and began writing.

The day before, I'd called Waterbury information and was lucky enough to get it right on the second La Monte. "Mel's busy," a woman, his mother, I thought, told me. In the background I could hear laughter. "It's prom night," the woman explained.

"Who is it, Mom?" I heard Mel ask. The woman put her hand over the mouthpiece and there was a garbled dialogue.

"He'll call you," the woman said when she got back on.

"Tell him it's Sally."

"Oh, yes, he's mentioned you. Good-bye now," she said before I could give her the number.

"I thought about him in bed, you know," I told Valerie. "I thought about my father, while Mel was making love to me."

"And how did that make you feel?"

"Sick."

"So that's why you cut yourself. You never told me—did this ever happen with Carey?"

"I think I was just numb with Carey. And he didn't know about Monkey King. He didn't even know where the scars came from. I told him I'd had an accident on a picket fence."

"Why do you think it was different with Mel?"

"I guess being sick made me weaker."

"Is that what you would call it? Being weaker?"

I looked at my arm, the right one, without the scars, at the curve of the forearm bone, the pronounced knob on the outside of the wrist like my mother's. My hands, of course, were my father's. I imagined the way his long fingers had held the chalk as he stroked characters on the blackboard for his first-year class. Though my mother was known for being strict, Daddy was willing to be led off on a tangent. What are the characters for planet? for comet? his students would ask. He'd put down the chalk and tell them the legend of the herdsman and the weaving maid, two stars doomed to be separated by the Milky Way because they had loved each other too much and forgotten the rest of the world. My father would have turned it into a moral tale. The weaving maid had deserted her father for another man and he had punished her by forever denying her what she desired most.

After my session with Valerie I caught the bus to Woodside Avenue. When I walked in, using my key, I could smell pot roast in the oven. Ma was at the counter chopping carrots. "Lally's coming to dinner," she announced.

"Fine," I said.

My sister was lying on the living room floor watching TV. "Hi," she said, not looking up.

"I tried to call you," I said. The sling was off, but she had an Ace bandage on her right forearm. It reminded me of the time I'd gone down to see her in Charlottesville.

"It doesn't matter. The emergency's over."

"What emergency?"

"I thought I needed a place to stay. Dennis was going to kick me out."

Dennis was the producer, the one she'd gone to France with. I said: "No wonder, if you spent all that time up in Vermont with some other guy."

"Bill's just a friend," Marty said. "But you know men. Anyway, it's all right now."

"If it's all right, then why are you here?"

"I'm still healing, stupid," she said.

I went back into the kitchen, where Ma was making the salad. "Sal-lee, please get the dressing from the fridge."

"I'll make it from scratch," I said. She watched suspiciously as I peeled a clove of garlic and chopped it, mixed oil and vinegar. When her back was turned I added mustard, ginger, sherry, soy sauce, and the scrapings of an old jar of honey I found in the cupboard. Then I ground some black pepper in.

"Don't forget salt," Ma said.

"Okay," I said, ignoring her.

"I talk to Aunty Winnie today, she's so excited."

"Well, Xiao Lu's her only child, it must be a big deal."

"I tell her, lucky he's a boy, she doesn't have to pay."

"Mmmhmm."

"I ever tell you about my cousin in Shanghai, she got a divorce?"

"Yes, Ma."

"In China this is unheard of. Her mother and father disown her. When they see her in the street, they look right through her. Like ghost."

"What is the point of this story, Ma?"

"No point. Just conversation."

Lally rapped on the side door and I went over to let her in. "Hey, sweetie!" she brayed, giving me a hug. "Boy, you look like you've been somewhere. Bonnie, did ya see how dark she is? Looks like a Malaysian, almost. Here, this is for you. To celebrate your birthday, but more importantly, your total and final recovery!" Never one to mince words, was Lally. I snuck a glance at Ma, saw that her mouth was set in a mean line. The gift was a pewter heart on a chain bracelet. "I got one for your sister too." Lally, like my uncle, had always wished for daughters.

"Thanks, Lally. It's beautiful."

"Go set the table, Sally," Ma said. "We eat in the dining room tonight."

When we were all sitting down Lally said to me: "Now, I want to hear all about you. How are things in that big bad city?"

"Sally lost her job," Ma said. "She quit, and she can't get it back."

"I'm freelancing," I said.

"Just another word for unemployed."

"Freelancing seems to be the thing these days," Lally said. "God, this salad dressing's divine, Bonnie, you'll have to give

me the recipe." She started going on and on about some
neighbor of ours who had a son who was a poet in New York
and doing legal proofreading nights to pay the rent. She asked
my sister, "And how did you say you made your living, dear?"

Marty yawned.

"She's a clown," I said. "She dresses up in a polka-dot suit
and juggles at the South Street Seaport."

"You have to start somewhere." My mother smoothed her
apron and smiled at Lally. "Now, how about dessert?"

After Lally left and Marty and I had loaded the dishwasher my
sister retreated upstairs and I went into the living room and
watched a couple of sitcoms. When I came into the kitchen
for something to drink my mother was sitting at the table cor-
recting papers. Flick, flick, flick. Marty and I used to imitate
her on our already corrected school compositions and then
hold them up shrieking: "I got a hundred!" It was one of the
few things we did that could make Daddy look up from his
newspapers.

I was leaning into the refrigerator and jumped at the sound
of my mother's voice.

"I call Valerie and she says you're doing fine."

"She said fine?"

"She said progress."

"That's a little different, Ma."

"Maybe you don't need her anymore."

My mother's stare was level, telling me nothing.

"I think it's too soon to quit," I said, trying to keep my tone
neutral.

"When do you think you're going to get better?"

This was what she used to say when I was a little girl, home
from school with the mumps or the measles. In the first hours
of an illness, my mother was tender and magnanimous, running out to indulge every whim: a special brand of orange
soda, a stuffed animal, another box of crayons. But then I'd

wake up one morning to her standing over me: "You've been sick for two days. When do you think you can go back to school?"

I could think of several answers to Ma's question: Therapy is a process, not an instant cure; someone who's just been discharged from a psychiatric hospital needs to be followed up; or even the desperate, I'll pay for it myself if I have to. They all sounded weak, unconvincing.

"It will probably take a little while. I'll let you know."

This was the wrong answer—I could tell from the look on her face.

"I don't say anything when you're in the hospital. I do all what Valerie says I should do, I even go to family therapy. But there's no result!"

"What do you mean, no result? What did you expect?"

"You still don't have decent job, you still see doctor all the time."

"Ma, it's only been a month!"

"I know all you do in Florida, your Aunty Mabel tells me. What kind of boy! Boy from the hospital!"

"Just leave Mel out of it."

"You're not so sick, you can fool around with this boy. You just feel sorry for yourself, I can tell. You think 'Poor, poor Sally' and you imagine everything that's happen to you, what I do to spoil your childhood, terrible things about your daddy."

"You didn't spoil my childhood."

"You're so selfish, I'm embarrassed to speak about you to my friends. They all the time talk about their children, this one gets married, this one goes to law school, and what am I suppose to say? I have a crazy daughter? I spend so much money and she is crazier than before?"

I'd never understood the expression "to see red," but now a faint crimson bar appeared in the middle of my line of vision, so that I could only see the periphery of the scene, and not the focus, which was my mother sitting in the midst of her papers.

"You are a horrible person," I said. "You are not even a human being."

I turned and walked out of the kitchen. Behind me I heard her shouting, "We do everything for you, we send you to the best boarding school in America," and it was as if Daddy were speaking. I found that I could tune it out easily—there seemed to be a switch in my brain designed specifically for this purpose.

I went up to my room and into my day pack I stuffed the following items: the carved wooden horse, my summer correspondence with Fran, the snapshot of Marty and me on the swing set on Coram Drive. Also a postcard from Lillith I found on my bureau—a photograph of a giant hot fudge sundae with a message I couldn't quite make out, something about feast or famine. From Ma's bedroom I called a taxi to take me to the train station and then I went down to the living room to wait.

My mother came to stand in the doorway. "What are you doing?"

"I'm going back to New York."

"Too late to take the train."

I didn't answer.

"I can drive you to the station, if you want."

I picked up a copy of *Newsweek* from the coffee table and opened it.

The next time I looked up she had disappeared.

I studied the room, as if seeing it for the first time: the wooden laughing Buddha seated cross-legged on his cushion on the stereo cabinet, the tapestry of the Great Wall over the sofa, the set of three porcelain stools with their elaborate raised red and green curlicue designs like script on a birthday cake; there had once been four, but Marty had broken one pretending to be a circus elephant. If I could have taken anything with me, it would have been the painting in the foyer. It was of a boy on the back of a water buffalo. The boy was so insouciant—he was playing a flute and looking off into the distance. I remembered the painting was a gift from Mr. Lin, and now it occurred to me that it was probably his work.

Across from where I was sitting was a low table displaying my mother's collection of framed photographs. My and Carey's wedding portrait, once in the position of honor, had been removed. There were my parents and Aunty Mabel and Uncle Richard all dressed up in a nightclub somewhere in Florida. A sepia picture of Nai-nai from her singing days, a perfect full-blown orchid in her sleek hair, her mouth a dark bow. Marty leaning against the front door of our house in Monterey—the photo was black and white, but I remembered the dress, a pale yellow, with navy stripes across the bodice. Marty as the Virgin Mary in the eighth-grade play, draped in blue and gold. Marty's head shot when her hair was longer, in a bob. In none of these pictures was my sister smiling, but there was something seductively relaxed about her look, the confidence of someone who was thinking at the moment her image was being recorded: yes, yes, I am beautiful, and I deserve to be adored, I deserve everything the world is able to give me, and more.

24

On Memorial Day weekend I finally saw Fran for the first time in over a year. We had both been invited to a cocktail party given by a friend of ours from boarding school. She came over early to pick me up, and when I opened the door my first impression was that despite being dressed up she looked haggard, a little hollow-eyed. But Fran was one of those people whom exhaustion becomes, it made her seem more alive, somehow. After we'd hugged, she plopped herself into the baby rocking chair. "Listen, kiddo," she said, "I just want to get this out of the way before we start catching up. You have no idea what you put me through this spring. It was a crime, what you did."

"Franny, you don't understand, I was like a vegetable."

"You know what suicide is? Murder in the first fucking degree."

"You have no right to judge me. You have no idea what it was like."

She was silent, rocking, and then she said: "I'm sorry I didn't come to visit you in that place. You know how it is with me." When we were teenagers, Fran's mother had gone through several breakdowns and she'd had to leave school to check her into Payne-Whitney. Fran would never talk about these trips, although once she told me that when she was nine, right before her parents got divorced, she'd found her mother passed out on the pantry floor. "Tranquilizers, of course," Fran told me. "Mom was never very original." As neither I had been.

"How's your summer job?" I asked, handing her an opened beer.

"Fucking corporate politics. All the other interns are up there, you know, working this long weekend. They got browbeaten into it. They all live in terror, essentially." Fran, who had been at the top of our class and graduated Harvard summa cum laude, had never known this kind of terror.

"You're not up there," I said.

"Nope. I'm taking my chances." She took a swig of her beer. "So how's it feel to be back outside?"

I'd tried to explain it to Valerie. Sometimes I still simply didn't belong on this earth. The triggers were everywhere. That morning when I was struggling back to my apartment with grocery bags, the glance of a strange man burned me to the ground and I'd thought: What right have I to be here?

And there was Ma, phoning practically every night. Sometimes I picked up, sometimes I didn't. Yesterday she'd asked what I was doing this weekend. "Go to a barbecue maybe?" She was being her most charming and I recognized the tone—it was the voice she used with Marty. I told her I wasn't doing anything special. "You know I don't get a bill from Valerie this month," my mother said.

"You won't be anymore. She's sending them to me now."

"I can pay, Sal-lee. I didn't mean say I wouldn't pay."

"It's all right, Ma. I'll take care of it."

There was a space full of her breathing and then she said, "Well, I just call to say Happy Memorial Day."

I thought of greeting cards.

"Thanks, Ma. You too."

Fran asked if I had cigarettes.

I found a pack and handed it to her. "Take it. I'm trying to quit."

She lit up and exhaled. Then she said: "I'm having an affair with one of my professors."

"Affair? You mean he's married?"

"She's married."

"Come again?" But I'd heard what I'd heard.

"Surprised?"

"Does this mean you're bi, or something?"

"Maybe. I don't think so though. I think this might be who I am."

I wanted to ask: What about that guy with the boat in Wellfleet you lost your virginity to? Or the French tutor you almost eloped with sophomore year? But I didn't have to ask. I already knew. Suddenly it made all the sense in the world.

"How long have you known?" I asked.

"Well, it was like there was this door in front of me and I kept thinking, What'll happen if I step through, and when I did I realized there hadn't been any door in the first place. Do you understand what I mean?"

"Kind of."

"She's very smart. Very verbal."

"Sounds great."

Fran dropped her cigarette into the beer bottle and began picking at the label. "I'll tell you, Sally, it's different with a woman. You don't have to *condescend*. Or worse, be condescended to."

"You seem very okay with this."

"The whole idea of coming out, well, it's so unpleasant, isn't it? Why do you have to announce anything? Why can't you just be yourself, live your life?"

"What does your mother think?"

"I haven't told anyone except you. The thing is, my mother probably wouldn't give a shit. My father would be amused."

"It's actually kind of hip."

"Hip to the outside world. To me, it's my fucking life. And don't worry, Sally," she added, addressing my secret thoughts, "I'm not attracted to you. You're not my type."

"That's a relief."

"I like more meat on the bone."

"Okay, okay." I thought about telling her about Lillith, what there was to tell, but I didn't. I felt lonely in a way I hadn't before.

"I can see you're ready to rock at Alicia's." Alicia, whose party we were invited to, was actually more Fran's friend than mine—they'd attended elementary school together.

I had on the hibiscus dress. "Yeah. What do you think?"

"Foxy. And that's just as well. I heard Carey might be there." Fran had always liked my husband.

"Oh, great."

"He has a new girlfriend."

"I know."

"I think he's still carrying a torch for you though."

"I doubt it," I said. "I got Alicia a bottle of Merlot. Do you think we should bring flowers too?"

"Relax, Sal. Wine will be fine."

"I'm sorry I'm such a nervous wreck. This is my first social event since I've been back."

I had never been to Alicia's apartment, which was on Beekman Place. In the old-fashioned wood-paneled lobby, a liveried doorman phoned up to announce us. He said, "Miss Fischel and Miss Wang." Fran tapped her toe on the slick marble floor. She looked like she belonged; I didn't. I'd had no idea how rich Alicia was until once when I was at the dentist I'd picked up a copy of *Town & Country* and found her name on the list of the most eligible heiresses in the United States.

Alicia herself answered the door wearing a fuchsia minidress and decadently high stiletto heels, in the style of the Latinas in my neighborhood. Why did all the women I know have such terrific legs? Her hair, which was almost as dark and straight as mine, was cut in a severe angled pageboy. Diamond drops fell casually from her ears. As she gave kisses to Fran and me, I saw that the love seat in the foyer was strewn with expensive-looking women's purses. One that particularly caught my eye was a clutch made of colored straw in the shape of a watermelon.

I wanted to turn around and go home.

But Alicia was already pulling us in and saying gaily, "Forgive the decor of this place, it's actually my stepmother's, she's really into this froufrou stuff."

I saw what she meant. The place had kind of a European clutter to it, valances fringed in gold, photographs in ornate silver frames scattered on tables and shelves, lots of small eccentrically shaped chairs and ottomans that I couldn't identify but knew were extremely valuable. In what seemed to be the main room stood a ring of people holding glasses, talking and laughing very loudly.

I offered my wine. "Oh, good," Alicia said, examining the label, and Fran and I followed her to the kitchen, where I felt safer. A kitchen was a room in which the agenda was obvious. You could always find something to do in a kitchen. It was also where the bar was. Fran and I mixed ourselves gin and tonics, using tall glasses that had levels marked off with pictures of different animals. The top picture was a monkey, and the bottom was a jackass. I made my drink strong, and after a couple of swigs I was able to follow Fran into the living room.

How many gatherings like this had I attended, where the point was to blend in, not to call attention to myself because I stood out too much? My father would have loved this, me at the party of Alicia Houghton, with all the sons and daughters of the establishment. He would have said that I had made it.

Fran waded right in, addressing a brawny man wearing shorts printed with coconuts and clusters of grapes, paired with a formal red linen suit jacket. She introduced him to me as Alicia's cousin, and to my relief he seemed to be the conversational type, probably due to the fact that the glass in his hand was nearly down to jackass level. I concentrated on smiling in what I thought were the correct places, and soon we were having a perfectly civilized conversation about a recent exhibition of Persian miniatures at the Met. The cousin actually looked interested in what I had to say, although it might have been just a facade. There was something so fatal about that WASP politeness—you never knew where you stood—although I had had enough practice with my in-laws to have begun to be able to decipher it. I was suddenly and sadly reminded of those vacations with Fran in the city when we'd gone out with those boys who consistently froze me out. The cousin might have been one, for all I knew, because I didn't remember any of their faces. He tilted his glass and drained it heartily. I watched the action of that white Adam's apple and thought, He has no idea how ridiculous that getup he's wearing is, how few places in the world would find it even remotely acceptable.

Fran got collared by a couple in matching white duck trousers, who both turned out to be lawyers and wanted to know what Harvard was like these days. I studied my friend as she stood poised there in her blue and green abstract-patterned cocktail dress, hair conservatively pulled back in barrettes. There was nothing the least bit dykey about Fran, unless you counted her intensity, or the way she walked into a room as if she owned it.

"So, can I get you another drink?" the cousin was asking me. Then, seeing that I wasn't quite finished—"Or freshen that one?" I handed him my glass.

"Thanks."

This was what I dreaded most, being alone at a party, it was the stuff of nightmares. Although I wasn't drunk yet, that familiar unsteadiness came over me. I imagined, not for the first time, that what I'd been feeling since I'd gotten back from St. Pete must be like the malaise people go through when they move to a new country, that continuing seasickness of immigrants. The sickness that, according to Aunty Mabel, my father had never gotten over. Longing for a cigarette, I sat down on the pink-and-white-striped window seat. There was a little marble-topped table in front of me displaying a collection of Limoges boxes shaped liked different kinds of fruit. Fruit was certainly the theme of the afternoon. I picked up a tiny clump of raspberries to examine it.

Alicia's breathy voice was in my ear: "Aren't they beautiful? That was my grandmother's collection. I gave her those raspberries the Christmas before she died."

I thought of Nai-nai's Limoges gathering dust in my mother's attic.

"Here's Charlie with a drink for someone. Oh, for you, Sally. I'm glad you two are getting to know each other."

"So you knew Lish at prep school." The cousin plunked himself down next to me. I marveled at the way he'd managed to make my drink—lime, ice, and all—with the level exactly at the monkey line. Obviously an expert.

Before I could answer there was a commotion at the door. Alicia excused herself and went over. I saw the copper flash of Fran's hair as she turned from her conversation with the lawyers to look toward the foyer. The new guest was a woman alone, an ice-blonde in an orange sheath. She looked vaguely familiar. Fran raised her eyebrows at me, tilting her head to the kitchen.

"What's up?" I asked her a few minutes later.

"I just wanted to make sure you knew."

"Knew what?"

"That woman who just came in. It's Carey's new girlfriend."

I felt sick. "Is Carey here?"

"I haven't seen him."

I said: "I think I need another drink."

"Sally. What a surprise."

"Carey." It was much, much later in the party. I didn't know where Charlie had gotten himself to, he was probably off with someone more his speed, someone who could hold their liquor. Astonishingly, Carey looked exactly the same, substantial, like a husband. He was wearing a tropical-print shirt and the khaki trousers we'd shopped for together at Brooks Brothers. He was so familiar I could almost believe that we were still married, that we would leave this party together and go back to our apartment on Riverside Drive. He had new glasses, I noticed, wire-framed instead of horn-rimmed.

"You look terrific," he said.

"So do you." Had my husband always had that pretentious accent?

"You here alone?"

"No," I said, trying not to slur my words, "I'm with Fran." I reached up and touched his shoulder in what I thought was a friendly way. "Where'd you get that shirt? I don't remember it. Is it from Hawaii or something?"

There was something in his look I couldn't read. He bent toward me and said into my ear, "Listen, I think it's time for you to go home. I'll take you if you want. We can get a cab downstairs. Let me just tell Sukey."

"Sukey? What kind of name is that?"

"Go wait in the foyer, Sally. I'll be right there."

"No," I said. "You're not my husband anymore."

He straightened up and squared his shoulders. "Where is Fran?"

"I don't know."

"I see her. Over there." Carey took me by the elbow and steered me through the crowd. I didn't resist. The room was swimming.

In the elevator the two of them discussed how lucky it was that the Memorial Day parade had been over hours earlier, so we wouldn't have any problems with traffic. Carey had his arm around me and I thought this wasn't appropriate but didn't say anything. Out on the street he hailed a taxi and kissed me on the cheek. "You take care of yourself." By then I was concentrating on not throwing up. At about Twenty-third Street I thought I was going to lose the battle. Fran reached across me and rolled down the window but it turned out to be a false alarm.

"Franny, I'm sorry," I said. "I've never done this before." It was true. I never let myself get too drunk or stoned, even during our summer on the Cape. I was too afraid of losing control.

"Forget about it," she said.

Miraculously, we managed to get into my apartment before I puked. In the bathroom I kept saying, "I'm sorry I'm so fucked up. I'm sorry you have to take care of me."

"I'm not mad at you, Sally," Fran said. "Why do you keep on acting like I'm mad at you?"

"I did this once for my sister. When she was twelve."

"That figures."

"Do you think Alicia will ever talk to me again?"

"You got sick here, not in her apartment. Besides, I happen to know that old Charlie was blowing lunch before we left. Sorry about that." Her hand stayed on my nape as I aimed my head over the toilet again.

The phone was ringing. I knew it was early from the angle of sun through the half-opened curtain, and I was afraid to get up to answer it, afraid to alter the equilibrium of my body. It couldn't be Fran, she'd left only a few hours ago, arranging the fans so they were blowing a cross-draft over me, a wastebasket by my head. The machine clicked on.

"Sa, pick up, pick up, I know you're there."

I slid out of bed, dragging the wastebasket with me, and practically crawled to the kitchen, where the phone was. "Marty?" I said into the receiver.

"You sound awful," my sister said cheerfully.

"Where are you calling from?" I closed my eyes and managed to slide my body down into a sitting position on the floor, my back resting against the under-the-sink cabinet.

"Home. Listen, Sa"—lowering her voice—"I have to ask you a favor."

"Would you please speak up?"

"I'll try, but Ma's out in the hall and I don't want her to hear."

"Okay, okay, what."

"Can you lend me some money?"

"How much?"

"A thousand."

"No way."

"Please, Sa. It's just to help me put down a security deposit and the first month's rent. I'll pay you back by the end of this year, I promise."

"What happened to Dennis?"

"Are you going to lend me the money or not?"

"I can't think now, Mar, I'm sick. Could you please call back later?"

"When?"

"I don't know. Just later." I hung up, opened the refrigerator, and got out a bottle of club soda, which I finished off in one gulp. My stomach roiled. I forced myself to my feet and hung over the sink, waiting. Nothing. Finally I went back to bed.

My sister had never hit me up like that before, she must be desperate. Maybe I'd give her five hundred. It was all I could spare, and not even that really. Why hadn't she asked Ma for a loan? I'd call her tomorrow, when I felt human.

I lay back and shut my eyes and concentrated on my breathing. I remembered Carey's arm around me. Fran rubbing my back in the bathroom. Valerie doing the same in the emergency room.

This was my dream: I was skiing with Carey, or rather, he was doing the skiing, and I was following behind him, no poles, my arms wrapped around his waist, as if we were on a motorcycle. My ex-husband's body shielded me from the wind and snow. There were no decisions to make, nothing to do but follow. After a while I realized that we were going to crash and I tried to extricate myself, but it was as if my arms were glued in place. Don't, I tried to say, but I couldn't speak, and we kept going, down, down. Then the dream changed. I was a little girl in Monterey, walking around the grass in the backyard. I kept falling. Every time I did, someone would pick me up by the shoulders, setting me back on my feet. All around us was the smell of jasmine.

25

The fallout from the party was not as bad as I'd expected. Fran called that evening from Boston to make sure I was okay, and told me that Charlie had asked Alicia for my phone number. Later in the week I got a message from Carey saying it had been good to see me, why didn't we meet for drinks at the Brown Club sometime. I thought this was a good idea. There was a lot we needed to talk about.

My hangover lasted for two days. There are lots of things you can't do well when you have a hangover, but painting isn't one of them. Artist friends of mine tell me they sometimes do their best work when physically compromised—with a fever, for instance. It's like the defenses are down. On the second day I got up and opened all my reds—cadmium, crimson, scarlet, rose madder, burgundy, geranium, ruby. I flipped through my sketchbook and studied the automatic drawings I had done in the hospital and St. Pete, and then I started to work.

Like my drawing at Willowbridge it came out fast and completely abstract. I shouldn't have been surprised, but I was. The background a silver-gray wash and on top of that incomprehensible graffiti that spelled out nothing, not even letters, most of the strokes slashing diagonally down, so that your heart would go the same direction when you looked. I'd been taught to be careful with red. The color called attention to itself, eclipsed all others, so that you had to use it sparingly. I wasn't sparing. I tacked up a second canvas and tried again,

without the background, for the shock of it on bright cool
white.

I would have used my own blood if it weren't for the limited
supply and the fact that it did not dry true to color.

By the end of the day my studio looked like a massacre had
taken place. I had to turn the canvases to the wall so that I
could sleep.

"Aunty Winnie says she looks forward to see you at wedding,"
my mother said on the phone.

"I don't know if I'm going."

"How come you don't go? Such an old childhood friend."

"Look, I'll think about it, okay?"

And I did. Sitting on the floor of my studio with the sun
pouring in, I decided, what the hell. But first I had to get back
into my life. Slowly, Sally, I told myself.

"Why do you think she keeps calling you?" Valerie asked.

"Control, of course. She wants to keep tabs on me now."

"Why now?"

"Before I wasn't dangerous. Now she knows I could hurt
her. I could tell everyone the truth about my father."

"And?"

"If I tell the truth about Monkey King, I tell the truth about
her."

"And what truth is that?"

"She let it happen."

"Yes. She let it happen." Valerie leaned forward, her chin in
her hands.

"She was a failure," I said.

"As what?"

"As a mother."

"What else?"

"I don't understand."

"What else was she a failure at?"

"Is this a trick question?"

"Wasn't she a failure as a wife?"

"Oh."

"Think about it."

Why was everyone always telling me to think about things? "I guess so," I said. "But why did she stay with him then?"

"Why do you think?"

"She thinks the ancestors will curse you if you get a divorce. She was afraid, I guess."

I wrote out a check for five hundred dollars to my sister, put "Loan" in the memo section, and mailed it to Woodside Avenue, with MS. MARTHA WANG in block letters so Ma wouldn't open the envelope. I didn't know why I did it. It wasn't like I owed her anything. But she was my sister, after all.

A few days later Marty called. She didn't mention the money.

"I'm coming into the city tomorrow," she said. "Let's have lunch. My treat."

"Where?"

"You live near Chinatown, don't you?"

"Fine with me."

"Good," she said, sounding like a little kid. "We'll have *bao zi*."

I went down early so I could stop at Pearl Paint beforehand. Since I'd gotten back I'd been deliberately avoiding it, but Pearl was the best and cheapest in Manhattan for art supplies, so I guessed sooner was better than later. I was apprehensive. What if back in February they'd caught me on tape walking out of the store with a bulge in my parka, or worse, actually slipping the tubes of paint into my pocket? When it came right down to it, I didn't have my sister's nerve. I put on the largest sunglasses I owned and the red lipstick I'd bought for pool

nights, tied my hair up in an uncharacteristically high ponytail. We all have our ways of courting luck, although maybe
this was more of a disguise.

I needed brushes, not beautiful calligraphy ones like my
uncle and aunt had given me, but the cheapest kind of oil
brushes, which I could abuse and leave paint on overnight. I
was going through a sloppy stage, working until the small
hours of the morning, when I was too exhausted to clean up.
There were piles of red-stained rags all over my studio, and it
seemed I could never get my hands completely clean. By then
there was no doubt in my mind that what I was doing was calligraphy. Sometimes when I squinted my eyes I could make
out familiar characters from Chinese class I thought I had forgotten. The stocky pitchfork strokes of the word for *mountain*,
the delicate voluptuous curves of the word for *heart*.

Nothing happened at Pearl. I just walked in and up those
precarious stairs like millions of others before me, chose my
brushes, paid, and left. The saleswoman didn't even meet my
eyes. The whole time my pulse was rabbiting as crazily as it
had the last time I'd been there. As soon as I got outside I felt
my knees buckle, and I had to go into a coffee shop so I could
sit down and have a cup of tea.

The block where my sister wanted us to meet had a string of
those tiny jewelry stores that my parents used to hurry us by
when, as kids, we would be caught by the displays of rings.
Marty seemed paler than the last time I'd seen her. For once I
was the tanner one. She was still wearing a bandage. Our
arms are our weakness, I thought.

"You look very fifties," my sister said. She peered down the
block. "I think it's the third store to the right, that one."

"What are you up to?"

"The best prices in town," Marty said. "I bet you didn't
know they're pawnshops too."

"No, I didn't. What are you thinking of pawning?"

"What else? Jewelry."

She had a little leather zippered bag, from which she withdrew her stash and placed it carefully, item by item, on the piece of black velvet the proprietor had laid over the counter. I noticed she was wearing the pink cameo ring. I hoped she wasn't going to sell that.

The proprietor, a grouchy old man, was impassive, grunting every so often. "No good" is what he said to most of what she showed him. And they were beautiful things, some of them. An aquamarine ring in a white gold setting, an opera-length necklace of jade beads, a half dozen hammered silver cuffs. But the man looked unimpressed until she produced a pair of gold grape-size earrings in the shape of lovers' knots, each trimmed with a tiny line of diamonds following the curves. He picked one up to peer at it through his loupe.

"Cartier," my sister said.

I could picture her strolling down Fifth Avenue with Dennis, both of them dressed in leather jackets and jeans. It would have been early in the relationship, maybe right after they'd moved in together. At the corner of Fifty-second he'd turn to her and say casually, "Sweetie, do you feel like stopping in here?" And so they'd push through those monstrously heavy doors with their entwined CC handles into the sepia interior, intimate and heavily carpeted, so unlike Tiffany's with its light and sparkle.

The proprietor gave her $350 for the things he wanted. This seemed criminally low to me, and when we were out on the street again I told her: "You should have bargained him up."

"It doesn't matter. I don't care about any of that stuff. I just want to make my first month's rent and security, and this will do it, along with what you loaned me."

"You already found a place?"

"Yeah. A share, on the Upper West Side."

"Why didn't you ask Ma for the money?"

Marty rolled her eyes. "She's gotten it into her head that I'm staying in New Haven. She'd throw a fit if she knew I'd even been looking for an apartment."

It occurred to me that my sister probably didn't have very many close women friends. In fact maybe I was it.

I'd forgotten exactly where the *bao zi* shop was, and Marty didn't have a clue, so we ended up going down a couple of wrong streets. Since it was Saturday there were lots of tourists mixed among the natives and as always I felt displaced, not being either. My sister made her way through the crowd confidently, somehow blending in, maybe because she was short. But I noticed that she distinctly favored her right arm, and I wondered how long it would take until she didn't. Would it be until the bandage was off, or a week after that, a month, a year, or would it become a tic, a vulnerability, the way she'd edge her left shoulder forward as she walked?

When we finally found the place I was shocked to see that they had changed it all around, refurbished it. The old Formica counter and stools had been replaced by little café tables, and you ordered from a waitress instead of the cheerful baker behind the counter. But there were still those old glass cases by the door, all steamed up with warm pastries, and I recognized the baker as he emerged from the kitchen shouting orders at a boy pushing a cart full of trays.

Marty gave our order in the sketchy Mandarin she'd picked up in a semester at the University of Vermont. It always made me jealous that she had finished college and I hadn't, that she was naturally more clever than me though she never studied. After the waitress had left, my sister opened up the zippered case and we inspected what the jeweler had rejected.

"You want any of this?"

"What about the cameo ring?"

"I like that, I'm not going to get rid of it. It was Nai-nai's, you know. Ma gave it to me."

"I didn't know."

"I deserve something from her, after all, she was always so hard on me."

"You think so?"

"I know so. I think she saw herself in me."

"Oh, come on, Mar, you're not a thing like her."

"I look exactly like her."

"You look a *little* like her."

My sister pursed up her mouth and said in a high, choppy voice: "You girls should be proud, you have Han ancestors," and the imitation was so perfect I had to laugh. She laid her left hand in front of her on the table, spreading her fingers out like a star, and we admired the precisely cut ivory silhouette on its dusty pink background. It was a Victorian lady's profile with a small bun at the nape. I wouldn't have been surprised if it had been commissioned especially for my grandmother. Sitting there with my sister, it was as if I could feel Nai-nai's stern eye on us, her disapproval at Marty's punk haircut. "That lipstick wrong color on you!" she'd say to me. "Not feminine enough."

My sister took out her Gauloises and offered me one. I shook my head.

"I'm trying to quit."

"Good for you," she said. I couldn't tell whether she was being sarcastic or not. She struck the match in a precise gesture, touched the flame to the cigarette end, and then I knew why I had lent her the money. It was bait, so she'd talk to me.

"Look," I said. "I'm just going to ask you this once. Why didn't you back me up in the hospital? About Monkey King."

Marty didn't say anything for a moment, but I could tell from her eyes she'd heard. When she did speak, I could barely hear her.

"It wasn't my fault, Sa."

"That you and Ma ganged up on me like that?"

"It wasn't my fault he did that to you."

My sister coming to wake me in the morning. When I wouldn't get up, she'd climb into bed with me, whispering like a chant: "Monkey King, Monkey King." This was how I knew it was real, not a dream.

"I never said it was your fault, Mar."

"When we moved to Woodside Avenue I started locking my door."

"But he never touched you."

"No."

The waitress had brought our orders—sweet bean for Marty, pork for me. I pushed my plate away and picked up my teacup, but my hand was shaking so badly that I couldn't drink.

"Did Ma know?"

My sister shook her head.

"Does that mean, 'No, she didn't know,' or 'No, you can't answer'?"

"Ma was the one who said there was something wrong with you. That's why we had to send you away."

"I wanted to go away."

"She cried all the time, that first year you were at that school. You didn't know, did you? She told me I was her only comfort. You were only home summers. Can you imagine what it was like living in that house day in and day out? I told Ma she should get a divorce. She said she couldn't leave him. You think Ma's so strong, well, that was her blind spot."

I thought: But you're her blind spot.

"Look," she said. "I know you're into being the victim and everything, but at least he paid attention to you."

"Jesus," I said.

"He never even cared what I did. Do you know what he said to Ma? That he was sorry I'd turned out to be so stupid. That it must have been his sister's genes—you know, the one who never finished primary school. The one who died. Can you believe it? He didn't even have the guts to say it to my face. And all that crap about a piece of meat, I was just a piece of meat."

"He called me that too. And that's bullshit about him not caring. Remember, you were the one he was talking about when he had the stroke."

My sister closed her eyes. "Oh God, Sally," she said. "You actually believed that. I made it up. Didn't you know?"

"Were you lying then or are you lying now?"

"It doesn't matter."

I wanted to strangle her. I could have at least slapped her face, right in the restaurant in front of all those people. But I didn't. Because the truth was, my sister was right. It didn't matter. I'd wanted her to say she was sorry, I had wanted to forgive her. It was clear to me now that this would never happen.

I said: "You know, if he had tried to do it to you, I would have told Ma."

My sister was silent.

"When he did it to me, I could stand it. For you I would have told."

"I don't believe you." Marty stubbed out her cigarette and lit another.

"You're my sister."

She looked away. It was the old story: Yes, I'm your sister but I'll never be you, thank God.

I said, "I give up. I guess it's just impossible for you to understand."

We sat in silence for a while before our untouched plates. Finally my sister asked, "So, you going to the lingerie shower?"

"What lingerie shower?" It was by the greatest effort that I kept my tone as casual as hers.

"The one Mimi Sung's giving for Grace."

"Grace?"

"You know, Xiao Lu's Grace. I met her, you know. Ma invited her and Aunty Winnie to tea."

"Wasn't Nai-nai's cousin named Grace?"

"It's just one of those Chinese names, like Pearl or Ruby. We're lucky they wanted us to be so assimilated."

"I didn't get an invitation so I guess I'm not going."

"They called people. I bet you're not picking up your phone again. Anyway, you have to go out and buy a piece of lingerie, size six, she likes red and pink. She looks like the type to wear sexy underwear. You know, like the magazines say, prim and proper on the outside and a whore underneath. I think we should get her a Merry Widow with a hole cut out in the crotch. Can you imagine Xiao Lu's face?"

"I have a theory about this shower," I said. "I think it's just a cover."

"What do you mean?"

"I don't think Grace is the one who is going to wear the lingerie."

It wasn't that funny, but we both started to giggle until we were out of control, until we were laughing so hard I thought our hearts might break.

I thought, She's not the only liar in the family. I had lied too. Both of us had lied all our lives, by omission and creation, about what our father was to us.

26

When I got back from Chinatown there was a message on my machine from Mel telling me to call him right away. His voice was higher pitched than I remembered, the tone a little distant. This time it was he, not his mother, who picked up. "How are you?" he asked.

"Oh, just dandy."

"I deserved that," he said. "I'm sorry I haven't called. I have some bad news. It's Douglas. He's dead. He killed himself."

"How?" I asked.

"They think he drank himself to death."

"What?"

"He was renting this cabin in the Poconos and when his lease ran out the manager went to see why he hadn't checked out. At first they couldn't figure out what happened, and then when they did the autopsy they found a lethal dose of alcohol in his blood."

I was thinking that finding a dead person must change you forever.

"Are you okay, Sal?"

"Yes. I'm surprised he didn't use a gun, that's all. Since he really meant it."

"His dad said they found an old bear rifle in the cabin, but it hadn't been fired."

"So God *is* capable of mercy."

"What?"

"Nothing."

"Sal, the funeral's Monday. I think I'm going."

"I'm sorry. I know you guys were friends."

"Are you interested in coming?"

"I didn't know him that well."

"I realize that. I'm asking for me, honey. For moral support."

"This is kind of sick, isn't it? Trying to con me into attending a funeral when you don't even bother calling to say hi?"

"Lillith is going to be there."

I didn't say anything.

"If you take the train up I'll drive you back to the city."

"All right," I said.

Greenwich was the first stop, an hour from New York. Since it was off-peak I got a triple seat to myself in the back of the car—I could tell that it used to be a smoking one because it was never possible to completely get the smell out of the upholstery. I thought of Uncle Richard and all our illicit cigarettes together. I'd sent him a postcard of the Statue of Liberty doing a jig, telling him that I had a feeling my fortunes were going to change. It's not coincidence that *fortune* means both luck and money, he'd informed me once.

There was a girl several seats ahead of me, sprawled out with her socked feet up on the seat. She was intently reading a Penguin paperback, making notes in it with a fat pen. She looked smart, serious, unstoppable. Her shoulder-length dark hair needed washing, and she had on a Yale sweatshirt. When the conductor came by she handed him her ticket without looking up. I couldn't remember ever in my life feeling as confident as she looked.

The other people in my car were a family, a mother and three kids—two young daughters and a baby whose sex was indeterminate because it was bald and wearing a yellow blanket. The two little girls, in party dresses with sashes and patent leather Mary Janes, kept getting out of their seats and running up and down the aisle. "How much longer?" "Where are we now?" they kept asking, and their mother said to me apologetically, "We usually drive."

They got off at my station, leaning out over the platform as the train slowed down, so that I automatically reached over and took the smaller one by the shoulders. She ignored me and began screaming: "There he is! Daddy! Daddy! Daddy!" As we got off, I heard the older one whisper to her mother, "Mommy, what's the matter with that lady?"

By the time the cab dropped me off in front of the church I had regained my composure. Standing at the back of the chapel, I spotted Mel in a pew toward the back. When I slid in beside him he smiled, took my hand, and gave it a squeeze. He was wearing a pale gray linen suit—I hadn't known he owned a suit—and the sapphire stud in his ear. The white cuffs of his shirt looked so soft and spotless I wanted to stroke them. Unlike me, he seemed perfectly at home in church. His parents were strict Roman Catholics. He'd told me once that he still felt guilty using condoms.

I didn't recognize the woman on his other side until she leaned and mouthed "Hi" and I realized with a shock that it was Lillith. She had gained at least twenty-five pounds, had her hair up in a tortoiseshell clip, and was wearing gold shell earrings, all of which gave her an almost matronly look. But her wrists and ankles and those tiny feet in their navy pumps were just as breakably delicate as I'd remembered.

My main feeling about the service was that it had little to do with the Douglas I had known. The old Episcopal chapel, chilly enough to make you shiver although it was over eighty degrees outside, the friends and relatives with their long faces that seemed designed for mourning, the dark burnished coffin with brass handles like furniture, covered with sprays of white lilies, like Easter. Subdued, conservative, in the best of taste—everything Douglas would have loathed. I tried to remember if my father's coffin had had flowers. Somehow I thought so, but I, who had such an eye for detail, couldn't conjure the scene up in my mind.

The minister kept calling Douglas "this young man," which made me wonder if the guy had even known him. "Let not this young man's sufferings have been in vain." I thought about that night in the hallway when Douglas had dragged me into the phone booth, the smell and feel of him, which was not so different from other boys after all. Then I remembered my last session with Valerie, when I'd told her about Fran and my irrational disappointment that it was not me she had fallen in love with. My shrink had said very gently: "Sally, there is caring and attention in this world that is not sexual."

I looked for family members and finally recognized Douglas's Jack Lemmon look-alike father in front, dressed in banker's dark blue. He seemed terribly pious, hunching down low for the prayers and staring blankly ahead the rest of the time. There were two dark-complected women in the same pew who matched the description of his mother, elegant, he'd sneered to us in group, so fucking elegant you could eat whipped cream off her asshole.

Family was fatal but they created you after all. Who would I be if it hadn't been for Monkey King, if I didn't have his breadth and bones and blood, if he hadn't made his mark on me? It was useless to try to imagine how things would have turned out had I been born to another family, not only useless but impossible. I was what I had come from. When I had tried to leave I'd ended up in other families that would define me in different ways—my friends at boarding school, Carey, my group at Willowridge, Aunty Mabel and Uncle Richard. I was destined to leave them all and at the same time never to leave. There was no escape, except for that one I had tried to take, that Douglas had succeeded in taking.

I imagined him planning this, giving his father's credit card number to reserve the cabin, packing the bear rifle into a duffel, his only luggage. On the bus down, sitting alone because no one dared take the seat beside him, not caring that people shunned him, because he was aiming so precisely now, aiming past them to the end.

One of the dark women got up to read the Twenty-third Psalm.

Yea though I walk through the valley of the shadow of death
I will fear no evil

I was thinking of a painting in progress, red with violet in it, the strokes as sinuous as the cold flames of hell, if I believed in such a place. But I didn't, and not in heaven either.

The minister said: "Let us say a silent prayer for the soul of Douglas Abercrombie and for all those dearly departed."

Although I could not pray for Monkey King, I could pray for my father. And while I was sitting there I thought of the others to whom I'd never had a chance to say good-bye: Nai-nai, Darcy, soon Uncle Richard, and of course, as Hopkins said, myself. Sealy. *It is Margaret you mourn for.*

Douglas's mother turned out to be the woman who'd read the psalm. She stood beside his father in the back of the church as we filed past to offer our condolences. "A tragedy," I kept hearing. I supposed there were a limited number of things to say in a situation like this, and Douglas's life, after all, had been so short. I tried hard to think of a correct remark. Had any of the mourners at Daddy's funeral been as ill at ease as me?

When our turn came Mel spoke for all three of us. "We knew your son at Willowridge. We're all so sorry." For all the father knew we could have been staff. I could see that Mel, as well as being comfortable in church, was familiar with the rituals of death. That was one of the advantages of coming from a large family.

Douglas's father extended his hand to each of us in turn, his grip firm but clammy. His mother's hand was limp and warm and lotiony and she barely looked at us. I could smell her perfume.

"Cold bitch," Mel said when we were outside.

"What do we want to do now?" I asked. It was so strange, the three of us standing there in the sunlight of this lovely woodsy town, stranger than it had been first seeing Mel in Florida.

Lillith shaded her hand over her eyes and said, "I've got to be getting back. I only have a two-hour pass." I still couldn't get over her plumpness. It was as if she were a different person.

"We'll drop you off at the train station," Mel said. The teal Oldsmobile was around the back, in the church parking lot. "Sorry about this old heap," he said to me, as if I'd never seen it before, as if we hadn't logged hours in it together. "Someday I'll get a silver Triumph."

"Don't," I said.

Because she was getting out first Lillith insisted that I take the front seat, and I had to crane my head around to look at her.

"Well," Lillith said. "He made it." Her tone was matter-of-fact. I knew what she meant. Douglas had made it where we had failed. I had tried only once, she had tried at least once a year since she'd hit puberty.

"That was bizarre," I said. "The ceremony, I mean. Meeting his family."

Lillith said: "It's always bizarre to meet the family."

"Was there any warning?" I asked. "Did anyone know?"

"He was pretty incommunicado," said Mel. "You should have seen him after you guys left. He looked like those people you see in pictures of death row, who don't give a shit anymore, don't exercise or anything."

"How come they discharged him?"

"Why else? His insurance ran out."

"They shouldn't have let him go."

"What could they do? His family isn't poor, but you know Willowridge costs an arm and a leg."

No one said anything for a while, and then I asked Lillith how she was doing.

"Same old same old," she said. "I'm a fucking walking chemical factory. There's this new drug, I can get it for free if I'm in the FDA trial, so they're giving me that plus lithium. It kind of spaces me out."

"Sorry."

She yawned. "Oh, and I have a part-time job. They make you, at this place. I tutor math at an elementary school."

"I didn't know you did that." It didn't seem, somehow, to jibe with Joan of Arc. Then I remembered. "I got your post-card. The one with the ice cream sundae. It took a while."

"I got yours." There didn't seem to be anything more to say, and I was actually relieved when we pulled up in front of the train station. I missed the old Lillith, not like she was at the end, unintelligible, but the zany girlie one who had made food sculptures and a string bikini and braided my hair.

After we'd let her out and watched her walk onto the platform Mel leaned back in his seat and stretched. "You hungry?"

"Not really."

"Maybe by the time we get to New York you will be."

"Yeah."

I felt his fingertips brush the back of my neck and got a lump in my throat.

"Hair's getting long," he said.

"I know, I keep forgetting to have it cut." We watched the train pull up and Lillith get on. "How's the prom queen?"

He didn't miss a beat. "Bethie? She's fine. She's decided she wants to go to dog-grooming school."

"Sounds like a hot career to me."

"Yeah, well, you know we're not serious."

"Like it wasn't serious with us?"

Mel was silent for a moment. Then he said: "You know I'd slay a dragon for you, Sally."

And I for you, I thought, but didn't say. Instead I asked, "You want your poetry book back?"

"What? Oh, that. No, no, you keep it. Think of it as a memento."

The drive to the city was much too short. Mel told me funny stories about the restaurant, where he was working that summer, and then tuned the radio to a salsa station and translated the songs for me.

"You speak Spanish?" I asked, and he nodded.

Miracle of miracles, there was a parking space right in front of my building. Mel eyed the street dubiously before we went up and then watched, incredulous, as I went through my ritual with the three locks. Inside, he shucked his jacket and draped it over the baby rocking chair. Everyone loved that chair. When he sat down he said, "This is more comfortable than it looks."

"It's stronger than it looks too."

"Are you implying that I'm fat?"

"Dapper little Mel? Who are you kidding?"

"'Little'? You're the queen of insults today, aren't you?" He pulled me onto his lap and we rocked, both our feet on the floor, our legs tangled up. I could never resist him.

"Just let me get out of this skirt," I finally said.

"Don't close your eyes," Mel said.

He made me come with his hand, telling me precisely and graphically what he was going to do once I did. Then he made good on his promise. This time it was Mel entirely, his lean face, his eyes with their charcoal-rimmed pupils, his boy smell, his patient artful touch. I was sitting in the chair and he knelt in front until I came again in a long drawn-out wave.

"I love you," I said as I came.

*   *   *

We were sitting naked in bed eating an omelette scrounged up from leftovers in my refrigerator. Since I only had one full set of silverware I gave him the fork and used a pair of chopsticks. I'd forgotten the beautiful way he ate, with such delicate bites.

"So," I said, "in your regular day, do you ever think about me?"

"All the time. You're pretty hard to forget."

"I miss you."

"I miss you too, honey."

"But we were right in Florida, weren't we. About it not working."

"Yes," he said.

"Age difference."

"That, and everything else."

"We could have tried."

"We did try."

"What if I said I couldn't live without you."

He ran his fingers over my bare shoulder. "I wouldn't believe you."

"Why did you want me to come to the funeral?"

"I told you. I needed you."

"And what if I suddenly called one day and said I needed you?"

"I'd be there for you, honey."

I sighed. "You're so young."

"Doug was my best friend there, you know, before he tried that first time. We told each other things. Like you and I do."

"You couldn't have saved him. Take it from one who's been there."

He picked up my left forearm and held it up to the light. The newest tiger stripe had healed nicely, but like the others it would never fade completely.

I said: "You know, there's one thing I've always wanted to ask you."

"Shoot."

"What's your real name?"

He made a sound like a buzzer going off. "Classified."

"Please. We might never see each other again."

He considered. "Well, I guess there's no harm. If you swear you'll keep it secret to your grave."

"I promise."

"Okay. Well, you know my mother's father was from Venezuela."

"No, I didn't know that."

"I was named after him. Carmel."

"That's where I was born."

"What do you mean?"

"Carmel-by-the-Sea, California. Near Monterey."

"Amazing."

"Isn't it?"

I didn't tell him I had known his name for a long time, that I had seen it one day on the tab of his folder in the nurses' station at Willowridge.

27

Another church, five days later, this one light and carpeted and a little too warm. Aunty Lilah Sung turned around in the pew in front of us and said in a loud whisper: "Sal-lee, *ni pang le!*"

"Thanks," I whispered back. Her daughter Mimi turned around too. I hadn't seen her since my own wedding, but I would have recognized that sweet smug smile of hers anywhere. Beside me my sister shifted, recrossed her legs. On her other side Ma fanned herself with her folded program. The last bridesmaid was making her way down the aisle.

Grace turned out to be slender and American-tall, towering over her father, and unexpectedly pretty. She had grown up in San Francisco Chinatown, which explained why her hair was "done" in the way the older women's were. Her earrings were pearl drops trimmed with gold filigree. Aunty Lilah turned around again and hissed: "Hong Kong jewelry. Her uncle gets it wholesale."

In the reception line, Grace's grip was as confident as her step down the aisle. "I'm so glad to finally meet you," she said. "Xiao's told me what a trip it was, growing up Asian in the burbs." Like Xiao Lu, she was an electrical engineer. They'd met at Berkeley; in a last-minute burst of rebellion, Xiao Lu had decided to forgo M.I.T. Grace's smile was open and intelligent—she was obviously a good girl, the kind of daughter my parents had wished for and never gotten. In his tux beside her, Xiao Lu looked like the cat that had swallowed the canary. "Hey, Sal, Hey, Marty," he said, kissing us as if we were old pals. It always surprised me that his voice was deep. Aunty Winnie was even scarier than I'd remembered, in rhinestone cat glasses and a French blue satin sheath. "Glad to see your whole family could make it," she clucked at us.

As we walked away, my mother grabbed my sleeve.

"Grace and Xiao Lu do this whole wedding theirselves. All paid, everything."

"Good for them," I said. Ma was wearing a new dress, tailored periwinkle silk, and her hair was cut in a becoming shag style. I could see my sister's influence.

The guests had formed a clutch outside on the church steps and their loud chatter rose up into the sultry Manhattan evening:

"This is my son the cardiac surgeon."

"This is my daughter, she's associate economics professor at U Penn. Only thirty years old, too young for the position, don't you think?"

"Roger is going to be in the Van Cliburn competition this year. Rachmaninoff specialty."

"My daughters, Sal-lee and Mar-tee, they decide to live in New York City, be close to their mother."

My sister was leaning against a pillar at the top of the steps, already flirting with one of the ushers, a white guy. She was dressed to kill in an old Pucci-print dress with a sashed waist and sheer black stockings and sandals with stiletto heels, even higher than the ones Alicia had had on at her Memorial Day party. I watched as she left the usher and strutted down the steps, swinging her arms like a dancer. No bandage, no trace of damage.

She came up to me and asked, "So whadja think?"

"Of what?"

"Grace."

"I feel sorry for her," I said. "Having Aunty Winnie as a mother-in-law. You're not supposed to outshine the bride, you know."

"Who's outshining? She's the one in fucking white."

Someone started giving out directions to the restaurant where the reception was going to be held, a few blocks away. The guests began surging forward in a mass that disrupted all other foot traffic on the sidewalk. "Why don't you just stay in Chinatown," I heard a pedestrian mutter as he was forced to step aside for us. At the restaurant we were ushered upstairs into a windowless red and gold banquet room with dragons wound around the pillars. "How tasteful," my sister said. There was no band set up or anything, just rows of round tables covered with plain white cloths and modest vases of pink carnations. The food would be the main event. My reception, which was held in the Yale Law School dining room, had featured a string quartet plus a menu of filet mignon and roasted new potatoes, a salad to start, and wedding cake for dessert. Ma told me the Chinese guests had complained bitterly that there hadn't been enough to eat.

While Ma went to find our table, Marty and I settled ourselves at the bar, scarfing up the honey-roasted walnuts they'd put around in little painted dishes. "How was the lingerie thing?" I asked her.

"Fine, although Mimi had a bug up her ass the whole time."

"What do you mean?"

Before she could answer there was a burst of applause and cheering—Grace and Xiao Lu were making their grand entrance as man and wife. The bride had changed into a floor-length crimson gown with a matching fringed stole. She lingered by the door, chatting to guests, and I didn't need to hear her to know that her Mandarin was perfect.

Marty and I had been seated with Ma, Aunty Lilah, Mimi, and old Mr. Lin. I hadn't even known Mr. Lin was still alive. He was shriveled like a dried shrimp in his chair, with those Coke-bottle glasses they have for people with cataracts.

It was never clear to me exactly how Mr. Lin had made his living. Daddy used to say, "He has beautiful calligraphy," as if that were enough to grant him distinction, a place in the world.

When a lazy Susan containing hors d'oeuvres was set down in front of us, Ma said, "Look, duck feet!"

"Calling them that is not the way to make people want to eat them," my sister said peevishly. She began drumming her fingernails on the table.

I decided to be polite to Mimi who was seated next to me and asked her how her dad and sisters were. "How come they're not here, anyway?"

"My father had to mind the store. And my sisters both moved to the Midwest." She didn't need to say married. I tried to remember what she did for a living. Some kind of medical thing. Physical therapy, that was it. I could see it. She had big, strong *hausfrau* arms and the right kind of incurable cheerfulness.

Aunty Lilah spun the lazy Susan around so the sliced eggs on their bed of cellophane noodles were facing Mr. Lin. "Hey! You take first, huh?" He scrutinized the eggs through his lenses and then waveringly approached his chopsticks and plucked out the biggest slice. Aunty Lilah leaned across Mimi and said to me: "Not too many girls look good in black like you, Sally."

"Thanks," I said, trying to figure out the barb inside this compliment.

"Actually I'm surprise you look so good. Your ma-ma tells me you have a bad time with your divorce."

"I'm fine now."

"Just remember, most important thing for woman in America is be financially independent. I keep all the books for the store, did you know that? If your Uncle Frank dies I could take over in a minute, no problem."

They were pouring champagne for the first toast. I got up to go to the bathroom. When I was at the sink washing my hands my mother came in.

"Ma, I wish you wouldn't do that."

"Do what?"

"Tell everyone about my life."

She went into a stall, slammed the door and locked it. Over the noise of her peeing she called out: "Everyone ask. It doesn't matter. You know how your Aunty Lilah is, so nosy, such a gossip."

"But I barely know any of these people. Why do they have to know about me?"

The toilet flushed and my mother came out and joined me at the sink. "You're like a sponge, Sally. You take everything in. Why don't you let bounce off?"

"I just don't like it, that's all."

"If you want me to talk good things about you, why don't you tell me good things? Every time you call, it's something bad. Getting divorced. Worried about money. Might get fired."

"I'm sorry if I can't be Marty."

"You and your sister two sides of the same thing. You complain, even when it's not so terrible. Your sister says everything's fine, when I know it's not so fine."

When we got back to the table, Marty was smoking in quick, short jerks, and I noticed she was the only one who had emptied her champagne glass. The Peking duck had arrived, sliced and accompanied by pancakes and scallions and sauce. Mr. Lin was constructing a crepe. For some reason he had taken off his glasses to do this. Although his eyelids were now densely wrinkled, I could see that they had once been double.

My mother and Marty were arguing about something. Then Ma reached over to the ashtray for my sister's cigarette to put it out. "It's not bothering anyone," Marty said.

"Bother me," Ma said.

Aunty Lilah jumped in with one of her non sequiturs. "Bau-yu, listen, you're still so good-looking. You should get married again."

Ma gave Aunty Lilah a look—*not in front of the children.*

Aunty Lilah ignored her. "Lots of eligible men. Widowers." We all looked at Mr. Lin, who was slobbering over his plate, and then we looked away.

But what Aunty Lilah had said about my mother was true. She was barely fifty, and with her new hairstyle easily looked ten years younger. Her complexion was still as translucently pale as it had been on her own wedding day, complemented by the luster of Nai-nai's black pearl earrings. She was still that contained aristocratic Shanghai beauty my father had fallen in love with.

"And you girls, if you want meet, just call me," Aunty Lilah went on. "I know many nice young men, Ivy League, good family."

Ma said to me: "Sal-lee, you don't take any *kao ya.*"

"I don't want any."

"This is wedding. You have to eat at wedding."

"I'm not hungry."

"Mar-tee, what about you?"

My sister didn't answer.

"Look, I make a sandwich," my mother said. "You take some."

"Okay," I said. "Just a bite."

"Just a bite for me too, Ma," Marty said.

Using her chopsticks, my mother cut the crepe exactly in half and gave one piece to me, one piece to my sister.

I leaned across the table. "Mr. Lin, remember the duck my father used to make for Chinese New Year?"

"Ah, yes," he said. "Such a talented man, your ba-ba. And talented daughter too. You still paint pictures?"

"Yes."

"Good," he said. "You're a good girl. Obedient to your parents."

The bride and groom came around to our table. Grace leaned over and said into my ear, "My old boyfriend has the biggest crush on your sister. He wants to know if she's free or not." Marty had gone over to the bar to have another cigarette.

"Your old boyfriend's the usher?" She nodded. "Yes, I guess she's free."

Xiao Lu was grinning in kind of a glazed way, so what came out of his mouth shocked me.

"These two Wang sisters were the bane of my existence when I was growing up."

"What?" I said. Grace frowned, wrapping her red stole tighter around her shoulders.

"It took me years to recover. I don't think you ever realized how stupid you were. Making fun of me was like making fun of yourself." Then he laughed, weakly, as if trying to turn what he'd said into a joke.

"Oh, all kids tease." Aunty Lilah to the rescue.

"Xiao Lu doesn't have any brothers and sisters," Ma said. "My girls toughen him up."

"Grace, I *love* your reception outfit," said Mimi.

"Thanks," said Grace. The photographer was setting up in front of our table and she put her arms around me and Ma and gestured with her head to Xiao Lu to come join us.

Snap. Everyone smiling, everything perfect.

"A bunch of us are going out to hear Zachary Richard. You wanna come?" My sister was refreshing her eye shadow in front of the ladies' room mirror. I watched as she dipped her fingers under the tap and then ran them through her hair to make it stick up in spikes.

"Okay."

"We're leaving right now. First show starts in ten minutes."

We went back to the table where Ma and Aunty Lilah and Mr. Lin were working on *ba bao fan*. "Don't wait up for me, Ma, I'll get a ride back," Marty said, leaning to kiss my mother on her greasy cheek.

"Okay," Ma said with her mouth full. Without thinking I leaned over and kissed her other cheek. I could feel her powder on my lips.

"Huh," said Aunty Lilah. "Too bad they didn't get a picture, all three of you together. That Marty, she hasn't changed a bit." This was Aunty Lilah's way of saying she didn't approve of my sister's dress.

As we headed for the door I asked Marty: "Does Ma know that you're moving back to the city?"

"Nope."

"Don't you think you'd better tell her soon?"

She rolled her eyes and didn't answer.

I ended up sharing a cab with Mimi and a couple of members of the wedding party. Poor Mimi. The photographer had caught her unsuccessful lunge—Grace had aimed perfectly into the arms of her maid of honor. As our driver slammed on his brakes for the fifth time, Mimi turned to me. "How can you stand to live in this city?"

"I don't drive."

Mimi lowered her voice. "My mother told me about your trouble. If there's ever anything I can do to help—"

"There's nothing you can do," I said. She looked so wounded that I added, "I'm sorry, but I just don't feel like talking about it."

"I understand," she said, in her best social worker manner.

When we got there the warm-up band, a couple of twangy girls with acoustic guitars, was just finishing their set. Marty and the others had arrived before us and managed to secure a table in the corner. They waved us over. This was lucky because by the time Zachary Richard got onstage it was standing room only.

The music was zydeco with a strong rock influence—great for dancing, and pretty soon Marty got up with the usher. I could tell he didn't know Cajun from a hole in the ground but was good-naturedly making it up as he went along. When he twirled my sister the skirt of her flimsy dress hiked right up to her garter belt snaps, giving every guy in the room a bird's-eye view.

Beside me, Mimi was getting drunk. "This music is SO GREAT," she shrieked into my ear. "Why aren't you dancing?"

"Why aren't you?" I asked, and she laughed, tilting her head toward the man sitting next to her. I couldn't tell what this meant.

When the song ended Marty's partner kissed her hand and she gave a little curtsy.

Mimi said to me: "I thought Grace was beautiful. That train—it had little diamonds cut out in it. Did you see?"

"I didn't notice."

"It's amazing that Xiao Lu ended up with someone Asian at all. All through high school he was obsessed with the blond cheerleader type."

The band had begun playing a slow song, a lullaby, with what sounded like Cajun baby talk. *Fais do do.* It was very sexy. I wanted to close my eyes and just listen but there was Mimi yammering in my ear again: "Did you know Xiao Lu lost his virginity with me?"

"Really?" She was drunker than I'd thought. "And you with him?"

"Uh-huh. And I threw that fucking lingerie shower for her."

"You're a good person, Mimi."

"I am, aren't I." Her gaze was caught by something on the dance floor.

I turned and saw them too. *Fais do do.* Marty and the usher, his hands on her waist, hers locked playfully around the back of his neck. She was laughing, but when wasn't my sister laughing as if the whole world were some colossal joke? She reached up and pressed her cheek against the guy's and then said something into his ear.

I turned back to make a snide comment to Mimi and my forearm accidentally brushed my half-full beer. It went crashing to the floor. I found myself mesmerized by the jagged shards swimming in the rapidly spreading puddle. Why had I never thought of broken glass—surely it would make a spectacular scar, unlike the neat little controlled surgeries my tiger stripes were. I could even aim for a vein this time.

I thought this and then I got up abruptly with no idea what I was going to do. I stepped carefully around the beer and broken glass and began negotiating my way through the crowd. As I passed the dance floor, I saw the usher cup my sister's chin and turn her face toward him. Marty looked disoriented for a second, from liquor or coke or whatever she was doing, and then, like the actress she was, recovered and smiled up at him. It was her most winsome smile, the one she used when she was in big trouble or when she wanted something very badly.

But the stage lights were cruel and brought out the lines around her mouth and across her forehead. She had Ma's complexion, but unlike Ma had not shunned the sun to protect it. In that moment I saw this: that despite her beauty, my sister was after all very ordinary.

I left the club, knowing that she could take care of herself. I wasn't worried about Mimi either. Maybe she'd have a great one-night stand with the guy next to her.

It was a week until the first official day of summer, but with the sulfur smell off the sidewalk, the scanty way people were dressed, you'd have thought it was already in full swing. I turned south, into the hoi polloi of the Village, the angled streets crammed with cafés and strolling couples, calm, as if I could keep walking forever. Eventually I found myself on Hudson Street, where the breeze freshened off the river, which I could glimpse each time I passed a cross street.

I had just enough left in my bank account to meet my July rent and living expenses. I knew I'd never see a cent of the money I'd given Marty. On Monday I'd call my boss, commit to some freelance I could do at home. It was time.

Three months ago I'd wanted to leave this world. In the hospital they told us that pain is something you experience and then put behind you. I disagree. I think you hold everything, pain and pleasure, in your heart, and that memory only deepens the next experience.

In painting, it's gesture that counts. Prime the canvas and use anything, a dirty brush will do, to lay out the first strokes, and then whether you realize it or not you've begun the rhythm. When it's dry, a finished piece, what onlookers should feel is the tension of your wrist cocked as you fed leaf blades into whiteness, dipping again and again into your palette, the precision and confidence of the three seconds it took to draw the curve of a limb with your brush angled like a pen nib. All the steps of that particular dance, as well as the particular whole.

The morning I'd tried to kill myself, I'd stood on the curb of the driveway looking down at the backyard, and what I'd felt, finally, was failure. Whatever would I have done with that pale New England sky, the spreading boughs of the pines etched so mercilessly upon it, how could I have expressed the simplicity of the black walnut so that it would have meant anything to anyone but me? I wasn't good enough. I wasn't nearly good enough. I wouldn't even know how to begin. It was my doom to be able to see, to feel like this, and not be able to translate.

Still, at that moment I'd known: this life is exquisite.

Epilogue

I never told anyone, not even Valerie, what I was dreaming about when Ma woke me up that Saturday afternoon after she got back from New York five hours earlier than she'd planned. She'd known, my mother, as she sat through her alumnae lunch, because she excused herself before dessert and hailed a cab to Grand Central to make the 2:05. When she saw me she began to scream, and miraculously they said, I was jolted back to consciousness.

I didn't want to wake up. At first it had been like any kind of going to sleep, except more serious, I could even feel my heart slowing down, my breath becoming shallow. I was dreaming of Carey, more of a feeling than a dream, of lying in a narrow bed with him, the long bones of his body pressed against mine like those times he'd held me the last few days, before I moved out, after we'd quit having sex, but the warmth of him was something I still craved.

And then I dreamed of a pattern, repeated over and over: white bears carrying pink and yellow balloons on a light blue background. I hadn't seen it in twenty-six years, but I recognized it instantly: the walls of my crib in Monterey.

Finally I dreamed I was flying. Not by myself, but on the back of an enormous white crane, up into the eye of the sun.

That's when she called me back. OPEN YOUR EYES. OPEN YOUR EYES. THIS IS YOUR MOTHER. OPEN YOUR EYES.

*   *   *

Before he died, Uncle Richard sent me a present, a key chain with a single charm—a little silver greyhound. Like Nai-nai's hairpin, I keep it with me always, because, even with the way things turned out, I need all the luck I can get.